ELVISSEY

ELVISSEY

Also by Jack Womack

Ambient
Terraplane
Heathern
Random Acts of Senseless Violence
Let's Put the Future Behind Us

ELVISSEY

□ □ □

JACK WOMACK

Grove Press
New York

Originally published by Tom Doherty Associates, Inc.
in 1993
First Grove Press edition published in 1997

Published simultaneously in Canada
Printed in the United States of America

Library of Congress Cataloging-in-Publication Data
Womack, Jack.
    Elvissey / Jack Womack.
        p.   cm.
    ISBN 0-8021-3495-5
    1. Presley, Elvis, 1935–1977—Fiction.   I. Title.
PS3573.0575E48   1997
813'.54—dc20   96-32015

Grove Press
841 Broadway
New York, NY 10003

10 9 8 7 6 5 4 3 2 1

All my love
For Carrie

1

□

"Elvis died several years before he saved me from drowning. My late husband's chihuahua, Betty, fell off the pier and I dove in after her, forgetting I couldn't swim. As I sank beneath the waves a strong hand pulled me out. Though the glow of His suit blinded me I saw His face, bathed in beatific light. Averting my eyes before His glory burned me I realized that without my having to ask He'd washed me in His love and I'd walk with Him ever after. As I dropped to my knees He ascended into the clouds, shining like the evening star. I didn't understand why He didn't save Betty but I know there must be a reason, there has to be."

—from "Postludinal Testimonies,"
The Book of E (Vegassene)

Ascension, I craved; my husband dreamed of descent. At our meet that set our seal.

"Zen," Conrad repeated. "Zen, not zinc. Zen, zen, zen."

"Think philosophy, not metal, to correctly phrase," said Weber.

Aware that present is bearable only when future makes it past, my husband and I often found ourselves creating images of what we believed our marriage had been, or of the people we once thought we were. But I was unable any longer to take comfort from holograms of the spirit, for when I tried clasping their shimmers against me, they dissolved under touch as reflections in water.

"Crui*sin'*—" I replayed, following my teachers' lead.

"Zen," Weber said.

We'd tried timeover to regood ourselves; perceived, we thought, that we never would. Then our company gifted us, heaving an assignment our way, rippling our stasis; we believed it our last chance to recover what we'd had as we plunged in, heedless of depth.

"Cruisin'—" I repeated; they nodded. Conrad and Weber were forensic philologists, adept in resuscitating dead languages so that, once alive again, the words might be appropriately vivisected. For my husband and myself, in preparation for our assignment, they ran their class, Slang Lab—Slab, I rephrased. Slab underwayed on Philosophy Hall's fifth, at Columbia, on Morningside Heights, under Dryco aegis. We all worked for Dryco, for whom there were no betters to work; no others, in truth, whether regooded or not. "Cruisin' for a bruisin'."

Words skidded smooth off my tongue, however their friction, at intervals, burned my tutors' ears. This time, having mimed proper, I'd delighted them. "AO," said Conrad, offering what John called a switchblade smile. "Demetaform."

Metaphor meaning, they meant; I considered all likely interpretations, deciding upon one that personally pleased. "One finds trouble when and where it's sought," I said. But why seek trouble when it finds you so easily?

"Apt," said Weber. "Next," he requested of his monitor; its blue eye refused to wink. "Phrase me."

"Moderate tone to effect interface—" Conrad began to say.

"Phrase," Weber commanded, his voice and color deepening. "Please," he added; at last received response. Hieroglyphs emerged from the blue as Venus rose from the sea. Staring doorways as Weber deciphered, longlost argot ringing twixt my ears, I glimpsed a woman hallwayed, downbound, carrying a veiled container; one of the artists, I reckoned. A workperson, too, strolled amid students, bloodying her orange coverall with reddened hands. During the month my husband and I trained oncampus, razored vines were loosed from all college walls that ivy might again shoot unslashed veins along clot-colored brick, revealing regooded structures fit to house regooded souls. Regooding proposed to make all that was long-wrong rainright once more.

"Ah," Weber murmured, studying the text at last revealed. "Comprehended."

By regooding, Dryco proclaimed to all that security was assured. In my mind it unimagined that security could ever be secure. "Bonney," Weber continued, addressing me. "Hear and replay."

Isabel, my mind rephrased; my name is Isabel, that name is my own. Isabel Bonney overran my boundaries; admitted my husband, my other who sat so near, too dangerously deep into my being. I loved him; there were none I loved as I loved my husband, but his is not my name. Call me Isabel.

"I be boppin'—" Weber began.

"I be boppin'—" I replayed. My husband—John, his name—said I knacked lingo; he didn't, and sat lipstill in Slab, eating apricot slices from his bag of dried fruit, which almost exclusively made up his daylight diet. One of us had to master background; it essentialled plain that we understand what the natives were saying when we confronted.

"—at the high school hoop," Weber concluded.

"I be boppin' at the high school hoop—"

"Hold," Conrad interrupted, extending a hand the shade and texture of undyed surimi. "Errored."

Weber's face so reddened that stroke seemed readied to cut him free. "Sourced here, sourced there," he said, fingertapping the screen.

"Don't," his monitor voiced in woman's gentle tones.

"Excuse. Sourced all the same, Conrad," Weber went on. "Midfifties term, present in all media. In *High School Confidential*, plus—"

Conrad shook his head. "1958 cinescript jumbled into low vernacular black English, urb class." He paused, as if only now noting my own urb class; eyed my lightening darkness, the yet-evident kink of my hair. Convincing himself he'd not offended, he proceeded sans exegesis or afterword. "Inapplicable for situation. Next."

"Demonstrable proof available," Weber insisted. "Stand corrected."

"Ignore, Bonney," said Conrad. "Proceed, Weber."

That linguists so incomprehensibled as they did didn't surprise; their degreed specialty was the Elizabethan period, not America's nineteen-fifties. But if we were to return to our world with anyone—as Dryco intended—it wouldn't be Shakespeare; at Dryco's demand, they adapted for the duration of our prep.

"Proof postsession," Weber said. "Waste time, want time. Next, then. Phrase me, please."

John's hands trembled as if palsied; his rising fear evidenced pure. I watched as he attempted meditation, appearing, after a moment, not to breathe.

"Complexities," Weber warned, examining the screen. "Replay tripartite with ongoing phrasing. Set?" I nodded. "*My baby*. Iterate, Bonney."

"My name's so unpronounceable?" I asked; wasn't answered. They so deafened to my words that I felt no greater than a lesser preposition.

"My baby," Conrad said. "Iterate."

"My baby—"

"Not be-be," he corrected. *"Bay*-bee. Replay."

"Bay-bee," I replayed. "My *bay*-bee—"

"Rocks me."

"Rocks me—"

John so stilled that others might have marveled that he be alive. A fly settled on his nose; stroked its legs against themselves as if to self-immolate, then wandered across his closed eyes; buzzed, and flew away. When John lapped his hands his knuckles whitened more than I'd ever seen them pale.

"—with a steady roll," concluded Weber.

"With a steady roll."

"Replay in toto," said Conrad.

"My *bay*-bee rocks me with a steady roll."

"She's got, she's got," said Weber.

"Demetaform," said Conrad.

If Dryco could regood itself—regood, therefore, our world—there was naught to believe that my husband and I would not eventually regood ourselves as well, in like manner, to like effect. This we told ourselves, timeover time, until we almost believed it.

"Ears open, Bonney," said Conrad, jarring me. "Demetaform phrase given as requested."

"Love bites when it strikes," I suggested. Again, they nodded. John's eyelids peeled open; he shuddered, seeming beaten by his dreams out of a restless sleep. He unpocketed a bottle of small blue pills; Dryco's standard eyedots and smile were imprinted upon each tablet. Three hours sole could pass between dosings, no more, no less. Swallowing dry, he fixed a doorways stare; shook, and resettled. There was so much he could have seen if he hadn't looked so hard. Meditation, medication; both essentialled, neither changed. Regooded or not, his unscratchables still itched.

* * *

"Which is the universe? Fortean or Joycean? Who tells?" asked Professor Mora, who taught Historical Inference; Guess and Grab, I rephrased. "The shadow world is, by its nature, shadowed." His room was on Schermerhorn Hall's ninth. The building was once a science center; in its womb the Manhattan Project conceived. "Notions of two spatial structures at once independent and interrelated were intolerable concepts until reality demonstrated other, fifteen years past."

We surely inhaled so much radiation, interiored, as exteriored. John and I transversed the campus topside, strolling along ramps inset for the physically challenged. Our fellow students formicated through tunnels underneath, battening their stores for winter. That afternoon, John and I stared into Jersey sunset, as if seeking literal, rather than metaphorical, blindness; sighted instead a herald, an unforecast spark, appearing as a match Godness struck against heaven.

Wish I may, John whispered as the spark faded. *Wish I might.*

We wished; in lieu of the doable that was all to be done. Fate, chance, kismet, term it as willed: to have seen, as we had, an old missile erasing itself against the atmosphere as its orbit knew inevitable decay was a vision as rare as that of a robin in springtime; most often they lowered over desert or taiga or sea, sprinkling the clouds with isotopes to later baptize us in soft burning rain. I fancied, at its sight; imagined Venus, rising on her own accord, the morning star slipped free of her perpetual transit's unbreakable noose.

"Science explains rotational balance essentialed to superimposed earths," Mora continued. "Accounts for observable non-Keplerian orbital dynamics. Explanations for similarity divergence between worlds and nonconcurrent progression of their respective human timelines are the concern of art, mayhap, rather than science. Certainly nothing in our history explains."

Nothing in history explains why something goes wrong.

John and I stared into the curtain before which Mora paced, seeing in its nub's sparkling texture a moonshadowed beach's color. Scrawling its dune with tracings of light, he inscribed dates; they washed away as he wrote them.

"What occurs there seems not always what happened here. Less so, as time passes. In the other world it is presently late April, 1954. Peopled expeditions previous-yeared yielded inconsistent data owing to mortality of all responsive participants save three. From the two Russians, little forthcame and less was told. From the third, Biggerstaff, we gained such awareness as we've possessed of that world's existence, one summer weekend in 1939. Their 1939."

In our fifteen-year transit through cosmic haphazards John and I slid across surfaces seeming smooth from afar, suffering irreparable scars in the flames our contact raised. Our similarity divergence developed as unexpectedly as it had for the two worlds, for like reasons undoubted: multitudinous though unguessable, foreseen yet Cassandraed, known because ignored.

"Mayhap inference and induction gained us not enough, it was thought. There inhered challenge, thus. How to answer unanswerables?"

Where did love for John end, and hate begin? How deep did each lie buried beneath anger's eversettling mud? Did love essential a coeval hate? Must those emotions deepen from acute into chronic so synchronically? Must only enough love linger to so pain its inevitable decay?

"Last month, in correlation with the E project, we at last broke off a new shard of their glass," Mora said. "An icicle fallen from a plane overhead."

Did we want our love to end? Did we need it to end? Did it matter?

"A minireceiver was guided through the Flushing Window, across the zone, for sixteen minutes, seizing and relaying the other world's radio transmissions in immediate range."

Chance attracted us, experience repelled; what bound us was as enigmaed as the true nature of that only-imaginable world.

"Reception peripheralled. Static and fade were unavoidable, enhancement notwithstanding. Keep minded of this, giving ear," said Mora.

As John's medication, taken the hour earlier, soaked into its hold, he first expressed nothing but inexpressible rage; then his look became no look at all. I turned from him, feeling my own anger flower; I couldn't save him from himself, by myself, and the assistance of others only hurt all the more. Underdesk I took my husband's hand, in my grasp feeling a fish snatched from water. Pressing my fingers into his numbness I fought to draw his blood through his veins anew, warming his graying skin if but for a shard of history, a shiver of time.

"Insert your present into theirs," said Mora, petting his machine as if hoping he could bring it to climax. "Hear the unseeable. Quilt the patchwork assembled. This is what awaits." Disarticulate voices spurted from the speakers, near yet afar, shouts across canyons lowed into ears. We heard silence; then, a song.

"Sh-boom, sh-boom—!"

Lessons memorized in Antecedental Ur-Beat class awared me that these voices, white as bones, were Crew-Cut notes, and not those of the Chords. Their song faded; medleyed vocalese drifted across the range.

"Pepsi-Cola hits the spot—"

"—every day at this time by Listerine—"

"—that doggie in the window—"

John's eyes refocused as he drew further inward, stealing from Mora, from me, from another world's words. He unjacketed a worn black book; studied its pages as if seeking answers to questions never guessed applicable.

"—and the prices go down, down, down—"

"—dozens reported seeing the saucers in the skies over Washington last night, and on radar screens—"

Jake oversaw Security during John's initiation, seventeen years past; upon graduation, following the blooding, John and all acceptables were gifted with Jake's hymnal *Knifelife*. In its pages Jake provided for his charges' inspiration enabling enough that they might ignore the day presently entrapping and look ahead to the one that, likely, would follow: one perhaps better, perhaps worse; a fresh day regardless, its evanescent security as yet unaborted by event.

"—as we join Reg Berman and the gang at the Marine barracks at the Brooklyn Navy Yard—"

Days after meeting John, at once knowing the love I'd never lose, however hard I tried, I met Jake, who avoided the look of others' eyes. Overhanging him I fancied a cloud so black as his suit was white; I realized only afterward that I was taller than Jake. He said little, and that gnomic; John told me that in justifiable mood Jake killed with a wink, and though I prodded, he left that remark to be taken as metaphor to be demetaformed as I chose. Jake vanished soon after, coming back from the place where we'd be going: in his class Mora had earlier recounted how Jake accompanied Biggerstaff on that initial transgression into that other world; how, returning, he'd been somehow lost, somewhere inbetween. Whether he lingered there, no one could say.

"—that the Spirit of Light should overwhelm the Sons of Darkness—"

"—nine out of ten doctors recommend Camels—"

John had been Dryco's Security Head for three years. He oversaw what had been, implemented that which was becoming; forever provided security to all save himself. Mora frowned, seeing John ignore the lesson; yet attempted no punishment, surely recalling responses of other guards, seen at other times. In the classroom dim Mora's face appeared so livid as John's, as if for his chieftain's funeral he'd painted it with ash.

"—travel the Interstate, you'll be glad you did—"

"In Berlin, Chancellor Speer—"

Regooding of Dryco Security's five hundred departmental units necessitated that they begin a program of medication to assist in curbing their long-conditioned reactions. One hundred and seventy-four had suicided in the six months since.

"Now's the time for Jell-O—"

Indirectly and overtly, my husband smothered me beneath more emotions than I could bear, killing me so surely, if not so slowly, as they killed him: still I stayed with him; couldn't abandon, felt compelled to accompany, wherever he went.

"Why, then—"

Whenever he went.

"Why, then, with all this strength," the voice said: Eisenhower's voice. President there too, we induced, and sounding enough like ours as to chill; again I remembered what was first told, that their world was no less real, nor more unreal, than ours. "Why should we be worrying at times about what the world is doing to us?"

Worry, rather, about what we'd allowed it to do. John continued to regard Jakeisms; I vizzed the page he studied, saw its single printed line: *Sharpest knives leave sweetest wounds.*

"—this increase of power from the mere musket and the little cannon," their Ike went on, "to the hydrogen bomb in a single lifetime is indicative of the things that have happened to us."

What wounds had we inflicted upon ourselves that we didn't even feel? Which had we asked for? Which, wanted? Which, needed? Which, deserved?

"They indicate, rather, how far the advances of science have outraced our social conscience."

Many moments lately passed when I dreamed of conclusion so immediate, and so thorough, as John desired. His pain destroyed us—my pain destroyed us—and all I could do in response was love: but love didn't limit darkness, wouldn't shape shadow. Our world shrifted love, ran screaming from its presence, at night turned from its light to fasten gaze upon the dark, lonely bed. We favored a notion so free of science as a history class: that the other world held the answer we needed, if not the one we wanted; that, smashing through our looking-glass, we might on the other side see ourselves true, neither as we wished nor as we feared we were, and so be able to decide, at last, whether we should disunite.

"—solution to the Negro problem cannot be found in legislation, but in the minds—"

Static exploded, shattering their world; all silenced, as if it'd never been. Mora stroked his machine to a stop.

"At that point the device was apparently observed. Expected response surely ensued. Prospects," Mora summed, "fascinate."

Not always sure I'd had one, I wanted life; John felt sentenced to his. As we sat there, while Mora gathered his papers, I saw John reread the book's closure, a quote attributed to John Donne. Once I'd been to London, and in St. Paul's seen the preacher's statue, his image sculpted as he'd desired: wrapped within windings, eyeshut as if asleep, smiling as if dreaming of every funeral followed; foreseeing his own, mayhap—the end of a long trial, with the outcome of the appeal ahead assured.

> *I run to death, and death meets me as fast,*
> *and all my pleasures are like yesterday.*

Jake's deconstruction followed; succincted. *When time comes,* he'd writ, *act.*

* * *

Class ended; before homing we descended into the crypt of Columbia's St. Paul's to attend an artshow. A marble spiral led to the display; at stairfoot stood artists, smoking and drinking cups of wine, chatting technik. By their abdominal convexities I gathered that they endeavored new projects even while conversing. The other designers, including the woman I'd earlier spotted, had galleried, hovering round their containers. Their sculptures, too, were tabletopped; among them were interspersed bowls of ikebana, lending color no less artificial, however natural.

"Ugly," an appreciator noted to his companion. Their first date, I inferred; each wore a forced disinterest in anyone's affairs other than their own.

"Art," she replied, ecstasized.

Background essentials: inbody pregnancy, when accidental, was inevitably if circumventially terminated; regooding upheld the edicts forbidding the wombed from being untimely ripped, amniotic forecast irregarded. Only through tubed cultures, suitably outbodied, was birthed perfection assured. Mutative nature's inescapables—chemical rain rich with acid and deviant ray, unseeables in food and drink, our radium-blue heaven—certified that trad gestation inevitably delivered into our world fresh deformities, sometimes quick, most often dead.

"One pill at daybreak, sixteen weeks running," an artist whispered to one of her protégées. Each wore earrings made of tiny silverplated feet, toes splayed apart by diamond chips. "Resulting varietals are of nobler invention than thalidomide's."

"Side effects?" asked a listener. "Yours, meant."

"Standard."

Fetal artists conceived as was once the rule, as deliberately exposing themselves to select media during pregnancy to most appropriately flesh their concepts, which could live only after they'd died.

"Solipsizers," said John, bareglancing, his eyes so deep-socketed that, had I not known, I could never have guessed them to be blue. "Let's shortterm."

"Hang cool," I said, forever now practicing, in speech, the rephrasing essentialled for our upcoming travels. "Loose, rather. Hang loose."

"Oh, Iz," he said, frowning so that only I would see. "Straightspeak with me if no other."

"Forgive," I said; could he? I wondered if for reasons other than chemical my eyes showed so drawn as his; began persuing what was displayed. Within each mother's tabled glass belly floated a freeform manifest, a maternal expression. Some were lava-lit, making the jars' small ones appear self-luminescent as they drifted amid glowing plasmas, resembling warning balloons lofted in advance of toxic clouds, giving all in harmway reason enough to run. Other babies presented to admirers internal organs origamied outward, or the look of ones dissembled and reconstructed by mechanics uncertain of the original arrangement.

"Unoriginal," a critic noted of one who was unlit, and bore a face emerging direct from a stubbed neck. The baby's arms drifted through its gel as if it attempted to fly.

"How so?" asked his accompaniment.

"Similar seen live, begging on Mercer Street, six months past."

In the eyes of some exhibits I saw duped the eyes of lovers longlost reincarnate, no less painful to stare into now than they'd been when I'd last taken leave of them. All the jugged children carried a feel of specimens recovered from those more distant worlds once imagined extant, far beyond visible stars, stolen from Edens as yet untarnished by the slither of snakes.

"Postambient," the holoed gallerist explained, her image afloat in room's midst. "As cubism rose from trad Afro styles. Brancusi, exampled. Prim remade proper; rebirth becomes any art."

The sculptures, I favored; those employed the interior

frames so that the design's more profound aspects might be fully revealed. The ribcage of one draped down over its femurs. Several small skulls evidenced cyclopean features; holiday lights were inserted within the expected openings, to whimsify onlookers. One sculpture, hued waste-green, stood balanced, seeming weightless upon its fourth foot's third, longest toe.

"Iz, I beg—" John murmured. I kissed; calmed, if didn't settle.

"Por fav, moment," I said; took his hand in mine, feeling no feeling. "Let's see who's cookin'."

"*Iz*—"

"Practice perfects."

The exhibit's centerpiece was wrought by an artist named Tanya, a provincial who'd been living in the Bowl, near the great Indiana dunes; no others so fertiled as she, either in idea or in technik. Tanya bore a look resembling my husband's, that of one who suffered for their art. Her child, whom I took to be one of outbodied origin, sat smiling nearby; she had honey hair, thick and tousled in the back, and skin so pink as to have been boiled.

"Wordless," others muttered, eyeing Tanya's bodiwork. "Doublestunned."

Half mobile, half collage, the art was contained within two transparent cones poised tiptipped; the topmost revolved unceasing by way of the gyroscopic motion of two intertwined catherine-wheels afloat within, both armspoked with ten bony lengths, digits directed viewer-outward, striking balance nature neither offered nor intended. In the lower cone four small ones, fullbodied if emptyfaced, circled round-rosied, their dance forever macabring.

"Years, making," Tanya said, responding to another's question. "I despaired, sometimes."

"How'd you bleach the bones?" I asked.

"China White," she explained. "After beetling."

Her little girl's face lit as if it, too, generated its own glow, reflecting much more than her mother's glory. "She loves her brothers and sisters," Tanya said, stroking her daughter's perfect hair and hands. "When you're old enough, sweetie."

"Cost?" I inquired.

Tanya shrugged; smiled. "If you have to ask—"

I thought myself no artist; imagined I could have been a good mother, but our marriage's anesthetic was unmarred by creativity. When I wed John I was awared at moment one that we were to remain childless. Though insistent guards, such as John, were allowed conjunction, Dryco's concern for familial stability demanded that from Security unions no progeny might spring, to be too early orphaned. By directive, not even seed could be gathered in advance to later plant, pre- or post-retirement; all guards were clipped before being diplomaed, the vasect required before they could receive Jake's book. Often before learning there was one I dreamt of a parallel world, where John was a good father and I, a good mother.

"Iz," he said, with stiff fingers touching my arm with fly's lightness; as had his old overseer, he avoided my eyes, as if undesiring to see what was lost. "Homeaway now. Age befalls the legs. I beg."

"Moment."

In that other world, would our counterparts be birthed? If they were, and if they married, would they create? Or, once joined, would they live as we had, sans art, a cozy couple separate yet equal, sharing an isotope's halflife, clinging to madness to which they'd most familiared, shielding themselves against vaster insanities whirling without?

Was that love? What was its cost? *If you have to ask . . .* Before homing I charged up an exhibit disk that I could review later at leisure, discerning what I'd overlooked; finding those unintended truths artists so well as critics failed to see even when shown, the ones most meaningful, because most disturbing.

"Love you," I told my husband, "overmuch." He nodded; he knew.

Aiming Bronxward up Broadway our car carried us home; through smoked windows we eyed tripleshifters deconstructing the walls between Harlem and Washington Heights as the northern, higher parts of Manhattan underwent their own regooding. So few still lived on either side of the walls that such security had for years been so superfluous as those who'd once lived there; I'd lived there, as a child. We'd grown together in Washington Heights, me and Judy and poor lost Lola, inloading info, streetsmarting, grasping our world's way in a moment's breath if and when essentialled; I regooded myself, once I left.

Looking upward through the roof I gazed toward Godness; saw no spark, no sign, no flare of St. Elmo's fire. Mundanities blotted the night: clouds aglow with searchlight-shine coagulated on high, no sooner taking the shape intended by those directing groundbound than breezes conspired to deface the fog-scrawled designs. Environads, when successed, allowed Dryco to emboss its logo upon land, sky and sea; that if tongues stilled, and screens blanked, the rocks themselves would forever sing a song of Dryco. Airtravelers descending through the yellow zone into the apparent clear vizzed highwayside forests grown on demand, controlling erosion while, in engraven greenery, foliating the corporate sign; streams raced along rechanneled courses that from far vistas the interested might glimpse our name writ in water; knolls were shaved and shifted into the familiar face's leer, eyed with boulders, smiled with a shrubbery curl, and spelling out in hedges circled round our company's rephrased ethos: *Do Good. Feel Real.* The word was too much with us, too soon: Dryco was the word, and our world was of the word, and with the word, and the world was the word.

"*Watch—!!*" John shouted. Our driver swerved slidelong,

rushing through the reds; at 156th escaped blindsiding by another Bronxbound limo. John clasped the man's shoulders, steering him curbways as he slowed to a stop. "You're risking," he told the driver, a reassigned Security staffer; as he told him that I knew that it was my safety, not their own, that so concerned my husband.

"Known," the man mumbled, barely audible.

"I'll cruise us," John said. "Shift." Stepping out, wheeling himself, John eased our driver into shotgun position; spoke to the dash so kindly as to his co-worker, and when the car responded we moved on: righting, lefting, rivercrossing, passing from the gone world into the one which would be.

Under Dryco guidance, at inestimable cost, our city rebuilded atop the Bronx hills, designed half trad, half in the style Eurotrenders termed Dreizinuovy. New New York's nightlight made lurid its host of shades, pastel and primary: apricot and aubergine, lemon and lilac, cerise and cerulean and deep emerald green. Betowered and lowdomed, the city showed so spired as a bed of nails; tubes bridged street-canyons eighty floors over, sodastraw elevators ran along building-sides toward rich azimuths bedecked with faux-curlicue and neo-arabesque. Clouds of tiny copters circled midge-like round those grown and growing hothouse flowers, our garden town. The Met, at intervals, displayed fading comic panels, whereupon more conservative appreciators of art would see inked, half a century past by those in the know, our city's image: sealed within a bottle, one candid among many miniatures lifted from a farrago of worlds.

Old New York would in time be sea-swallowed, as Chicago would go Nineveh as each daily dust-storm laid down another coat, as LA would in time smother beneath its Jovian atmosphere's weight; Moscow might crumble, Lagos and Karachi burn anew with nuclear fire, Cairo and Bangkok and Brazzaville depopulate at one hundred souls per hour. Yet as in Tokyo, as in Berlin and London, new New York would—upon completion—show as all in our world should have shown, had so many not slowed along the roadway to view the accidents previous onlookers caused.

New New York would hold a million. Its presentiment screamed the unstated, that its inhabitants had been retrofitted as well, to assure perfection. In outlanders' minds—in the Bowl and among the Coasters and down in the vast Southern delta—New Yorkers underwent a most complete regooding: they were reimagined as reflections, new Atlanteans plucked landward from water; their wet hair so blond as mine was becoming, their moist eyes so blue as my contacts feigned. We who lived here knew true; our hills' city provided only new jars for old specimens, who, when pricked, yet gushed red and not gold-vermilion.

John and I had a fiftieth floor place in a Concourse tower; twenty other families lived in our building. We sidewalked ourselves, watching empty trolleys race down the boulevard's gardened aisles, their ads' neon belettering the dark, the bulbed glow of Dryco's face tracklighting fore and aft, the sign of its word; everybody heard about the word. Our driver, deafened, sped into his night, two red lights on behind.

"How long?" I asked, watching his meteors skid out of sight.

"Week," John said. "He's edged. Let's up ourselves, Iz."

The seven million of old New York could have roomed here in comfort, high atop the hills. Mooted: in new New York, those not regooded weren't there anymore.

We lay in our single bed's separate worlds. John's wide white back lifted high on my left, its crags appearing as an iceberg around which I could never maneuver in time. He shivered; mayhap his own coldness chilled too bonedeep. Stroking him, pulling our comforter around us, I warmed him as I could.

"Sleepaway," he murmured. "Deepdead shagged, Iz. Dreamtime calls. Listen."

"Talk to me, John," I said. "Talk."

"Sleepaway, Iz," he repeated. "Places to go, people to be. Sleepaway."

Rolling off I eyed our ceiling's slate, an unreadable heaven too close to comfort. We lay separate but equal, together yet apart, one and divided; I wished he was with me, fearing he'd never be again. The living room's TVC came on by itself; it needed rechipping but a workperson essentialled for that and so we let it play as it wished. From the words I gathered that a speaker representing one sect of the C of E—that is to say, the Church of Elvis—was preaching; the congregants called out for their imagined savior, crying for him to step from his world into ours.

"E," they chanted, intruding themselves throughout our space. "Save us, E."

As I lay there I listened to wind scratching the window; then I heard the wind drop to the carpet and land on a shoe. Pressing on the light I soaked our room until all appeared freefloating within an amber sea. A mouse sought succor beneath my dressing-table.

"John," I said, shifting him with no greater ease than if I'd tried pushing a mountain. "The room's wildlifed. Heard and seen, present and accounted."

"Wildlifed," he replayed. "Two feet or four?"

"We're verminized," I said. "A mouse, undertabled. Go, do, please—"

"Untouchable, Iz," he said. "It's life."

"It'll breed and bedcrawl," I said. "Cruise it and bruise it, John. I beg."

The mouse's head appeared, resembling a shoetip; it froze, seeming fixed by my stare. I didn't move; it did, racing crossroom, vanishing under our bed. Awakened full I bounded high, tumbling John floorways.

"Godness, Iz—" His insomnia disrupted, John rose with clear, if troubled, mind.

"Ex it, John," I said. "It'll warm itself with us."

He stared bedways, considering my question even as I asked it. "Impossibled, Iz. Even with peewees. Can't think—"

"*A mouse!*" I shouted, balancing myself upon our mattress, alerted to sounds of scratch. "Try, John. Show it what for."

My husband stamped his good foot, rocking the room. Our intruder darted out, shooting into the quarter-meter's width between dresser and console. Kneeling, grasping one of my boots, I tossed it, jamming the heel into the mouse's only exit. Isolate now, it attempted to scramble up the surrounding smoothness, seeking grip, finding none, sliding floorways again and again, outsplaying tiny feet no larger than earrings.

"Send it up the flagpole and fly it, John," I screamed. "John, please, I beg, I don't want to have to—"

"Can't think. Can't. No—" he began to say; leaning forward, his sentence pending, clutching himself stomachways, he balled inward as if to keep his innards from gnawing themselves free. A medication side-effect was tenfolded gastric output at mere notion of violent response; if the notion prolonged, even sans action, he'd be eaten away so physically from within as I had been emotionally.

"Living must live," he said, replaying his new-learned lessons. "Live with purpose. Must live. Must—"

"*John—*" I cried, aware of what necessaried, were we to know peace. Something in the mouse kept it living against every odd; I'd hoped it would keel, but it didn't. John's white face drew deathshade as his blood streamed inward, seeking release.

"Iz," he said, sinking his teeth lipways, reddening them, "I can't. Can't, can't, can't—"

"I'll settle," I said, climbing down, smoothing his damp

hair. He attempted to go blank, eyeshutting, surely constructing in mindeye images of sunshine and meadows and all else neverseen, that he could recover enough to lie at rest without hemorrhage. I hated him so for my having to do what essentialled; pushed deeperdown my own rage with the ease experience brings. I was never so good at hurting as was John. "Rest, angel. I'll settle."

In my bedside drawer were scissors; my choice of weapon was no less impromptu than any guard's. I trod gentlefooted to where the mouse flung itself against the walls within which it was bottled. I clenched; lifted my scissors. Bringing them down, I realized I'd grasped them widdershins, as if to safely present them to another, who might then with ease stab me with my own gift. Feeling the points sharp within my hand, closing my eyes, imagining myself as a child again, I struck the mouse with the rounded handles; hit it repeatedly, allowing myself sight enough only to certify my strikes, that I didn't overdraw another's pain overlong, regardless of my own.

Done, then: the mouse lay fetuscurled upon the darkened carpet as if sleeping, its nostrils crimsoned. Cringing from sight of my handiwork, feeling no satisfaction of artistic accomplishment, I saw John rub his face sweatless against our sheets; wondered for whom I felt sorriest, feeling possessed with numbness I hadn't remembered I could so easily summon.

"It's doornailed," I said. My eyes were wet as the mouse's nose, as our sheets, as John's hair. "Angel?"

"Sorry," he said. "Forgive."

"No," I said. "Forgive me." No response. If John cried, his tears streamed unseen within. Standing, feeling my own head light of blood, I tore open two dusty condoms taken from the drawer and rolled them over my fingers; grasped the mouse's tail and ran with it to the bathroom, to jet it down the toilet. I watched the pink water swirl away; washed and rewashed and rewashed my hands, feeling as Lady M herself. Then I returned to our room, bedding again beside my husband. He lay wide-eyed; some nights, lately, he only halfslept, thrashing through undreamt dreams, recalling none at morningside.

"I've done unforgivables," I said. "I have."

"You weren't trained for such, even streetways—"

"No, John. With you, I mean."

"Nada," he said; I stared at his back. "Guilt undeserved scars spirit and soul, Iz. Never know guilt sans reason."

"You do constant," I said.

"Sans reason, said."

"You're lying, not truthing," I said; sighed. "Saming, not changing." I fit myself anew into my spot alongside him, touching his skin; he couldn't stop shaking, and I wondered if this was a hitherto undetected side-effect. "Better or worse, John. Love. You slay me."

"Never!" he shouted, rising as if to slap me down. "Never. Disallowed."

"Not literal, John. Misinterpreted. I'll demetaform—"

"Never hurt," he said. "Not you," he added. "No one," he sighed. "None."

"You're abandoning you, John," I said. "And me. Without fault of yours—"

"With fault."

"No. Oh, John, it hurts—"

"Mutualities," he whispered, "best unsaid."

"Least said soonest known."

"Over there," he said. "Difference will become us again as it did. I know it'll be so, over there."

"So hoped," I said. Pressing closer, I felt him warm: again glimpsed the shimmers, our bright reflections, the heatshine above the highway; imagined for an instant that Godness might indulge our prayers. He shifted, as if to face me; suddenly reached downward, his face wrinkling as if at once he showed a hundred years, each unwanted.

"What hurts, John?" I asked. "What—?"

"Leg—!"

Asiding our damp sheets, he flailed and pounded his knee with his fist, reslotting his joint. Since the ninth operation the implants never quite took, and rarely responded as desired, however much he concentrated when guiding their action. Guards, heretofore, forever required refitting; artificialities had merits but permanence was not among them. John's add-on leg would suffice several months to a year sans problems: then fluid dried, the marrow-channels bubbled, the cables knotted; down to the clinic he'd hobble, knowing well inevitable obsolescence's inescapable pain. He stilled anew, pillowing his head, gasping for breath.

"Are you AO?" I asked. He nodded. "I love you. I'm sorry."

"For loving?"

"Sometimes," I said.

His lips downturned, as if they'd been pinned. "Known," he said. "Understood. I love, too. Overmuch contained within. Overmuch to bear."

"Overmuch inexpressible?"

He nodded. "Spillage unavoidable, sometimes. Hurt to avoid hurt, unavoidable," he said. "Ergo, implode within. Better, because safer."

We'd had a friend in the trade; after graduation she was implanted with finger-razors which, commanded, sprang from undernail that with them she might lunge and slash. One afternoon while she was grating cheese for dinner they unexpectedly emerged, freezing in extremis. At her operative time, years before, such gear was bonegrafted direct; only through amputation could she have been loosed of her superfluous knives. Still, Dryco found her retainable for special use; in time such acts as turning doorknobs again came naturally to her. Upon regooding's instilling she foresaw her unavoidable obsolescence; the edict passed, and a week passed, and then one night she lay full-uniformed in her tub; resting there for a time, she must have made motions as if to adjust her collar. John once loved her, before our meet; I never jealoused. Love was love, however manifest.

"John—"

"It'll remake us. I'll exemplarize, and protect sans harm. The change'll come, over there," he said. I clasped his shimmer, fearing—his words notwithstanding—he was lost to us both, if not till endtime, at least for our present. Curling inward, feeling mouse-size, small and dark and bottled within smooth walls, I stared out into a wide white world. "Peace yourself meantime with dreams, Iz. Sleepaway."

Once sex netted us tight, giving life, renewing our souls as Godness so hoped; our love was Godness. Now I fancied that John thought if we were to swive he'd only shoot into me unneeded poison, embodying me overmuch with a readjusted virus. He shivered: I rubbed his stomach, felt his muscles and the curls of his hair, and held his penis in my hand. He never told me how he'd lost the tip.

The TVC switched on again. "E," the desparate called throughout our rooms; their pleas rebounded soft against my ears as I lay there, unswived, unsaved. "Return to us. Cleanse. Renew. We beg."

E would return to them, if and when we found his double in the shadow world; if our mission accomplished, and we stole that world's E away, bringing him into ours where he was so wanted, Dryco would present him returned anew, its soothing gift for its regooded world. Some at Dryco wanted—needed, in truth—E more than any of his believers ever had.

I wanted John so much; I couldn't say how much I still needed him. Avoiding my eyes, he looked elsewhere now. One suicidal stares at death to see who'll soonest blink. Too soon, morningshade eked through our bamboo curtains, and so I ascended. Mayhap, heavenbound, my husband could ride me.

2

□

"New always overcomes old," Judy said, sounding the words as if to convince not me, but herself. Judy, I called her; that was her name, and that was how I'd known her. Most of Dryco were familiared with her chosen pseudonym; as befit corporate etiquette, none save Mister O'Malley officially called her anything other than Madam. "New throttles old groundward, sighs and shudders, and tramps a remapped path. Nature's way, irregardless of old's needs." She drew in air as if each breath stung her throat; with pencil-thin fingers she smoothed her hair's gray cap. "John'll readjust or he won't, Iz. If he doesn't, you will."

"There's great unfairness in that," I said.

"Great unfairness in all," she said. "Regooding essentials that those in Security must readjust, if regooding is to effect. Cruelty no longer satisfies Dryco's intent. So says Seamus, at Leverett's request."

Through Judy's wallwide windows I watched pigeons and sparrows descending through clouds, swooping sillward, shelterbound. At touchdown they burst into blue bubbles; their leavings feathered the air.

"Since regooding underwayed John's gone holloweyed and withery," I said. "He'd have exed himself by now if we hadn't volunteered."

"He was awared of Security's needs at time of hire," Judy said. "Such deliberate positioning infers predisposing traits. Disregarding one's own life essentials to enable the undertaking of others. Prior to regooding, Security readied its members for their chosen hell, as was intended. Heaven doesn't become them, Iz. You knew that when your wedlock clamped."

"I never imagined this."

"Nor did I," she said. "Seamus reveals like patterns daily, and his training never so thoroughed as John's, or the others. If your husband breaks, he breaks. Accept that."

"He's failing, however hard he tries," I said. "It's so hurtful to watch."

"Blind yourself," she said. "I disapproved from moment primo, Iz. You deserved better. Where do they have him, this morning?"

"Clinicking," I said. "My turn, after. Such an awful place. Such awful people."

"Professionals all." She avoided my look. "So Leverett reminds me when I mention your complaints. I've long suspected those in the clinic are hired once they're proved too disturbed for Security. Still, this passage he's coursed for you demands full health."

"Mental health, too?"

"Nonadherent to *this* project," she said. "Absolute madness. Nada comes of breaking a mountain over a mouse for gravel."

"Mister O'Malley's unyielding?" I asked, relieved to assume that he still was.

"Leverett's silvertongued his ears shut."

Judy's surety in our project's purpose was considerably

less than absolute. As her assistant, I was positioned prime
to take the bait before any others; but Leverett had, after all,
recommended that John and myself would be best suited for
assignment needs. As vice-president overseeing New Projects, Leverett had conceived not only the policy of regooding; he'd as well originated the concept of our mission,
bypassing Judy in mothering his idea, slipping it along to
Mister O'Malley direct. Judy controlled Mister O'Malley as
no others did; he'd bestowed full favor before she could call
halt.

"The sole plus," Judy said, "Leverett's so occupied by
these mechanics he hasn't time for his usual plots. He'll be
dealt out unless this results as he pretends."

"You're hostiling so," I said. "You weren't so upset earlier—"

"You're needed here," she said. "But he's got you in the
midst of this. You've unheeded all warnings—"

"My decision," I said. "We volunteered."

"At whose prompt?" she asked. "Your worser half's, or
mine?"

"My husband and I are mutualed. Change essentials,
Judy, but I don't wish to asunder, and he'll not last if we do."

"What fears you most, then?" she asked. "His desire to go,
or yours to accompany?"

"Neither," I said. "Both."

"You've worked for me too long—"

"There's much unsaid," I told her, unable to say what it
was. "We need togetherness. He's adrift unless I anchor," I
said. "We've never tripped in simulcast." Her stare evidenced no sign that she would ever comprehend my love for
John; so often, lately, I couldn't either. "I fear we'll return
unchanged, with finis stamped through and through."

"If you return."

"Judy—"

"Forgive," she said. "Danger overwhelms all aspects of
this. Pointless imbecilities."

"It does frighten at immediate level," I told her. "With John unable to act as might essential—"

"That's unconcerning me," Judy said. "I've seen you both act. His was learrned. Yours was born. If emergencies arise over there, you'll handle. I've seen you handle before."

"Years before," I said. "I'm no child any longer, Judy."

"Known," she said. "Don't mirage yourself, Iz. Our beloved enhance bad so well as good. Certify whose thoughts you're thinking before you act." Standing, she walked over to embrace me. "You're missed," she said. "Such a color you're turning, Iz." Her hand was dark against my cheek, as it had never been before; the six weeks treatment of Melaway they'd dosed me with had lightened my skin as if I'd been painted with milk. "Plainly a sister still, and here you leave two days hence. Problematic. That world's no place for our people, and it'll do you no good to show. Biggerstaff'll aware you of that—"

"Leverett's told me of that. They all have," I said. "I've inklings it's doing more than what's desired. Aches and pains rack me. They deafen to my complaints at the clinic."

"Tell Leverett. He raves so of the drug's worth, and I'd never heard tell of it. I suspect he'd like to dose me with it, to lessen his discomfort when I direct him and his peers," she said, laughing. "Time's here, Iz. Fond farewells await."

"Mister O'Malley?" She nodded. "What're my lines?"

"Mute yourself. He's nonresponsive, lately, to most," she said, stepping hallways; I flowed after her in her wake. "You smile, I'll transmit."

Abandoning Judy's office, we drifted through Dryco's new halls. A month before, as we underwayed our training, the Bronx headquarters finally opened, and all operations uptowned from Manhattan. The building's saffron spear stabbed heaven, scattering clouds; appeared altitudinous enough to be struck by rockets as yet unglared. Dryco Tower epidermed perfect; its innards yet transitioned. Topladen containments crowded passages, farragoed workstations

cluttered all around; rugs awaited laying, charts wanted
posting. Not all elevators elevated, yet all yawned at command to admit the unwary. Three days earlier, an executive
marketeer in charge of Dryco's Indonesian sphere—suffering work-induced insomnia, entering her third foodless
day—had misstepped, and expressed one hundred floors;
incompany looselips gossiped that she dropped not by
chance, but choice. Regooded Dryco gifted her husband
with the cost of her urn.

"What's meant, he's nonresponsive?" I asked; wondered
what prevented her gown's hem from sweeping the floor as
she walked.

"He's introverting," she said. "He'll word me, or his sister,
or the damned computer—"

"Alice?"

"None other. Even when he words us, he words us sole in
Ambient talk."

"Serious?" When we were young we'd heard such talk,
down in old Loisaida, where they hid; in secreting their
gloriously misshapen husks from the world, Ambients secreted their speech as well, burying thought in the brambles
of a clotted argot. Some believed their cant melodied pure;
its garble headached me each time it hit my ear. None spoke
it any longer, I'd thought; weren't all Ambients, like
Loisaida, gone and lostaway for years? Certainly Ambients
would never have stood to be regooded.

"And so I reply likewise. And Alice now words to no one
but him. If I say something he chooses not to hear, he
deafens; Leverett's plugged him twiceover. So no one listens,
and sense goes unheard. Such complications madden, Iz.
Fuckall. A better job I'd choose, if I druthered. But then
Leverett would only see greater chance to grab. I'll see him
six under first."

"Then he's not speaking to Leverett—?" I asked.

"Never did," she said. "Leverett speaks, he listens. That's
what's downfalled."

Judy superiored Leverett, as she superiored all, though
he'd been the sole Dryconian who'd been at his position
since before her arrival. For years he'd worked his duties,
unseen and unheard; then at once some short time before,
he enlivened as if possessed, as if another had crept into his
bed one night to supplant his being as he slept.

"Where'll my office be?" I asked, realizing I'd not been
shown it during my initial visit. Judy didn't immediately
respond; waited until we turned a corner, and faced a humming white wall.

"We'll decide after this project's put down."

She twisted her bracelet, twice to the left and once to the
right. As the hum ceased the wall opened and Mister O'Malley's outer office revealed itself, free of furniture, executaries, or any corporate accoutrements. Judy proclaimed our
arrival as we entered the space, shouting her name so that
those listening might hear.

"Avalon," a man's voice responded, crying out from unseen speakers. "Behold me."

Mister O'Malley's doors parted, sans sound; peering sanc-
tumways, we beheld. I'd not seen him in eighteen years; in
the old building his entrances and exits were separate from
all others. Here, twenty meters distant, he sat desked, staring
south through the glass behind him, across his Bronx garden toward a dozen multistory trellises with covers but half-
encircling. We crossed a lake-size maroon rug isled with
stains of coffee. Dryco's owner was John's size squared; his
sagging shoulders and wrinklepuckered eyes falsified his
look as John's age quintupled. John had seven years advantage over his superior; or disadvantage, depending.

"Friends, Seamus?" asked a woman at Mister O'Malley's
deskside. His sister, of whom I'd often heard, though again,
never seen: as legended incompany, it passed that she'd
been in some way treated, and wasn't quite right. She evidenced more years than me, though like her brother she
might have held fewer; her biceps were larger than my

thighs, and she could have tossed her sibling at command, if she wished. Drapes of auburn hair curtained her eyes, and her smile belied content.

"Friendsall, Enid," he told her, swiveling round to confront us; his voice-pitch was higher than his size would have led to expect. "Tell," he said, regarding Judy.

"Watched pots ready to boil, Seamus," Judy replied. "Our pigeons keen to fly. Pose last wishes, and so beglow the chosen."

"Then give ear to the wind and hear the hurricane. Regooding demands redemption," he said, his stare losing its focus in the gap between his eyes and ours. "Lovers love, journeyending."

"He wishes well. Hopes all settles, husbandwise," she retold to me. Extending his hand, he motioned for us to come forward; I noticed that his right forefinger lacked its first knuckle. A micromonitor broke his desktop's plain; I estimated that daylong he gazed into Alice's blue mirror, awaiting answers, perhaps recalling old secrets, slipping away from the day. His sister's head jerked as she craned her neck, as if her form were guided by strings. She spoke, keeping an expression seeming tacked to her face.

"Who are your friends, Seamus?" she asked, with fourteen-year-old's apprehension; with taloned fingernails she raked pink designs into her legs.

"Co-conspirators," he told her. "Night's fellow travelers."

"They go to your school?"

He nodded. "Our rails parallel at close range, commingling as one once horizoned."

"Word as preferred, Seamus," Judy said, her voice commanding obeisance. The company he kept was Dryco; as CEO, the company was hers as well: Judy had heretofore fulfilled all Mister O'Malley's wishes while furthering her own designs; they had always symbiosed well. "Bestill all fear. Grant your tongue to flap. The blind need one-eye sight."

"Sight betroubles those who viz too clear," he said. "Pluck loose lying eyes, and cast skull's dry sockets over green, pleasant land."

"Seamus?" his sister interrupted, rubbing spittle-foam from her grin's sharp points. "Lunchtime. Take us to lunch."

"Hushabye, Enid," Mister O'Malley said; turning to us, employed a softer voice. "Lookabout. This wicked world befuddles master and servant likeminded. Chaos fences tempers round. Millions cling to dead past longbegone, sucking dead hosts, spending like moths in unseen flame."

"Old hinders new, flying in fact's face," Judy translated. "Time to move on."

"Elvii misbeliefs dry bones' marrow," he continued, "rend purse and pocket. They convene their daft congress, heedless of our own sessions, wetdreaming absolution from one incapable. Deadeyed to light, they opt for dark." He shook his head. "Lemmings racing cliffways, and here we stand stillfooted, marveling at the cold gray waste."

"E's fools breathe our needed air," Judy said. "Distract multitudes with tales of vague return. Sense demands we settle." She annotated with a whisper. "My sense says we'll not."

"All Elvii bewail their lot," he said. "Grow bony by feasting on fancy. Digging oases of pain in deserts of comfort." Mister O'Malley blinked, gazing into his desktop; stared more intently, as if into a pool whose mirror, unexpectedly, revealed another's reflection, one not immediately recognizable. "Such jabbernowling frets and hinders. Our good works go out sans gratitude and all suffer. Therefore, if the converted won't reconvert, their master, or one so guised, should undertake to play our tune. A touch of truthache essentials, lest sharper drama too soon becloak our stage, and weary our watchers of our play."

"Options sole," said Judy, "our neck or theirs."

"Friends," his sister said, interrupting once more; a

thread of spittle hung from her mouth. "Seamus, friends?"

"Friends. Yes, Enid," he sighed. "So if in seeking that other world's obscure object you find him, then the Elvii's savior can be awarded bespoken, and shall pronounce as we wish, calming all with his words. His lightning rod shall drain heaven's wrath, leaving sunlight clarified clear. Our new dawn's fingers shall stroke with lover's touch until they fade to black. The Elvii deserve their desired, as the bright-minded deserve us." He eyeshut, as if to sleep, and dreama-way; reawakening, he spoke of what he'd dreamed. "In the gone world, similar once was tried, to sad result."

"Dryden attempted the like sans E figure," Judy said, and again, added commentary. "This'll result sadder, sure."

"Friends, Seamus." His sister thumbedged smiling, circular faces in the dust atop Mister O'Malley's desk. Mentally challenged, mayhap; she knew her logo so well as any. "Happy."

"Yes, Enid. Happy." His sister slapped her knees with her hands as if joyful with her noise, staining her palms crimson as they touched her newmade scars. "Then fly break-necked," he told me, his eyes at last seeking mine, "over there and back again. Guise yourself in stealth's cloak, and cross. Seek. Find. Return. Afterward, lucked, their new shall regood what's left of our old."

"If successed," Judy transposed, "we be messiasized."

With his hand Mister O'Malley traced his face's knobs and valleys, as if sanding his fingertips upon his stubble, to make his grasp more delicate, therefore undetectable; as if assuring himself that he was still there. Examining me twiceover before reaverting his eyes, he momentarily incarnated my husband's face upon his own, expressing sans word that he'd closer neared what each—all—sought.

"All good," he concluded. "Till time's lovely end."

Windowways, beads of blue fire flared; dropped from an ever-restrung strand. "Sooner," I heard Judy mutter, as we backed away from his desk.

*   *   *

Between elevator and exit I vizzed the thousand faces of
Dryco; its glories manifested throughout the new red lobby,
upon its stone floor, beneath its vaults and arches and
groins. So chambered, I knew entrapment's feel: jailed
within a whale's heart, or in the bloodied womb of Godness.
Blasphemy, mayhap, to so meld spiritual metaphor with
secular truth; but mine is a faithful blasphemy. Mother
Church thralled John and me: we took the Visions of Joanna, Revised, as truthed; when desperate, found—could
find no longer—comfort in Her grace; believed as any believed in God and Godness, the Two in One, who preserve
Their world that, when Day comes, They might destroy all
and enact a cosmic regooding.

Their competition was present in guise, if not spirit. E's
gilded statue revolved atop a pedestal, amid all else which
Dryco had gifted unto its world; his icon was shipped from
the Dryden estate after Mister O'Malley's redevelopment of
the property and, prepping for what was to come, reinstalled
here. E's dead eyes stared blind upon his potential worshipers; his vast sculpted belly held a world's weight. His congregants outnumbered, and outshouted, those who followed
Godness; my fellow heathen and I knew no escape from the
King.

Elvii were as locusts: harmless, even funful, when singled,
and suffocating, massed. They swarmed into their services
and into the mass gatherings they termed ElCons, praying
for, talking about, listening to and posing as the King for
days on end, segregating themselves from the world to cele-
brate their increasing strength; then, recharged, they'd appear amid the unafflicted populace, proselytizing sans
cease, berating their co-workers, distributing illiterate tracts
and zines, deadheading computer lines, vandalizing walls
and screens with their deconstruction of the word. Dialogu-
ing with Elvii became, inevitably, monologuing: they under-

stood no referents but E, and all else existed but to be measured against his greatness and found lacking. That *they* believed didn't satisfy; to their eyes all should want him as desperately, and to the exclusion of everything else.

Millions wanted the King now, wanted without cease, fullfaithed and overt; but which King? The C of E was one church become many; its mitosis ensued at conception, and seemed primed to split, divide and resplit unto perpetuity. Each new denomination contained from its birth fresh infidels, keen to look askance and thereafter contrary: take, as exampled, the Prearmyites. Within their ranks were souls believing the rhythms of E's songs to have been irredeemably tainted, once accompanied by drums; others certained that in recording's act an impenetrable firewall came down between singer and hearer; the sect's fundamentals affirmed sans admittance and argument that between song headheard and throatsung, the shadow showed: that not even the King himself comprehended his deepest glories.

And the Prearmyite denomination was but one: amongst the Elvii were the Hosts of Memphis, the Shaken, Rattled and Rolled, the River Jordanaires; the Gracelandians, the Vegassenes, the Gladyseans; the C of E Now or Never, the Redeemed Believers in Our Master's Voice, the Church of the True Assumption of His Burning Love, and a hundred dozen more. Each schismatrix knew their King true, and saw their road as sole and only; their only given was that, for whatever reason, and—they supposed—at no one's command, the King would return.

There were no longer overt Elvii in the tenth and ultimate circle of Dryco as there had been in the Drydens' time; Judy, for one, I suspect, would have preferred that all Elvii be neutralized in oldstyle manner. But regooding forbade elimination, necessitated appeasement. By suggestion of Leverett, by command of Mister O'Malley, against Judy's every wish, it was Dryco's given that if E returned, John and I would bring him, in the guise of his other world's counter-

part, that he might be tossed into his crowd and so docile
them, if not in rejoining quotidian life, at least into departing fully from it. That was the theory as we'd thus far heard
it. His exact material form in that other world immaterialled: his new overseers would reengrave the image
stolen into desired shape, pleasing his followers in whatever
way they wished; but pleasing Dryco, first of all.

"Denude," I heard my doctor's voice demand; I did. "Table
yourself."

Her image fluttered as a windblown flag, revealing only
multihue blur free of formal line. Even when my medicis
onscreened true it remained uncertifiable that the women
seen were the women speaking; Dryco invariably hired pos-
ers if their look better suited perceived prejudice.

"Arms over and above," my nurse's monitor voiced.
"Spread."

As per the employee plan, females were treated by females
in Dryco's health clinics, dissecting and probing and poking
with neither less sympathy, nor greater kindness, than would
have males. Their names were nonessentialled info; I never
knew what to call them that might lull forth an unwitting—
any—response. Once unshelled, I reclined upon cold metal,
wincing at its heel-to-head burn, suspecting that when I
departed the clinic this time—as I suspected, every time—
my toes would be tagged, my eyelids sewn shut and my sheet
wrapped tight around me.

"Inhale."

Their machines's songs ascended Eastern scales, warming
into vibrant modality; once revved, they wailed as banshees.
A host of utensils emerged from tabletop, prepping to examine and prod. Metal baffles lifted, encompassing me, that
during treatment I could not meet their surrounding stare.
Steel bands unribboned, cuffing my wrists; clamps took hold
of my ankles and extended upward, angling my legs forty

degrees upward. "Physical underway," my doctor noted her record, and then spoke to me. "Relax."

Our docs never neared living patients; needless exposure to such vectors of transmission inevitabled otherwise-avoidable infection.

"Circulatories, normal," my nurse said, descending the list. "Gene stimulations, uninterrupted. Transmissions, steady. Respiration, acceptable. Lymphonic conversion, responsive. T-cell progressions, negative. Neural response, appropriate. Cell regrowth, positive—"

"Perspiration, hypertropic," my doctor noted. "Adrenaline output elevating. Blood pressure rising. *Relax*, Bonney."

Both nurse and doctor seemed to speak from Mars. Ceiling reflections of machine-light shimmered as if watercast.

"Rectal readings," my doctor said, "suitabled. Throttle up."

"Boosters ready." A dozen needles speared me, piercing my arms, my legs, my bottom, neck and spine. Immobilized as I was, all I could do was scream.

"Administering vaccinations and reboosts as per program: measles A and B, hepatitis varietals, gamma-g, typhoid, Sabin, DS, DPT, malaria, HIV one through six, coryza series, TB, influenza, smallpox, RecomStrain, yellow fever, Carcinomile, RNA screens, pneumonics. Contraindications noted, no unpredicted danger foreseen."

"Catscans?" asked my nurse.

"Demonstrate patient's continued viability. Prepare for pelvic insertion."

My legs, assisted, reached greater altitude as their separation increased, and then the table intruded itself into me; its rod felt to have been chilled for weeks. My fingers grasped at air as I felt myself split. A year-long minute passed before either nurse or doctor spoke.

"Examination proceeding," said the nurse. I saw a yellow light blinking.

"Celibate state not contractually demanded," said my doctor, after perfunctory observations. "Cycles abnormalling?"

"No."

"Louder, please. Detail reasons."

"Husband," I said. "His mood lacks. I'm hurting—"

"Pain responses within boundaries. Discharge evident. Ovulation patterns suitable. Dermal reactions—"

"Relax," the table's loudspeaker voiced, sounding with a man's ingratiating rumble.

"Pacify yourself to lessen discomfort. Silence, please. Sedative application proceeding," said my nurse.

"Don't dope me. Don't—" But their additives already coursed through the needles; momentslong, my head lightened, and as perception altered I watched the overheads waving as if they'd taken on a semblance of life. Shortly, the pain was almost describable, if not bearable.

"Melanin production abeying as predicted in British studies of Melaway," my doctor noted. "Caucasian similitude attainable on schedule as desired. Continue avoiding noonday sunlight."

"This drug," I tried to say, "Affecting more than—"

"Corrective agent," she reworded. "Drugs heal. Corrective agents correct."

"Term it as suited," I said. "All's incorrective. Headaches, daily. Nausea unavoidable, every morn. Vomiting and cramps. I jointache as if bonebroken. Melaway's causing all, I know—"

"Expected. Silence, please. Health dissemination proceeding."

"Relax," the table said.

"Expected?" I replayed, hearing my words slur as I enabled them to crawl over my lips. "Every effect?"

"Not unexpected," my doctor said. "Further questions?"

"AO. At treatment termination I'll darken anew?"

"As detailed earlier," she said. "Original skin pigmenta-

tion redevelops within three weeks following cessation of
treatment with Melaway. Exhale."

"Certify harmlessness," I said. "These effects—"

"Total harmlessness uncertifiable with any experimental
corrective agents. Silence, please. Further elaboration inessentialled within program guidlines and can only result in
patiental intensified confusion induction. Inhale."

Their thing slid deeper into me. "Get it out," I shouted,
not wanting to cry.

"Tear salinity, acceptable," my doctor said. "Calm yourself, please, preparatory to withdrawal. Greater pain may
result otherwise."

"Ready automatic release," said my nurse.

"Ready," said the table.

My wrists, fresh-accessoried with blue-black bracelets,
slipped loose of their bonds. My intruder slipped out as I
rose. Glimpsing a red jewel newly adorning its chromed tip,
I felt my throat bile over. As I dragged myself off the table
I nearly collapsed, feeling physical agony as intense as my
emotional pain, and would have tumbled groundward had
I not caught myself. The room spun round me, as if to
launch itself skyward with I, its fuse.

"Smile," my nurse's voice said. "Your day awaits."

"Madam still thinks mass movements undocilable, eh?"
Leverett said; aiming a finger toward his temple he twirled
it, and smiled. "Unreason's sleep breeds madness, poor
thing. We'll calm the Elvii too, whatever she imagines. Regooding works in all areas of human endeavor, depending
upon approach."

Leverett, sixty-six, appeared fifty; he'd overseen Dryco's
New Projects division since soon after century's turn. His suit
looked as if he'd bought it the summer after graduation, and
had slept in it every night since, though all knew he had
them made to so impress; his hair was tousled artfully by one

of many assistants who were appointed to come by and tousle it. Leverett's suit and hair were of like hue, though I couldn't immediately distinguish which had been dyed to match.

"Marvelous weather," he said. Eyeing windowways I watched a waterspout kilometers distant take root in the harbor's gray field. Leverett's office was splendidly plain: its bleakness was enhanced by one desk, mismatched chairs, a stack of printout, a Harvard banner and portraits of his position's two predecessors. "Hairs the chest."

"Undesirable," said John, leaning forward in his chair; as he shifted closer to Leverett's desk a flock of paper clips flew from their nest and rested on his shirtfront.

"How'd they magnetize you?" Leverett asked as John plucked the clips loose. My husband, as did all in Security, had strips of Krylar dermally implanted across his torso, that missiles might be deflected without recoursing to bulky outerwear; Security once did all that was possible to stress-lessen its workers in body and mind.

"Passing side effect of morning's tests," John answered, "I'm told." I'd met my husband after clinicking; John's session had been no more enjoyable than mine. "Departure date solid yet?"

"Wednesday next. Expectations must be mounting sky-high, considering what lies ahead," Leverett said, smiling so unceasingly, if with more subtly evinced awareness, as Mister O'Malley's sister. "Travelready?"

"We're hep, dad," I said, demonstrating the command I'd gained in properly wording those whom we might encounter. "Keen to lay rubber."

Comprehending my rewordings without overmuch confusion, Leverett allowed his smile to broaden until his skull seemed set to drop from his jaw. "AO, Isabel. Clear as air," he said. "Plaintext English suffices here, needless to say. What necessaries remain, at present? So many tracks, my train gets lost sometimes."

"Evening meet with Biggerstaff set for this eve," I said. "Course finals, Friday."

"Fine, fine. Your teachers prepped to apple?" We nodded. "Couldn't have selected better than you two if we'd tried." Fisting one hand, he struck his other, rejoicing at the sound of skin hurting skin. "Oh, Godness. Superfluous to say where I'd go, if I wasn't essentialled here—"

"Where?" John asked, employing Jakeish methods: inquiring of the obvious where no inquiry was expected, that unpracticed reactions might be studied, and appraised, and filed into memory for possible later use. "Where would you go?"

"*There*. Over there," said Leverett, his smile unchanging. His simplest reaction impressed me as long-practiced and heartknown, if not heartfelt. I didn't distrust Leverett more or less than any for whom I worked, supposed co-believer of ours in God and Godness though he might be; John, of suspicious mind, forever reattuned to those around him, and so kept greater distance. Once I termed Leverett avuncular; John said he'd never allow him near children, whosever they were. "It's a dream mission, truly. Over there you'll see how we all could have gone."

"I've concerns," said John.

"Allow me to mentor," he said, his eyes dog-eager and as dark. "It's what I'm made for. No policy better than honesty. Detail deepest thoughts. What's felt?" I silenced, lipstill; by then numberless tests had come so unexpectedly, so often, that I considered at length the simplest inquiries. "Relax," he said. "No answer wrong here. What troubles?"

"The polarization," John said. "Madam's disbelief unyields, yet with each meet your spiel intenses till we seem stopping short of reinventing wheels. The difference troubles overmuch."

"Mister O'Malley approves full," said Leverett, reclining in his unpadded chair. "All have opinions, his matter most." He gestured toward the portrait of his male predecessor, a middleage man of unsettling look whose painted stare blistered whomever his eyes sighted. "Timeover there've been questions and qualms incompany over method and purpose. Mister Leibson always contraried if the betterment of the company demanded. Timeover he was proven right."

"He was exed, nonetheless," John said. "Might history repeat?"

"It was an interfamilial matter," said Leverett. "Mrs. Dryden. Mindaddled. You know the tales. A tragedy, nonetheless. My blessing, that I was mentored by one so great. Mister Liebson enabled Dryco to be what it became."

Leverett's other predecessor was female, and named Joanna, or so worded the frame's inscription. Her face interested me more than Liebson's; her fear, unlike his, directed not out but in. Hers was a twentieth-century face, haloed with blond hair, staring with sleepless look, countenancing lightbright with unaccepted pain. She'd suicided as well, or so Leverett told; yet another mindaddled, he said.

"Then what so necessaries Dryco's regooding?" John asked.

"Changing circumstance," Leverett said, "as told. Regooding's a simple process. Minor readjustments, a clock's winding, new soles on the shoes. Some improve at will," he said, looking at me. "Elvii, sadly, respond to no prompts other than their own. As Mister O'Malley has said, sense goes unheard. Ergo, we'll calm them as they wish, since nothing else suffices."

"A corresponding E's existence is unassured," John said.

"Statistics evidence an eighty per chance." said Leverett. "Numbers' comfort satisfies."

"Statistics lie, told to lie," John said. His damp forehead beaded, and he tempered so, that I feared he'd forgotten to medicate. I took his hand, hoping to calm; he slipped free of my grip. "If the goal's nonexistent, all's pointless."

"Nonexistent? Unknown unless tried," said Leverett. "We'll tack a different course in event of unsuccess, but one attempt's demanded. Ends justify means, however the turn-out. What concerns so, as the date nears and all plans ready to engage?"

"Promotion's assured?" John asked, pointing towards me, seeming unmindful of his own proposed raise. Leverett sat back in his chair; examined us—still smiling—as if he were our father, and was disappointed we'd found it necessary to ask about something promised, however often he'd reneged in the past.

"Doubled salaries in either circumstance," he said. "If all successes, unimaginable fulfillment is certified as contracted. Our world and all its wonders will lay platterways before you."

John shrugged, quieted. A different concern beset my mind. "I discussed particulars of medical problems with Madam—"

"She awared me," Leverett said, his smile narrowing. He reached into his desk, taking from a secured compartment two pill-filled tubes. "Had to roundabout a bit on these. All doors open when one knows the knock," he said, laughing, passing me one of the containers. "This will intensify Melaway's recomplexioning process. A like formula, similar to what you have. Take one each night till departure, along with your other dose, neither more nor less." He handed the second tube to John. "For you."

"Added dope?" he asked, pocketing it.

"I wouldn't call it that," Leverett said. "Should assist your trials. Again, take along with what's prescribed. There, now. Further questions?"

"What if we find the other world's E," I asked, "and he's disinclined to return?"

"Would anyone deny proffered godhead?" Leverett asked, his facade agleam with a child's astonishment. "Choose a limboed life over one spent in something approximating heaven? If he's there, and if he's found, relate your truth predeparture, if necessaried. Cliffside him, and show him his awaiting cities. Hold any carrots you have close to his nose." His smile engorged, revealing rows of whitened teeth. "If he still doubts," Leverett said, eyeing my husband as he rattled his bottle of pills, "well, you'll convince. My trust implicits."

"General Biggerstaff—"

"Luther, please. Formalities never suited," he said. "Listen as I tell. Point of transferral was here." He tapped Russia's gold meadowlands with coppery fingers. "Point of emergence, here." Adjusting his touch as if to better please a lover, he stroked Pennsylvania's rosy mountains. "You've been awared of the displacement effects of high velocity, surely. Shouldn't expect similar, moving at slower pace."

"This globe," John asked, vizzing the world before him. "Dated when?"

"1939," said Luther. "Summer. It's of our world, of course. Eye Germany, there. Austria and Czechoslovakia already annexed. Poland not yet overrun, and the future just over the edge."

Imprinted upon the orb were splotches of pink and green and yellow, lingering evidence of lands long lost: Tibet and Madagascar, Baluchistan and Siam; Chosen, Tannu Touva, the Belgian Congo and Nyasaland. What were Nyasas? Where had they gone? Were they sent away by others, or had they packed themselves off en masse, that they alone might perpetrate the erasure of their memory? Standing in his living room, staring at his globe, I studied our world's face as it once showed itself. Did the resemblance to theirs still hold true, or had, unbeknownst to us or mayhap even to them, a third world emerged from the mix?

"Enumerate their world's dissimilar manifests," John said.

"Innumerable," said Luther.

"What were your impressions?" I asked.

"Tragic beauty. Grateful loss. All descriptives are contradictory. My opinions are meaningless, after all. Rewrite the book according to your wishes as you read."

The Biggerstaffs were forty-seventh-floored in a new Dryco building, on One-Eighty, near the park. I remembered going as a child to the old zoo, seeing animals so lost as Nyasas or Baluchistanis. Those living in the surrounding neighborhood, prior to its levelling, hadn't yet killed them all. I trepidated that evening upon entering their apartment; his wife, we were told, was from that other world, and no one briefed us as to how she would show. Luther greeted us singly, appearing to hold fewer years than in truth he actually held. After a half hour passed in his wife's absence, I relaxed enough to almost forget she was there.

"This'll show at borderbreak?" John asked, studying a framed photo ahang on a wall that pictured a sharp white spear and marbled ball.

"Your guess, my guess," Luther said. "We tore ours down. They have their own style."

As did Luther; the photo was contemporaneous with the decor. Throughout the apartment were century-old antiques: Kodachromed postcards of erased American streets, stony, gargoyled towers, and restaurants guised in animal shape; bloodshaded tumblers, lamps with smooth chrome curves, skyscraper-sleek bottles, stepsided clocks faced with angular, unreadable numbers; tins logoed with non-Dryco insignia, the silver moons of hubcaps affixed to peach-pale walls. Atop an oversized wooden radio was an insecticide sprayer, its shape reminiscent of streamlined male genitalia, recast in dented tin; the painted letters FLIT underlay the shaft's rust.

"Your museumpieces astonish," I said, eyeing it all. "Such a collection."

"It's a bloodsport like any other. The past pleases overmuch to be entirely healthy," Luther said. "My wife needs dinner. Excuse me."

Luther trod catfooted, glancing through the doors he

passed, moving as John moved: those tarred with the Army
or Security brush forever revealed their conditioning, however they tried to hide it, stepping as if each movement
might bring blast, hooding their eyes against what didn't
have to be seen.

"You crossed unaware of what lay before you," John said.
"What resulted?"

"Expect your own shocks," said Luther, switching on kit-
chenlight; pausing before he entered the room. "They've
prepped you so well as possible for this, I gather?"

"We're doubleprepped," I said. "Classed in linguistics,
sociobservation, popular artifacts, cultural anticipation, historical processes—"

He masked his face as he spoke, revealing nothing.
"They're bleaching you? That's wise. They've absolute apartheid there, and nothing inkled that it was about to
change—"

"Forewarned, forearmed," I said. "I'm prepped to slough
away hurt."

"It'll slough like burnt skin," he said. "Excuse present
company, but whites are worse than devils over there. You'll
be in New York, I reason. Unimaginable what the rest is
like." Luther extracted a wrapped tray from the freezer and
slid it into the unit. "Can you tell what essentials this trip?"

"You weren't briefed?" He shook his head, and sat down
at his table, gesturing that we should sit as well. "Forgive and
understand, we can't relate—"

"Understood," he said. "I was outcompanied till retirement, to all intent. Jake was held irreplaceable by the company, but he chose not to return. I'd have been happy to
bring him back, regardless. Blame must sleep somewhere,
and Dryco found my bed best. When would it be over there,
now?"

"1954," I said. "May's first week."

He nodded. "Keep minded. The longer you're there," he
said, "the worse it'll become."

John's expression shadowed, as if his curtains drew tighter, hearing of that other world's limited blessings; he appeared unsurprised by Luther's warning. "It took you long to readjust, postreturn?" he asked. Luther's expression inferred that the thought had never occurred; that, mayhap, he'd never readjusted. The unit's bell rang; he walked over and reset the warmer for an additional minute. "Wanda likes hers burnt black," he explained.

"Your wife is here?" I asked, recalling her theoretical presence; unexpectedly, I discerned her spirit near, and shivered with the sense of feeling a cool draft, or ice brushed along my spine.

"She keeps to herself," Luther said. "Consider this question personal rather than corporate. What concerns you most about your trip?"

"Returning," I said.

Luther nodded. "Don't expect to."

The chime rerang; Luther extracted the tray from the unit and flayed away its glittering skin, easing back from the steamjet so as not to scald himself.

"Understood," John said. Luther slipped on kitchen mitts before lifting the tray. "You knew Jake well?" My husband's voice came unexpectedly soft, as if we were alone.

"Did you?" Luther asked. "My wife needs feeding. You'd care to meet?"

"She's from the other world?" I said, hoping that he'd deny. He nodded, raising the tray before him with shaking hands, as if in offerance to one who might slap him down. I perceived in him the penultimate result of our unavoidable syzygy with time; how its touch changed over years from that of lover to that of snake, its embrace crushing as it hardened, stealing all life but for that upon which it needed to feed before crawling away.

"Her own world," our host corrected. "If you do return, be mindful," he added. "Whoever passes, changes."

We followed him through a passage lined with old gray

engravings of Manhattan scenes, etched as if with needles of smoke, capturing glimpses of our own lost world. Even at their moment of existence those places and people were made of stuff less lasting than what had seized their shadows; concepts of the other world never seemed less empirical, nor more evanescent, than the irreality of our own.

Luther slid open a door at the hall's end. Beyond was a darkened room, full of light. Twenty wall-installed monitors girdled his wife, each set to different channels. Each set's volume was audible enough that thirty babblebits of language might be misunderstood simultaneously. Luther's wife sat statue-still in a chair, facing most of the screens, her eyes so unblinking as theirs. Multitone spectra rainbowed her black face.

"Wanda, honey," Luther said, kneeling beside her. "You hungry?" She muted, too enraptured by her visions to heed the world beyond her illusionary ring. "Wanda," he repeated. "Chowtime, honey. Open wide."

He lifted a strip of potato impaled on the tines of a fork to her mouth, prodding her lips apart; she made mouthmotions as if, drowning, she wished to suck in more water. Luther's wife never took her look from the sets as she admitted the fork; when he extracted his instrument, she chewed what he'd given her with care, as if she were conscious enough to want to avoid biting her tongue, or lip, or the inside of her cheek.

"That good?"

She nodded. Momentslong he knelt there, free of word; it evidenced that his attentions redirected themselves solely to his wife, when they were bound in one room. He smiled, regarding her with television eyes, skycolored and endowed with induced life. I fancied that after endless exposure to unspeakable broadcasts, he'd settled upon this single channel, one showing all he could still bear to see.

"I'm so sorry," I said.

"Why?" Luther asked, plainfacing puzzlement over my

offering; his voice's tones placing inexpressibly distant as they landed in my ears. "She's happier." His wife laughed; she'd seen something funny on one of the screens. "Don't bring souvenirs, if you return," he said, losing his smile. "Nostalgia's worse than any drug."

3

□

"You anticipate with pleasure a trip unassuring guaranteed return?"

"Not unassuring hope," I replied. A crack, ceilingways, appeared to my upturned eyes as a hair in milk. A chlorine scent permeated the room, as if it had contained a pool recently drained.

"Because return isn't guaranteed?"

"Nada," I said, correcting; regathered my thoughts and expressed something I believed I knew, at least until the moment I expressed the belief. "I've no wish to suicide."

"Your negatives are most positive."

"My husband so wishes."

"You think he wishes to die?"

"An unwavered yes." Unwavered; still, I could answer true for only one of us. Vizzing downward, I regarded the space between my feet. The clock's readout awared me that this final session was but half-done. Drafts rustled the wall-cloaking drapes that muffled all outroomed sounds.

"Why suspect your husband of thanautopian desires?"

"His actions evidence plain, as recounted timeover. Expressed thoughts and deeds demonstrate as well. His words and facial affect hold a matching slackness evident to all."

"As you interpret."

"As they reveal," I said. A poster of a Magritte work affixed to the curtains on my right reproduced the artist's green apple filling a tiny room. The wording announced a retrospective at the Postmodern, two years earlier. I'd not attended; surrealists' work was too mindfully suffused with tradition to suit my preferences. There were throughout Dryco's building, along with portraits of incompany notables departed and present, multicultural artworks of five centuries, all selected by Mister O'Malley, each possessing some private relevance; creating in toto once their details were examined and collated—or so Judy informed me—a pattern overt to none save Mister O'Malley.

"This depresses you?"

"Overmuch," I said, "sans relief."

Throughout those quarters buzzed a barely-heard hum, semblancing lifesound more effectively than white noise generally did; sounding as bees in a nearby yard, a sick kitten's purr, neighbor's latenight noise discerned through the bedroom wall or the digitalized aspiration of artifical lungs.

"A pleasurable depression, or one best avoided?"

"Depression can be pleasurable?" I asked.

"For some, when enhancing dreams of self-enacted conclusion."

"I take no such pleasure."

"So stated. This belief impresses full?"

"As a song in the brain."

"Who does the singing?" I was asked. "Depression scores its own fantasia, with fortissimo drowning truest truth. In such a state imagined leitmotivs, previously unheard, swell up from the noteflow. How does the listener know if they're truly in the score?"

"Unknown," I said.

"Self-analysis's perils proven."

"Doubtful, regardless."

"Attempt another approach. What is your fantasy about your trip?"

"You mean what I hope will happen, once we're done? Or while we're there?"

No response forthcame; lying on the couch, seeing in the ceiling, as in clouds, faces of loved and hated alike, I wished as ever for an ever-absent clarity.

"Which?" I asked. "What's meant?"

"What is your fantasy about your trip?"

Before answering I closed my eyes; considered my most honest response, if not the one I'd have preferred to give. "To reengrave our image," I said. "Make all that was, whole again. The attempt matters. True?"

"What is your fantasy about your trip?"

"Why was what's said inapplicable?" I asked; again, silence. "I only want us bettered. Of late we've only worsened, seeming with our wishes. A remade life, that's what's desired. But it'll never pass if—"

"Your fantasy? Your fantasy? Your fantasy?"

Troubled by my interrogator's new-erupting obsession, I turned over to confront fullfaced, wanting to disturb it as I had been disturbed; saw phrased onscreen unexpected, unsurprising, words:

DOWNBLOCK ERRORED / SYSTEMIC FLAW /
ANALYSIS PROCEEDING.

"Your fantasy. Your fant—"

My analyzer continued its rewrought analysis, so unwitting as any patient of its most obvious compulsion. A frayed wire, or encased dustmote, prevented me from goodbyeing one who'd so kindly simulated care. I'd allowed this particular chain to enwrap me so close that now, loosed so unexpectedly, I felt no freedom; only bereftness.

Would my husband miss his chains more than me? What if I were the one who loosed them? My head ached as if it were being hollowed out from within. Uncouching myself, I left the office, shutting the door behind me.

In the lobby I met John, embraced his stillness, shivered at his chill. The light crimsoned us, and, standing there, I wondered how long we had left to bleed.

For two hours that afternoon we reresearched, reassuring familiarity with the construct of E: instilling ourselves thrice-over with given truth gleaned from memoirs of cousins, guards, percussionists, psychic hairdressers, and all those who, while earthed, remained close to the heavenly one; reheard tales told of the Dutch Devil, recounted by Goldman (the more respectable sects of the C of E, thinking themselves freethinkers, referred to the latter only as *the Jew*); reexamined news accounts entered into computer files so obsoleted that only Alice was enabled to rosetta their lost linguas; reread sources deemed apocryphal by the faithful, telling of revelations so unlike accepted texts, and so unsettling to fundamentalists, that even sans critique they held, for infidels, the greatest credence.

During our training John and I daily monitored, drenching ourselves in image, studying eleventh-generation footage; vizzed fuzzedged clips stolen from a black and white youth, eyed midcareer films so faded as to limn his skin orange, his hair blue. Vids shot during his penultimate months most disconcerted, ambering onstage moments when—as went the word of Elvii—holy spirit so infiltrated his being that, mid-song, he would segue into drooling glossolalia. In those most special moments E did appear possessed; by what, I hesitate to say.

Yet in his essence was a mystery barely theological. E's musical expressions—the sole hard reality we had of him, however secondhand—were consistent; but never in either

print or image did the same E twice appear. Both the Elvii
and those opposed advantaged this, timeover. That the am-
bulatorially-unabled might walk, the visually-challenged
see, the speech-inhibited shout when he beheld them
seemed, to many Elvii, undeniable; skeptics viewed him as
the Confederacy's final, and most effective, blow against the
Union. Those needing E most—including Dryco—came to
him freighted with preconceived notions of his anatomy,
that they might thereupon fashion a skin most preferable to
lay over those unavoidable bones; an act of creation not so
dissimilar from fetal art, it occurs to me now.

Does a beloved's actuality matter, while the image carries
comfort enough? In such circumstance is actuality ever admitted, or even recognized? Who suffers profoundest regret,
then, when truth rears ugly head: the worshiper, or the
worshiped?

John and I disbelieved in E's divinity; doubted even his
worth. That served as demonstrable asset when Leverett assigned us. Still, during our training, while E's presence was
daily extruded into our lives, it unavoidabled that we be
baptized in his flood, however unwillingly. Feeling myself so
drown, my surety sometimes wavered: it uncertained,
whether if in so unyieldingly admitting my chosen messiah,
I'd needlessly lost the grace of others more saving; I wondered whether my messiah as chosen had the look I wanted,
or the one I needed.

John's eyes no longer held any look; could either of us still
save the other? Did we still want to? Pick messiahs, and
spouses, with care.

"How powered?" John asked, standing with me that afternoon as we examined our trip's transport; the garage was
several levels beneath a generating plant, five blocks off
Pelham Park Boulevard. Tak, the engineer—a slender man,
Korean-descended, who evidenced only teenage years—

opened the auto's hood, that we might admire his work, and
placed his hands into a shiny box to let its air shake loose
their grime. The engine seen was a relic, agleam with mirrored flatware, with gray metal spotted and dabbed with
white ceramic, spaghettied round with blue and red wires.

"Employs standard batteries set, normally moded," said
Tak. "In third gear, mainline engages, assuring full thrust.
Speed one-twenty, top. Miles, mind, not k's."

"The potemkin's single-batteried," said John. "It's car-
buretored. The look's Smithsonian."

"You're vizzing style sans substance. Actual motor se-
cludes beneath in order to fool casual onlookers. Doubled
weightload resulting, so adjust as needed when circumstanced, as on wet roads."

The car's diamond eyes and metaled smile recalled an
idol's look; I considered the sacrifices that must once have
been offered unto it. As I circled its shell to open the driver's
door, I gazed at the roof's parabolic slope, the chrome-
streaked sidewalls and black leatherette innards. "It's a total
recreation?" I asked.

"Only within," Tak said, wheeling himself within his
handiwork. "1953 Hudson Hornet body, provided from the
Dryden collection. Steel, coldrolled. Two tons' fun. Rust-
proofed. Reconditioned especially for the trip."

"And bedecked in Brazilian funeral colors," John said.

"Huescheme's reproduced from period ads. Blame's not
mine." The car was duotoned bruise-purple below waist-
level, breadspread-yellow above; it resembled one of those
tropical beetles occasionally used by jewelers.

"The dash design couldn't remain so trad," Tak explained, beginning to decipher the two dozen dials. "Multiple readout devices are guised in old format where possible.
Observe, por fav." John and I followed the route of his finger
as it mapped the terrain. "Speedometer, here. Recompensa-
tor. Lightrod inserted here, to allow better nightsight; pulls

out when needed and automatically ignites. Battery gauge. Compass."

"Compass? Where're the geographics?" asked John.

"There'll be no satellite on that side to atlas in with," said Tak, prodding a stubby rod attached to the steering column. "Automatic transmission, three gears and reverse. AM radio, guaranteed against fadeout or sunspots." Switching its knob, he tuned in, bringing up the news.

"—missile fell this morning in Mexico City exurbs sustaining minor damage. Seven hundred missing—"

"Five hundred HP," Tak said, pressing the ignition. We tried to hear the actual engine's gentle whir beneath the soundtrack, a loud, rhythmic pounding. "Authentic V-8 engine sound. Inbuilt Lasereo on and offswitches automatically. Handy if otherworlders give ear as it's running. This is the flux monitor. Digitalizer, with necessary graphs available on demand. Geiger counter. Agitators, inside and out. Compensator. Tachometer. Area meteorologics panel here—"

"What's this?" John asked, tapping a blue ovoid bolted onto the steering wheel.

"Necker knob," said Tak. "Original accoutrement."

"Purpose?"

"For onehanding the wheel, freeing driver to fondle willing companions without dysfunctioning driving." Tak pointed at a red button located below the radio. "*Most* important. Your plan calls for returning to original entrance point after completion of mission, correct?"

"AO," said John. "If possible."

"If OEP is unreachable, employ this. *Only* if danger demands. Otherwise, consider it nonexistent."

"Why?" I asked. "What is it?"

"Concealed as overdrive," Tak said. "In truth, an Alekhine device. Upon employment, transfer immediately effects and car crosses back to this world. Trauma to vehicle and occupants will be great upon application, increasing proportionate to speed at the instant of transferral. Inferences suggest that this method caused, if in unknown manner, all previous terminations. The Alekhine device kills as it cures, authorities believe. But—"

"If needed," I said.

"Pay up and chance," said Tak. "But there it is."

"This screen," John said, fingering a blank rhomboid bordered by chrome ribbon. "Catalytic readings? Reconnaisance tracker?"

"Clock."

The pills Leverett provided drained away my lingering dark with indecent haste; ten hours after I'd dosed, my skin's gray vanished beneath a wash of pink and crimson, as if in night an artist, possessed by artistic inspiration perhaps believed divine, came upon me while I slept, and bespattered without warning the canvas there found.

"Bedaway, Iz," my husband said, calling to me through our bathroom door, on our predeparture evening. "Tomorrow'll be yesterday too soon."

"Hold the horses," I said, disrobing. Rinsing my flatironed hair a final time, rubbing added blondness into every strand, I concluded my bleach. Standing naked before the mirror, I saw myself through blue lenses, recreated as desired, an artist's delight: Venus atremble at seaside, another regooded resident to best suit our eternal city; one showing neither black nor white, but golden. I eyed my new and forever-unfamiliar image, troubled and attracted, wondering how long it would take me to forget who I'd been. Would my persona change to match my appearance? Had it already changed?

Prolonging my look overmuch, I began fearing that this metamorphosis was, rather, metastasis; soon enough supplanted that fright with a new one. Stepping into our bedroom, I allowed my husband to behold me. John lay bedded, staring ceilingways, confronting the dark.

"Iz—?" he whispered.

"Think I'll pass?" I asked, reclining alongside him, corpus to corpus. Rolling over toward me, he twitched as if galvanized; raised himself on one elbow and eyed me long, saying nothing. John studied me so closely as I'd studied myself, vizzing and revizzing my ashen hair, my watery eyes, my bleached skin. "Preferred?"

"Yes," he said. "No. Yes—"

"Which?" I asked.

"Both. All. Iz—"

He caressed my shoulder, as if to demonstrate to himself that I was more than cloud or nightmare, though no more harmful than either. Leverett's pills sedated John so efficaciously as had his old prescription, yet not to such degree, and those emotions he retained intensified anew. His lassitude ceased at once, that afternoon. By evening his soul seemed nearly to reemerge.

"You've cat-tongued," I said. "Blurt."

"Confusion overwhelmed. You appeared ghosted."

"Foolish," I said, and smiled. "Grave matters you're minding, as ever."

"Iz, it's—"

"What's thought, then? Is my look better or worse?"

"Unsayable," he said. "You're neither nor. You're a third."

Rolling stomachways, pressing my face into my pillow as if to snuff breath, I wished I had a confessor near, who by telling me what I should think, would enable me to say what was thought.

"What troubles, Iz?" John said. "It's told as seen. Unsayable because—"

"I'll renew as I was, once returned," I said. "Bear up and blind eye till then."

"Unsayable because neither. Better, worse; inapplicable. Different, nothing other. Beauty surpasses, irregarded."

My thoughts perversed: *whose beauty?* With careful movement, John shifted his legs; during his clinicking the medicis finalized him for our trip, certifying him limber, reoiling, restringing, and rehanging all joints. Hauling himself onto me as if onto a raft, he clasped my face as if holding ostrich-fruit, kissing me; I responded, full. Momentslong, all was nearly as once before; I rolled with him, wrapping myself round, and he held and crushed and pounded. But as I lay there beneath him I troubled anew, sensing sans reason that he'd gone elsewhere again, perhaps thinking of others or even of me as I'd been. This notion disconnected me, and however much I should have preferred to remain within my own body, I didn't, and allowed myself release. As in what children call cyberdreams, real enough to heartseize, I saw myself hovering above our bed, observing sans expression our thrashes below, wondering how it must feel.

"Iz—"

"Yes—?" I asked, uncertain from which of my figures my voice issued.

"You there—?"

"Why?"

As he pushed himself inside me, he descended each time with hammerblows. I'd thought that as he raged the sickness would arise, and slow him, yet each violent shove only made more mindless his thrall. Without warning or desire, my soul lurched back into my flesh, cleaving body with spirit till both were bloodied.

"Hurting," I shouted. "You're hurting me, John—"

His eyeshades fluttered, flashing the blank white windows they hid. My husband muted while he bruised, vising me into immobility, giving no sign of hearing my pleas. My fright was rising high when he unexpectedly burst, shaking as if he were bombarded land. Coughing for several minutes afterward, he enabled air to reinvade his lungs. Reaching around his great shivering whiteness, I clutched my husband twoarmed; then, as mindlessly, tried squeezing his breath out, as if to kill him while I could.

"Iz—" he said, gasping as he broke my hold.

"*John,*" I shouted; recovered. "Bestill. Calm, calm yourself. John—"

"Where were you?" he shouted, his air regained.

"Where? With you—" He sighed; lay becalmed across me, his eyes pinching shut, racking and reracking, wetting my skin with tears. "You hurt me, John—"

"You absented," he said. "I felt you go."

"Forgive," I said, "Forgive, John, forgive, but you hurt me."

"All's nulled when only one's pleased. Why did you fly?"

"I thought I wasn't me. I didn't think I was. The feel's as different as the look."

"You inspired so—" he said.

"A blondie in your bed inspired as I never have."

"You, you, only you—"

"I could have been anyone," I said. "So your actions evidenced. You've never hurt me before, John, especially not bedded."

With scarred hands he dried his eyes. "Not with you," he said. "Not deliberate, never. Never. Forgive, Iz, forgive—"

"All we've done is forgive sans forgetting," I said. "It wearies."

"I blanked, Iz. I never meant to hurt. Not you. Never."

"So you blanked, I blanked. Lovemaking at last, and nobody home."

We lay there listening to our sounds. Mayhap that explained his drugs' noneffect; he'd have bled himself into coma had true violence inhered. Mayhap a blinding exuberance of emotion astrayed him, the love of another surpassing all sense: nothing more, I retold myself, believing as I could. My husband appeared helpless as a beached whale as he lay there, his respiration gradually slowing as his sobs slipped away. The clock clicked midnight; our departure day arrived, and as it did, John spoke again.

"Will we ever regood ourselves, Iz?"

"I don't know," I said. "Forgiven, forgotten," I said. "Two renewed virgins who'd let their technik lapse. Nothing more."

"Supposed," he said, petting my face. I wouldn't pull away, but didn't feel able to touch him again so soon. "Twelve hours till leavetaking, thereabouts."

"Scared?" I asked.

"No. You?" I shook my head, lying as he did; traced my fingers along an old riverbed topographing his cheek, regretful that he'd made hate rather than love to me. "Say we pass over, Iz, and naught changes between us. What then?" he asked.

"Abey hopes while traveling, John," I said. "Don't dwell overmuch now. Earplay as we go, and we'll reconsider all, once returned. This may suffice, or may not."

"It's facted I'm positive about this trip," he said, sounding unnervingly insistent, anxious for belief. "I've no negatives. Not one."

"Known, love," I said. "Return first, then we'll see. Work as commanded till then."

"Return's not guaranteed, Iz," he said.

"Known."

Laying his head on the pillow next to mine, engulfing my hand within his, John stared at me; I knew he saw into me as I saw into him, however much we forever fought our mutual trespasses. "The advantage, after all," he said. "Be near me always, Iz. Always. Will you be near me always?"

I knew the answer he wanted to hear; it couldn't be mine, could never be mine. Death should hinge neither on another's desire, nor on the lack thereof, but should arrive accorded as it sees fit; as naturally, and unexpectedly, as love. "I'll try," I answered; but softly, minutes later, and I wasn't sure he was listening; but in his mind, he'd already heard.

* * *

At morningside we donned our traveling clothes, bespoken for our journey; the researchers judged them era-appropriate. John wore a black double-breasted suit, white shirt, gray hat and a tie imprinted with neon swirls; I was ensembled with a blue pillbox hat and boat-necked sheath dress mid-calf-long, clinging to my shape as burlap drapes potatoes. The shoes given me had toes so pointed and heels so spiked that they pained, merely to see; wearing unbeared, but I adjusted.

We were driven to Dryco; while John and Leverett readied our car for removal, I went to see Judy, who'd wished to meet once more, predeparture. While waiting for her to unlink from her conferencees, I wandered through her office's inner reception area, hidden from executaries' stares, struggling to think of anything other than John, or our assignment; a new shipment of design elements awaited dispersal throughout her suite. I wondered where my desk would be, afterward.

Judy stepped from her chamber; paused at her door; stared at me as if I were a stranger. "Iz?"

"Howdy," I said; she frowned. "What's thought?"

"That's apparel, over there? Their poor women," she said, eyeing me updown. "Such seachanges in you, Iz. None unknowing should see through the guise. Leverett said his candy'd perform its tricks, and for once he truthed."

"It's unnatural," I said. "A stranger in myself. I feel inhabited."

"You always have," she said.

"Inhabited," I repeated. "Not inhibited."

Crossing the room, she neared and embraced. "I've a secondary failsafe for you. In case." Thrusting her arm through the crook of my own, she led me into her chamber. "Mum it with Leverett, it's no matter of his. Scared, Iz?"

"Greatly," I said.

"Wise," she said, nodding. "Last eve I gutspilled to Seamus anew about this madness. But all're mindset, so all goes ahead. Nada to be done then but ready for disaster, and so lessen cost.'' Redecoration was underwaying, within her office. A sail-size portrait had been hung above her faux-log fireplace. Her drapes were drawn wide, and looking window-ways I saw impenetrable layers of cloud without, streaming and bubbling and flash-lit by lightning.

"When it rains here, does it rain there?'' I said, posing inquiry to none who could answer; keening to know, all the same.

"Leverett assures me these conditions are perfect. He's assured of all, except when he's not. Here, now,'' Judy said, handing me a small green compact. She glanced round-about before conversing anew, as if even here others' eyes might peer onward. Her habit, I thought, but I waried as well. "Additional backup,'' she said. "As personally requested by me. I'll not hazard you overmuch, however care-free he clads the danger.''

"What is it?''

"Another Alekhine device. If the Window's unreachable from wherever you wind up, how'll you cross back?''

"The car's equipped. We were enlightened yesterday—''

"If the car's stolen? Crashed? Commandeered? Additional backup, as I say. Purse it, let it slip your mind unless called for. Paint with it if desired; it's usable for that as well. A button within, mirror-hid, must be pressed for ten seconds to engage device.''

"Timeover we're told that uncontained transferral is impossibled,'' I said, slipping her gift into my purse. "That if we did, we'd freefloat between forever. As happened to Jake, they said—''

"They know?'' she said. "Situate yourself in something beforehand, then. By all accounts their world's unfit for brown people, however, white you show. The place inbetween might be preferred, if perchance you're uncovered.''

"It'll work for two or more?'' I asked.

"For one, certain,'' Judy sighed; shrugged. "Who's to tell,

Iz?" She paused to insert her teeth, as if prepping to greet
family members. "For the duration Leverett's hands will
steer you. His project is to be overseen by him as Seamus
wishes. Mayhap it'll work as proposed, but I'll not turn blue
waiting. After your return, my hands can reach you once
more, and if Leverett aims you or the company wrong thereafter, I'll hash him sure when the moment comes."

Unexpressed rage tightened her face's muscles; veins in
her temples throbbed as if to split. Only two years separated
us, truthed; the look she'd grown into aged her a dozen
more. "Such oldline thoughts bear regooding, I'd be told,"
I said.

"And I'd be telling. Do as said, not as done." She eyeshut,
and sighed; breathed deep as if to take the pipe. "This is a
house of the damned, undoubted, Iz. My time's forever
spent staring at shadows, seeing what moves. Cleaning others' messes, boiling others' stews. Stepping on razors, all the
while, and who's to help? Seamus is mindlost, and no longer
hears what needs hearing. I'm fit to spring."

"Judy, I—"

She opened her eyes. "Excuse, Iz. You've concerns aplen-
ty. Mine's an untempered tantrum, nothing more. All's not
overmuch, once faced and considered. The worst's longb-
ested, blood under the bridge. Look there." She aimed her
finger toward the fireplace's painting as if feigning aim.
"Reinstalled after twenty years. Distance enough at last regained."

"Who are they?"

"The Drydens," she said. "Bless their black hearts. Two
tries the artist took before pleasing, it's told. The Old Man
thumbed it, first time round. Demanded that he and his
blood be captured as they were, not as they wished."

"This pleased?"

"This captured." Three oiled Drydens posed in a woodpa-
neled room. Judy anecdoted as I vizzed each one in turn.
"Susie D." Mrs. Dryden lounged in a wingbacked chair,

squeezed twixt her men fore and aft, glaring at her onlookers with eyes appearing borrowed for the occasion. Her sky-gray gown was so haphazardly pleated as to resemble amateur's origami. "Rewired Mona Lisa with a surgical smile. Nasty bitch, she was. Sowdugged and flabby." Mrs. Dryden's hand rested in semblance of blessing atop her teenager's brow, who sprawled on the carpet before her, his head brushing her knees. "Sonny." His leggings' shadows revealed an untoward bulge, as if mother's touch comforted more than was proper. "He liked to play the girl, and me Mandingo," Judy said. "I'd strap on a peacemaker, and work him till he bled." Thatcher Dryden stood behind his wife as if he'd crept up to surprise. "The Old Man. None like him." His face appeared to blaze from within; blue fire lit his eyes. In none living had I ever seen such unhealthy self-assurance. He wore his hair long, and leaned upon a baseball bat as if it were a cane. "His American pasttime," Judy said, laughing. "That was them, and this is now."

"No descendants to reclaim a grip?"

"Sonny and his wife spawned a son, wet-eared and awful." Her laugh decayed, and, at first seeming set to continue, she instead tangented, or so I believed. "Lessen competition, the Old Man told all timeover, lessen competition. He mottoed by that. Seamus and I, when time came right, we lessened." As Judy lingered her look over the Drydens, her expression stilled; her eyes gleamed wet as if, against odds and expectations, she missed her onetime owners. "You want your husband, Iz?"

"Always," I said, contexting his word to my preference.

"I wanted this." She eyed the clock. Blue light bounced off her windows. "The deadline's nearing. You'd best off. Aim expectations low in all matters, Iz. Return, and all else is clover. Just return."

"Why'd you hang them here?" I asked, reading the inscription brass-plated upon the Drydens' gilded frame: IN LOCO PARENTIS.

"To remind of what I've faced, pasttime," she said. "All else is minor, compared. And history demands honor, however dishonorable its participants."

"Money spins the world," Leverett told us during the drive to Flushing; he, my husband and I rode backseated in our company car. Our transport was trucked over following their check, preliminarying our arrival, that all equipment might be again reexamined at the departure point.

"Long-learned," said John. Rainsheets opaqued our windows; I pressed mine down, to clear air so well as sight.

"While tripping, meant," said Leverett. "I've funding here, prepacked and document-accompanied." Giving John a wallet, he handed me a billfold. In both were licenses, IDs and three hundred paper dollars, green and gray crinkles free of holo, strip or mark, and each bearing a century-old date. My white gloves went unsmeared by their feel. Most were ones; two were tens. "Copied from models returned from Biggerstaff's visit. Excuse the unwieldy thicknesses."

"Usable to recover parents' deferments?" I asked, flashing my new-printed Venezuelan resident card. Leverett grinned without smiling.

"IDed names imprinted match your own," he answered.

"Pseudonyming's undesired, undercovering," said John. My wad crowded my purse overmuch, but fit. "Attempts to keep in character brainrattle, sans purpose."

"Be none but yourselves," said Leverett. "No advice betters. Suggestion, Isabel. Subtle your makeup."

Daily cosmeticking was my exception, not rule; accurate colorization of my new skin still challenged, lending new befuddlements each time. With tissue I softened my rouge, slightened my lipstick; studying my redesigns in my green compact's mirror I marveled, seeing yet another strange face.

"American-fresh," said Leverett. "Remember image impressions. With such a look as previous, prices might be asked or offered, depending on who eyes the paint."

"What's meant?" John asked, forwarding as if setting to avenge insult.

"Nada, nada," said Leverett. "Idle social commentary, pertinent only to upcoming surroundings."

Our windows defogged, easing our vision. On the East River a full-loaded garbarge hove toward Hell Gate and the Sound's dump beyond, drifting through the flames. Yellow scratches in the shipsides etched our corporate name above the waterline. Boatworkers clad in protective suits appeared through riversmoke as orange flecks sprinkled over foaming, nut-brown wastes.

"Mind, John," Leverett said, "your hosts may phrase in untoward, because unfamiliar, manner. Your subject, when found, may especially do so. Ignore, unless harm appears meant. Then react as able."

"Known," he said, sounding stringtaut. I'd watched him dose himself that morning; if I hadn't, I would have believed him slipping somehow into old mode, so tense and set to blow he appeared without; yet so innerpeaced, and loving toward me, all the same. "All ignorable, once understood."

"Isabel?" Leverett asked. "Expectant?"

"Rollable," I said; corrected. "Ready to roll."

Leaving Bronx behind, we pulled onto the Triborough Bridge, unbombed throughout the Long Island vicissitudes; the Home Army preserved the span that troop transferrals might speed across with greater ease, to more immediate result. The war was so long over that its memory returned, ofttimes, as no more than dream, but if willed I recalled nightlong cannonades, false dawns in the east; remembered the look of my friends' older siblings departing, and their look when and if they returned, demonstrating full a reversed regooding. Judy's two sisters and three brothers, all older, all went willingly to serve their nation's masters; by thirteen, Judy was an only child.

"Perfect weather," said Leverett, peering downriver, as if to discern the gray overlap where cloud kissed water. "Overcasting sharpens the Window's apparency, illuminating the route."

The river hightided: shorelapped Long Island, crept along its sidestreets; flooded ground floors and scattered vehicles' shells wherever water broke against land. Manhattan's faraway towers appeared as afterimages in the wet fog, scars left unerased by regooding's surgeons, that present would not forget past's pox. Our car downramped, clattering across patches of metal; turning onto a cratered expressway, we passed kilometer after kilometer of charred walls and dry sockets, the places where houses were pulled. My mother grew up in Queens; from the look of the borough's leftovers, its remaining children could as well have grown up on the moon.

"Expectations heightening?" Leverett asked, slapping his own knees.

I nodded; new-experienced nausea's leavings roiled my belly. "Heightened enough," said John.

We approached Flushing Meadows. On our left the old stadium's manglings lay oceaned round by shattered asphalt; brownleafed trees with anorectic limbs erupted between girders. All nearby was woodland or desert; the onetime park overgrew wherever prolonged shelling hadn't barrened the land. The red ribs of the Unisphere perched axised on a concrete dot, its continents disarrayed; North America, drifting far, lay crumpled beneath Antarctica. Army guards slowed us as we neared; we transversed their barricade beneath a razorwired roof. Some distance beyond, the sky ripped apart, fluttering and flapping independent of windwrack.

"Behold," Leverett said. "The eighth wonder."

The Window wasn't so much a window as a tear in the atmosphere's curtain. Behind its folds lay a blizzard's white; until we drew closer it appeared as a cloud attached at base to earth, and pinned at apex to a star. We stopped several hundred meters short of the Window, parking alongside our purple-and-yellow transport. We'd been shown photos and vids; nothing forewarned of the Window's immensity, nor of its awfulness.

"Step clear," said Leverett, throwing himself coatless into gale's midst, hopping out bareheaded; his hair held its hold on his head. "Something, yes?"

A dozen smock-and-uniform-clad officials waited near, sheltering themselves with wind-imploded umbrellas. Ozone perfumed the air; breathing in, I dizzied, and my stomach churned anew. Steadying myself, I noticed my hair, everyone's hair, uplifting as if staticked. Tingles shivered through my neck's nape; I uncertained if they quivered with electric's buzz, or with fear's. Birds of indeterminate species flew around the Window, their cries calling over rain and thunder; stragglers drawing too near its flaps vanished in midflight.

"Their birds or ours?" I asked, flattening my hair with a scarf.

"It matters?" Leverett answered. Deadeyeing the Window, staring straight in, I saw nothing; the whiteness blanked all beyond. Our world horizoned plain on either side as if naught interrupted its line. Red and gold light-blobs floated from the opening's edges, skittering skyways, bobbing groundward; appearing and reappearing with the unpredictability of soap-bubbles.

"Plasmas?"

"Plasmaesque, undoubted," said Leverett. "Magnetic apparitions. Specters of the cosmos, looking for tables to tap against. Harmless, probably."

A lightning-bolt flashed, rebounding along the Window's line; shot back into the overhead, new-streaked in blue and pink. When the lightning struck its birthplace a thunderpeal rang out to bleed all ears in hearshot, and my own drums felt set to pop, not with sound, but pressure. The Window had its own voice, I discerned, a headaching blend of hiss and sizzle, so lowpitched as to come through sole as subliminal throb.

"Bizarreness overwrought," said John, his hair shining beneath rain's cascade. "It's unreal."

"Real enough," said Leverett. "Invitation to adventure."

"What stays it in place?"

"Unceasing operation of the othersided Tesla coil that split it open, the lab says. Something about field fluctuation. They're mute to detail more, if they know. Science's socalled wondersense leaves my mind forever desiring. Missionways, all's unmattering, however it's put."

"People," a smocked woman said, shouting over thunder. "Proceed apace, please." I recognized her; she once addressed our physics class, and I'd not understood a word.

"Timeframe's moving as planned," Leverett said. "What's problemed?"

"We're rainsoaked," she said. "Please proceed."

"Delays unnerve," said John. "Let's lookingglass."

Climbing into the Hudson, fronting myself beside my husband, I marveled that a full meter nonetheless separated us, so spacious was the interior. Leverett and the scientist fingertapped the driver's window; John fumbled for a moment before finding the necessary opening knob. When he rolled down the glass the scientist thrust in her head, showering us as she shook herself dry.

"Excuse," she said to John. "Give full ear. Drive lightfooted, as up a driveway. Five miles per transports at secure rate, allowing passage sans location displacement. Visibility returns, following whiteout. Speed at emergence point won't top thirty."

"Certain?"

"Certain. Proceed as per plan, tracking symptomologies at all times with twicedailied healthchecks."

"All grasped and understood," John said, onehanding the wheel. He switched on the windshield wipers, sweeping clear a semiview; between the Window and ourselves the air heat-shimmered, throwing no mirage equal to what lay ahead.

"Mind, too, as told," Leverett said. "Minimize interaction with all. Readied?"

"Readied."

"Whatever results with primary goal, fulfill secondary," he reminded us. "Retrieve contemporary history text wherever availabled, to satisfy info needs. Facts forever best inference, however circumstanced."

John pressed the ignition. "Later, alligator," I said.

"Begone, then," said Leverett, slapping the roof. "Behave. Return."

We unbraked; our car lurched ahead, bumping along a length of rutted concrete that led into the Window. Those seeing us off raced for their cars, tossing their umbrellas behind them, all but Leverett; he stood unmoving, his suit dark with rain, as if to ascertain that, attaining point zero, we wouldn't grow chary, and at the last moment reconsider, and steer away.

"Handling easy?" I asked my husband.

"Coasting, thus far."

The rain's pelting loudened, as did the everpresent hiss; sounds of crackling audibled round, as if our air crumpled over us. Plasmas skated over the car's hood, leaping skyward, gravity-heedless as a fire's embers. From eyecorner I glanced clockways; expected without reason that I might see its numbers reverse, or transform in some manner, as we closed in, and of course saw only the seconds tick off as before. The Window loomed ever larger overhead, blotting our world; the rapping on the roof grew louder, and came faster; our tires skidded on the road.

"What's falling?" John asked, demisting the inner windshield with his sleeve. "Hail?"

"Frogs." All manner of unlikely events occurred mid-worlds—*in the fence*, our professors put it, theorizing—and so it evidenced. Hundreds of tiny frogs, likely extinct with all others in our world, showered onto our car, all spring-green, none larger than coinsize; they splattered the glass and crunched beneath the wheels, appearing no less surprised than were we. The fall tapered within the final few meters of our approach, and, as we brushed the Window's edge, ceased entirely.

"Iz," my husband said, "I love—"

"You too," I completed. As whiteness enclosed us, I imagined we stopped; knew at once a frozen feel, as if we'd been sealed within a glacier. Neither John nor I worded during that motionless eternity; as void swallowed us, my worries left me for the first time in months, and peace overwhelmed. The thought that this might not be so dissimilar from death struck deep; would this be so bad, after all?

A smile came to my lips; without intended effort stretched into sneer, and then grimace. When I attempted to draw breath, I couldn't; felt myself pressing into the seatback as if flattened by unseen Godness. A harsher light flashed, half-blinding us; I heard a scream, and as my breath returned I saw our car smashing through a fence, and a uniformed man flying off the front fender.

"*Iz!! Hold—!*" John braked our car, steering left, his hands slapping the wheel; burning rubber's odor extinguished ozone's and we stopped short of plunging into a long reflecting pool. Sunlight's glare shone upon our backs as we stared into night; it wasn't raining on the other side. "Thirty per," he shouted, highvoiced, as if in transit he'd recovered so many years as to be left prepubertied. "Sixty-plus, rather—"

Wheeling right, he steered us onto a roadway alongsiding the pool, and floored the car, accelerating full. "You're safe—?" I asked.

"Our casualty," he said, fixing eyes on the straightaway, speedheedless. "Moving? Dead? Others seen?"

Rolling down my window, staring behind us, I saw a kneeling silhouette evidence sustained, if shaken, life. "Moving. No others visible."

"What's that light?" John asked.

"Drive!"

Beyond the actual fence through which we'd crashed, a house-wide pillar of light shot skyward from our arrival point, tossing sparks, streamlining as it flowed; at azimuth, it split and medusaed into churning coils of lightning. As we further distanced, I clarified that the yellow-white current streamed groundways, rather; poured down from a framework encircling a tall spire's tip. The spire and its alongsiding ball familiared; Luther kept their correspondents' photo on his wall. Here, however, the Trylon had no red warning lights attached, and the Perisphere was not illumined as to resemble a globe; imprinted upon its curve was the single letter T.

"This way to exit?" I asked.

"So believed. Still no followthrough?"

"Nada." Looking out, letting my hair fly as it never had before, I felt this world's breeze blow twenty degrees warmer. Stationary searchlights, interspersed amid shrubbery, outlined the road ahead, showing it as a high white hallway; over the distancing electrical roar I heard a flapping at the front tire, a sound resembling wings beating against glass.

"Give a noisecheck, once cleared," John said. Two large windowless buildings faced off across the road, exit-near; along their smooth cornices ran backlit black letters reading NEW YORK CONSOLIDATED POWER AND LIGHT. No workers or guards showed, no sirens sounded; we drove through the gate, a brick archway outlined with small incandescents and topped with a figure limbed with lightning bolts, crowned with a lightbulb head. Slowing, feeling more secured, we moved undisturbed along the streets beyond, passing long rows of small buildings, and smaller houses; all must have semimatched Queens's onetime look. "Iz," my husband said. "We're—"

"Safe," I said. "Pull over. Let's exam."

John curbsided and stopped the car, switching off the engine. Closing his eyes, inhaling as if to hyperventilate, he slid closer, took my hand and kissed me. His hand's tremble ran body-wide.

"All'll better now, Iz," he said. "All's recoverable again."

I eyed the street updown, certifying that we'd not been trailed by the man we'd struck or any others after speeding away from where we'd crossed. Neither cars nor passersby showed; we were as alone in this world as we were in our own.

"None to interrupt."

"We'd best damage-assess," I said, opening my door. Judging the lightening east, I estimated dawn wouldn't be long in coming. John got out and lowered himself to examine underwheel. Staring past the Trylon's glowing discharge, sighting New York's skyline lights, I saw that they outlined so much lower here as to seem another city's.

"All's fine," John said, favoring his leg as he stood; I suspected the day's earlier damp was working delayed effects upon his joints. Limping around to where I stood, he embraced me. "Love, Iz."

"Yes, John, love," I answered. "It'll not harm to pause momentslong. Work enough awaits."

I held him until at last his shaking ceased, and assured calm came to him anew. None trailed us, and for a time we sat sleepless in our car, resting upon each other as dawn brillantined the city's skyscrapers. Their America lay beyond, and in it, if lucked, our E; if blessed, our reunited soul, its unity once more a given.

4

Having transversed the middle passage safely, I attempted to reset my mindwaves, that I might process all thought in the words of their lingua, turning my tongue so white as my face. As I employed their wordpatterns—those rambled phrasings, rich with prepositional flow and adverbial complication—I thought I must have learned the lines as a child, so naturally did they come to me. By thinking in their mode, I allowed a penultimate layer to be flayed from my soul's skin; it essentialled that I become what I beheld.

"Situate me, Iz," John said as we drove away from where we'd rested. "We're westbounding?"

"On Northern Boulevard, I believe. Hold, I'll assure." When I unfolded our period-vintage map it fragmented, crumbling in my hands, as if having accumulated so many years it couldn't withstand losing them. "Northern Parkway, on this side," I said, spotting a sign as I rained map-flakes floorways. "Similar route, evidently. Cross at the 59th Street Bridge, then over to Fifth and from there down to the library."

"It's assured there're phonebooks to peruse there?"

"Library provided such service once, they said. If there's one for Memphis we can certify his existence before moving on."

John glanced out his side window as we aimed toward Manhattan. "Iz, eye that," he said, nodding leftward. "What is it? They've walled off Brooklyn from Queens?"

"There'd be no reason here," I said, gleaning through a haze's shroud what appeared to be a high concrete barricade, stabbing between buildings, lofting over roofs. "It's an expressway, I think. The old LIE, could be. There's a bridge in the mid-thirties here never built in our world. Possibly that's its feeder."

Above Manhattan the haze patinaed the sky sepia. Some few familiarities poked through the ocher clouds: the Empire State and Chrysler buildings, Dryco's old shaft, several others familiar enough though long-erased. Lemony morningshine bronzed their brick, transmuted their stone into gold. The 59th Street Bridge emerged from the strata ahead, its iron webs blood-red and fuzzed, appearing as a primeval relic confronted in some island swamp.

"Fog's an eyeburner, however thick the glass," said John, rolling up his window. My lenses stung me till I readied to pop my tearing eyes from their sockets; the pain almost supplanted my nausea, for which I was grateful. I'd eaten nothing to so unsettle my stomach. "Check the color," said John. "Toxicity plus in that. A spillcloud, mayhap."

"Peasoup," I murmured to myself, recalling a phrase of my mother's.

"Soup?" he repeated. It surprised that he caught my mutterance over the metal roadway's hum, a beebuzz raised by our tires' spin. "Hungry, Iz? I've fruit—"

I shook my head; marveled at the myriad untried paths to misunderstanding we would surely discover here. As I eyed their Manhattan our trainers' warnings came again to my mind: that, if thoughtless, we would look upon theirs not as a separate world, but rather see within it our own as it had once shown, enabling insidious nostalgia sans reason for a place never known to affect our actions. But even as the strange spires clarified before me, I knew I was reading my wishes into the city's image, as I did into my husband's, chancing again that perception, for once, could roughshod reality. Leaving the bridge we bumped over 59th Street's cobblestones, entering a cliff-walled stream along with a thousand other cars.

"Careful now, Iz," said John. "Caution essentials hereout till we're countrysided."

"We're already sunk," I said, grasping at once a prime problematic. My couture unhauted to such a degree here as to be laughable. It evidenced that this world's women garbed themselves in nothing resembling my sheath; wore instead kneegrazing skirts puffed out by starched slips, ensembles apted more for revelation than concealment. Women trotted along on heels higher than mine, and I couldn't imagine how they walked with such hooves.

"What is it? What troubles?" John asked.

"Your executive drag'll do you right," I said. "I'll never pass go. Check the dolls."

John shifted his look from curb to curb as we crossed Park Avenue. "None match you," he said, pleasing me enough to reassure, if but momentslong. Watching the women struggle to keep their skirts from flipping up in the wind gladdened; nothing enslaved me, fashion least of all. We lefted onto Fifth; we'd reached Rockefeller Center when I realized, looking downtown, that the expressway we'd earlier seen crossed Manhattan aboveground.

"Godness—"

"Iz," John said, seeing what I saw. "Evident misprediction. There's a backup plan?" The public library's building still stood in our world, if in ruins; here, it and its site had gone missing, overrun by concrete supports twenty meters high, bearing the expressway westward. A car-clogged ramp alongsiding the columns ascended from Madison's direction, rising toward Sixth. A green directional affixed to the overpasses read: *Al Smith Midcross Arterial / To Long Island / Interstates 1–11 / West Side Hwy.*

"Hang right. Look, phone boxes," I said, spying wooden windowed sheds aligned along 42nd Street's northern pedway. "Pull over. I'll tap into info."

John curbsided our car in a spot evidently legal. Once outside, inhaling air both purer and dirtier than that of our New York, I hacked myself blind, choking on the chemical tickle in my gullet. When I recovered I pulled, then pushed the doorhandle of a booth and stepped in. John sat finger-tapping the wheel while he watched cars slog up the ramp to the roadway. After dialing the operator I heard a short ring, followed by a click.

"Information, help me," I blurted into the receiver, conscious to word as they would. "Get me Memphis, Tennessee."

"Moment, please," said a woman's voice. Hearing undigitalized tones surprised me; I'd not expected to speak to something not programmed. "What number in Memphis?"

"You got me," I said. "There's a listing for Presley?"

"Moment, please." Detecting a rustling sound above the static, I fancied that she might be thumbing actual directories, however impossible that would have been. "First names of your party?"

"Vernon," I said, "or Gladys."

"I have neither a Vernon nor a Gladys Presley listed in Memphis, Tennessee," she said. "I do have an Elvis Presley listed."

"Shoot me," I said.

"Pardon?"

"Address, I mean. Please." She recounted; I transcribed. "Crazy. Many thanks." Extricating myself from the booth after hanging up, I returned to our car; shouted to John through the open windows.

"He's there," I said. "We're on."

"Seat yourself and let's fly."

"A map's essentialled," I said; glanced behind me. "There's a magazine store. They'll supply."

"Hasten," said John. My skirt hobbled me from rushing; as I tried to dash I sensed a lightheaded feel, as if I were airshort after only a few steps. The store was small, no wider than three meters; the single window was curtained by rows of magazines held with metal clips. Within, racked magazines papered one wall; stacks of newspapers laid atop a radiator bulwarked the window. The proprietor looked to be seated behind a barrier of candy, and it was a moment more before I realized that he stood. His other customers, two prepube boys, pawed comics and stared as if they were mentally denuding me.

"Hi ho," I said; the proprietor stonefaced me. "I need a road atlas. Can you give me aid and comfort?" He pointed an ink-blackened finger toward a shelf near the boys. "What's the damage?"

"Half a buck," he said. "You can't read, lady?"

"Fifty cents," I repeated to myself, trusting that I could accurately convert. Finding two silver quarters in my purse I handed them over, and he slung them into a wooden box; they chimed, landing atop previous receipts. "And a newspaper," I added, seizing one of the smaller atlases.

"Okay. Which one?"

Nine stacks of different titles awaited my selection. "This'll do," I said, retrieving a *Daily Mirror*, gathering from its mast that it was national, not local.

"Nickel." The ones I had bore a bust of an Aboriginal-American on one side and an animal on the other. He sneered at my coin. "Lady, this ain't a nickel."

"Sorry," I said; another error of research. From my purse I withdrew a dollar.

"Nothin' smaller?"

I shook my head; as he coined me in return I examined

one of his nickels, but couldn't recognize the figures depicted. "You haven't history books, have you?" I asked.

"Why would I?"

"Would anyone nearby? I'll pay through the nose."

"Hey lady, you want a history book?" one of the boys asked. His voice broke as he spoke; from his look I'd have judged his age as no more than eight, but his sound suggested fifteen. I wondered if they went manly sooner, over here. "You can buy mine," he said, passing me a hardcover he carried. Its torn orange cloth bore the words *The Growth of the American Republic, Fourth Edition;* the author's line pronounced it writ by Casner and Gilbert.

"You don't need it?" I asked. "For schooling?"

"I'll tell 'em I lost it. How much you give me?"

"A fin?" I suggested, slipping him one of my tens.

"Yeah, swell." He and his friend evidenced no suspicion as they admired the bill; I sighed, relieved that it suited, and gratified as well that our mission's minor task had been successed so soon. Taking my buys, I readied to depart. "Hey, lady," the child said.

"Yes?"

"How much for this?" He drew his forefinger in and out of his mouth, slurping as if lunching up noodles. By his laughter I gathered that the proprietor appreciated the boy's mimesis; I didn't. Walking out sans reply, I briskfooted as I'd entered, returning to our car.

"Police roundabouting," John said, shifting into drive as I seated myself. "Our look peculiars in unguessed manner, I'd reason."

"Let's take that big road," I said, peering downstreet; at 42nd's terminus was a tangle of ramps, resembling a razor-wire barrier tumbled groundways. "Onload there. It'll send us soonest, fastest."

Neither police nor any others approached as we merged into traffic; at Ninth Avenue John steered us onto the Jersey-bound ramp. Cars ahead stopped, started and stopped again; walls on either side of the ramp blinded our view of what awaited, and it was only as we readied to blend that our chosen course showed plain. The Midtown Arterial carried twenty lanes; cars, trucks and buses hurtled by at unnerving velocity.

"This wasn't forewarned," I said.

"Little has been," John said. "It's an Indy racecourse. Brace, Iz. We'll thunder road."

We were over the river, on the highway's towerless bridge before we commingled with the traffic flow; the water was unseeable from where we'd laned ourselves. "Aim me, Iz," John said, twohanding the wheel, stilling the wobbles raised by car-wind. "Which way?"

"Moment." Opening our new atlas I studied the metro map, marveling at the network charted. "John, it's so different—" Two express routes—I–1 and I–2—cut across Long Island, splitting into four crosstowns before entering Manhattan; another pair, I–3 and I–4, came down from New England, slicing the Bronx and Harlem before they, too, divided.

"*Shit,*" John said, his stare fixing roadways. "Iz, it's hellbound. Viz this, would you?"

The six Manhattan crosstowns shot into Jersey, coalescing atop the remnants of Weehawken and Union City, thrusting an eighty-lane boulevard into the blurred horizon. Not even LA had such roads in our world, in our day.

"What's the speed limit?" I asked as he floored. "Hypersonic?"

"None, as evidenced," said John. "We're topping out." He held our car within our entry-lane; around us vehicles bearing like look to ours, though of subtler hue, paced and overtook us sans seeming exertion. The preponderance of cars were a smaller model that was no more than a bulge with running boards; appearing, grouped, as insects swarming over the highway's gray hide. Some lanes were used

solely by double-length trucks and buses, moving so fast as
the cars though they held ten times the mass.

"Where now, Iz?" John shouted. "Inform! Hasten—!"

"Hold," I shouted, glancing forthback, attempting to
overlay the print grid with the one through which we mazed.
High steel towers, each shingled with a dozen directionals,
stood at roadside every hundred meters, forecasting which
lane would carry which vehicles where; in our rush their
words were indecipherable. Oversized billboards began lining the expressway's low outbanks, spaced every twenty meters, positioned at an angle visible, if unreadable, to all who
drove by. "I'll have it, momentslong—"

"Which way?" Seven lanes on our right plunged earthward as their course redirected north.

"I-3, bearing south," I said, fixing our position on the
Jersey map. Staring through the overcast I eyed an upcoming tower's signs; sighted the guidemark needed. "Go left,
ten lanes across."

"Ten?"

"As told," I said. "John—!" One of those buggish cars
almost slipsided us as we underwayed our sidle. My husband
jerked the wheel; I cycled my feet against the floor as if,
against reason, I might assist in braking us. Horns blared,
sounding as a flock's migratory blast; no one struck our car,
however close they came. As John swerved the car into the
proper lane I saw his arms shaking; he was so pale as to look
leeched.

"Straight on from here?" he asked. "Iz—?"

"A direct slipstream, the map claims." Our lane elevated,
shooting off into the south. It shocked to see how ivoried I'd
turned; my hands looked as if they belonged not solely to
another, but to another's corpse. I tried untensing by studying the roadlining ads as they showed, one riff per second,
gleaning such phrases as I could: IT'S FUN TO PHONE/WHEN IT
RAINS IT POURS/DOCTORS RECOMMEND CAMELS/BREAKFAST OF

CHAMPIONS/DIXIELAND ONLY 275 MI/"ONE MORE" FOR THE
ROAD? MAKE IT RUPPERT'S—

"There but for grace," John said, staring past me.
"Below."

Our road lifted us ten additional meters above the in-
bound lanes as they curved away from the mainline; following my husband's nod, I looked down and watched an
ongoing accident. Vehicles piled up as if they'd been
dumped out from a bag, blocking fifteen lanes; oncoming
cars and buses sutteed themselves upon the pyre sans cease.
Through the black billow I re-reregarded New York; the city
was already unseeable, blotted not so much by the smoke as
by the haze which, I now saw, hung heaviest above the interstate. Our lane rejoined earth, alongsided nineteen similar
and carried us away.

"They'll back up to Pennsylvania," I said, hypnotized by
the plume of the accident. Closing my eyes, I felt my aches
anew; whether brought on by fear, by stress or by ozone, my
head's pain doubled as if my brain was swelling beyond the
confines of my skull. "You're calming?" I asked my husband.

"By comparison," he said. "Should we have prepped at
all, considering? None of this is as they said."

"They estimated, nothing more," I said. His voice's tremble matched that of his body. "We're safe enough for now."
When I attempted to stroke his shoulder, he shook me away,
as if my touch might sear.

"So they believed," he said, nodding back toward the
flames.

" 'The Federal Interstate Road Network,' it says, 'designed
by Robert Moses in 1943 in accordance with the transportation directives of President Willkie's Provisional War Orders
of 1942, continues to serve the nation as it never needed to
in war—' "

"They're built to carry tanks, then?" John asked. I flipped through the atlas's intro. "Does it detail?"

"No theory, only fact," I said, glancing across each page; returned to my reading. " 'Built between 1944 and 1953 at a cost of—' "

"You adjust to it with such ease," he said, one unshaking hand at rest upon the wheel; with his other he plucked fruit from the bag he brought. "A smoother ride's unimagined."

My husband's apparent peace intensified mine; I put away the atlas, and gazed windowways. Between the unending ads I glimpsed Jersey suburbs, the treeless redbrick veldt. Forest-patches dotted the undeveloped stretches that remained, resembling a futon's stuffing aburst at the seams. It struck me that the billboards commanded, rather than sold; they told this world's consumers to sleep eight hours nightly, brush their teeth with chlorophyll paste, fulfill civic responsibilities whenever called, smoke tobacco products, marry the right girl, keep regular, report suspicious behavior and visit Dixieland.

"Dixieland's a city or country?" John asked, seeing another of its ads; this one had as centerpiece an upright pig playing a violin as it hoisted one trotter skyward. SOOEE, its words read, YOU'VE NEVER SEEN ANYTHING LIKE IT.

"A song, I thought." The interstate narrowed to fourteen mirror-smooth groundbound lanes between cities; but at Trenton's outskirts, at Philadelphia's and Wilmington's, it reascended, cleaving each city's heart as it unthreaded, multilaning ever upward as if to the moon. One billboard, seen repeatedly, proclaimed *Three Days Coast to Coast by Interstate* and it must have been so; we reached Baltimore in two and a quarter hours.

"You medicated again before we left Queens?" I asked John, noting his lingering pallor, fearing that this world's germs had stormed his defenses.

"I'll redose this evening." The time approached eleven; by our clocks it should have been that night, or the next morning. I uncertained which; my circadians hadn't yet attuned to the off-beat.

"You've a bloodless look," I told him. "Aware me of any complaints, John. Inoculations notwithstanding, unknowns could be infecting even as we speak—"

"No complaints while partnered," he said, his voice so gentle that I barely thought it his. "None to file. Look roundabout, Iz. This is as it should be."

Whether John referred to the world without or the world within our car was unguessable, and he didn't elaborate. How much of his calm resulted from faux-nostalgia's sedative was unguessable as well. Were imagined memories of this illusory past endorphing him with thought of tranquil comfort, or were we simply feeling ourselves reborn as teenylovers, run away from an unendurable home? I couldn't pin my own feeling, much less my husband's; continued studying this world's fossils, frozen in the amber air. I wondered if one recalled a lover's lost qualities as one rebuilds, in mind's eye, a lost house or school or street; were the true lines inevitably remodeled when seen again through a haze made heavier by years?

"That history'll content them, you think?" he asked, pointing to the orange book I'd bought.

"Copyright's 1948," I said, opening the pages. "The text begs excavation. Give ear: 'The United States leads the struggle for democracy. It has faced problems, and met challenges. It leads those people of the world who believe in freedom—' "

"It whitens and brightens," said John, recalling an ad's demand.

"It's bonedry and simplistic. Authors seem as brainchallenged as their readers. 'Agents of the worldwide Communist conspiracy have been active and are active still in the United States. Some have been trusted officials, and there is no telling who may be one—' "

"Paranoiacs," said John. Without vocalizing, I continued

to read: " 'Under Trotsky, the Soviet Union's weakened state has not put a halt . . .' "

"What's the newsheet hold?" he asked.

"Indecipherables," I said, glancing over and rereading the *Mirror*'s lead for Saturday, May 8, 1954: "GO AX YER MA"—HE DID. "Conrad and Weber can patholinguistic as desired. It's a New York pub, it turns out, not global. I've gleaned a page or two. It's all illiteracies."

John's copy of *Knifelife* protruded from his jacket pocket; he'd packed his own read. As the road ahead unshuttered anew, penetrating Baltimore, he switched on the dash recharger, replenishing half the batteries as we cruised; we'd kept such pace as to drain power at twice the rate expected. Slouching against the seat's thick padding, I vizzed those passing us; all others, drivers and passengers alike, appeared cheerful, well-fed, and uniformly caucasoid. Their look bored; I eyeshut, and dozed for what seemed a second or so; when John awoke me I saw by the clock I'd been out fifty minutes.

"Washington," he said. "A Siamese, as evidenced."

No ads blocked the capital's vista; the obelisk and dome appeared as our own. The highway riversided the Potomac as its sixteen lanes obliterated Georgetown. "Nearly," I said. "No Lincoln Memorial." No Lincoln, here; Mora had informed us that his assassination in 1861, in this world, was seemingly the initial pebble in the pond, rippling our histories thereafter. Here, Luther discovered, there'd been no Civil War, no emancipation of enslaved people until 1905. But if they'd let my people go, where had they gone? I'd seen none of color in New York; saw none but snowbirds during the several hundred kilometers thus far traveled. By all accounts segregation in this America was more elaborate and overt than it had been in ours; how far had they refined their methods? Recalling my perception of the store proprietor's unreasoned dislike, I worried if perchance my false skin didn't incog so well as I thought it should; wondered if through some technique unknown to our world, my ethnicity nonetheless showed its signs. It displeased me to think how easily I'd become a racialist toward myself.

As the road crossed the river south of Arlington's leafless trees ads reappeared, blocking our view of what semblanced as the Pentagon, though theirs appeared twice the size of ours. Another of those tall directionals stood to the right of the bridge's exit; attached to its steel was the greeting, *Welcome to the Old Dominion. Interstate Bus Check Next Exit.*

"Hunger building, Iz?" John asked. As we passed the exit I looked to see what might be getting checked; a long line of buses parked before a low building were surrounded by uniformed men. "We should stop soon and feed you." As the haze at last thinned I saw, distanced, shimmering pools appear and disappear on the roadway.

"At a suitable place," I said.

"Particular suitables."

"Where we can minimize interaction," I said. "We'll stop long enough to eat and then depart before we're uncovered."

"You're enhancing, Iz," he said. "We're round pegs in round holes here. Fretting overmuch'll show you all the sooner, it's a given. I know the game. When undercovered, go as if the world is yours. It is ours, for now."

"My dress is wrong," I said. "My skin too, mayhap."

"Your skin?" John asked. "You're specterish. An X-ray of yourself."

"It's the absence bothering me most," I said. "I miss me."

"You're unchanged but for your skin," he said. "And hair and eyes."

"That's me. My skin's me. I mean I'm more than that, but it's me all the same, it is—"

"Iz," John said, keeping the road eyed while showing his concern as he could. "It's known you're still you. I know."

"I'm addling," I said, calming anew; was paranoia pathogenic, over here? "Never mind."

"Reassure yourself that we own this world, presently," he said. "Facted true."

I smiled; wished I could have settled myself with such ease as he'd settled me. A sign much larger than the others hove to view at roadside. A comic-balloon spouted from the mouth of a gaptoothed boy; his mien suggested lead poisoning at an early age. Within the balloon were the words: THEY'RE HERE, PA! NEXT EXIT DIXIELAND.

"We can lunch there," said John. "Scan the natives close."

"With minimal contact," I reminded.

"Reaction time'll improve if their actions are observed beforehand."

"All right," I said, wondering why I'd agreed so readily, why action observations essentialled if John was unable to action in return. As we eased into the exit lane we saw Dixieland appear; the ramp sped us directly into the parking lot, a sunglared ocean over two kilometers wide. Dixieland appeared as an agglomeration of two-story log shacks spread across the middle of the concrete flats. To the left of the shacks were pens aflocked with animals; to the right, roller coasters, ferris wheels and smaller amusement rides. Entering the lot, we drove beneath an aluminum archway neon-blaring the motto, *Where Folks Are Friendly;* at its crest spun a house-size jug insigniaed with three Xs. We slotted our car on the lots' outskirts; as we stepped out, the humid air sponged us.

"This heat's assaulting," John said. "Let's threshold."

I saw my first elephant in the Dixieland Children's Zoo. The ones in the Bronx Zoo were killed when I was young, before my mother could take me there. Elephants' visuals preserved in my head faded against pachydermic reality. The beast was but a baby, and badly treated; as it limped toward its onlookers it showed a great sore on its back. Two young men flicked cigarettes at it sides. I stilled all the same, confronting extinction.

"These animals," John said. We stared at cows and pigs

and sheep, freeranging as if they'd never be called on to reproduce. There were also birds and animals never seen before on screen or in life, and whether they'd once existed on our side was unknowable. "They're gone, Iz."

"Known," I said, and we continued walking toward the main buildings, passing the last cage; there were three over-sized wingless birds within, so large as turkeys though considerably uglier. At close range the buildings' logs showed as metal siding. The entrance's doors were simulated wood as well, set in concrete painted to resemble stone; they parted as we trod upon a red rubber carpet leading up to them. The AC flashfroze us as we stepped inside.

"It's a bazaar," I said.

"A madhouse, more like." On all sides were cubicles of varying size, topfull with bounty being pawed over by milling hundreds. The peddlers offered quilts of Met quality and stuffed animals for children or adults; dishes and glassware, plaster statuary cast in the form of gnomes; smoked meat, small jugs similar to the one spinning above the entrance; oversized hats and eyed hoods, American flags, guns of every caliber, cheap cotton dresses and Coca-Cola. Three-quarters of the crowd smoked cigars and cigarettes, and the air was so poisonous as the open road's.

"They're dressed as if for bed," I said, eyeing the crowd between my coughs.

"They're butterballs," said John. "A plane couldn't carry more than two per load—"

"Quiet—"

"Five-figure daily calories, certain—"

"Bestill!" I said, hoping that none heard. The fattest wore the tightest clothes, as if through such display they could reveal the wealth of their folds. Farther down the aisle I sighted a cubicle whose goods appeared, at distance, rather more attractive. "That's not so innocent. Let's viz."

Fabulous Fifties sextoys were so unenlightened as I expected, though in not the relentlessly misogynist style, say, of

Nasty Nineties pop. The rapebait photoed on the material
wore diapers, or corsets or pants tourniquet-tight; printed
messages were subtexted solely through double-entendres.
There were as well simulated anatomies in every type of
plastic, hard and soft. I lifted a thin rod to which plastic
breasts and buttocks were loosely attached, and wiggled
them before John's nose.

"Nipply goodness and bottomy treats," I said, laughing.
John kissed my cheek; I marveled at the warmth of his lips.

"They've postcards of Dixieland in this next booth."

"I'll gather added visuals," I said. "Leverett'll appreciate."

After selecting various ones depicting the buildings, the
rides, and the zoo I paid the cashier, a thick-necked man
wearing a white tee. Sweatbeads dropped from his prickly
roof of hair. "What are these?" John asked, noting represen-
tationals arrayed along the side counter.

"Those're banks, folks," the cashier said. "We sell a lotta
that one. Try one and see for yourself."

The plastic tableau depicted a black man standing on a
box beneath a single-limbed tree. A thin bar ran between his
neck and the branch. John slotted a coin. The box dropped
into the bank's base; the figure's wide eyes shut, and a red
metal strip emerged from the white lips. SORRY, SAM was
stamped along the bank's rim. The hair on my neck lifted,
as if in an electrical storm I felt lightning ready to strike me.

"Iz?" John asked, noting my distress, taking my arm.
"What is it?"

"Let's eat," I said. "Now. Come on, John."

"That bank?" he asked, once we'd stepped out of the
cashier's earshot.

"Horrible," I said, trying to slough away what I'd seen, as
I'd assured Luther I could do with such confidence; each
time I eyeshut I saw the figure's face again. "There's a place
to eat across the way. Leaving essentials, after. Come."

We entered Dixieland's Oldtime Country Kitchen

through a doorway bracketed by statues of bonneted women wielding rolling pins; the room could have sat five hundred. Short-skirted waitresses scurried around the space, balancing plastic trays overbrimmed with glassware. We sat ourselves in a booth near the entrance, one along the hallwall, which was glassed through so that we could watch the place's goings-on while eating. A waitress greeted us; her hemlength was so high and her heels so lifted her feet that her goosebumped legs looked genetically stretched. She handed us meter-length menus.

"Hi, folks," she said, smiling so rigidly as to suggest she'd had facial nerves cut. "Figure out what you all want and I'll be right back."

We unfolded the plasticked pages and examined the offerings. Before either of us had read even half of the list our waitress returned, her heels clicking against the worn wooden floor.

"Made up your minds yet?" she asked. "Everything's good."

"I'm hep," I said. "Recommendations?"

"Lookin' to have breakfast or dinner?"

"Neither," I said. "There's chicken in a Big Cluck Deelite?"

"And a whole lot more. You want one a those?" I assented. "Anything to drink?"

"Mug us with joe," John said, startling me as he appeared to startle the waitress; I hadn't thought he'd soaked a single phrase during our training.

"Coupla cups a coffee, you mean?" our waitress asked.

"That's right," I said. "Unmilked. I mean black. I'm lactose-intolerant."

"Egg me," my husband added. "Deyolked and mashed."

"You mean scrambled?" the waitress annotated her pad, forbidding confusion from affecting her smile.

"It matters that yours are the whitest eggs on the Eastern Seaboard?" John asked.

" 'Scuse me?"

"That's what's claimed," he said. "I wondered why?"

"Oh, that's just somethin' they put on there to make it sound good," said the waitress. "You all from up north?"

"Vacationing," I said. "Taking the low road."

Taking up the menus, her smile so fixed as it had been, she walked back to the food prep area; her skirt bounced up and away from her hips with her every step. The phrase *Sweetiepie* was woven onto the seat of her pink unders.

"Let me communicate, John," I said, leaning across our formicaed table. "Multivoicing'll disrupt them."

"Two can game at this," he said, smiling. "AO, Iz."

Through our booth's window I looked out into the building's central artery, at the setup of the initial attraction of the amusement room across the way. Players stood before a low counter, throwing balls at a wooden wall three meters distant. At intervals a boy would thrust his head through a hole in the fence, pulling it back as quickly. Glimpsing him, I thought at last I'd seen one of my people here; but as he reappeared I sighted his shock of blond hair, and noted that for unknown reason this white boy had painted his face black. The areas in the wood around the holes were gouged and chipped, as if heavier projectiles had been hurled in the past.

The waitress returned with our order. "May we pay now?" I asked.

"If you'd like," she said. "That'll be two dollars. Ma'am, can I ask a question if you don't mind?"

"I'm mindless," I said, moneying her. "Ask."

Her attendant's smile was supplanted by a genuine grin. "Don't y'all ever get out in the sun up north?"

"What's meant?" I asked; as I looked around the room it occurred to me that I was so pale in comparison to all others as to appear dead. "Oh. A family affair. Nothing contagious."

"I didn't mean to pry, ma'am," she said. "Some a my

friends were just wonderin' if you was an albino, they wanted
to meet you if you were."

"No, that's all right." She departed. We ate what she'd
brought us; I was as grateful that what I ate had no discernible taste. Halfway through my sandwich I noticed John's
stare drift past me. "What's seen?" I asked.

"Sporting," he said. "That way. Boys being boys."

Another waitress was attending to two oversized men in
their thirties. While she tried to take their order they reached
beneath her skirt, clutching at her legs; it astonished me that
she neither ran away, nor hit them. The heavier man
laughed as she shoved his hand from her knee. As she leaned
forward to do so the other man grabbed her bottom, squeezing it until she cried; then he splashed coffee onto her legs.

"Unsensed harassment," said John, placing his spoon on
the table. "Where's the militia?"

It tore me to see such abuse; yet I lifted my hand, to
forestall my husband's actions. "Ignore, John. We can't interact."

However, interaction had already occurred. "What're you
staring at?" one of the men shouted across to my husband.

"You," John said in a voice as loud, setting aside his
cutlery and standing up.

"That's it," I said, rising. "Come on, John—"

"Why don't you come over here, tell me what's eatin' you,
boy?" the man said, hauling himself from his booth; I interposed myself between them so that neither could see the
other's expression. "You got a problem?"

"No problem at all," I said, returning my attentions toward John. "We're leaving. Now. Come on—"

"I didn't ask you, missy," he said. "Boy, you got some
problem you need to talk to us about?"

"Talking's nonessentialled to gynoterrorists," John said,
his stance unwavering as I tried pushing him along; he
flatfooted, and held his place.

"What the hell'd you say—?"

"Goodbye," I said to the man, and anyone else who cared to give ear. "We're leaving." Most of those in the restaurant were staring, and some laughed. "Police'll interact, John," I said, whispering to him. "Move."

My husband stared at the man a moment longer; then turned toward the exit. The man spoke again, coming toward us.

"Got anything to show for yourself, boy?"

John's rage so overwhelmed that, as I took his arm, I felt his quivers rippling through his suit; it incomprehensibled to me why he evidenced no oncoming sickness, why his medication seemed not to hinder his thoughts of violence. "Ignore him, John." The man followed us into the hall, closing in. His fat didn't move when he walked.

"Your wife's the one protects you after you start trouble?" the man said. "You queer or somethin'? Answer me, y'ignorant?"

"Don't answer," I said. "Ignore, John, please—"

"Whatcha do if somebody did somethin' to her? Huh? Whatcha do then—?"

John circled to confront, and only my stare appeared to hold him back; gentling my motions, I guided my husband toward the exit, hoping that the man would not be foolish enough to lunge. As we exited, he remained inside, shouting after us until everyone stared.

"Faggot," the man shouted. "Chickenshit."

My husband silenced while we crossed the steaming asphalt, averting his glance to prevent my reading his eyes. His face purpled; he shook bodywide, and his touch was so hot as the lot beneath our feet. Upon reaching our car he unlocked my door; walked around to the driverside. I waited for him to board before seating myself. Wordlessly, he slammed his fist onto our car's roof, cratering the metal, flaking the paint. His face's color disappeared at once, reappearing in his hand; I statued, having seen him so edge but once or twice before. He climbed into the car and pressed the ignition. After I got in we drove away from Dixieland, continuing south.

Between bouts of slumber I read; by late afternoon we'd traveled so far as western Virginia, and I'd reached the late nineteenth century.

> Nor were the slaves unhappy in their cabins; there were shade trees nearby, and vegetable gardens, and chickens in the coop. The slaves sang when they worked because they were happy with their simple life.

I–9 branched away from I–3 outside of Richmond, tearing across Virginia through Tennessee toward Memphis in an unvarying straightaway, indifferent to natural barrier. As the Appalachians horizoned I saw that the road shot through their worn folds as if they'd not been there. As we passed through the cuts it evidenced that hills and knobs had been scooped from the earth in preparation for the interstate; our car's geiger counter noted lowlevel radiation as we drove through the widest gouges. The mountain ranges remaining were stripped of soil and flora, and resembled the photos of Mars.

"We should overnight soon," I said, laying my book aside. "We've gone sleepless at least a day and a half."

"Next exit, then," he said; he'd talked little since leaving Dixieland, stirring at moments only to retrieve a piece of dried fruit, or to ask me how I felt. By his demeanor I understood that he wasn't mooded to talk of what had happened, of why his anger had so risen without being thwarted. We exited as we crossed Tennessee's border, coming down onto a twisting two-lane, its surface blackened by mud washed down from the hills. Unpainted houses stood alone in roadside depressions, or beside stagnant ponds, suggesting that the area was yet inhabited. Not long after sunset we drove through a small town. One or two people walked its main street, windowshopping shuttered stores.

"Isn't it Saturday here?" John asked. "All appears plagued. The natives'd restless tonight, I'd think."

We found the population when the street became road again, outside of town. Dozens of rusting cars and minitrucks were parked near several square, windowless concrete bunkers. Through their open doors streamed the townsfolk; circles were drawn over most of the entranceways. Some distance from the others was a rambling shed; on its roadfacing side, a crude painting of a rattlesnake entwining its coils around a cross.

"Keep driving," I said. "All're busy here." Downroad, far from those crowded boxes, an assemblage of frame cabanas encircled a gravel lot; above the gateway were neon letters spelling TO RISTS.

"That's us," said John, and we drove in. Lightning's reflections flared the dark above the farthest hills. As we walked toward the office we saw another sign, one that read *White Only.* A woman with a barrel's proportions stood behind the counter inside; an unseen TV echoed racket wallround.

"Stayin' overnight, folks?" she asked; we nodded. "Glad to have you all visit us. Hope you have a pleasant stay." Her voice sharpened as she opened the guestbook. "Cash up front and proof of marriage." Our U.S. driver's licenses impressed her enough; she handed John a key after we'd paid. He stared at it long enough that I elbowed him, trying to distract. "What're you New Yorkers doing down this way?" she asked. "You coal people?"

"Vacationing," I said. John crossed the room, walking up to a Coca-Cola machine, a tall red-blood box. Slotting coins, he opened its windowed door and withdrew two bottles.

"Sounds nice," she said. "Goin' far?"

"Memphis, Tennessee," I said. "We're wondering how much more of a row we have to hoe."

She blinked her eyes, as if they stung. "Take the Moses Road when you leave in the morning, you'll get there by afternoon. Checkout time's nine-thirty. Say, mister, the opener's on the front of the door—"

"Accomplished," John said, thumbing off each cap.

"Well," she said, "have a good night, then." She backed away from the counter as she moved into another room, eyeing us all the while; we exited into rain. John's leg prevented him from running so swiftly as me to our cabin, but the clouds hadn't yet burst and we weren't soaked through. The place was no larger than our bedroom; contained but a concave bed, dusty table and lamp. The bathroom was no less lavish. As I toileted I rubbed myself with the thin towel provided; no sooner was I dry than my parchment skin wetted anew. The harsh light illuminated my veins so well that I didn't have to search for them as I performed my medicheck. As I watched the strip go pink, assuring a negative response, I listened to rain brush its beat against the roof. The downpour intensed while John bathroomed himself, and I lay listening to it until he emerged, and we faced each other stripped.

"It's honeymoon two, Iz," John said, evidencing desire, looking lovely; but my stomach ached, my head throbbed, and the memory of pain from our last encounter overcame my libido. The floor groaned beneath my steps as I walked over to where he stood; I reached up and brushed his damp hair from his brow.

"Let's lie for now, John. We'll play at morningside if able."

He nodded; stroked his chest as we bedded ourselves atop the sheets. A red and blue vine enscrolled his torso's Y-scar, his sole tattoo serving to disguise the Krylar's insertion-line. Gravity rolled us toward one another, pressing us together in the depths of the bed. He held out his palm that I could see his evening's dose, the standard baby blue and one of Leverett's white triangles.

"Medicheck's AO?" I asked, watching as he swallowed his pills dry.

"AO. Yours?"

"No infectives," I said. "Headwobbly, all the same. Stomachturned. I'm dragging axles waltz-timed."

Lightning lit our room with blue flashes as the rain increased and thunder upvolumed. I petted his elbow's inner curve, touching the lumps left where his bones had reknitted. "Regooding doesn't become me," John said. "All efforts to change my ways within unavail. Appletrees don't grow oranges, Iz. Are they blinded to that?"

"Not all of them, surely," I said, suspecting that they were. "The man at Dixieland. What happened?"

"I keened to ex him, Iz."

"Obvioused," I said. "You should have sickened unto death, as prescribed," I said. "You didn't. Why?"

"Unknown," he said. "I'm medicating, you watched—"

"Thank you for showing."

"I knew you worried," he said. "It's beyond me, Iz. Tolerance levels overrode, possibly. Mayhap the rite of passage affects the innards somehow. Psychovirals in the air. I don't know but—"

"But what?"

"It's matterless, Iz, I'm regretting nothing, not even the interplay. This world's rewired me." He smiled without my having to cue; I couldn't remember the last time that had happened. "I'm alive."

"Understood. It's good, John. Earplay your reactions, all the same," I said. "You've calmed now?"

"As a morning lake," he said. "But wide-eyed. I'll not sleep tonight, I can tell."

"It frightens me to see you so upset," I said. "When that other face turns toward me, I know it's not your own."

"It is."

He stroked my neck so tenderly that I lay almost unmindful of the ease with which he could have broken it. "Sleepaway, then," I said. Telling myself that for the nonce I was satisfied with our lot, I listened to the rain. Beneath its rhythm I noted an unrecognizable cacophony, previously unheard. "What's that?"

"It's an outward sound," John said. "It's loudening. Listen." The gray sheet stuck to me as I got up. Peering out the room's window into the woods behind the motel I saw—far from the road, but close to our cabin—another of those concrete blockhouses, this one scarred by neither mark nor sign. A full house seemed in attendance within.

"Some ceremony, you think?" John asked, staring through the trees, seeing no more than I could. We heard exhilarating screams and tambourine's rattle rising above the raindrone, against a three-quarter-time stomp; those inside began chanting, their phrases sounding as *Kana*-lea, *kana*-lea, *kana*-lea. After a minute the chant ceased, and all silenced; then, the congregants began singing an a capella hymn.

> *"O! what a wretched land is this,*
> *That yields us no supply,*
> *No cheering fruits, no wholesome trees—"*

"Is it religious?" John asked. "A ritual?"

"A southernism, mayhap."

The worshipers boomed forth as they undertook the chorus, their voices lifting is if overjoyed.

> *"I'm glad, so glad, I was born to die."*

There were eleven additional verses, and as they concluded the last those in attendance screamed and laughed as drunks, intoxicated by spirit, besodden by the love of grim thoughts. John smiled, hearing their words, as if even before

he listened their spirit had found its way inside of him. My
fatigue overtook me; we lay down again, and after a short
time I fell asleep. As he'd foreseen, John remained wakeful
nightlong; he was lowvoicing as I drifted into my darkness,
humming the song's chorus to himself.

Through the next morning I read, all the way to Memphis.
Read *The Growth of the American Republic:*

> Now this basic force, the secret of the sun, this
> energy beyond comprehension has been found.
> The atom has been split, and mankind stands at
> the threshold of a future no one can foresee.

Attempted to decipher the *Daily Mirror:*

> PUT ANOTHER ROSENBERGER ON THE GRILL
> DOES REICH HAVE BOMB? NEIN, SAYS SPEER
> IKE DENIES SAUCERS OURS; PHILLY BUZZED

Idly thumbing *Knifelife,* found a quote from Edmund Burke:

> No passion so effectually robs the mind of all its
> powers of acting and reasoning as fear; for fear
> being an apprehension of pain or death, it oper-
> ates in a manner that resembles actual pain.
> Whatever is terrible, therefore, is sublime, too.

"Memphis, five miles," John said, gleaning a towered directional outskirting another factory complex. The country-
side west of Nashville was exclusively given over to industry,
contrarying what we'd been told we'd likely find. "Twenty
minutes, accounting for traffic."

"Mayhap we should verify their presence, prearrival?" I
asked. "It's Sunday, they could be churching."

"Best not to lessen surprise," John said. Though his face was still flushed with new redness, his features had taken on the oddest cast, perspiring sans sweat, as if his skin had been waxed and polished. He'd medicated again that morning, predeparture; again, I'd watched, to certify.

"Is anything troubling?" I asked.

"Not at all, Iz," he said. "Life's renewed."

Memphis skylined on the horizon. On our left, some kilometers south of town, I saw industrial chimneys several hundred meters high; the heavy black smoke issuing from their spouts besmeared the clouds floating in from the west. Within the city the highest building held only twenty floors; suburban steeples jabbing up from all quadrants pricked the sky. Some were crucifixed at their points, but most were apexed with open circles such as the ones enscrawled above the doors of those boxes back in the mountains.

"The address's mapped?" John asked as we unramped from the interstate where it slashed into downtown. We stopped alongside a Piggly Wiggly store; I was uncertain what might have been sold at a place so named.

"We're directioned true," I said, examining the atlas. "Go right, and eventually turn left. It's Alabama Avenue we want."

For twelve blocks we drove up a treeless commercial strip of one- and two-floor brickfaces storing groceries, laundries and other small shops. The city's populace appeared as if they'd been floured, showing almost so colorless as I did, though the sun was hot enough to blister. Halfway along our course we glided past a windowless beige building, recently built; its grounds were fenced and guarded by men in blue uniforms. An Army-green bus, its windows painted and rear door soldered shut, was pulling out of its driveway as we sped by. Along its side was stenciled the legend, *Memphis Department of Rehabilitation.*

"A correction facility, I'd hazard," John said.

Seeing the sign for Alabama Avenue, we lefted onto its

rutted pavement; yellowed grass grew in the avenue's gutters. Neither sidewalks nor streetlamps lent civility's appearance; judging from the houses' condition, none in the
neighborhood had ever been monied. Junked cars were
parked in barren yards; children scrambled over their rusted
frames, staring at us as we rolled by. John parked our car
before number 462, a two-story frame with encircling ve-
randa: paint eczemaed from its boards, curling away in long,
dry strips; an upper-floor window was patched with brown
paper. The gutters sagged away from the roof, overweighted
with wet leaves. No one evidenced as we exited and tramped
across the muddy yard; ascending the porch's rotting steps,
we sighted four battered mailboxes.

"Presley," I read. "Number two."

"On the side," said John, looking round. "After you." We
lightfooted as we stepped across the porch, hearing the slats
splinter and groan beneath our shoes. The unpaved driveway was emptied of cars; dogs were barking in the next street
over. The air was thick enough to pour. "Door's unlocked,"
he said, touching the knob. "I'll precede."

With his fingertips he widened our passage, pushing the
door open; wordlessly motioning that I should follow. The
Presleys' living-room walls were newspapered with sheets of
the *Press-Scimitar*, affording them as well the sole library
seen. The windows were open, and unscreened; flies beaded
every surface inside. A doorway led into a short hall stacked
with unopened cartons; the kitchen showed, beyond. I
glimpsed a white refrigerator streaked with gray and yellow
stains. When he came to the end of the hall John jumped
away from the kitchen, bumping into me as he raised his
hands over his head.

"Excuse," he said, to one unseen. "Harm's unmeant."

"Who're you?" I heard a young man say. "*Who?* Let me
see you."

I trailed my husband as he entered the kitchen, stepping

over a woman who lay on the floor. Her appearance was that of Gladys Presley; she seemed to be asleep, wearing what I imagined at first to be a red apron over her white cotton dress. Elvis had a gun.

5

□

He barely resembled the icon with which we were familiared. If, while drunk and guided solely by a blurred snap, one attempted to mold with one's hands the features of Elvis onto a nongender-specific passerby, one could as easily have reproduced the look of this world's E. His hair was flat-brushed, with strands snaking down with humidity's weight; acne bubbled up from his face, poxing him with blisters. E's pink and black *blouson* buttoned with bone-white metal snaps, four on each cuff; its collar drooped from his craw as if unwilling to abut his skin. His black baggy trousers were sideseamed with yellow sequins. His hand shook as he leveled his gun at us; he bit his nails, I could see, and though his weapon's size was moderate I couldn't guess its caliber.

"Who the hell're you people?" he asked, liplicking. A daft anger inhered in his eyes, as if he readied to kill for having sneezed on his shirt. "What're y'doin' in my house?"

Trailing as John led, I froze, and listened to my husband's voice reveal nothing. "We overheard in passing," he said, appearing as calm personified, feigning that confronting an armed adolescent didn't fear him. "An accident, we thought. Then we looked."

E stepped nearer; his bath powder's scent sickened. "Y'like what y'see? Huh?"

"Then it was an accident?" John asked, softspeaking, lulling me with verbal opiates if not E; he spoke as if to a baby he wished to make unconscious without exertion.

"Yeah, a *accident,*" E said, his voice upscaling into a child's petulant whine, adding to his threat. "Might be another accident. Tell me who you are."

"You're threatening?" I asked, keeping minded such distraction techniques as I knew. "Why would you hurt us?"

"Why wouldn't I?" E's fabled charisma was absent from his double; still, however disappointing his look and manner, there was no mistaking the voice. His wordsound identicalled with that of his counterpart, though E's drawl was mud-thick. Hearing him speak, I noted anew the sensation felt when I'd heard this world's Eisenhower; that of an awe so encompassing as to terrify rather than astonish, as if I tried standing in hurricane's midst. "What's that accent? You're not Germans, are you?"

"Why Germans—?" I asked.

"*Warum Deutsch?*" John said, trolling for reactions.

"Sure's hell not police," E said. "Keep your hands up and get up against that wall there. Go on."

My hands stuck to the wall, it was so grease-bespattered. Flies bombarded me as I stood there with my husband, restraining my shakes as I turned away from our host. In the instant between our circling and his touching I anticipated all the places where he might lay hands; then he pawed my shoulder. "What'd your mother do, Elvis?" I asked, thinking he must have stung himself as he jerked away his fingers.

"How'd you know my name?" he asked, recovering at once enough to position his gun-barrel's tip behind my ear. It uncertained, what my husband might be reading in E's actions and stance; I feared overmuch that our quarry would, at any second, ex us sans qualm or reason, and so I couldn't distance myself enough yet to judge. Seeing John's lack of motion assured me but little; guaranteed that, as circumstanced, there was naught to do but waitwatch.

"We're looking for you," I said.

"What for?" E asked, pressing his gun against my head, pinching my scalp. "You all government?"

"You're hurting me," I said; simultaneously felt his free hand pushing up my dress, and his fingers kneading my hip.

"Turn around here," he said; I spun, ready to slap. As he gazed at me fullface I watched his features shift. I was older than his mother, after all; however toned and tucked I'd been, however bleached I showed, my age evidenced clear in the corners that needed dusting: in the wrinkles around my eyes, at my lipcorners, at my neck's root. E drew his hand from under my clothing; took the gun far enough from my head to allow air to circulate between them again. "Just checkin' to see if you're armed," he said, as if to apologize. "Have to."

"Don't hurt me again," I said. "Or touch me as if I were property."

"I'll do more'n that if I haveta," E said. "What're you lookin' for me for if you're government? We're not commies or niggers."

"We're not government. We came for you." E attempted a sneer, but hadn't yet perfected its angle and pitch, and so he appeared not so ominous as mentally challenged. "We want you to hear our proposal," I said.

"Better hear mine first," he said. "I'm tireda this bullshit. Hey!" E goosed John with his gun. "Face me but keep those hands up. Who sent you?"

"Our employers," John said as he turned toward E, his voice so untensed as before. E placed his gun-barrel at my husband's lips, stilling them.

"Y'all gonna do what I say," E said. "Dig me?"

"Duggen," I said. "Don't do that."

E replaced the barrel against my lips, brushing its coldness against them as if to add color. "Y'all got a car?" he asked.

"We do," I said as he took away his gun. "Why'd you kill your mother?"

"That's none a your business, ma'am. Don't ask me why. Just do it."

"Understood." Looking at John, steeling myself against kneeshake, blinking stinging sweat from my eyes' lenses, I saw his wink; grasped sans analysis that he would do nothing until E threatened overmuch: how much threat might that be, I wondered, if a gun at my head and a hand up my dress didn't inload emergency into crisis? It occurred that mayhap his medication had at last effected, doubling his coma, leaving him loboed.

"Let's take a ride," E said. "Tireda sittin' in here with that."

"Your mother?" E frowned; fumbled through a drawer with his free hand until he found a length of white cord. "Might others have heard as we did?"

E untwisted the rope, straightening its coils. "Everbody round here's at church. They're all Christians."

"What are you?" I asked.

"Hey, you a rough crawler, son?" E said, ignoring me save to hand me the white rope; he slapped my husband's back as if to judge ripeness. John said nothing; remained unmoving. "You tie'm up now. Go on. Tie'm tight with that clothesline. Don't do no slip knot. I'm watchin' you."

"Why's it necessary to bind him?" I asked, holding the line in my hands.

"I don't want no barrelhouse," said E. "Your friend here's no spring chicken but he's solid. Go ahead, now. Tie his wrists together. Loop the clothesline through his belt."

John nodded, allowing permission; he placed his hands at the small of his back. I was no scout, and knew nothing of knots; I attempted to secure my husband's arms tightly

enough to satisfy E but not enough to prevent bloodflow. I
stood back, enabling E to examine my handiwork; as he
gripped the line he yanked it, almost unfooting my husband.

"Don't," John said, evidencing upset.

"Don't tell me what t'do." Reaching into the sink E extracted a rag from a dish-stack and threw it at me. "Gag'm."

"I won't—"

"Will," said E, placing his gun at my temple. I wound the
cloth round my husband's head, fitting it over his mouth
before knotting it. E readjusted the rag, stuffing its folds
between John's lips; then moved a step or two away, turning
him toward us. While he kept his gun on me E lefted John's
stomach, felling him. Once my husband floored he booted
his ribs, smiling all the time as if keening to hear the snap.

"Don't!" I shouted, heedless of whether he shot me.

"I'm not wearin' hard shoes," E said. He laughed until I
wished to hurt him more than he'd hurt my husband; John
glared at me, willing that I still, evidencing that he'd not
been overly harmed. E hadn't kicked hard enough to dent
John's underlay; if bruised without, he remained whole
within. "Hell, you act like he's your boyfriend or somethin',
you—"

"He's my husband," I said. "Don't hurt him again."

"You're married?" E asked, staring at us. "That beats all.
Okay, then, help 'im get up."

"Don't touch him."

"Won't if I can help it," E said, laughing, rubbing his
fingers along his gun's grip, caressing the stock as if his
touch brought mutual joy. "Looks kinda pitiful there like
that, don't he?"

As I righted my husband I recalled that our world's Elvis
was one of twins; his brother was born dead, as he would
have been a century later. Speculation rifed as to what the
nature of Elvis's mirroring brother might have been; the
Jesseans, truly, pronounced the dead baby to be their messiah, and were thus excommunicated by all other sects of the

C of E. I fancied that the E with whom we were dealing in this world might in ours be the twin who'd not lived, a survivor who'd taken on or been given the name of his brother.

"Let's go," said E, raising a battered valise from beneath the kitchen table, lifting it over his mother's husk. "You go first. Don't try nothin'. Where're y'parked?"

"We're fronted."

As we left the kitchen E shifted his bag beneath his arm and pulled a sheet off the living room's worn sofa. He paused sidelong at the front doorway as we porched ourselves, eyeing the street updown. "That Hudson's yours?"

"None other."

"Nobody's around," he said. "Go on. I'm right behind you, don't do nothin' stupid." We crossed the grassless lawn, followed close by E. "Unlock it if it's locked and lay him down in the back seat." While I opened the car's back door I watched E overlook its polychromed metal. "Damn. Y'all get this thing off a nigger?"

"That word's unwarranted," I said. "Bestill its use around me. Why the question?"

"The colors—"

"They're summery and pleasant." He stared at me as if witholding a smile while I guided John into the back, assisting him as I placed him on his side, careful not to disengage his leg's mechanics.

"Where the hell y'all from, lady?" E asked, tossing his valise into the front seat.

"North," I said. "New York."

"Oh, yeah?" E billowed the sheet over John, cloaking him. "All laid out," he said. "All he needs now's coins on his eyes. Might get 'em yet."

"He'll overheat like that," I said. "Remove it."

"Not while we're in town. People'll think he's bein' kidnapped."

"He's not?" I asked. "A covered body won't arouse suspicions?"

"You know how to drive?"

"You don't?" During our training I'd been taught; as a New Yorker I'd never learned.

"Yeah, but not one-hand," E said, waving his gun, motioning for me to move. "Get in. Let's hit it."

E clambered into shotgun position as I wheeled myself, planting his foot on my purse; his white shoes were so scuffed as a Bolshoi dancer's. His valise sprang open as he floored it, scattering colorful shirts and magazines. As he seated himself he struck his head on the doorframe; I readied to pluck up his gun if he dropped it, but he didn't.

"Dammit," he said, massaging his forehead; he must have noticed my smile. "Dammit, go on. Drive."

"Where?"

"Where I tell you."

"My husband," I said. "John. Tap your foot if you're AO." Looking in the rearview I saw only his sheeted midsection. I pressed the ignition, revving the soundtrack as the batteries silently charged; heard beneath its roar his shoes rapping against the side of the car. I kicked off my shoe; rested my foot on the accelerator and shifted to drive after assuring clearance.

"Watch for kids, pullin' out," E said. The car was a smooth runner, but I didn't want to drive those interstates. "Hang a left at the light." He positioned his arm against his knee, tenting his gun with our newssheet. The signal changed from orange to blue as we approached, and I steered the car left, toward the town center. "What kinda Hudson is this?" he asked, studying the dash's gauges and dials. "Looks like a fighter jet in here."

"You're familiared with jets?" I asked. "Were you blue yondered?"

"Can't you talk straight, lady?" he asked; I wondered how

many anachronisms were slipping into my speech. "I seen pictures a jets, who hasn't?"

For a short distance the neighborhood upscaled. Midsize houses stood newroofed and clear-windowed, polished cars shone in the sun, residents clipped green grass before breaking for one of several daily meals. "What's the destination?" I asked, switching on the AC so that John wouldn't broil.

"Mississippi," he said. "I'll be tellin' you how to get there."

"Why Mississippi?"

"Cause it's not Tennessee," E said. "Quit askin' so many damn questions, lady, I don't want to shoot you."

"You shot your mother," I said.

"That's nobody's business but mine and hers," he said, his voice uninflected. "Left again, at this stop sign."

I steered the car onto Third Street, entering the commercial zone's outskirts. Three blocks distant, the interstate's overhead provided a long, cool tunnel; when we emerged we were in downtown's thriving midst, its streets lined with office buildings no higher than a Westchester cineplex. Memphiseans—caucasoids all—thronged the wide awninged sidewalks as their cars and buses gridlocked the avenues. Most stores' signs were illuminated as if it were night, flashing multihued neon displays. Its small size notwithstanding, Memphis's center semblanced an urbanity I'd known only from films, here seen technicolored and holo-sharp. My dress was no less unstylish here than it had been in New York; most men wore wrinkled seersucker, stained between the shoulderblades. Standing outside the ornate entrance of a larger structure called the Peabody Hotel was a metal placard in bird's outline, announcing that all should *Come See the Ducks.*

"What ducks?" I asked.

"They come walkin' cross the lobby there ever' day to go swim in a fountain inside," said E. "Hotel makes a big to-do 'bout it. President, movie stars come to town, mayor takes 'em down to see the ducks. It's sorry, but true."

"Why do they have ducks in a hotel?"

"Think I run the place, lady? I don't know." Even he seemed surprised by his anger; he settled, staring window-ways, allowing his eyes to unfocus while he reveried. "When I was a kid there was a boy lived next door to us in Tupelo. His parents, they were Christians, they gave him some baby ducks for Easter." To the right, blocking any riverviews, stood a number of sprawling stone buildings whose forbidding designs inferred that they housed government functionaries. "He took 'em out in the back yard, buried 'em up to their necks and then run over 'em with the mower."

"That's senseless," I said. "Did he murder, later on?"

"I said, you want to kill 'em, just kill 'em," E said. "No need to make a big thing out of it. Crazy mixed-up kid."

I eyed the placement of the Alekhine button on the dash, in the event immediate transferral essentialed; glimpsed the magazines strewn among his clothing as they spilled from his bag. Limned upon one of the covers was a man wearing a winged helmet and staring into what appeared to be a TV screen programming a shot of an aerodynamically improbable rocket.

"Science fiction?" I asked, nodding downward. E lay his shoe upon the magazine as if to hide it. "You read it?"

"It's not what you think," he said, grunting his reply. "It's not all made-up." Beyond a number of older houses on our left was a larger stone building with columns. A sign impaled in its surrounding greensward announced, in badly drawn letters, *Tonight's Lecture: How Red Is The Little Red Schoolhouse?*

"That's a school?" I asked.

"Library," E said, chewing at his lips. He facaded calm, whatever roiled within him, and it seemed unlikely that he would kill me within the next few minutes. Still, whether he replayed within his mind the reasons for having shot his mother, pondered how to dispose of our bodies, or simply thought of what he'd had for breakfast as he sat there was unguessable to me.

"You got gas in this car?" E asked.

"We're fueled."

"How much money you got on you?"

"Much as you need," I said.

"Nobody's got that much money, lady," he said, laughing. "Where is it?"

"It's pursed," I said. "Down there."

E retrieved my clutch from where I'd left it and dumped out the contents. Unbilling my wallet, he shoved my money into his pants. Finding John's copy of *Knifelife*, he picked it up, and perused its pages as we drove on, a book in one hand, a gun in the other. "What kinda book is this?" he said. "They're talkin' about how t'kill people in here."

"That's intended," I said. "You need lessons?"

"Damn. 'More solid than stabbing a pillow so long as ribs—' " E dropped the book, as if by touching it he'd heard a victim's screams. "That's sick. That is."

"It's my husband's book. A trainer's text."

"Like a schoolbook?" I nodded. "He's not a gangster or anything, is he?"

"A businessman," I said. A sign in a window passed announced the arrival of new model television sets, some with built-in bars. "You shouldn't literal all the text, I'm told."

"Good thing. Some of it reads like science fiction but the rest—"

"There's nothing in it of moons or Martians," I said.

"I mean the attitude," said E. "I can handle stuff with Martians in it. I been readin' *Amazing Stories*, all of 'em, since I was a kid." His attentions shot elsewhere; uprighting himself, he smoothed the newssheet over his gun, and glanced back at John. "Shit. See that police car over there? Don't do nothin', just keep drivin' or I'll shoot." The police's black-and-white passed us, heading downtown; the cop within stared ahead, as if debating whether to respond to a call. He held the look common to all enforcement junkies, a wash of ennui so absolute that only the greatest levels of violence, experienced either actively or passively, could stir them. John considered police the worst sort of amateurs. As the car distanced, E sighed; he'd held his breath as we brushed.

"He must be going to see your mother," I said.

"Maybe," E said, closing his eyes. "Don't wanta talk about it."

"John?" I heard two taps in reply, and spoke to E. "Your gun's unneeded. Please stuff it."

"Won't fit in my pocket," he said, and I thought he japed me; when he said nothing more, I discerned that he believed his reason valid. "Almost outta town. That's good."

"What do people do in Memphis?"

"Get out of it, first chance they get," said E. "Just stay on this road."

On the road's right side was a prime familiarity. "This is recognizable," I said. "I've seen pictures." Visible behind a high fence and grove of trees was a stone house standing atop a hill. "Graceland," I said, sounding the word, seeing the shrine as it stood in pre-Presley days. The roof sagged, many windows were broken; the columns needed paint. Its setting was nearly rural, entirely unlike the house's grounds in our world, reconstructed and prettified and circled round by tetzeltowns, where all manner of indulgences were peddled to the coin-ringing faithful.

"That old barn," E said, glancing over. "It's not as old as I am and it's already fallin' down."

The road Graceland faced, the route by which we departed Memphis, had been renamed Elvis Presley Boulevard while its namesake still lived. I debated whether this moment suitabled to point this out, and aware E of why we'd come for him; decided that, as circumstanced, he was probably in no more mood to hear than I was to tell. The road narrowed as we left town; its two lanes straightarrowed into deeper south. Clumps of brown pine and bare-leafed deciduous were interspersed between gas stations, diners and shacks, and I espied the interstate and its accompanying atmosphere coming close. Its wall curved toward our road, rising above the fields some two hundred meters off to the left, paralleling our route.

"When can we untie John?"

"That's his name?" E asked. "Drive and don't worry. It's air-cooled in here, he's comfortable enough. He's really your husband?"

"Why would I lie?"

"I didn't say you did. He looks ten years older'n you."

"Two."

"I said he looked it," said E. "Can't say I buy that, ma'am. Pretty woman like you wouldn't marry some old dog like him."

"Don't macho me," I said. "Did your mother do something to you?"

"Lady, it's nobody's business but mine—"

"I'm involved in your business."

"You got yourself involved, walkin' in without knockin'," E said. "Nobody ever teach you manners?"

"Manners? You murder and you talk etiquette to me—?"

I noticed he'd slackened his grip on his gun—seemed, in truth, almost to have forgotten he held it. Lunging for it while driving seemed to me an unsound response, and so I didn't attempt seizure. As I sized him sidelong, my glance repeatedly returned to his eyes; I was almost certain that he'd mascaraed his lashes, as had our world's Elvis. Without doubt I suspected that he used his mother's makeup.

"I don't wanta talk about that," he said. "Damn women—"

"Women? You're alive, she's not."

"Alive in body," he said. "Hell, lady. When you get acted

on, what're y'gonna do? Devil owns this world, you know that. Man can't do nothin' 'cept take it as it comes."

"You're talking as if you're scripted," I said, estimating it best that I continue to assuage and misdirect, talking him into deeper distraction. One approach I could have taken was one John couldn't opt for; but I imagined no condition which would cause me to attempt seduction. Recalling so well as I could my younger days, when Judy and I conned as willed those we wished to bend, I earplayed my way through, drawing upon technik I'd forgotten I had. "You're disassociating blame. No devil killed your mother."

"You don't get it?" he asked. "You Christian?"

"What are you?" I responded.

"Damned," he said, intoning with such melodrama as only a teen can muster. "Might as well talk to the wall, then."

The road countrysided, passing flat fields on the right; the riverplain must have been some unseeable distance beyond. The interstate's wall rolled on, leftward, as before. High oak and loblolly pines erupted along the borders of lots. Six small signs no larger than floorboards sequenced along the shoulder, each bearing white-lettered sentences enscribed upon a sunbleached red field, and reading WITH GLAMOUR GIRLS / YOU'LL NEVER CLICK / BEWHISKERED / LIKE A / BOLSHEVIK / BURMA SHAVE.

"What's Burma Shave?" I asked. "An art project?"

"Lady, you kill me," E said, smiling as if he liked me. "Tell me where you're really from."

"New York, told as said. That's our city's newssheet, true?"

"Looks like it," he said, opening the *Mirror*'s pages. However loosely he held his gun, his aim kept true. "I've heard people from New York talk before. You don't sound like 'em." He snorted, as if his lungs imploded.

"Are you choking?" I asked.

"Laughin'," he said. "Listen to this. 'Panty raid turns violent. Twenty University of Kentucky coeds assaulted,

three dead.' Just havin' fun, says—" He paused. "Partici-
ple—"

"Participant," I said, reading the word which so troubled.

"My kinda fun, sounds like."

The incident's charm eluded me; then again, so had his.
"That's monstrous," I said. "Those poor women."

"Hell, they just didn't interview the ones that liked it."

"Mayhap those were the ones killed," I said. Rearviewing,
I glanced at John's middle as it shook with the roll of the car.

"They musta asked for it—"

"As we did?"

He gazed my way; smiled. "Maybe."

"What are you going to do with us?" I asked. E pressed his
gun's muzzle against my side and scooted closer to me,
pushing its tip against my ribs.

"You never did tell me how you know my name," he said,
"or why you're lookin' for me."

"We've a job for you," I said. "We came to flagpole the
idea and see what flies."

"Jobs're a drag, ma'am," E said. "I've had enough jobs."

"Once you're captured they'll work you in prison,
surely—"

"Goddamnit, shut up—!" The vehemence with which he
slung his demand intimidated as intended. I muted, and
readied to brake the car if he began flailing, but he didn't.
A billboard on our left advertised the Ditty Wah Ditty Tourist Court's clean cabins, six miles downroad. Allowing him
time enough to calm, I waited until he again appeared at
comparative peace before conversing anew.

"Why do you ma'am me sometime and lady me others?"
I asked.

"Your husband didn't act like a businessman," E said,
ignoring my question as if I'd not asked it, pronouncing *biz*
as *bid.* "Acts like a teacher I had back in high school."

"A teacher?" I repeated, astonished by the concept that
my husband could so image. "You mean in a reformatory?"

"Yeah," he laughed. "Humes High. Teacher I had, he taught biology. Mean ol' sonofabitch. Just looked down on everything and everybody."

"You've misread my husband, then—"

"Turned out he was a commie," E said.

"How uncovered?"

"Had a map of Russia right there in his house. Nobody was surprised."

"Who was looking for commies?"

His lip drew up as he laughed again, evidencing delight at my having to so inquire. "Must do things *real* different up north," he said. An overalled man guided a plow as his horse clomped through a yellow field on the right, rutting dirt; I perceived by his stance that our appearance startled him as his amazed me. We'd never been awared as to how recently the peasantry had subsisted in such ancient manner in the veldt. "Doesn't"—pronounced *dudn't*—"Doesn't this feel good now, just runnin' down the road like this?" E asked; I shook my head. "How long you been married?"

"Fifteen years."

"How old were you? Fourteen?"

"I'm forty-four," I said.

"I don't believe you," said E. "You don't look it. He does. Looks like he's been sewn up so many times they can't find a place to stitch."

"Generally they do," I said.

"Why's a good-lookin' woman like you married to an old gorilla like him?"

"That's none of your business," I said; once more felt him shove his gun against me.

"I think it is," he said. "Don't be tellin' me otherwise."

"My business doesn't matter and yours does, that's what you're telling?"

"Come on, don't get upset—"

"Take that gun off me," I said; he did. "Did your mother tell you what your business should be all the time?"

His face slackened as if he'd been sedated; he moved away from me, and was wordless for a moment. "I loved my mother."

"You snuffed her, all the same."

He nodded, as if one shouldn't preclude the other. "One time she told me it was harder than I'd ever know, raisin' me. I told her I didn't try t'make it that way but she said it didn't matter, I did anyway. Nothin' I ever did was right, hear her tell it."

"Where's your father?"

"I don't know," E said, his color fading until he was almost so pale as me; he so monotoned as he spoke that a stranger might have thought he was talking of someone else's family. "He passed some bad checks. Got caught, went to jail. Never come back. It tore mamma up. We'd just moved to Memphis. She kept sayin' if it hadn't been for that we mighta been all right."

"What was her job?"

"Mamma worked for a while as a nurse's aide at the hospital. Mopped floors. Emptied rich ladies' bedpans. Quit once or twice, said she couldn't do nothin' with a bad back."

"So you worked, then?"

"Yeah. Didn't want to. Hell, what choice's anybody got?" he said. "Where's the radio in this car?" I switched it on, cautioning my actions so that he wouldn't think I threatened. After he situated the radio he took control of the knobs, moving through the spectrum's static, blurring sound into garble.

"That problematicked between you and your mother?" I asked.

"I don't wanta talk about it." He ceased his search when a flourish of strings wafted up, backgrounding a singer. "Dean Martin," E said. "He's okay." However unmemorable the song might have been, E knew the lyrics, and as we drove he began singing along. It evidenced at once that his voice duped exactly the earliest sound of our world's Elvis. Dryco would have no trouble foisting him off on his audience so long as he did nothing but sing; I was grateful that the regooding of the rest of him would be left to them, so long as we got him back. The song ended, and he quieted; the announcer started spieling for an upcoming program.

"Your voice is one of a kind," I said. "We're music people."

"Up in New York?" he asked. "What's this job you were talkin' about?"

"Singing. Performing. We'd heard word of your ability."

"Heard from who?" He foottapped the floor as an instrumental came on the radio; John added his own counterpoint, assuring me by producing his own percussion.

"Word rounds," I said. "What goes, comes. You've sung in public before?"

"One time in Mississippi, last year," he said.

"Tell."

"What for?" he asked. "I'm still up for this job?"

"So long as you don't hurt us," I said. "What happened?"

"One weekend I took off 'n hitchiked down to the Jimmie Rodgers Festival in Meridian. I was born in Mississippi, that made me eligible to play. I brought my guitar. Sang a couple songs. I didn't play country, though. They started booin' and laughin' at me. Sonsabitches—" His voice broke before he quieted, lending his voice greater youth than it already held.

"Everyone thinks themselves a critic," I said. "Why didn't you bring your guitar along with you?"

"I smashed it upside a tree after I got off stage," he said. "Couple old rednecks said it was the best thing I coulda done with it. If it'd still been in one piece I'da beat 'em blind with it—"

"Then you've no instrument—"

"Aw, I could always rig up a diddly bo if I needed somethin' to play. It's not necessary to—"

"What's a diddly bo?"

"Take a board, drive some nails in it, tie string between 'em. It'll do the trick."

"You didn't play country," I said. "What did you play?"

"Blues," he said. "They don't care much for it in Mississippi, I guess."

The interstate's wall apparently shielded the local industries from view; every few kilometers more of those cloud-high chimneys towered above its length, spewing blackness. Scattered along the right roadside, interspersed with clapboard shacks, were oversized houses encompassed by verandas; gleaming copper cupolas supplied their green in lieu of that of the naked trees surrounding. The houses must once have been plantation HQs, I thought; their matches, in our world, were undoubtedly torched during the Civil War, or left to rot into the soil once their support systems were emancipated. But these places looked museum-preserved, appearing new-built through the netting of gray moss hanging from their yards' stripped trees, as if my ancestors were still being used to brighten paint and glaze windows.

Where were my people? WELCOME TO MISSISSIPPI, read a directional beyond the road's intersection with a narrow dirt lane; our car wheels dusted the asphalt as we sped on. Possibly, I thought, they'd all been painted as I'd been, washed of their color to better satisfy someone's notions of decor; mayhap, like Nyasas, they'd hied themselves away before others took charge of their relocation. I conscioused of another's touch, mid-reverie; E stroked my arm with his free hand's fingers.

"Don't," I said, drawing back, feeling as if roaches were still strolling across me. I slowed as I bumped the car over a wooden bridge; the brown water below resembled dirty honey. Afternoon sun shimmered the horizon; pools of water appeared and disappeared on the concrete distanced. Heat rippled the air above the red and ocher flatland. E flipped through one of his magazines, aiming his gun at my side; looked up when he noticed me judging its angle.

"What's your name?" he asked.

"Call me Isabel."

He laughed, sounding as if he'd just returned from a panty raid; it appalled me to consider how much longer I would have to semblance calm. I tried to think of ways I could convince him to release John. "Figures, way this car's painted—"

"What's meant?"

"Nothin'," he said, softening his drawl. "I like this, Isabel. I like ridin' with you."

"The weapon's nonessential, I'd think," I said.

"You're thinkin' wrong, then," he said, looking at his magazine once more. The article he read was entitled *I Remember Lemuria.*

"That's science fiction you're reading?"

"No, this is true," E said. "It's about the Dero. I read this'n lotsa times before but it's good. Mamma wouldn't let me bring magazines into the house when I was little so—"

"Dero?" I replayed. "Dero what?"

"You never hearda Dero?" I shook my head. "This fellow named Shaver found out about 'em during the war. Dero live in caves and in secret hideaways. They kidnap people and take 'em down below and torture 'em, kill 'em sometimes. When they're not doin' that they cause everything bad that happens in the world. They must be minions of the Demiurge."

His allusions were absent of understandable referents, and I was thoroughly baffled. "I see . . ."

"Some think they're the ones in the flying saucers, the ones that aren't Germans."

"What do Germans have to do with Dero—?"

"I think they might have hooked up together, myself. You've never seen one a the German flying saucers?" E asked; I shook my head. "We see 'em down here all the time. They make 'em in the Farben plant, outside Memphis. They won't own up to it of course, but everybody knows whose they are. Fellow I met told me one swooped so low flyin' over him he saw a swastika on its underside."

"Swastikas?" I said. "Germans are still Nazis?"

E stared at me, his mouth agape, as if I'd spoken of my own Dero. "You don't keep up on these things in New York? What the hell do you think they are—?"

He eyed me as if, reapprised, he now distrusted anything I told him. "You hear about them re-forming all the time," I said, hoping to reassure. "I'd not figured they'd ID things such as those."

"Yeah, usually they lay low," E said. "I don't trust 'em myself, whatever they say."

"Better red than dead." As I said it I realized I'd transposed, but let it go; he seemed not to notice.

"I read that there're buildings in New York where if you press the right button in the elevator, you go down to where the Dero live. You never heard about that?"

"No," I said. "You say Dero cause all that's bad in the world?"

"That's what they say—"

"But they didn't kill your mother."

E lifted his gun, placing it against my cheek as if he readied to fire. "Uh-uh," he said. "Won't be the ones killin' you either if it comes to that."

"Put it down, Elvis," I said, keeping my eyes fixed roadways, hoping to see any car approaching, spotting none. When he didn't take away the gun I gradually flatfooted the accelerator, speeding us up to sixty miles per. "Shoot now and we'll crash and we'll all die. That's what's wanted?"

"My mamma doesn't concern you—"

"There's no reason for shooting her." I heard John tap his foot against the door, awaring me that he was conscious, if unmoving.

"You weren't there," he said, putting the gun away, thrusting its barrel between his body and his waistband, drawing his shirttail over the bulge. I brought up my foot, slowing to reasonable speed. "You don't know, you weren't there—"

"What happened, then?" I asked. "Detail."

"Nothin' happened," he shouted. "Not much. We had an argument. I brought her a present for Mother's Day and she didn't like it."

"That's why you shot her?"

"No," he said. "I bought her a Hank Williams record. She said she didn't want t'listen to it, and I should be ashamed a myself for—"

"For what?" I asked; his face purpled while he muted, recalling, but when he began talking again he'd recontrolled himself, and his words came bereft of emotion.

"She started tellin' me how no-account I was to be buyin' her records when I had a voice better'n anybody else. Told me if I'd just start learnin' country songs I could start playin' in public and makin' a livin'. But I can't sing that country shit, I hate it."

"It's blues you want to sing—"

"Exactly. And who wants to hear that? Nobody, that's who. But she started sayin' I was like my daddy, no good, and I kept tellin' her to shut up and she wouldn't, and she hit me, and so I ran back into my room and got my gun and—" He paused; blinked once or twice, as if emerging from a trance. "That's all she wrote."

"Your temperament entangles you overmuch," I said. "It hazards sans reason."

"What'd you just say to me, Isabel?"

"You can't respond to others so unthinkingly," I said. "You'll kill others and regret later."

"I don't regret nothin' I've ever done, you know that?"

"You will, with age," I said.

"I'm tougher'n most," he said. "I don't take any guff. You know what I did to a fellow I worked with at Loew's theater?"

"Kill him?"

"I caught him while he was changin' clothes. I cut him all

to pieces. Knocked him down, kicked him in the jaw while he was on the floor. Then I kicked him in the stomach. That was the least I could do. He was screamin' like a dog."

"How'd he upset you?" I asked.

"Told the manager I was gettin' free candy from a little girl workin' at the candy counter. I got fired for it. Went right downstairs and dealt with him straight. He got fired too, after that."

"The usher lived?"

"Yeah," E said. "What'd you think I am, anyway?" He appeared deeply troubled that I'd thought it necessary to ask. "That job was all right. I liked the uniform." He patted his thin chest as if he still wore it, and wished to display its buttons. "That set you straight about me?"

"I'd say you overkilled," I said. "You're trying to impress?"

He attempted his sneer, again doing nothing more than puckering his lip. "What'd I wanta impress you for?"

I shook my head. "We should get something to eat," I said. If I could loose John from his bonds once we stopped, we stood a chance of recontrolling the situation as we desired, thereafter returning sans delay. Ridding ourselves of E was all I wanted to do.

"I'm not hungry," he said.

"I am. John's certainly starving—"

"All right," he said, his voice highpitching. "Next place you see that's open, we'll get something. Not many places gonna be open on a Sunday. We'll go on a little ways somewhere else to eat it. Gettin' late anyhow."

Several kilometers along I eyed a frame building larger than most of the shacks we'd passed. A handdrawn sign hanging on a pole beside its parking lot's entry showed two frogs standing upright, holding an outstretched banner between them; upon its length were the words, GREEN FROG RESTAURANT / CHICKEN DINNERS / FROG LEGS.

"This looks good," E said. I turned the car into the gravel

yard, stopping at the lot's far edge, alongside a fenced meadow.

"What do you want?" I asked, shutting off the engines and the soundtrack.

"We'll both go in," he said, reaching across me and opening my door, deliberately drawing his arm over my breasts. "Get out."

He kept his gun waisted as he pulled himself up from his seat. Emerging, I thought I felt rain; realized that the air was so saturated that it wet my arms and face with moist sunshine. "I want to see if John's—"

"He's fine," E said. "You can see'm once we're clear. Come on."

The gravel burned my feet through my shoe-soles. Venetian blinds shaded the restaurant's windows; E held the screen door open for me as I entered. The interior was no larger than the Presleys' apartment had been, and sheltered only three unoccupied tables; two young men stood behind the unpainted wooden counter. Both wore smudged white caps; the taller one was missing several teeth, while the other rubbed his palms against his pink, draining eye, smearing both. The odor of frying fat overpowered me almost enough to sicken.

"What can we get you folks?" said the shorter man, taking his hand from his face and wiping it on his apron.

"Can we get us a couple chickens?" Elvis asked, interrupting me before I might order frog. "Maybe couple pieces a peach pie to go with it. And a couple cola drinks."

"Three of each, please," I added.

"Sure thing," said the man, stepping through a doorway into the kitchen to assemble our order. In his absence the man with dental troubles eyed us updown, his stare engorging with warm dislike. I could think of nothing we'd done to bother him. Flies buzzed through the still air; E rocked forthback on his heels, whistling underbreath. In a few min-

utes the other man returned to the counter, carrying three
brown, greasestained bags.

"That'll be three ninety-eight, mister," he said.

I fretted for a moment, realizing that I'd left my purse in
the car; then recalled that E had thieved my money. "You've
got it—" I started to tell him; watched as he pulled out his
gun, aiming it at the men.

"It's to go," E said.

"This some kinda joke, buddy?" E snatched the bags from
the man and handed them to me. The man's smile faded as
E unsafetied the gun.

"You laughin'?"

The man had started to reach beneath the counter when
E fired; he gurgled and dropped, clutching the hole in his
neck. The greasy bags slipped from my hands; I slumped
against the countertop, watching events cascade as if in
slomo. The other man impaled E's unweaponed hand with
a two-tined fork as he rested it upon the countertop. One
tine pricked E below the knuckles; he screamed as he pulled
his hand away and fired again, bullseyeing the other man's
mouth. Something gritty and damp splattered my face, and
I vomited. E thrust his gun back into his pants and grabbed
my arm with such vigor that he bruised it, dragging me out.
"Come on," he shouted. "Dammit."

"Idiot," I said, choking, continuing to heave. "Fool. We
had money—"

"*Shut up!*"

"We had money!" I shouted back, but my stomach so
pained and my throat so burned that I silenced. Even at the
time I didn't remember running to the car and throwing
myself in; E pushed his way into the driver's seat, shoving me
across the seat as he wheeled himself.

"Where's the key?" he screamed, pressing his bleeding
hand against his shirt. "Gimme the key—" I pressed the
dash's button, engaging the batteries, upping the soundtrack. He'd watched my actions while I drove, evidently, and

quickly found the shifter, guiding it into reverse. After backing out we sped out of the lot, skyshooting gravel in our wake as we tore downroad. I cleaned my face, staring through the windshield; noted that the interstate's wall ended in a cleared swath ahead and to our left. That stretch of the road was still under construction, I saw, at last sighting as well some of my people. Ten to twenty black men carried bags of cement across the clearing, overseen by uniformed guards wearing hard-hats; the men wore striped clothing, and appeared roped together in some way. As we flew by I realized that a long chain beaded them; they were attached by rings fastened around their necks. A work program, I told myself; prisoners at hard labor, whiling away their appointed time. That hardly explained the absolute absence I'd noticed, all the same, and as E took us farther into Mississippi, I began to wonder if they'd stored us all away somewhere.

"What'd you do to soup up this car?" E asked; lefting the wheel, he turned us down a narrow road several kilometers south of the construction site. "Ever' Hudson I ever drove was a piece a shit but this thing runs like a dream."

"Why?" I asked, ignoring his question, sickened by him and by everything I'd seen. "Why'd you kill those people?"

"Look what he did to my hand." He raised it, showing me; the puncture was small but deep, and a thin red stream trickled from the hole.

"They were defending," I said. "You senseless fool—"

"Shut up, I told you," he shouted. "I'll wreck us, I swear I will—"

"Fuckall," I screamed. "Do it! Do it! Do—"

Tree branches scraped the sides of our car as if attempting to restrain our flight. I examined my dress, seeing my stains, angering so as to hold in all tears. Throughout our marriage John had never involved me in his work; I'd not witnessed violence at close range since childhood, and it traumaed now as it traumaed then, its remembered familiarity notwithstanding. I hated E for dragging me into his madness so much as I regretted John burying me beneath his. Staring at the Alekhine's red button, I considered pressing it, hurtling us back into our world; calming, told myself repeatedly that I had no wish to die, however much I'd earlier pleaded for a wreck. The will to preservation but barely soothed; turning around, I looked over to where John lay on the seat. He'd worked the sheet off his head, but his gag remained where E had stuffed it. I started reaching over, wanting to untie him; E swatted back my hand away.

"Don't do it," E said, onehanding the wheel, nursing his injury. I glimpsed his gun protruding from his pants, not reachable unless I chose to send us into spinout. Again, I caught myself thinking unthinkables. "You're in this deep as I am now."

Keeping my hands lapped I turned to look at my husband, thinking again that we might, after all, be optionless in the face of E; that in some manner I would have to risk us, and should therefore consider our survival an uncertain possibility. John twisted his head, jerking it up and down, working the sheet farther away from his face. He winked at me, as if to assure; I smiled, understanding at last why he so wished that we'd go together when we died.

6

□

When I faced front again I sought the dash's compass, wanting to ascertain our placement, only to find its needle down-dangling; though I couldn't certify what had dysfunctioned it, I suspected our borderbreaking had produced this untimely effect, and I wondered if anything else had been damaged. I flinched as the car sideswiped pine branches, racing along the road; troubled deep over John's inexplicably cheerful mood. He'd conceived a plan, I tried to convince myself, ignoring as I could my fears that his drugs had erased my husband's mind, leaving him so braindead as Mister O'Malley's sister. My heart doubletimed; bile bittered my mouth. "Stop us," I shouted to E, unable to bear another minute sealed with him in the car. "I'm maddening—"

E swerved, bouncing us off the trail, steering our car through a junk-strewn meadow before stopping at the edge of a bordering woodland. "All right," E said. "How's this thing turn off?" Laying my hand on the steering column, finding the button, I shut down the engine. E tore away a strip of his shirttail and wrapped his injured hand; I exited sans permission, rushing rearward to fetch my husband. Opening the door, lifting him from the seat, I pulled the gag from his face and kissed him, uncaring of complaints E might register.

"You're AO?" he asked me. "Iz—"

"What about you?" I heard the door slam shut as E got out. "You must be dying. Oh, John—"

"What ensued when we stopped?"

"Murder," I said. "A breakaway essentials, whether with him or not. Let me untie you—"

My head was suddenly whiplashed; E fisted a length of my blondness, sprawling me backwards. As I lay on the ground I vizzed him in reverse, as if he hung upside-down from the sky above my head, appearing from this angle something less than simian. "You better not untie 'm, Isabel," he said, taking out his gun.

"My hair's not yours to touch," I told him as I hauled myself up. "Nothing of mine is."

"Keep 'm like he is," E said. "I'm not gonna be watchin' both of you—"

"I'm going to talk to my husband and take him out of the car. I'll leave him tied. Agreed?"

"Don't gab too long." E lowered his weapon and strolled far enough away from us that he couldn't hear our whispers, though he eyed us all the while.

"He shot two at the restaurant," I said to John. "Completely unreasoned. It'll alert authorities area-round, certain."

"Three bullets left, likely," my husband said. "One for each."

"He's murderous, John. He triggers at slights. He'll ex us both if we're with him much longer—"

"You'll have to disarm, then."

"Impossibled," I said.

"He'll act if I attempt, and I'll not see you bloodied—"

"And what if he bloodies me as I'm disarming—"

"He won't," John said. "He's fingerwrapped by you."

"I'm not trained as you are—"

"You're mine. I'm yours. Like attracted like." His features beatificked; I'd not seen such a look on his face since our wedding, though I'd always known it was there if he chose to show it. "You've proved timeover with me, Iz. You can act where I can't."

"You finished jawin' yet?" E shouted over to us.

"No!" I replied, at equal volume; returned my attentions to my husband. "Can't you break loose? Por fav—"

"The Achilles slipped my heel," John said. "Long as I'm bound I can't unshoe to readjust, and he wishes me tied. Do as you're doing, he'll distract soon enough. When he stresses over you can disarm with ease."

"John—"

"It's doable by you," he said. "Once he's weaponless I'll loose myself and we'll fly—"

"Time's up," E said, sauntering back to the car. "You want 'm to eat, you can feed 'm now—"

"Feed him what?" I asked. "The food's back at the restaurant, along with your leftovers—"

E reddened, and booted the side of our car, scuffing its paint; by his grimace it evidenced that he'd pained himself with his kick. "I gave 'em to you to hold and you dropped 'em—"

"Idiot," I said, uncaring to expend energy enough on him to shout; then blabbed other terms as I'd been taught them, wishing to degrade and insult as I could. "Peckerwood whitetrash redneck—"

He fired, shooting the ground at my feet. I muted in the shot's echo and remembered John's estimation; if there were two bullets remaining, at least one of us would remain if worse was to worsen. "Don't you call me that," he said, tantruming. "My people worked hard, they're not trash—"

"So claimed," I said, turning from him, gambling that he wouldn't shoot again. The sun was setting; enough light lingered that when I eyed our surroundings I realized that we rested in the midst of something utterly alien to my experience; possessing an unexplainable familiarity, all the same. "Where are we?" I asked, looking around. "What is this?"

"Nigger graveyard," E said, slinging that word at me again. "Thought they'd all been plowed up by now. They musta missed this'n."

Hollowed gourds were attached to treelimbs overhanging the field, twirling idly, spun by the breeze. As our car came to rest it slashed through these grounds so recklessly as the interstates carved the cities, shredding forty-odd patches of the cemetery's quilt. Favored leavings and fetishes of those who lay at rest delineated each mound's edges. Some plots were marked with colored glass bottles and pottery shards; tarnished spoons, white pebbles or shattered light-bulbs; dulled knives, broken bowls, conch shells, armless dolls and sets of choppers. Coins frosted several beds, comforting the sleeper with a cold blanket. A mirror topped one mound, framed with red mud, appearing as memory-pool and reminder, reflecting the stare of those who came to mourn. Headstoning another grave was a faced clock, its hands frozen at twelve, as if to mark Judgment's hour. Some few concrete lumps sufficed as markers; only one bore a message, and that with letters finger-inscribed in the cement as it dried. These were the words thereon:

> *Cecie*
> *Eighteen years a slave*
> *One year a wife*
> *One year a mother*
> *Then I lost my life.*

"Burma Shave," I whispered to myself, in lieu of eulogy. "What'd you mean you were surprised they hadn't plowed it up? Why would anyone deliberately desecrate?"

"To get rid of 'em," E said. "Like they did with Beale Street. Like they did everwhere." He ceased his annotations, as if there was no reason why I shouldn't comprehend. "Haven't seen one a these since I was a kid—"

"You're befuddling me," I said. "Who got rid of them?"

"They didn't Randolph 'em all up in New York?"

"No," I said. "What's meant?"

"After the strike," he said. "Riots and war crimes. I was little but I remember 'em all talkin' about it."

I keened to know more; between his lines I inferred the situation of my countryfolk, staying mindful at all times of what we had been told, predeparture, concerning this society's opinion of them, fifteen years before. Deliberately, I stilled my questions, unwilling for illusion's sake to illustrate my ignorance and cause him to doubt all the more that we were truly of his world. I enfolded my arms around myself, feeling chilled in the air's oven, grateful, now, to have had my color removed for our trip.

"I don't think much of it," said E, toying with his gun; I hoped he had it safetied. "What the hell. Can't stop progress, can you?"

Standing ringed by the final homes of those departed, I wished only to home it so soon as we could, and be rid of this place unto endtime. "Put that gun away," I said.

E nodded; eyed my husband lying in the car, not ten meters distant. "Something I need to do first."

Before I estimated his intent E walked to our car; I watched wordless as he bent down to slug my husband on the head with his gun. "*No!*" I shouted, running to the car, shoving E out of my way; sliding into the car, I rested John's bleeding head in my lap, fingercombing his hair until I found the flow's source. Pressing my hand against his scalp, I staunched his leak in minutes. "Why?" I screamed at E; petted my husband's face, attempting to wake him. His breathing steadied; he groaned as if surfacing before sinking

down again. I flipped on the ceiling's overhead, suffusing
our car with light.

"I didn't trust him not to try somethin'," E said. "He'll
come around, don't worry. I didn't hit 'im that hard."

"You'll regret if he doesn't," I said, shoving down my rage
until it pierced through my stomach. "You'll regret overmuch."

"I usually do," he said, backing away. E walked over to the
field's edge, looking away from the graves into the woods. As
the moon rose it showed as an overripened orange against
the violet sky, looking as it so usually looked over New York;
had we not spent so much time breathing in the interstate's
poison I would have thought its color here merely an atmo-
spheric quirk. Transferring to the front seat, I withdrew the
lightrod from its housing. As I alongsided my husband again
I twisted the rod's end; its tip glowed as it heated, warming
enough to burn. I pushed up his eyelids, and brought the
rod close to his eyes; his pupils pinpointed against the light,
and I was relieved that there appeared to be no lasting
damage. Switching off the rod, I slid it through my hair once
it had cooled. Removing John's shoes, I massaged his heel
until I felt the tendon-cord snap back into place. He remained unconscious, in seeming sleep; seeing no other escape, desirous of living up to his faith in me, I redarkened
the interior, and went to settle E.

"You're always this way?" I asked, once I'd reached him.
"So violent, and stupid?"

"Don't call me stupid. I'm not stupid," he said, proffering
nothing more than verbal threats; his gun was in his waistband, out of my grasp. "My mamma called me stupid."

"Another reason you shot her?" I asked.

"I asked her not to."

"She'd called you that before?"

"Lot more lately," he said. "I don't know, it's all messed
up."

"Always?"

"No," he said. "We useta get along real good. When we moved to Memphis looked like we were gonna be all right for a change. Then daddy went and got sent away. Screwed everthing up." He paused; looked away from me as he continued to speak, so that I couldn't read his face. Whether deliberately or inadvertently, he angled himself in such a way as to keep me far from his gun. "Excuse my french, ma'am."

"Isabel," I said.

"Yeah," he said. "Maybe it didn't change a lotta things, just sped 'em up. When she'd get sad Mamma useta always tell me we'd never get ahead, we had a black cloud over us. She kept tellin' me that till finally I believed she was right." He looked at me, but his eyes were unseeable in the dark. As he started walking forward, toward the woods, I paced him, keeping a few steps behind. "It's something, isn't it? However hard you try, there's no way out."

"How's your hand?" I asked as I followed him from grass onto breaking twigs. "You should be hospitalled, likely."

"You a nurse?" he asked. "Thought you told me you were in the music business."

"There's a way out for you, Elvis," I said.

"I don't know if I'm cut out for singin' in public," he said.

"What are you cut out for?" He shrugged; said nothing. "Our company wishes us to bring you back to them. Back to New York."

"Little late for that now, I'd think. I'd say there's not much chance a either one of us goin' to New York—"

"I say there is."

As we moved deeper into the woods the branches overhead shadowed the moonlight, darkening our steps. I slipped the lightrod out of my hair, readying it for use.

"Careful where you walk, I bet there's snakes in here," he said. "Don't see how you can say we can still go to New York. Even if they don't get you for bein' an accessory after the fact at the restaurant, they'll still put me away—"

"You want them to?"

"I did shoot 'em," he said. "Somebody's gotta be in trouble for it."

"We can get you out of this, if you do as we ask."

He nodded. "I thought so. You all are hooked up with gangsters then, aren't you?"

"Indirectly," I said. "We've other ways to remove ourselves from this. I'll demonstrate. Untie John, give me your gun, trust us and follow our lead."

He laughed. His mention of snakes upset me; twisting the rod's end as I held it up, I adjusted its shine to that of candlelight, enabling sight while retaining useful shadows with which I might cloak my actions.

"What the hell's that thing?" E asked, his eyes widening as he stared into its glow.

"I like to see where I'm going," I said. "What's your response?"

"Have to think about it," he said. "What'll I do if we get to New York, then?"

"Our company will prepare you. Periodically you'll sing and make public appearances. You'll be housed and paid."

"How much?"

"Whatever you needed," I said, "you'd have." My light illuminated a small circle around us; I listened to insects' white noise, and a recurrent croaking that I guessed was frog-spawned, though I'd heard their voices only as recorded, and never live. E said nothing; I became aware of a light above our heads, brighter than stars or moon. Peering through a strangle of branches I saw three plasmas skittering through the air, their edges blurry against the dark; they descended, revealing their circular forms at closer focus.

"Godness," I said. "Those are flying saucers—?"

"I told you they were testing 'em round here," E said. "There they are." As we watched they banked leftward, turning sharp and silently, disappearing from view. "Couldn't see anything on 'em. Could you?"

"No—"

"German," he said. "I'm positive. It'll all come out, one day." E stopped, and sat down on a windfallen tree after scraping a seat clean of bark and moss with his shoe. "So you're sayin' that even under the circumstances you'd be willin' to take me to New York?"

"More than willing," I said. "You'd try singing again, wouldn't you? Singing in public?"

"I'd haveta?"

"At times," I said. "You told me you sang blues?"

"When I could get away with it," he said. "Mamma said I sounded just like a nigger when I sing. I haveta be careful about that—"

"Another condition of employment," I said. "Don't use that word."

"What d'you call 'em up north?"

"People."

"That's not what I've heard," he said. "Hell, it's just a word. They usedta call each other that all the time, I remember hearin' 'em."

"It's a word like *whitetrash*," I said, "or *stupid.*"

I watched as his face hardened, hearing those terms, as mine must have done each time he spewed his epithet. "Don't call me stupid," he said, pulling out his gun. Conversing with E was not unlike attempting to sculpt fire without suffering burns.

"I didn't call you stupid," I said. "If you shoot me I think anyone else would have every right to, though. Give me the gun."

"No," he said, lowering it. "It's mine."

"Don't shove it at me every time you're upset," I said. "Why'd you pasttense, moments ago?"

"What're y'talkin' about now?" he said. "I'm sorry, Isabel, but don't call me stupid."

My light tanned him, and smoothed his face's bumps, and

for an instant E appeared nearly as his counterpart had shown. He replaced his gun beneath his billowing shirt.

"You used to hear the blues sung as well?"

"Back in Tupelo there usedta be some old boys around when I was a kid I'd go listen to. First year we come to Memphis they hadn't torn out Beale Street yet and I'd sneak out and go down to their clubs. Crawl up in the attics to get in, or sneak in backstage. Listen to 'em singin' and playin' all night. Mamma never liked me goin' down there. Said they'd come for me too one a these days."

"Could you sing a blues song for me?" I asked, hoping that as he sang he would distract enough that I could make a grab. My own stress was whelming over; I worried if John was recovering, I feared E's rages, I wanted to go home. Again, I found myself desiring the risk I readied myself to take, uncaring of outcome so long as I could break the situation's stasis, intoxicated with the rush of deathchancing. It occured to me that John must have always felt this way. "You're not instrumented—"

"Don't need no guitar to sing," he said. "What'cha wanta hear?"

"Your preference."

"Mamma'd never let me sing the ones I liked best in the house."

"Sing one of those, then," I said. E smiled, and cleared his throat. He patted his foot on the ground slowsteady while he acapellaed, shutting his eyes and bobbing his head as if he were blind when he began to sing.

"Well when I marry, now I ain't gonna buy no broom,
She got hair on her belly, gonna sweep my kitchen, my dinin'
room."

His pitch tracked unerringly by the first verse's end; in his tone and phrasing I heard a precise match of the Master's voice as we'd listened to it, replaying timeover in our ears.

E's youth notwithstanding, he'd already developed his tricks fullbore: the unexpected swoops from aching tenor to rumbling baritone, the sudden elisions as if the notes had been greased. E's songstyle shifted from primitive to mannerist and back again, containing the pluses and minuses of each extreme, and all else inbetween.

"Well, it's two, two more places, baby, where I want to go,
Baby, that's 'tween your legs and out your back door."

To watch E singing astonished me as I'd never been, seeing the vids of his double. Though I tried to believe it no more than a light-trick, he nonetheless countenanced what could only be called a religious glow; all the while he shaded his lyrics with secular threat, undertoned with a vengeance so subtle that its scalpel couldn't help but seduce as it sliced.

"I say belly, belly to belly, and skin, skin to skin,
Well it's two things workin' and ain't but one goin' in."

Against my will, I was fascinated; he knew he had me tranced and he rose, still singing as he approached me, fixing me where I stood with naught but voice and glare. Dryco would snare an unimaginable bargain if we were enabled to return with him; so long as he did nothing more than sing, the laity of the C of E would surely follow him wherever he led, and rush to do whatever he commanded. He fancied love in his eyes at me as he stared, appearing mayhap as Romeo eyed Juliet; as Jack the Ripper must have studied his first whore before closing in.

"Well, I asked her for her titty, or gimme her lovin' tongue,
She said suck this, daddy, till the goodie come."

As he finished, I snapped awake, recovering at once, thinking I heard a noise in the meadow; a slowrolling crunch, as if the remaining graves were being crushed flat by something heavy. I glanced behind me, looking through the woods to ascertain the noise's source; E suddenly embraced me, pressing himself against me, rubbing his tongue over my teeth as if to brush them. "Kiss me quick or a snake's gonna bite you," he said.

"Off," I said, breaking his hold. "Don't touch me—"

"You're sweatin', sissie," he said, bunching my dressfront in his hand so swiftly I hadn't seen him move. "Put out that candle. You must be gettin' hot in that dress." Ripping downward, he rended my shift to my waist. "Hell, yes," he said, brighteyed and gawking. "You know you want to. Let's rock."

"*Don't—!*"

"I'm not askin', Isabel, I'm takin'—"

Caution essentialled while using a lightrod; maxed, its length heated to sixty degrees centigrade. Sans hesitation I ironed mine across E's face, pressing his cheek; he stepped back, his pain muting him, and I fisted him square in his soft stomach. As he fell I booted him, trying to leverage my kick enough to send his jewels up his throat. With one hand I gripped my lightrod's cool end; with the other I drew his gun from his pants and unsafetied it as I rammed its tip against his ear. I'd instincted as John believed I would; as I feared I would. As my soul returned to me from its brief but necessary absence I saw E wailing as if he'd been orphaned.

"I'm untouchable, hereout," I told him, forcing the gunbarrel into his ear as if to plant it there, stilling my desire to trigger and blow. "Understood?"

"Understood—"

"You're *stupid*, Elvis," I said. He grunted, continuing to clutch himself, but responded with nothing resembling anger. My power over him heartened enough that I found myself readying to finger and fire away; but before I could, I stood up, heaving the gun into the woods so far as I could throw it. I seized him by the throat with an adrenaline-charged grip, bringing up my light-rod as if intending to sear away his eyes. "Astonishingly stupid," I said, barely recognizing my own voice's snarl. "I'm untying John. We're leaving. You, too—"

All at once we were absorbed within a near-nuclear whiteness, as if without benefit of the Alekhine we were transferring back. As I eyeshut against the glare, blinded by green afterimages swimming beneath my lids, I heard a voice that wasn't my husband's calling out to us.

"Put your hands over your head and walk out here into the light," the man said. "Don't try anything."

By fixing my stare at trees I was able to eclipse the glare's source as I helped E stand up and walk out. We moved slowpaced but steady, arms up as if to snatch heaven, until we came to the field's border. Two of our four visitors rushed from their car and grabhanded us; they wore gray uniforms with sleeve insignia that IDed them as Mississippi State Patrolmen. The other two men stood farther away, lurking near their vehicle; the searchlamps mounted atop the hoods of their cars attracted and sizzled uncountable moths.

"Looks like we got ourselves couple lovebirds here," said the patrolman who restrained me, bending my arms behind my back as if attempting to dislocate them. "Didn't have a chance to get all the way unbuttoned yet. Hate to break 'em up, they looked mighty cozy."

"He was lyin' down and she was leanin' over 'im," said the one who'd seized E; he was considerably fatter, and rested a long-barreled pistol along E's back, aiming it at the back of his head. "Hate to interrupt the matin' season, folks—"

"They armed?" said one of the other two, walking toward us. His accent was placeless; sewn onto his black uniform's sleeves were American flag patches.

"Not now," said the fat patrolman, grinning as he tightened his grip on E.

"Search 'em anyway."

"You know this is private property, people?" the fourth

man said; he was also in black, and evidenced as the senior authority. "You're trespassing."

"Didn't see no signs," said E.

"Could you a read 'em if there'd been signs, boy?" the fat patrolman asked, driving the end of his barrel into the base of E's neck. The four were well-armed; each carried a pistol, and the black-clad policemen shouldered rifles. The senior officer eyed our car, leaning slightly away from me; white letters stenciled upon his back's black field initialed F H P.

"Who's that in the Hudson?" he asked.

"My husband," I said. "It's explainable, officers."

"Try," said the patrolman behind me, grinding his midsection against my hips while he jerked back my arms. One of my breasts emerged from my torn dress's folds.

"I'd call those a pair a 45s," the fat one handling E said, laughing as he ogled me, throwing E against the hood of his car sans warning. "What'd you been doin' to that girl? You gonna answer me or you gonna play deaf and dumb?"

The men in black stared at my chest. The patrolman behind me pulled my elbows together, keeping me from covering myself. "Do some explaining, then. Why's your husband tied up?" asked the senior officer, raising his rifle as he stepped closer to me.

"We were kidnapped," I said. "Please let me go."

"You're both under arrest." I saw that their jackets' initials were spelled out in white letters on the doors of the black car: *Federal Highway Police.* "Charges, trespassing, public lewdness, indecent exposure, resisting arrest—"

"Let me go—" I shouted, trying to twist free. The senior officer thrust out his rifle as he approached, resting the end of its barrel against my breast, inserting my nipple into its muzzle. As I felt its chill shiver me I silenced, thinking how much safer I'd been with E.

"You stop at the Green Frog Restaurant on Highway 51 couple hours ago?" he asked, smiling; a stone set in one of his incisors sparkled. "Did you?"

"We did," I said.

"Charge murder, three counts," he said. "Sergeant, pat her down."

"Three counts?" I said. "There were two in the restaurant—"

"And one in your car," said the other Fed.

"He's not dead," I said. The senior officer lowered his rifle, and pushed me against the hood of their car as the patrolman held me; then, clutching my hair, slammed my head against the metal. I fought to keep from going coma; slipped in and out of awareness for several moments, thinking the pain would asunder my skull. Wetness warmed my forehead; my nose bled as freely.

"Ma'am," the senior officer said, "we want to keep you pretty if we can. Do what we tell you to do."

"Come on," the patrolman holding me said as he reached down and shoved my legs apart. "Spread."

"My husband's not dead," I told them. "I'm unweaponed. Don't, please—" The fat one was cuffing E's hands behind his back, preparing to search. My guardian patted me up-down as the Feds stared on, kneading my thighs beneath my dress, pawing and poking as if uncertain of what was sought. "He's not dead. Please untie him. You'll see."

"He doesn't respond," said the senior officer. "Bob reached in, shook his leg."

"He's stiff as a board," said Bob, the other officer in black. "When'd you kill him? This morning?"

"He's epileptic," I said, feeling the patrolman bruise me as he grasped my hips. Blood dripped into my eyes. "Fits, every day. He conniptions."

"What?"

"He's just blacked out. Untie him, and he'll tell what's up."

"All right. Go back there and drag him out, Bob," said the senior officer. "Raise the dead."

"You say so," Bob said, sighing; he walked off toward our car, disappearing from sight within the white glare.

"Stop hurting me," I said; the patrolman searched places he'd searched twice before, seeming unwilling to stop, having started. I eyed leftward; saw the fat one bodypunching E, giggling after each slap.

"We're just searchin' you, ma'am," said the patrolman. "We never hurt anybody doesn't bring it on themselves."

"Hell of a mess you left back there at the restaurant, lady," said the senior officer. "You know who found the bodies?" He held my chin in his hand as if it were an egg as he lifted up my head; after a moment's stare he slapped me so hard that I blinked one of my lenses out. "You want to know?"

"Who—?"

"Their wives found them," he said, pinching my mouth open; trying to spit on him, I only wet my lips. "They brought their children by after Sunday school to see their daddies at work. You know what they saw?"

"Stop—"

I thought I felt my teeth loosen as he tensed his grip; nerveache ripped through my cheeks, and I shook free of his hold long enough to keep from fainting. "Weren't both your eyes blue a minute ago?" he asked.

"What—?" asked the patrolman pinning me.

"I'll be damned," said the senior officer. "Her eyes. One's brown and one's blue. Look at this."

The patrolman turned me around and perched me hoodways. "Something's funny here," he said, putting his face close to mine. "Look at her features."

"What are you talking about?"

The patrolman touched his thumb against the tip of my nose, tapping it; pressing against it, spilled more of my blood. "Feels like split cartilage," he said. "She coulda dyed her hair. Looks like it's been straightened, you ask me—"

"You people see darkies under every bed—" said the senior officer.

"That's our job. Looks like we got ourselves an albino here tryin' to pass—"

"*Bob,*" said the senior officer. "What the hell you doing back there?"

"Blood'll tell—" said the patrolman. His face hung over me, washed pinkish gray in the searchlight; in the next second it reddened, and was gone. Shutting my eyes against the spray, I heard the blast; as I reopened them I saw the man slumping, tumbling groundways. I leapt off the hood; saw the fat one staring into the glare, stumbling sidelong toward me. "Valentine Almighty—" I heard him say; when I circled to see where he looked, I saw the senior officer firing his rifle, blasting my husband at midchest as he emerged from the light; he lifted airways, his flight reversed, and glided back to earth with a skid and a roll.

"*Sonofabitch,*" the senior officer said, running to where my husband lay waiting. He acted before I had time to worry; as my torturer neared John's legs my husband slapped his thigh, releasing a spring he'd once demonstrated for me. His limb shot up, impaling the officer's groin, flinging him forward. John reached up and seized the man's shoulders as he sailed over; slammed him headfirst into the ground.

"Isabel," John said as he stood, nodding toward the fat patrolman. "Take him."

I knelt down to seize his late companion's unused truncheon; as at the restaurant, I viewed what ensued as if from above. The fat one brought up his pistol, readying to shoot my husband; I swung twohanded, catching his nose. He dropped, and I hit him again; once he'd grounded I flailed away, letting my mind go, responding as I'd learned to do years before when I roamed Washington Heights with Judy, exing our tormentors before they might hurt us again. When at last I quieted I stared at the remnants of the fat patrolman's head, realizant I'd known deeper pain the night I'd killed the mouse in our apartment. When I felt my husband's heartpound as he embraced me and allowed the truncheon to slip from my hand, I was awared unto endtime that as my own chosen regooding had utterly failed, there was no reason to mourn that John's, enforced by others and not by himself, should not have been any more longlasting.

"Love," my husband said, wrapping around me with inordinate, if desired, force, evincing sans words a belief that were we to impress together close enough we might at length meld our physicalities, if never more our emotions after this moment. "Love you, Iz. I love you. I worried—"

"Godness, no—" My eyes flooded, and the flow was such I thought I'd never stop crying again. Tears washed away the blood; staring at my husband's face, ashine in the policelights as if it threw heat, I saw I'd reddened him with my new lipstick. Drawing away for a moment, taking deeper breaths, I more closely eyed the ragged hole blown through his clothes; his wound was large enough that I could see myself reflected in the crumpled Krylar beneath his skin.

"You see, Iz," John said, cradling me. "We unisoned. Simulcast action, simulcast thought." He shook bodywide, as if with malaria. "Oh Iz, we're renewed. I love you—"

"I'm no killer," I said. "I'm not—"

"You are," he said, kissing me with youth's passion, reading his own exuberance into me. "When I saw you act I knew our world as ours again. I love you," he whispered. "Let's love our life. We're renewed, Iz. We've successed."

"Are we?" I asked, thinking of E. "He's been bloodied. Let's retrieve."

"He's moving." E lay fetuscurled alongside the Mississippi patrolmen's car, chanting a murmur underbreath, lowvoicing his mutterances until it was unguessable whether he actually phrased words. Shock's opiates dulled me; I loosed myself from my husband's grip, so that we could recover our charge.

"He's traumaed," I said. "Let's take him and go."

"They hurt you, Iz?"

"Yes," I said, staring at the bodies we'd left. "You're hurt, too."

"Fleshwound." John stared at me as I attempted to pull my dress's torn fabric across my breasts. "Who ripped your clothes?"

I hesitated before answering, weighting us everafter with that instant's thoughtless pause. John compressed his smile, hiding his lips, and stared at E with a look such as he'd never allowed me to see on his face before.

"What was done?"

"We were in the woods," I said. "That's where I disarmed—"

"He *assaulted*—?"

"No, John—" I said, but his reflexes had already tripped. "Wait!" Before I could move to forestall him he'd reached E, lifting him from the grass one-handed and throwing him, still cuffed, onto the hood of the car. E catatonicked, allaying all movement and word, allowing my husband to prop him upright and do as desired. *"Stop!"*

"You raped her!" John screamed as he beat E, landing jab after jab. E's face convexed on one side, concaved on the other; his eyes were blackened, and closed so tightly as clamshells. My husband continued hitting E, pacing himself at one blow per second. "Detail sins. *Detail!*"

"You're killing him!" I shouted, slapping John's back with my own fists, trying sans success to disrupt his rhythm.

"Known." John noosed E with his hands, throttling him before smashing him through the windshield. "Why'd you rape her?" he said, pounding E's face into the glass. "Why? Why? Why—?"

"John!" E's blood drained, matting his hair, reddening his face and clothing. His jaw had was so swollen I couldn't tell how badly it had been shattered. He no longer appeared human.

"Why?" Again, I let slip my own controls; still beset by anger earlier felt toward E and the policemen, bilefull with

rage long abuilding toward my husband, I swung as if to hurt all who'd ever hurt me, fisting John's cheekbone, hurting my hand, knocking him back from the car. He let go of E as he footed his balance, trying not to fall; my action effected so well as a torrent of cold water. As he calmed he reimpressed as my preferred husband again.

"Iz," he said, gasping. "You hit me."

"Your attack's unwarranted," I said. "He didn't rape. He attempted and failed. I prevented attack."

"He tried—"

"And I prevented. We've suffered all this world throws at us to bring him back and as we're set to depart you'd leave him lifeless. What's purposed in that?"

"What was tried?" John asked, watching E writhe atop the spattered car. "Tell me—!"

My anger flared at the tone of my husband's demand, rage all the more intensed for being infused with my guilt rising for being attracted to E as he sang. "A kiss he wanted. A childgame. I tossed and unweaponed, and as I readied to haul him out the police showed. They hurt me, as you see. He despoiled my dress, no more."

"You're truthing?" John asked; I'd never seen him so nervefrayed.

"I'd lie to you?" I shouted. "Supplant anger with logic, John. A quick return's essentialled. Backups'll follow to see what's ensued here." Glancing round to see if other police were arriving I saw the cars parked amid desecrated graves and policemen's pulped husks; the searchlights whitened the woods, appearing them as a photo negative, as a forest of bones. "Forgive me for hitting," I said. "Something needed doing. I adhocked."

"Forgiven," he sighed, lying; he lied so infrequently as to give himself immediately away. It was ungatherable at that moment whether he falsehooded at will or sans consciousness. It frightened me that John was so uncontrolled; having been commanded not to act upon his slightest desires, he now appeared willing to revel in his deepest. "Is he viabled?" John asked, as if having only come upon E, and expressing the polite curiosity gentility demanded. I circled back to where our charge lay bleeding, approximating life.

"Elvis," I asked, trying to find an unwounded spot so that I might touch him, and comfort as I could.

"Take me home," he whispered, mumbling as if his tongue was too swollen to suitably articulate.

"Can you move?"

"Don't know," he said, seeming to fade. "Who are you people?"

"Why did you hurt my wife?" John asked, staying his actions, lowtoning as if to seem capable of lesser harm.

"Back!" I said, shouting at my husband.

"You killed those cops," said E. "The Feds. They shot you and you got up."

"I know how to fall," John said, monotoning as before.

"You're not human," E said. "Are you?"

"Human as any," I said.

"You're Dero—"

"From down below," John said, nodding; he'd evidently overheard E's earlier recounting. Raising his hand, he traced his thumbedge around E's swollen lids as if marking the orbits for an anatomy class. "What beautiful eyes."

"Stop it!" I slapped John's hand away; it hurt overmuch to realize that, at least for the moment, I could no longer trust him not to do harm. "We're not Dero," I told E. "Pay him no mind."

"You are," he said. "I know you are. What are you gonna do with me—?"

"Take you home," I said. "Our home." He wailed, shouting through the night. Carefully sliding my hands beneath his back, I readied to move him; a voice furred with static blared from the police car's radio.

"Car 43, come in," the voice said. "Car 43. Please respond, Car 43. Over."

"Time to blow," I said, struggling to raise E without damaging him further. "Rapido, John. Engage the device and let's home it."

"Point of emergence's preferable for transferral back, as told," John said, assisting me, supporting E's deadweight as he hoisted him. "We'll make New York by tomorrow night."

"We're transferring here if abled," I said. "Not a moment longer here."

"I like this world, Iz," he said. "And the in-car device's emergency sole—"

"All cars, please respond. Car 43—"

"We're emergencied," I said, helping John to guide E's bonebroken form into the back of our car; after certifying that his feet were out of the way I shut the door, securing our prisoner.

"We'll need distance, and a matching road," he said, wheeling himself as I ran to the front. "It's unassurable where we'll come out if we transfer from here." Rising in the distance was a long, steady whine; the sirens distinguished themselves as they drew nearer.

"They're surrounding," I said. "Come on, John—"

But before he did anything he kissed me again; I pushed him away from me, saying nothing, wanting nothing less than loving so long as we might still escape. "AO," he said, pressing the starter, engaging the engine. "Iz—"

"What?"

"I understand, Iz," he said. "You'll tell me, in time." My husband's condition of paranoiac insecurity was gathering greater strength as it momentumed, and I said nothing, estimating my protestations would only assure him that I belied all truth. The sirensound neared; nothing yet showed in the rearview. He ran his hand along the dash until he found the Alekhine's red button.

"Press it, John. Let's away."

I eyeshut, desiring of blinding myself against that midworld nothingness, trusting that I would never know if our transferral was unsuccessful. My ears continued to gather sounds of insect and siren, and when I opened my eyes I saw the sharp-shadowed woods, and the field, and groundbound red flashes speeding toward us in the distance. "It's lemoned," my husband said. "No go."

"I've something to use—"

"Floor yourself, Iz."

As I wedged myself beneath the dash I felt for my purse; remembered as I found it that E had dumped the contents while taking my money. John shifted the car into drive and spun the wheel; from my viewpoint I was unable to tell where he was aiming us. I ran my fingers through my debris, shoving aside E's valise, trying to find the compact Judy had given me.

"Ready yourself, Iz. We'll have to smash them head on. That'll hash the leads—"

"They'll be shooting, John," I said, rummaging through tissues, pens and pillbottles; farragoes of makeup never wanted, never used. "The glass'll give." Nothing I touched held the right shape; I thrust my hand beneath the front seat, finding naught but additional clutter so well as E's magazines. "Drive us away from them, not toward."

"Ten oncoming," he said, slumping down in the seat, allowing himself vision enough to see through the spokes of the wheel. "Hold on."

He floored us, tearing across the field; I thought of the people beneath our tires as we inflicted one last indignity upon them. Hearing gunfire and the ring of metal hitting metal I trembled; felt a cold, flat roundness in my palm. Fingerclamping tight, I brought out the compact. Bullets beat against the car, sounding as a thunderstorm, a rain of metal frogs. "They're trying to take out the tires," John said, wheeling rightways. "They've encircled. What've you got?"

"Release," I said, breaking off my nails against the compact's rim; the seal seemed airtight. My hand so shook I could hardly hold it.

"Together, Iz," John said, slowing the car as the rear window shattered. The gunfire ceased, and I heard shouts. "We'll go together—"

"Agreed," I said, flipping open the compact's lid as something heavy thudded against the hood of our car. Glass rained over me as I thumbed the pad's center, counting off ten seconds. Looking above my head I saw a uniformed arm passing through the broken windshield, aiming a gun at my husband. Then the car's interior whitened with light; all sound tuned out but for my husband's scream.

"Hold me," John said; I clambered onto the front seat and held him down against its fabric before he could be drawn out of the car. A policeman was slipping away from our vehicle, appearing to swim backwards, mouthing words sans sound; as he glided into absence his colors became translucent, and his dissolving form pinpointed as it blended into the whiteness. As I braced one arm against the dash, holding fast to my husband's legs with the other, I sensed myself drifting toward the opened windshield; had I slacked my arms I surely would have slid through, transversing the glass, losing myself in the space beyond.

There was a moment more of motionlessness, floating in that timeless freeze; then at once we reentered our world as if slapped awake by an intruder. Our sun, carcinogenic and welcoming, pricked us with hot needles. I looked through the windshield, seeing that we'd come to rest on several lanes of concrete; two multistory glass towers trellised with brown vines from ground to roof stood opposing, on either side of the road.

"Iz—!" John shouted as we were broadsided. Our world's freeways were not so expansive as theirs had been; our cars, nonetheless, sped nearly as fast. Most of those oncoming missed us; the one with which we collided had slowed enough to prevent our outright exing. We had emerged at a right angle to the road, blocking two lanes. John sustained full impact; our car pinwheeled down the highway, goosing the rear of one of our fellow travelers before caroming through the guardrail down a low embankment and coming to rest in a kudzu bed. The car didn't fourth-of-July on impact; I gathered that nothing of mine bled overmuch. I didn't fight to remain conscious, now that it no longer essentialled. Before fogging I recalled glancing through the unglassed windshield at the vine-entwined buildings overlooking us; around the cornices the foliage was chopped away, that nature, least of all, should hide Dryco's logo. E was viable; his screams assured me. As I looked over at my husband lying red amid our wreck, I wondered how much he regretted surviving. It didn't take our company's reps long to find us.

"Inhale." I did as demanded. "Exhale."

Dryco's clinic tables were so chilled after our return as they'd been, predeparture; the overheads blinded as before, the familiar odorless stench permeated the air, and my medicis evinced the same warm concern which I'd come to expect. Outpatienting, nonetheless, didn't inflict so much trauma as was sustained during their treatments. Following a week of isolate, intensive care, I was released; afterward naught essentialed but my whiling an hour in their bondage daily so that they might chart my recovery rate.

"Circulatories, normal," my nurse said, tallying. "Endoc-rinations, uninterrupted. Neural charges, steady. Respira-tion, acceptable. Lymphatic conversion, responsive—"

We'd returned a fortnight before; the New York observers, eyeing our dot on their screens as we reappeared, worded south to assure that, minutes later, our overt damages were being treated in Mississippi. Copters came and medevacked us direct, and an hour after our pickup we were each single-bedded in the Bronx, in Montefiore's Dryco wing. That eve-

ning I wavered momentslong into consciousness, unconcerned by my strapped limbs or my wired head once I realized where I was; I felt tubes inserted into my neck, and I
puzzled over why they were there; once I recovered I accessed a library text and comprehended that my blood had
been vacuumed from me so that it could be supplanted with
a purer vintage. As I considered my state, startled to still be
alive, a nurse noted my wakefulness and sedated me anew.
My physical injuries were slight: a concussion, sprained ankles, contusions and a fractured knuckle, sustained when I
hit my husband.

"No infective signs," concluded my doctor. "Melaway
treatment ongoing as required."

"I want my color back," I said; they ignored. "Why is
treatment ongoing?"

"Addictive factor of Melaway demands a three-week withdrawal program, once treatment is deemed inessential."

"Who essentials it?"

"Inapplicable question unanswerable by this department's representatives," said the nurse. "Silence, please."

John, too, had been released; only E remained in hospital,
secured on the wing's uppermost floor, still sealed away
from all eyes save those of his doctors, and Leverett.

"Detail troubling symptoms, if any," my doctor said.

"Headaches, as told before," I said. "Of lowgrade intensity and unceasing."

"Accounted for by concussion's lingering effects. Continue."

"I want magnetic resonance to certify. Cat me."

"Clinic policy cost-inhibits use during outpatient period
unless circumstances warrant, as explained," said my doctor.
"Unwarranted here. Detail other symptoms."

"Nausea upon rising," I said. "A prolonged bloat, and
menstrual abeyance."

"Believed to result from prolonged usage of Melaway.
Conclusive results regarding remaining related tests will be

available to you tomorrow morning between eleven and twelve, Lab Five, Desk Nine, Patient ID 74651135—"

"I'll not recall," I said, interrupting her reel. The machine nearest the table vomited from its slot a printout sheet.

"Use directionals supplied to locate. Present yourself at Lab Five, Desk Nine, between eleven and twelve tomorrow morning."

"Update concluded," said the nurse. "Report here at ten, morning. Rise."

"Which test results remain?" I asked, directing my question to the corner intersections of wall and ceiling from where their voices issued; again, no response. I loosed my robe, letting it fall floorways; eyed the flashings of machine-lights as they blinked on and off, poxing my goosebumped skin with spurting reflections. My skeleton semblanced in greenline upon one screen's black field, duplicating my structure's shifts as I moved. I'd not noticed before how unerringly its blended dots mimed me; placing my stance before the screen, I drew up my arms and flexed my legs so that I could watch my inside at play.

"Refrain from gesture stylization, please," my doctor said, startling me by returning so unexpectedly. "Move normally while clothing yourself."

"What's wanted?" I asked, pulling my shirt over my head, fitting its collar around my neck. "Why?"

"Self-conscious motions pattern falsely, throwing the observers' controls."

"Observers?" I replayed. "Who—?"

"Medical observers from appropriate fields," said my doctor. "Incognitoed, as awareness of presence inevitably affects patiental behavior."

As I backed against the table's cold edge I tugged my shirt down over my hips. "I'll not be eyeraped!" I shouted, uncertain of who stared where; wondered how long and how often I'd been onceovered. "Why are you watching me?"

"Observation assists research needs," she said. "Research purpose is inessential information."

"It's invasive," I said, forcing my feet through my trouser-legs so quickly as to nearly rend the inseam.

"Patiental commentary inessential," said my doctor. "Silence, please."

Retrieving my shoes and underwear, I rushed out of the room, not sliding the door closed behind me, knowing I'd never return after the next day, when I could gather my test results; results for tests whose purpose remained enigmaed. I shamefaced as I halled myself, forbidding tears, guilting sans reason as I always had whenever another assaulted me, as I'd done after unblanking my memory of the patrolman's probing; as when John went missing while we made love, or as Judy had known me before she knew me. But the rape for which I blamed myself most was the one that never occurred.

Late that afternoon, unenjoying my remaining moments of unscheduled time, safe from any eyes but those I desired might stare, I studied the disk I'd purchased at the fetal art exhibit. When I looked again upon the pieces they reentered my head half-forgotten, as if I'd seen them years, and not weeks, before. I studied their holoed images, reappraising my first looks, deciphering subtleties too cloaked to grasp even after years of study. Tanya's voice audibled clear over the unit's phones as I allowed all mundanities to slip from my mind, losing myself in her work.

"Violence against another is doggerel, not poetry, however developed its structure, no matter the comforts of its theory," she said. *"But there inheres to the aesthetic of violence against oneself an unassailable truth, that the greatest art bestows upon its onlookers, and its artist, the sublimity of pain."*

"Iz?" I heard John say.

"What, sweetie?" Switching off the unit, I freed my ears to better hear my husband. He'd suffered greater injury than I had in the smash; still, much of what was harmed was partially if not totally artificial, and so his recovery progression had matched mine. He trod catfooted upon his improved leg; his freshest scars were unbasted several days before. His Krylar implants secured his innards so well as shielded, and though he'd taken full impact he'd sustained only minor internal damage. In rebuilding his bone-shattered arms his doctors strengthened their lengths and joints, restringing new tendons so that both his fists might sound fortissimo chords, if he was ever again allowed to play.

"I've interrupted," he said, readying to exit. "Forgive—"

"Stay and speak," I said, patting the chair next to me. He sat himself with caution, slowing his motions so as not to harm what remained to be healed. "What's troubling?" I asked. "You've medicated?"

"I singled at half past." He lifted his head, revealing his oldest scar, one gained in teenage; a whitened furrow usually hidden within his neck's folds, close to but not touching the carotid. "I can't doubledose, Iz," he said. "It blanks me. That's life sans life—"

"It's essentialled," I said. "That's known."

"It's undoable, whatever's demanded," he said staring at dust-motes aglitter in the room's fading sunstream.

"They unanimoused, John. It's temp, all the same. A shortterm requirement, we were assured—"

"Retirement doesn't become me," he said. "I can't regood, Iz. I should have stayed—"

"That's not our world, John," I said. "It momented pleasant to you in some ways. At the end it was prepping to swallow us both. You weren't you, there."

Through my window I saw an adblimp sail by, puttering toward Jersey; bedecked along its bulges were all the marks of Dryco. From its fins a banner fluttered, iterating the company motto in letters twelve meters high. Leverett, fulfilling Dryco's promise, had had our salaries doubled after assuring that we'd not only met our goal, but returned with him. Debriefing our overseer two days before, I'd detailed the ensuings of our travels; demanded as well explanation for why my husband's medication hadn't acted. Leverett guaranteed a full investigation, and sent me homeways; that afternoon John was notified by nameless ones deep in Dryco that, for contrarying against regooding regardless of cause, he was suspended with pay for indefinite duration.

"I was me," he said. "You've not glimpsed before."

"No," I said. "You did as trained, John."

"Trained no longer," he said. "I'm redundant. They're unphasing me."

"Tomorrow I'll be conferring with Judy," I said. "I'll make your plea, I know she'll hear."

"I'm maddening, housebound."

"You're not imprisoned," I said. "Come and go as willed in my absence."

"I can't, Iz," he said. "It's impossibled—"

"You're fearful going alone, nothing more."

"More," he said. "I'm tongue-tied, trying to tell. It's—"

"It's temp," I said, fearful that it would be longer; lying to him came easier to me now, came almost so easy as breathing. "Once he's healed you'll be returned to the fold. Till then we're together. Mayhap we can vacation, at last—"

"Vacation's done," he said. "What if I am redeemed? It's obvioused they can't change me, whatever we do. We'll all be gone, once all's regooded." He stopped; mouthed soundlessly as if he was stroked, holding his hands out before him, waving them as if to swim. "It's halflife here, Iz. The feel's unbearable."

"John," I said, entwining my fingers with his; shuddered, feeling his grip clamp as if onto a trapped animal. "Ours is full life if you allow it. Please allow." Seating myself in his lap I embraced him, feeling once again the chill he'd had before we left, the icy distance; no sooner did he begin to warm than the phone rang. Sighing, I switched on the remote.

"4370," I said, spilling our number and no more across the room and into the speaker.

"Isabel," Leverett said, bellowing his voice through our quarters. "Recovery's complete, I'm informed."

"Not entirely." I stood, although he couldn't see us; we'd disabled the screen the day the phone was installed. "Any answers yet?"

"At any moment," he said. "All's being processed. Your success has doubled my workload, I've been end-over-end—"

"What's wanted, then?" I asked.

"Meet me at Montefiore at morningside," he said. "There'll be a car for you."

"I meet Madam at ten," I said. "My return day's tomorrow."

"She's been awared of our needs, Isabel," he said. "It essentials. Ten-thirty—"

"I was claimed our assignment's done—"

"Your assignment continues shortterm. Details tomorrow. Tally-H."

As he clicked off I heard behind me a splintering sound, as of a falling limb. My husband stared at the wedge of table-top he held in his hand. Dropping it he stood and walked out, his face unmasked, if emotionless. I laid aside my disc-player, and gazed windowways, skywatching for shooters plummeting earthward.

Only after my discharge was I told of E's state: his splintered ribs and collarbone, his back's torn muscles, his wounded hand's suppuration. John had so remodeled him as to leave his head little more than a skull with flesh bagging over its bone, and following his initial repairs the specialists began plasticking a new look for him. Our air poisoned him, as feared; he soaked in its bugs as if he were a sponge. His cold drained into flu, and then into pneumonia; allergies swelled

his face prior to its restructuring, appearing it—I was told—
as a red, featureless balloon.

E's room was on our Montefiore wing's highest, sealed
floor. When I arrived the next morning Leverett stood outside, conferring with whitegowned figures who must have
been medicis; I marveled, seeing them semblanced in
human form. "Isabel," he said; the others scurried off when
they saw me, as if light startled them. "You're aglow with
health."

"Why am I so essentialled here, Leverett? Matters need
discussion—"

"We'll have the time to talk en momento," he said, smiling and sweeping a shock of gray from his forehead. "The
situation demands your presence, Isabel. You're uniquely
positioned to assist as the E project progresses."

"What's meant?"

"He's disconcerted, now that he's on recovery road. He
deafens himself to our words and shrivels at our touch. Your
name liptrips from him hourly. In dreams he begs for
you—"

"He'll beg on," I said. "He tried rape and pillage on me.
Berated and degraded and caused my husband to mind-
lose."

"You're our icebreaker, Isabel. He demonstrates a fond-
ness for you the docs perceive as curative. A short confer, no
more. The human touch essentials."

"Leverett, I'm to return to Madam this morning, to my
standard position—"

"Would that our jobs ended at five," he said. "See this as
an aspect of your ongoing special task. An unexpected aspect, yes, but the able goflow when called."

"The special task's completed, I was led to understand—"

"Your safety's secured," Leverett said. "A brief meet to
comfort, no more. It may not essential again, not immediately. What's replied?"

"Is he comprehending his surroundings yet?" I asked,

refusing to respond. "I confabulated all that I told him, and John—"

"John's tales plainfaced the subject, as it were," Leverett said, regarding me with dying-calf eyes. "Regrettable, truly—"

"Something contraindicated his treatment," I said. "He reacted as trained. You've been aware, and naught's been done. These investigations—"

"Are ongoing. Mind, Isabel, I'm faultless in this. Moreso, I assured his continuing salary. Defended his actions, even as circumstanced. Some insisted he be . . ." Leverett paused, allowing his pridebeam to outshine anger or remorse. "It would surprise you, what was said by some. Who said what would surprise you more. But I deflected all. Later, I'll detail—"

"Do," I said. "What of E? Is he recovering? Truth me—"

"It's iffed. He's incohering. Beset by deliriums and fever dreams, muttering senselessness full of thunder. Your name solely softens his roar." Leverett paused; eyed E's door. "What are Dero?"

"People who live in caves and in the pits of elevators," I said. "Once we seized him—"

"After John beat him," he said, interrupting.

"He believed us Dero," I continued. "Thought we'd come for him."

"You had," Leverett said, nodding to himself. "Usable, perhaps. Communication's been impossible since he cleared. Mayhap he thinks we're all Dero. How'd he so notion such a concept?"

"He reads science fiction."

"Contributes nothing to the image," Leverett said, his eyebrows lifting. "Another untoward habit to break. Still, it'll ease your explanations if you employ that. Put fact in fiction's terms."

"My explanations?" I replayed. "I'm to explain his state to him—?"

"Isabel," he said, taking my arm. "Let's visit."

Fingertapping the door, Leverett awared it of our presence, so that it might slide away. Within a small antechamber were two guards, unweaponed and plainclothed; their unemotioned features revealed their provenance. The inner door opened; I blinked at the brightness within the windowless room. E lay bedded and bottlefed, bulwarked by machines, netted with wires. Bandages swathed all of his face but for his eyes; his neck was collared, placing his bones as he healed.

"You've a visitor," Leverett said, seating himself across the room as I approached E's bedside. "As promised."

"Isabel," he said. "They told me you were comin' but I figured they lied."

"That's unfigurable," I said. "Here I am."

"Where you got me?" he asked. "One a your caves?"

"You're hospitaled," I said. "It's not evident?"

He shifted his head on his pillow; stared at me from beneath his wraps. "How can I know for sure it's you?"

"What proof's required?" I asked, thinking it unconscionable, how I wished that he'd died in the wreck. "I'm not Dero and I'm not gaming with you, Elvis. I'm as you see me. Content?"

"Your eyes're different." I'd not replaced my lenses, and no longer colored my hair. During each daily appointment the clinic dosed me with Melaway, though I'd tossed my own pills away the day I went home; I suspected Leverett of being the one insistent on my remaining unhued, and reminded myself to find out why. "Turn a little to the right." I did, presenting my profile. "It's you all right. I'm glad t' see you."

"You're recovering?" I asked.

"I hear nurses but don't see 'em," E said. "Where're they hidin'?"

"They're shielded for your protection," Leverett said, interjecting. "Assuring rest—"

"Who's he? Sonofabitch's been in here ever day, bullshittin'. He's your leader?"

"Call him Dero dad," I said, stonefaced. "We're *people*, Elvis. Different people, that's all." From my jacket I removed my wallet; opened it to reveal family pics and ID. "Look. That's John and me ten years ago," I said, pointing out a shot of us standing before the razorwire surrounding our old apartment house, in the Upper East Zone. "My sister-in-law's daughter. We're people like you, truly—"

"I wanta go home."

"You're home now," Leverett said, interrupting again. "You're familied here traditionally and spiritually—"

"What the hell's he talkin' about?" E asked me. "This supposed t' be torture or somethin'?"

"Not deliberately."

"Not at all—" said Leverett.

"Excuse me a moment," I said, turning around. "Leverett. A word without, please."

"Talk, talk. We're secretless here," he said; after a moment, reconsidered and stood. "Of course, Isabel. Pardon us, Elvis."

The door closed behind us as we stepped back into the antechamber. The guards stared on as if they'd not noticed that any neared, offering threat solely by their presence. "Quit thieving my lines," I told Leverett. "You're acting as if I'm not even there."

"I can assist in guiding the dialogue—"

"I'll guide or I'll go," I said, lowvoicing so much as I could. "Agreed?" He nodded, lifting his hands as if to protect himself from my charge. "Now level. Has he any awareness of why he's here or what's being done to him?"

"Not as such," Leverett said. "Mind, Isabel, he's only been online since yesterday. We've concentrated on assuring viability, not information."

"So that I could inform," I said. "Let's go back. Keep tightlipped."

One of the guards sat leaning forward, handclasping; as we turned to reenter E's room I noticed a spittle-thread hanging from the guard's lower lip, and wondered if at intervals maintenants came round to dust them.

"We're back—" I said, returning to E's bedside.

"Y'all gonna talk about me, you best do it to my face."

"Our talk concerned unrelated matters," I said. "You're not all we talk about."

"How come those niggers're sittin' out in the hall?" he asked. "You all catch 'em and bring 'em down from up above?"

"Hear me," I said, leaning across him; if I was to teach, I'd discipline as well. "That word's unusable here. Never say it again. Understand?"

"What's with you?" he asked. "I was just wonderin' why they were out there, that's all. Damn, Isabel—"

"They're certifying your safety."

"Safety from what?" E asked. "The anointed never fear."

"Excuse?" I asked; as expected, he didn't clarify.

"You say you're not Dero. You told me you were in the music business."

"That's one of our many fields."

"Remember what you were tellin' me? When do I get outta here and start livin' the high life like you were talkin' about?"

"All'll occur in time."

"Dero always lie," he said. "That's a fact. I'm not gonna listen to you." E shifted so much as he could, resting his wrapped face against his pillow. "I'm tired, Isabel. Leave me alone awhile."

"As you wish—"

"Fine, fine," Leverett said, rising. "As much alonetime during recovery as desired. Come, Isabel. She'll be back, don't fear."

"Get outta here."

I looked at him lying there as Leverett drew me away; he'd

placed his free arm over his eyes, appearing to see us no more than I wished to see him. We passed the guards, and stepped back into the outer hall.

"Discussion now," I said to Leverett, catching him before he could rush away.

"Of course, Isabel. What's troubling?"

"Him, for one," I said. "He's flipping. I'd not give him half a month."

"That's why your assistance is demanded," he said. "You're a preventative, it seems. He hears, when you speak. The project needs you, more than before—"

"Our assignment was to end upon our return," I said. "My job with Madam awaits. My work—"

"Your job there'll await you still, once we're done," he said. "You've proved your potential, now live up to it. A shortterm responsibility, nothing more—"

"What's timeframed for project completion?" I asked.

"No more than a few days, if lucked," Leverett said. "Week, possibly two. Time enough to ground him. Not overlong."

"If I agree," I said, "will that reinstate my husband any sooner?"

"Sans doubt," he said. "Dependent upon final decisions, of course. Isabel, mind his behavior. Interaction was to be minimalized, and in that regard he not only slipped but plunged—"

"He preserved us all by plunging," I said.

"There's no excusing what he did to our subject, his suspicions notwithstanding," Leverett said. "I'll word well all the same. The means are almost justified. If you'll assist freewilled I'll certify his clearance, topspeeded."

"Agreed," I said, and lifted my arm to his eyelevel. "What of this? The clinic tells that I'm to stay white until they're instructed otherwise. Why's it essential I stay bleached?"

"Isabel," he said, lowering his voice, "you heard him word as he did toward the guards. The mindset's plain. Imagine if he was to see you as you are right now. Imaginable, isn't it—?"

"Understood, but undesired," I said. "He'll have to know, Leverett. I want off it, I'm awared there's an addictive factor and my sicknesses linger—"

"Only for a short time longer. Allow him regooding time. For all of us? Please? You lull him so well, Isabel, and he'll be traumaed otherwise."

"It's my skin—"

"The color becomes you," he said. "Be thankful it did. We're undertaking study of your reports, and the surviving materials you brought back. The discoveries and inferences pertaining to that world overwhelm. They aren't as we are, Isabel."

"Known," I said. "I was there. That phrase of his, 'the anointed.' What's meant?"

Leverett frowned, appearing thoughtful. "Some subcultural reference, mayhap. I hoped you'd know; it's not the first time he's used it. Take this," he said, handing me a thin yellow folder embossed with our company's grin. "Initial conclusions and inferrals regarding the shadow world's recent history as per the text you obtained. Deconstruction of his Bible is proceeding—"

"His magazines told of Dero."

"They crumble, under touch, as does the newsheet. The transferral process adverses woodpulp paper. We're seeking archival matches presently."

"It's essential I meet Madam, Leverett," I said. "Excuse me—"

"With your help, Isabel, we'll cream this skim milk nicely. I'll schedule you for daily visits to our boy. Return this afternoon. Visit again. One on one him."

"Schedule—?"

"I'll have it by day's end. Mindful, Isabel, it's shortterm. I swear it."

"This wasn't contracted," I said, reminding him. As he

loosed himself from me, he sidled down the hall, keeping his back wallways.

"The capable adapt, Isabel. The rest—" He shrugged, and walked away.

Judy and I met in her office for lunch; neither of us ate. I'd not seen her since our return, although she'd phoned several times. Her suite's redecoration was complete: drapes cloaked sunlight, chairs gathered dust, cameras onscreened visitors and monitored hallways, every bibelot was placed and forgotten. Her assistant's office, secluded beyond the reception area, held only an empty desk and its accoutrements; I wanted nothing more than to sit there and work.

"Iz," Judy called out through her open door. "Come here."

I walked into her office; she sat there staring at a chart unrolled across her desk, held down at one end with a brass paperweight. She rose as I approached and embraced me for several minutes, rocking with me forthback as we stood there. "It's good that you're back, it's so good," she said. "I feared you wouldn't return, however I assured us."

"I'm here," I said, releasing myself from her grip.

"Did what I give you assist?" she asked, lowvoicing.

"That's what returned us," I said. "Otherwise—"

"As told. Here, Iz. Eye this."

"Eye what?" I asked, looking down at the map on her desk. Isobaric lines overlay an unspecified area's geographics. "A weather map?"

"From the twenty-first," she said, tugging one edge of the chart, unfurling it further. "On the twenty-second, a Bowl reclamation facility was to be dedicated here, in Illinois. An environad was to be created overhead to suitably sendoff. Study the lines. Hot air mass atop the region, cold front coming. TV weatherpeople could forecast this likelihood. Our manipulations only intensified the effect. The resulting tornado killed or injured all present and caused ten million dollars damages to the new facility." As she released her hold on the map, it snapped up as might an old window-shade. "Leverett's decision to go-ahead."

"You can't oversee all," I said. "We've headrammed that timeover."

"When all others guide what's run groundways, it's essential that someone tries. He's irrepressible, and since you returned successed, Seamus deafens to all concerns save Leverett's E project. All else is waysided. That's why you're not here, now. Leverett sent word he still needed you, and my needs were overruled."

"How's he wording Mister O'Malley—?"

"He can write Ambient, if not speak it," she said. "He sends it direct sans blockage by Alice. So, until his project croppers—"

"What if it works?" I asked.

Judy downcast her look; then, eyed me as if my having had the notion was a betrayal. "You're set in either instance, don't you think?"

"Working here's what's wanted," I said. "I'm being bound with E against reason and desire."

"Is he still so stable as I'm told?"

"You've not seen him direct?"

"I've seen the invisible man, bedded atop Montefiore. Aren't appearances supposed to deceive?" she asked. "I know my eyes well enough not to trust them."

"All signs contrary Leverett's opinions, whatever he's told," I said. "E's looned. All this is only worsening him."

"I'll lunch with you often enough to hear truth, so long as you'll tell it."

"Why wouldn't I?"

Rather than answer me she sat back down in her chair, and studied the fogged skyline as it showed through her window. I took a seat on her desk's far side. "This project rolls with its own momentum now," she said. "Momentum carries off all before it, however all might wish to stay placed. You may be wishing, but you're as well in its way. I know you, Iz, you'll not be crushed." When she turned to face me I untensed, seeing her features soften. "Until he fumbles there's naught to be done," she continued. "Is the ruling against your husband impacting your judgment?"

"It's concerning me."

"I gather he's miseried at present?"

"Dangerously so."

"He is your husband, so I did as I could," she said. "Mayhap he's most dangerous to himself at present. But if he seeks other targets, ready yourself to jump."

"His medication ineffected," I said. "Otherwise—"

"He's uncontrollable in any circumstance," she said. "It's as he was trained, so why surprise inheres, I couldn't say. It was recommended that he be termed for his actions there, you know."

"By whom?"

"Leverett. You didn't know?" I shook my head. "The need to conspire overwhelms even the need to conspire against. It's plaintruth."

"He says you're mindlost and you say he lies," I said.

"And who truths?" she asked; shrugged. "Both or neither, depending on what's initially believed. If something's not seen that doesn't mean it's not there. You know your eyes. Should you believe me any more than I believe you?"

The longer we talked the more we seemed to doubt each other; I drew away, thinking of what she'd said, listening to jingling bells. I circled round in my chair to consider their source. Centered on a side table within the AC's currents was a fetal art sculpture; I recognized the style as Tanya's. The skeleton held no pronounced deformities; it dangled from a weightbent black metal rod rooted in stone. Miniature bells hung from toes and fingertips, musicking the air. The slender bones were aqua, matching the walls; it uncertained whether the room was toned to fit the art, or if the art was dyed to suit the room.

"When did you discover them?" I asked. "It's a surreptitious field."

"Their work fascinates. It's so uncooptable by men."

"It's Tanya's work?" Judy nodded. "We met briefly at a showing, predeparture. Barely a word had chance to pass—"

"I've supplied her with studio space in Riverdale this year," she said. "You should meet her, and talk, if Leverett's scheduling allows you a spare minute."

"I'd like that," I said.

"He'll have you on twenty-four-hour call once he's rolling. I'll give you her number. Contact her. Slip my name, she'll host you well."

"Gracias," I said; quieted for a moment, wondering if I should leave. "You've known me thirty years, Judy. I'm so untrustworthy now?"

"No," she said. "Anger displaces in bad situations. He has me raging, Iz, and some spills over. Forgive, por fav. Time tells truth."

"I've something else to tell," I said. "Before coming here I stopped at the clinic and received additional test results—"

"What's discovered?"

"I'm pregnant."

For a moment or two I feared the news left her reactionless, and regretted bringing it up; then her eyes widened, and she opened her mouth as if to speak. "You're not," she finally said. "Wasn't he clipped?"

"I'm told it happens," I said. "We loved before leaving, and it took."

"I'm muted. You're assured you're babied with his?"

"Who else's?"

"Your husband reported you were raped," she said. "Inferred that if you denied, it was because you'd blanked it. I doubted, Iz, but—"

"John's errored," I said. "That's what so unleashed him.

Misunderstanding, nothing more, but I couldn't convince otherwise in time. I thought I had, since—"

"The beast didn't assault you?"

"He touched me, and suffered for it," I said. "But it's undesired, being around him. The baby's John's, none other save mine."

"Then you'll abort?" My moment to silence came, and I did. "You don't mean you'll carry it?"

"They'll track its growth," I said. "It's miracled that I conceived, Judy. Miracled that John could plant. As circumstanced, I might birth proper—"

"None do, nowadays," she said. "And his as well. Iz, reconsider. You've so hardened your life, don't worsen it now."

"I'll chance it," I said. "My decision's made. It's our saving grace, mayhap. Nothing else will hold us as one."

"That's what's wanted?"

I nodded. She came around her desk and hugged me, warming my body with her feel. We held each other, secure against all others. She stroked my back as she had years before, on nights when we sheltered offstreet, secluded from horror; I'd allow her to comfort and pleasure, and she promised to look after me always, however many years we had left.

"I'll certify your care, Iz," she said. "I can't certify John's."

"Do what's possibled," I said. "If he stables he'll see he can bring life so well as death—"

"If he wants to see," she said as we sat on her deskedge. I stared at her earrings' holoed inserts; two small corporate spheres smirked back at me. "You've much to discuss with Tanya, then, if otherwise evented."

Before I could consider what she'd said a buzzing startled me; Judy touched her intercom. "Identify," she said.

"Delivery, Madam," a man's voice answered.

"Delivery's unexpected. Identify further."

"Martin," he said. "Presently stationed in general HQ

Security. Assigned to Miss O'Malley prior to regooding, Madam."

"Of course," Judy said. "Recalled. Prepare to enter." Reaching back, stretching her arm across her desktop, she flipped several switches. "Iz, close in. Your feet."

"Excuse?" I said, drawing up my legs. As I did the floor yawned around the desk; transparent baffles lifted, surrounding us. As they rose they curved inward, closing round until they met at the top, sealing us up as if we were within an oversized bell jar.

"My suggestion," she said, pressing another button. "Your desk is supplied, too. Enter, Martin."

No more than half the guards were ever recognizable to me by sight. His single-breasted suit was in standard, unbesmirched, corporate blue. He'd knotted his necktie in an impeccable four-in-hand. The man stared at us with doll's eyes, glassy and wobbling. "What's delivered?" Judy asked.

"Goodbyes," he said. As he began racing across the room toward us, before he slid his weapon from beneath his jacket, Judy engaged another switch and the back of the sofa facing her desk returned fire. His Krylar underlay held as he flew floorways, skidding back. When he rerose, his intention cleared; aiming his weapon at Judy's window he let fly, breaking the glass. Leaping up, he threw himself through, hanging on the edge of the air as they do in cartoons; then gravity intruded and he plummeted, wordlessly traveling one hundred and six floors. The wind rushing in blew printout off her desk; a pigeon fluttered in between the shards and landed on the roof of the dome above our heads. Alarms rang buildingwide, and cover-smoke poured down from the roof's vents.

"They'll regood when I will, Iz," Judy said, starting to cry until I thought she neared breakdown. "It's too much."

* * *

I sat alone with E in his room when I returned, late that afternoon. "That guy's really your boss?" he asked me; I sat far enough away to be unreachable, his condition notwithstanding, mindful of the monitors forever reading whatever actioned within.

"For now he's overseeing me," I said. "I work elsewhere, regularly."

"He acts like a boss. Old know-it-all." E studied the drainage tube as it emerged from beneath his hand's gauze. "He ever talk straight about anything?"

"I'm told he does."

"Don't believe everything you're told," he said. "That's what my mamma always said to me. Don't know what you Dero get told."

"You truthfully think that's what we are?" I asked. He shook his head; his eyes were unreadable, shadowed by the bandages. The lower half of his face was visible now, as it hadn't been that morning; I saw no sign of scars, and his skin was so clear that his complexion no longer suggested that he lived solely on paste.

"I guess not. You all aren't like me, that's for sure."

"Leaving off Dero, then, did you read much science fiction?"

"Some," he said. "Stuff about space ships, Mars. Travelin' through time to hunt dinosaurs. Long as people got killed and went flyin' off somewhere I liked it. I had a idea for a story once but I never wrote it down."

"That's good—"

"This space commander and his girl scientist land on Mars. It's in the future," he began. I closed my eyes, wishing my headache might overcome me, so that I wouldn't have to listen. "He goes outside to explore, she sees this ol' Martian comin' up behind him. Big ol' sucker, got long arms and all green, scaly, goofy-lookin'. She puts her head through the porthole and shouts and warn him. He runs off but she gets

her head stuck like in a fence and then the Martian sees her
and—"

"The spaceship's portholes are open?"

"After they land."

"There's no atmosphere on Mars," I said. "No Martians,
either."

"You know?" he asked. "Y' been there?"

"What do you think of where you are?" I asked, keen to
distract him from recounting the rest of his tale. "What does
it resemble? Anything you've seen or read of before?"

"Kinda," he said. "You gonna tell me you took me into
the future?"

"Not your future," I said. "Time travel's impossible."

"Nothin's impossible—"

"But you are in our future."

"What're you talkin' about?" he asked, laughing. It disturbed me to see that in reconstructing his lips, the surgeons
had so adapted his embouchure as to allow him to form
without seeming effort the perfect Elvisian sneer; the expression reappeared too often to be deliberate, and I wondered
in what other ways his body had been recut to suit.

"You've read stories about parallel worlds?" He nodded.
"Where you lived exists parallel to our world, and resembles
ours as it was almost a century ago. Do you believe me?"

"Hell, no—"

"The concept's understandable, though."

"This world's like mine but it's in the future, and it's not
my world, right?" I nodded. "So this's what the future'll be
like in my world?"

"Probably not," I said. "Your past doesn't exactly corre-
spond to ours. The worlds are similar, but separate."

"Why're they similar if they're not the same, then?" I
shook my head. "How'd you all come over and how'd we go
back?"

"We have a method of transferral," I said; I still had it.

The compact was returned to me along with all materials in my purse recovered from the crash.

"This is the only parallel world?" he asked.

"One's not enough?"

"Damn," he said. "This's worse'n science fiction—"

"Because it's real," I said. "Hard to explain, harder to understand."

"You're crazier than he is, Isabel," E said, frowning. "If you all are Dero, course, then you'd tell me all kinda stories."

"We're not Dero, Elvis—"

"Maybe not that you'll own up to," he said. "I'm not gonna listen to it."

"It's essentialled that you do—"

"Damn you, I don't haveta do nothin'," he said; had he not been so harnessed by wires and tubes I might have taken his anger more seriously. From my bag I retrieved a disk I'd obtained from research that afternoon, one heard timeover during our training.

"Here's something for you to hear," I said, slipping the disk into my player and switching it on.

"I'm not fallin' for it," he said. "You're just like the rest. Lyin' to me through your teeth ever' chance you—"

He ceased his rant when he heard his voice blaring around him, permeating the room.

"I wish I was—in the land a cotton—"

Approaching him, I lifted the disk's container and held it before his eyes, allowing him to see himself as, mayhap, he would one day be. The sleevephoto was of this world's Elvis, jumpsuited and forty, many kilos heavier and closing in on his life's end. E's lips curled away from his teeth as he listened, forming neither sneer nor smile; expressing emotions more along the line of anguish, or fear. "As he is, so you'll be," I said.

"No," he said. "Turn it off. Go away—"

"This is your counterpart's voice as it was," I said, incomprehending my position, trapped in one room with the Once and Future Kings simultaneously. "As you'll sound soon."

"I don't look like that—"

"You will."

He tried pulling his arms loose of their bonds, to stop his ears against the song. "Leave me alone—" I took his wrists in my hands to keep him down; he struggled, but was too weak to break my grip. "Please turn it off. Turn—"

"You believe me now?" I asked as he tired and ceased his fight; perspiration dewed his upper lip, soaking into his face's gauze. "He was here. You're there. Two and the same. Two worlds. Two of you."

"Where am I?" he pleaded, beginning to cry. "I wanta go home—"

"This is home now," I said. "Answer. You believe me?"

"Yeah," he said; he cried. "Please don't—"

"You'll listen to what I tell you now?" I asked. "Will you?"

"Don't hurt me. I didn't mean t'hurt her," he unexpectedly said, inarticulating through his sobs. "She wouldn't stop fussin' at me."

"Killing never essentials," I said. "Hurting people never essentials."

"Don't hurt me, Isabel. Please don't hurt me—"

"I won't," I said, switching off my player; taking his damp hand in mine, I held it, standing at his bedside interrogating myself while he cried himself dry. I knew I had to break him, but didn't know why; did making him suffer content me? Had I taken vengeance or pleasure in my act? I'd rarely looked for answers, fearful of what I'd find; one question led to others until, at end, nada certained. Had John's mindset affected mine more than we could admit, or was it as Judy believed, that my stone was harder than his all along?

E settled at last; what I could see of his face appeared as

a boy's, which he was, after all. "My sooties're cold, Isabel," he said. "Cover 'em up for me."

"Your what?" I examined his blanketed form, unsure of what might be exposed; saw his stubby toes protruding from the edge of his sheet. "Sooties?" I asked; he affirmed. I tightened his bedding around his toes, thinking I'd prefer to tag them. Aware of too many untoward emotions coming to me, I filed them all away.

"Thank you, Isabel," he said. "You'll come see me tomorrow?"

"Yes," I said, replaying the word *sooties* in my aching head. "Tomorrow. Sleep now."

As I was driven home that evening I studied the filed material Leverett had given me—translating its obfuscatories as I read—regarding the other world's recent history as found in, or inferred from, the history text we'd brought back. In that world's 1939, as we knew predeparture, the immediate future grimmed: the Depression was unending, Churchill and Roosevelt were dead, and Stalin—during the first borderbreak Alekhine kidnapped and returned with him to our world—was absent, leaving naught to roadblock Hitler.

World War Two came there, as here; Germany invaded the whole of Europe, Japan swept through Asia. Trotsky returned to Russia from Mexico in Stalin's absence, taking power, reorganizing his Red Army and converting factories to war production. A separate peace, agreed to by King Edward and drawn up by Prime Minister Butler, was rigged between Great Britain and Germany; that done, Hitler readied his soldiers to invade Russia. A week before their assault was to begin, Trotsky ordered his own attack. For two years the forces stalemated along the Eastern Front.

In America, President Willkie, foreseeing unavoidable involvement, reinstituted the draft following his inauguration in 1941; declared war on Japan and Germany after the at-

tack on Pearl Harbor, later that year. Matters progressed, for
a time, in like pattern to what had happened here. Then
Willkie coronaried on D-Day, as Allied forces were landing
at Marseilles; Hitler was assassinated by his officers the next
month. A cease-fire was called by Trotsky, new President
McNary and Chancellor Speer. The war continued in the
Pacific; Germany agreed to a conditional surrender and
withdrawal to its original borders. In August 1945, fourteen
atomic bombs were dropped in one week on Japan by America, destroying Tokyo, Kyoto, and other cities; the war
ended.

Our experts inferred, from what I'd told them concerning
E's statements regarding Germans, and from the McCarthy-
ish manner in which communism was spoken of within the
text, that a relationship between Germany and America developed as both readied themselves for possible attack by
Russia, some day in the future.

But what of my people, over there?

The book's later chapters, which I'd not read, told how A.
Philip Randolph, the union leader, called for a general
strike of all black workers in early 1942, threatening a halt
in wartime production unless the American apartheid system was dismantled. They struck, at least in the north, but
not for long. After the riots were calmed an emergency
measure was enacted, interning as potential traitors all black
Americans for the duration of the war. The text never overted what underwayed, but stated that the measure was still
in effect; our experts suspected that after the war German
specialists were consulted regarding the treatment of difficult populations; there, as here, they were likely experienced in such matters.

I cried as my car pulled up before our building, and tried
to imagine a world without me.

* * *

John was asleep when I found him; since his release he'd spent much time in slumber. His copy of *Knifelife*, its black cover bleached by battery-acid spillage, lay open before him; I read the passage, related in Jake's words.

> *When one kills another, two die. Never forget this.*
> *Even when no blood is shed some inevitably spills. The*
> *drops collect around you over years; each action deep-*
> *ens the pool. Once the bottom is lost, the surface is*
> *unreachable. Accept your drowning time.*

"John," I said, tapping his shoulder. Not for the first time an ever-present possibility intruded itself into my mind, that in my absence he'd finally lost himself in his pool. "Love—?" Subconsciously, he seized my wrist; readied to snap it. *"No!"* My shout awakened him; he blinked once or twice, staring at me as if needing to remember who I was before he released. It surprised me that his fingernails were so darkened; my housekeeping wasn't so bad that he'd dirty himself, sleeping.

"Forgive, Iz, forgive—"

"Forgotten," I said, massaging my wrist, looking at the purple welt rising from my deadwhite. "Bed yourself, John, you'll stiffen."

"I have," he said, smiling, lifting himself from his seat. "Love me, Iz. Please."

When he enfolded me within his arms I initially thought of fending him off; shortly decided I didn't want to, and returned his kiss. Babysitting E would allow me too little time with my husband, and my condition would soon pre-vent such play; I wanted to enjoy what moments together remained to us. Holding one another, we went into our room. He didn't hurt me; as we loved I stayed inbodied, consciousing myself full as I once always did when we loved, as if premonitioned that the next morning's events would forever steal one of us from the other, and wishing to plea-sure so much the last time as we had the first. Afterward we

were so commingled as to be immediately uncertain whose
limb belonged to whom.

"What ensued at Montefiore?" he asked. "What's Leverett
want?"

"I've been apprised of new situations."

"Involving?"

"I'm informed E needs an overseer he trusts," I said.
"Against reason and desire, he trusts me. My arguments
inessentialled, and so went unheard. Leverett's drawing my
schedule now."

There was too much darkness in our room for me to read
his expression. His voice was another's, when he did at last
respond. "You're to guide him after what he did to you?"

"He did nothing to me, as told," I said. "His attempt went
for naught. He tore my dress, nothing more."

"Leverett's request's unsupportable," John said. "Action-
able."

"It's part of my job," I said. "I've never impacted upon
yours, whatever you did. Show equal respect."

"What's essentialled in this?"

"To comfort while they train him," I said. "By agreeing,
Leverett assures he'll hasten your—"

"Comfort how?"

"*Stop!*" I feared; when his moods were on him he acted
first, considered later. "You'll not suspicion me like this,
John. He did nothing to me. I'll do nothing to him. Settle
yourself before you go missing. It's unbearable."

As he sighed I heard his air rush from him as if he were
attempting to empty his lungs. "His behavior maddened."

"He hurt you, not me," I said. "If that angers, so be it.
Understand, John, this difficults overmuch. Leverett'll have
me scheduled daylong on this for who knows how long. But
I'm with you, John. Even when I'm not, I am."

"Understood, Iz," he said, intending to silence. "Understood."

"I want to be with you, John," I said. "No one else. But I'm told this essentials. Even Judy's helpless to act."

"Certainly she could," he said. "There's a reason she won't. You'll not know what it is."

"I know her, John," I said. "She's helpless, trust me. She'd act if she could."

"If said, so believed. This'll ongo how long?"

"Unknown," I said. "There's something I've not told you yet, of overriding importance."

"Told me what?"

"We're gifted, John," I said. "You know there're improbabilities and impossibilities. How the unlikely can happen, so long as it's not impossible."

"What's meant?"

"Remember our making love predeparture?"

"Memoryburned," he said. "Forgive me hurting you. Forgive—"

"Forgiven then, forgiven now," I said. "It accomplished, all the same. It's Godness's gift. I'm pregnant."

"Pregnant?"

"Perfection's unassured but there's the chance, and I'll chance it for us. Oh, John, if we parent we're forever bound. It's near-miracle, it's our blessing, it's—"

I shushed, feeling his shake begin. "John?" He muted, quivering as if readying to erupt; then slowly settled again, at last so stilling that I imagined he'd been brainstruck. "John, what is it?"

"It's his," he said, rolling away from me, saying no more.

8

Elvis sang; E listened. "What's thought?" I asked. During the three weeks since I'd first exposed him to his counterpart E had adjusted to the voice's sound, so long as it was musicked; those passages where Elvis tonguespoke still unnerved him enough that he refused to listen to whatever was being said and not sung. I was as glad; Elvis's talk, as preserved, bespoke a public mind so banal that I would go coma before hearing two sentences in sequence.

"He sings good. It's what he's singin' that I can't handle." That afternoon we were listening to the soundtrack of *Clambake* as we worked chronologically through the recorded bible. "You say a lotta people like this stuff?"

"Your counterpart is very popular, E," I said.

He studied the diskbox's photo, a shot from the midsixties; Elvis's features were so heavily airbrushed as any postcard icon's. "They got'm lookin' pretty good here," E said. "Some of 'em he looks like a big ol' hog ready for market. I'm not gonna have to look like that, am I?"

"It's the preferred look for many," I said. "Not for us."

His bandages were off, revealing his look as we'd made it. Dryco's workmen had so retrofitted E that at certain angles he appeared even less realistic than his dupe did in the treated photos; in daylight his skin and hair looked to have been supplanted by colored polymer and acrylic. "That's crazy. How could anybody like somethin' looked like that?"

"It's love," I said. "Look any way as wished, say whatever's desired. It won't matter. You know how it is when you're in love." He muted; it occurred to me that mayhap he never had been; possibly the occasional rape sufficed.

"I had a girl, once," he said. "She was all right."

"Tell."

"Her name was Dixie," E said. "We met at church. She was a pretty little thing. We'd get together after school."

"What happened?"

"Her family didn't like me," he said. "Her mamma and daddy thought I was white trash. Didn't want her goin' out with me but she snuck out anyhow. We'd go downtown or out on Mud Island. Got along real good." E lay down on his bed again; now that most of the machines had been taken away his hospital room looked to have been doubled in size. "Her brother Jimmy was a sorry bastard even before I started hangin' out with her. He was in my class, one a the guys'd go out nights and kick possums to death for the hell of it. Always called me queerbait. Trip me when I'd be goin' down the hall. I had to ignore him, though. He and Dixie were real close. Couldn't figure out why but they were."

"You finally interacted, I assume—?"

"One afternoon after class I went in the washroom. Jimmy and some a his boys came in and caught me there." E's face darkened; I couldn't tell if anger or embarrassment most responsibled for his purpling. "Not gonna tell you what they did. So next mornin', before school, I took a piece a hose and filled it up with sand. Jimmy was sittin' in home room when I got in. He was laughin' when I walked past 'm.

Laughin' up a storm and then I sapped him with that hose. Went down like a bull in the slaughterhouse."

He smiled, telling of his most memorable act of revenge; his features and tone evidenced that this particular anecdoting wasn't intended to impress.

"Was he killed?"

"Hell, no. But he was out three days and never was the same after. He and his boys didn't bug me no more but I got that gun after that just in case. I wasn't gonna let nobody do nothin' to me again and I haven't."

"Certainly not," I said.

"That's when I got kicked out a school. Dixie, she wouldn't have nothin' to do with me after that, she'd just be hangin' on her brother makin' sure he always knew where he was goin'. Last time I tried talkin' to her she just called me a name and ran off."

"When was that?"

"Couple months ago," he said. "Well. Lot longer ago than that now, I guess." Picking up a remote he switched on the wall's TVC, across the room. "Let's see what's on the fireplace." With quick motions he zapped through the hundred and forty channels, silencing as we soaked in image. Each channel was commercialling as he called them up; most ads were for Dryco products, though there were a few PR spots, which inferred with metaphysical certitude that the ideal behavior patterns Dryco recommended that all follow would, perhaps, steer the viewers toward a life convincingly semblancing an idealization of contentment.

"You've always felt alone?" I asked.

"You get used to it." E blanked the screen and closed his eyes as we conversed.

"You'll rarely be alone here," I said.

"Can't say much for that either," he said. "None a this seems real, it's all crazy. All of it. You must feel crazy all the time, you've been in it so long."

"It's best if you take none of it seriously. You'll be able to do that in time, to some degree."

He smiled. "I can't ever take Leverett seriously," said E. "He's always goin' on—"

"And always will," I said. "Take him seriously."

"He as crazy as he acts?" E asked. "Level with me."

I hedged, before replying, knowing it a surety that our words would be replayed and noted, later on. "There's little they want of you, after all."

"More'n I want t'give, I think," E said. "These appearances you keep talkin' about. I don't think I'll mind gettin' up before people long as they're not gonna start laughin' at me—"

"Stand there and let them love you," I said. "The sole requirement."

"What if they blow me up too?" E said. "Like they did Hitler?"

"Doubtful," I said. "You'll have an easier time of it here than your twin had. You'll better understand what's expected."

"Maybe," he said. "What are they gonna think I am, Isabel?"

"God."

That was the first time I'd so overted what I'd tried, over weeks, to infer. For some moments he was reactionless, as if awaiting followup laughter. Even now I recall his expression when he understood that I truthed, saying that. He paled, and drew away from me as if I'd hurt him more than his girlfriend's brother, or his father, or anyone, even his mother, ever could have. "God of this world?" he asked, whispering as if we'd been caught in illicity.

"What other—?"

"They think I'm like that?" he said. "That's how you want me to be?"

"It's metaphor," I said. "Approximate, all the same.

When I say your predecessor is worshiped, I mean what's said."

"No." He began to cry; I'd no idea what so set him off. "I'm bad, but I'm not that bad. I'm not, I'm not—"

"E," I said, rubbing my hand along his shoulder, unwilling to embrace him even as he wept. "What is it? What—?"

"You all think I'm worse'n a murderer," he said. "Worse'n Hitler. My mamma didn't even say I was that bad."

Without warning he threw himself upon me again, as I always feared he might do were I allow him to approach too near; but there was nothing of lust in his clutch, this time. E sobbed, impressing utter bereftness, seeming to have broken as I'd predicted he would. Still, however helpless he was, however pitiable was his presence, I struggled to extricate myself from his grasp, so disgusted by his touch as I had been that night in the woods. I unsuccessed; he clung to me as if to a crumbling mountainside, or a raft in the midst of the sea. Sighing, accepting my lot for the moment, I responded, hoping to calm; hugged him, trying to keep minded that I was dealing with one who, in too many ways, was no more than a child. "You're not bad," I said, searing my tongue with lies.

"Don't call me God, Isabel," he said; he anguished so that I barely heard his words. "Please don't. Please."

Twice weekly Leverett called to his office all involved with the E project save E himself, conferencing with us, assuring that any problems arising might be swiftly solved before he could pretend he'd never known of them. Some were Dryconians, some came as consultants or subcontractors; all appeared to take joy from their labor only in that it served them as license to argue. I was the sole woman; in aggregate the group exuded that oppressive pheromonic air common to such manly lumps, however weedy and asexual they singly appeared. Though I spent so much time with E as any of

them, none but Leverett ever inquired me regarding my
opinions; they merely noted my observations as I recounted,
smiling as if hearing an unreliable, though amiable, passerby. The afternoon before I'd left E calming, if not wholly
recovered from his upset; during the following morning's
meeting I thought it essential to point my view between their
eyes to certify they saw as I saw.

"Any answer he gives is gansered," said one whose name
I constantly blanked, a sociopathologist affiliated with
Princeton. Several of the others nodded, as if they under-
stood.

"Demetaform," I asked. "What's meant, gansered?"

"Referent to Ganser's Syndrome. Subject consistently re-
plies to questions with approximate answers. A behaviorism
common to psychopaths. For example, when asked if he
missed his father he responded that they never had stamps
in the house."

"Understood," said Leverett. "I asked him if he wasn't
glad to be alive and he told me he couldn't say, he hadn't
been dead yet." They chuckled. "What's the point, then?"

"Nothing he tells should be entirely trusted," said the
Princeton SP. "This must at all times be considered."

"So we'll earplay his words," said Leverett. "Mother him
to quiet, father him otherwise. As you did yesterday, Isabel."

"Problem one demands immediate action," said Telford,
who taught Comparative Elvisisms at Harvard Divinity.
"What Ms. Bonney tells us facts our theories. The matter
must be confronted, otherwise project possibilities could be
nullified before he's even publicked."

"So describe problem one," Leverett said. "You've been
circling around it twenty minutes. Aim and fire, please."

"To best serve as a messiah figure," a bearded man I'd not
seen before said, speaking for the first time that day, "re-
quires of the figure a belief in essential messiah concepts."

"Professor Aponte, isn't it?" Leverett asked; the man nodded. "And your field—"

"Neopost Gnosticism," he said. "Doctor Telford contacted me this weekend past, detailing inferences made in direct observation. I've been overseeing deconstruction of the subject's Bible and was developing my own conclusions. Now, the lady tells us of this matter of his not willing to be even a metaphor for God. The subject, I fear, lacks a key essentiality."

"Detail," said Leverett. "No problem overwhelms."

"Professor Mora," said Aponte. "Historicize."

"Awared as we are from these studies that similarity divergence between worlds seems to have intensified, rather than begun, at the 1945/1861 coeval timeframe," said Mora, who appeared no less glad to see me now than he had during our class together, "it evidences that unforeseen complications upset prior predictions regarding the subject's response accordanced to his historical context—"

"Dejargonize," said Leverett, his smile unwavering.

"Prior to the Middle Ages, in our world," said Aponte, "numerous branches of Gnosticism coexisted with Christianity as viable belief-models throughout Eurasia and northern Africa. The Catholic church, over centuries, liquidated all who adhered to Gnosticism, ridding the world of those whom they considered the worst of heretical competitors. Only in the last fifty years have the beliefs remanifested themselves overtly in Western society."

"Macaffreyism, as an example," said Mora. "My wife believes."

"As do many," said Leverett, allowing no hint of his own supposed belief to be revealed. "So our boy's a Gnostic? Make him all the easier to handle, I'd think—"

"Not at all," said Aponte. "Macaffreyism, taking that example, is a neopost variant similar only in the base concept of dual deities, one good, one evil. Extrapolating from the subject's Bible and from interrogation of the subject—"

"Keeping minded of his propensity to ganser," said the Princeton SP.

"—it would appear that in the other world Gnosticism was not erased but thrived, and that the Valentinian sect became in fact the predominant religion of the American South. Correlating his response on the eschatological curve with the texted material, we discerned the potential problem—"

"I'd almost forgotten there was one," said Leverett. "Detail, please—"

"The messianic concept is alien to the subject," said Aponte.

"And? What of it?"

"The core belief of Valentinianism is that knowledge and self-awareness save the soul," said Aponte. "In this particular faith the creator manifests as a female deity, Sophia. She birthed the God of this world, the Demiurge, who created the world and who is unable and unwilling to lead either itself or humanity out of darkness. In our subject's religion old Christian beliefs are topturveyed. To his mind, people redeem their creator in the act of redeeming themselves. Humanity will save God, to be concise."

"He believes that?" Leverett asked.

"Evidently," said Aponte. "So to suggest to the subject that people here want him to contain the God of this world within himself inspires the unfavorable reaction observed." Aponte shrugged. "Heretofore he's believed that, however bad he was, he'd still one day be able to—"

"Regood himself," I said. Leverett nodded.

"So when he finds that others believe he contains God within himself, a God whom they expect to save them, he imagines not only that those who worship him call evil down upon themselves by doing so, but that by living as their worshipee he'll never have the chance to overcome his own evil."

"Keep the ganser factor minded while assuming," said the Princeton SP.

"Such religious beliefs must be politically quite useful, in their South," said Mora.

"What am I to do with him, then?" I asked.

"He'll mindshift, everyone does," said Leverett. "Reality's most adaptable thing there is. Talk with him about it. It's reasonless why he can't pose as one god while believing in another."

"I'm uncertain, Leverett—"

"He should viz his followers at close hand before we intro him en masse of course, so he'll know what to expect from them. I've a plan for that in any event. The forewarned forearm. We'll roundabout this."

"It may be difficult," said Aponte.

"We'll see. Adjourned for now, gentlemen. See you Thursday, same time. Isabel, remain."

While the others filed out Leverett fixed his stare on mine with such intensity that I believed he might be attempting to hypnotize me, as the late Colonel was said to have done so effectively with the King. "Your hair, Isabel. You didn't tell me of your intention to change."

"I saw no need to tell," I said, twirling relaxed strands of black between my fingers. "I've had enough of blondness. My natural look's called for."

"But what will he think?"

"It's unmattering," I said. "He'll adjust if it troubles, as he's adjusting to so much else. I've missed myself, Leverett. I want to be as I am—"

"His reaction could disrupt the project if he sees you're not as he's believed and then acts accordanced to his background," he said. "We've discussed this, Isabel, you're magnifying superficialities."

"It's not superficial—"

"I don't see why you've not adjusted better to your look," he said. "It's—"

"Preferable?" My shout must have upset him; he shook his head so vigorously that I thought he might send it sailing. "I'm devoting half my life to him for you, Leverett. He can take me as I am. I want to cease Melaway intake."

"He's racially backgrounded," Leverett said. "You can't, Isabel, it's unquestioned."

"I want to cease Melaway intake—"

"You have to make it so damned hard for me?" he said, his voice rising only enough to infer an anger with which he was growing too familiar. No sooner had he flared than he calmed anew. "You're deliberately not understanding me. We've got success by the throat. If you recolor now, Isabel, that could handbasket all to hell. Please, a short time more. That's all I ask."

"How long?"

"A short time. Trust me as he trusts you."

"Not enough trust," I said. "I'll stay housebound, then, like John. I've ceased home intake already."

"Isabel—"

"If he trusts me, he'll trust me however I am, once he understands," I said. "If this is unsuitable, then fire me. Now."

His eyes widened; for a moment I saw far enough into him to discern how afraid he was before he blinked, and reshuttered his soul. He leaned forward in his chair, clasping and reclasping his hands as if wishing to pray and forgetting how. "I understand this is important to you," he said. "Very well. I'll aware the technicians so they can begin overseeing withdrawal. But—"

"What?"

"I'd think you'd be concerned for your baby. For the effects withdrawal might have on it. Even if you're unconcerned for me, or your company, or the project—"

"Meditexts inform that Melaway withdrawal won't impact my baby," I said. "Proven, Leverett. Don't guilt me."

"Then if that's what's desired, I'll notify," he said, thrusting his lower lip out, as if evidencing a sulk. "You'll not reblacken overnight, true. Mayhap he'll adjust. Tell him you're spending more time in the sun—"

"He'll not believe that, Leverett—"

"If he upsets," he said, "if the screen blanks, your responsibility topmosts. That's understood?"

"Understood," I said.

"Fetal development thus far normal," my doctor said, concluding my check, several days later. If a computer died and returned in ghost's form to haunt its former office, its night cries would echo with like tonality, possessed of being sans soul. "Disruptions generally evidence after the initial month, as forewarned. Nothing can be assured until then."

"Awared," I said.

"Melaway withdrawal proceding sans untoward effect on either subject or fetus. Graduated reduction assures against unnecessary systemic shock. Have all options been reconsidered?"

She was forbidden to mention termination, as termination was illegal; still, as the law could be with ease bypassed by Dryco if circumstances demanded, the procedure could have onwent as I lay there, so long as through her phrasing I gathered her inquiry's subtext.

"No," I said. "Can the parentals be genied yet?"

"As of next week," said my doctor. "Fetal contamination risk rises tenfold with such procedure, as warned. The test's desired?"

"Desired," I said. "But I'll not chance. What of my headaches?"

"Indirect result of pregnancy along with nausea, as explained. Reappoint for tomorrow, then. Avoid all teratologic factors and mutagens as recommended."

"Including air and water?"

"Not unless you wish to precede your child," my doctor said. I lifted myself from the table. Tugging my jacket closer around me, I stared at my browning hands.

* * *

When they rehoused E the next week they moved him to the seventieth floor of a Concourse building, a lime-green spike driven through a century-old six-story base. The first time I met him there he sat on the floor by one of the windowwalls, staring into Manhattan's sea-haze and the strata cottoning the tower.

"What's sighted?" I asked, walking toward him after the guards nodded, allowing me entry. The rooms were so depersonalized as a hotel's, and nothing within was as it showed: stone was plaster, brick was vinyl, ceramic was polystyrene, and glass was lucite. E didn't stand as I approached; I knelt on the floor beside him. At that point we'd been so proximitied for so long that I suppose I could have kissed him hello; I didn't.

"What'd you do to your hair?" he asked, staring at me. I'd dyed it black the night before, prepping myself to see him as John lay silent in our bed. The darkness only paled my skin all the more, delaying any full realization he might yet make.

"What's thought?" I asked.

"Looks good," he said. "It's all right. You sleep on it wrong or somethin'? It's stickin' up real high in back." Lifting my hands, I patted my hair smooth, reshaping its lengths. I'd not yet readjusted to its unironed kinks. "What've you all got planned for me today? Am I really gonna get outta here? This's no different than the hospital."

"Soon—"

"*How* soon?" The room's cameras whirred, sharpening their focus at the source of the shout, taking account of movements. E's treatment during the preceding month had domesticated him enough so that I no longer disliked being alone with him; still, he hairtriggered, so that my guard never dropped, and at all times I readied to contain him if he bolted. It never came to that; generally all that was needed for me to do was glower, and that would still him. I imagined that his mother's look, too, must once have had that effect.

"Leverett's arriving shortly," I said. "You know as much as I do. Let's ask him."

"He's not gonna tell me anything. Like talkin' to a brick wall." He regarded the outer world once more, the odd towers and silhouettes eking through the clouds. "I never saw pictures a New York where it looked like this."

"It's a different city," I said, finding it unsurprising that he couldn't yet locate himself in either space or time. "Years later, as well. And over here, not there."

"Looks like somethin' on one a my magazines," he said. "Those little helicopters atomic powered?"

"Hardly. Wouldn't be ecobuddiable—"

"This's all like a dream, Isabel," he said. "I don't get it, I really don't. What is it y'all want me to be?"

"Being you suffices," I said.

"I'm not nobody and it's hard enough bein' that. You want somebody supernatural. I can't be that, nobody can. It just doesn't happen."

"People here believe it does."

"They believe crazy, then." He muted and, closing his eyes, handrubbed them, as if to prolong his awakening so as to assure that he wouldn't still be in his dream when he reopened. "It's all crazy, Isabel. Valentine tells us, anybody comes sayin' they're not a this world, they're either lyin' or they're a demiurge come to do mischief and harm. How can I pretend to be Satan?"

"You're not," I said again. "That's not what's thought—"

"I'm not no Dero," he said, "and I'm sure's hell not nothin' bigger."

"That's not the spec here, E," I retold. "By being here and being yourself you'll do so much—"

"What can I do for anybody?" he said, standing and walking away from me, toward the northfacing windowwall. "Can't even help myself. People'd be fools to wanta get anything outta me. I can't give 'em anything."

"You don't have to give," I said. "You just have to be. That's all that's wanted, nothing more—"

"Don't you mean they want me to be him, not me?" said E. "How can I do that? He wasn't even him, near's I can tell."

"You're advantaged," I said. "He had no expectations of what would happen. No warning. All that ensued overwhelmed until he mindlost. But we've awared you of what's ahead, good and bad."

"You're the only one talkin' to me 'bout anything bad."

"The bad's seeable to any who look," I said. "You've looked." He nodded. "You're prepared, and he wasn't. But your life's your own, and will stay your own."

"Not to hear Leverett tell it," E said. "He showed me this schedule he's cookin' up for me once this act gets rollin'. He's got me flyin' here, runnin' there—"

"Leverett's unhappy unless he sees everyone else being so busy as he believes he is," I said.

"Won't know if I'm comin' or goin' or already been there." He sat on a purple sofa and propped his feet atop a glass table. "And nobody t'talk to but you, the whole time."

"That's minded?"

"Doesn't do much good," he said. "You're married to a mean bastard, Isabel. I'm not gettin' in his way if I can help it."

"Friendship's the most I'm offering," I said, feeling my answer wasn't entirely truthful even as I gave it. Still, I wasn't willing to elaborate, as I wasn't certain what I'd already offered. "That's not enough?"

"Isabel, you're, I mean—"

"You're attracted to me?"

I awaited his response, suspecting I knew the answer even if he didn't. We looked at one another, eyegazing; he turned away first, and lapped his hands as if to hide them. "You're older'n I am, Isabel," he said, and his sneer reappeared on his lip; estimating it unintentional, I didn't personalize.

"And you're married, like I said. You're really pretty, you are, and I—"

"What?"

"I don't know," he said. "Maybe I do like you, Isabel. I never met anybody like you before."

"Understandable, I'd think—"

"I don't mean all this. I mean the way you are. It's not like anybody I know."

"Detail," I said.

"I never knew anybody who was in control of themselves before," he said. "Not my mamma or daddy. Nobody at school. Me, least of all. But you are."

"You think I'm in control of myself?"

"You don't?"

I smiled, considering the notion so alien as to charm even as it befogged me. Whether I'd been utterly misviewed or, like my husband, E could at intervals discern personality traits inevident to all others, including the personality's possessor, I couldn't guess. "Rarely," I said. "The river rises, and I float with the flood. That's all any can do."

"You can do more'n that," he said. "Don't let 'em fool you."

"Understood," I said. "You've a lever here too, you know."

"What're you talkin' about?" he asked, looking around.

"If you don't participate, the project hangs. If the project goes, you should have some say in what's done. True?"

"I don't see I got much choice."

"Mayhap I haven't either," I said, examining my deepening tan; remembering how easily Leverett rolled, once I pushed him. "Tell them what you choose before they tell you, if you can. It's bargaining, after all. Two steps forward, one back, two forward—"

"What if you're walkin' through a swamp?" E asked. Before I could reply I heard a buzzing echoing through the rooms, followed by the ring of Leverett's voice.

"Conversing well?" he asked, entering the room as the door slid away. E turned his eyes upward, as if to look into his head and see what might remain there that was still his. "What a view, isn't it? In clear air you'll see New Hampshire from here."

Clouds dampened the glass, obscuring the sight of all that lay without. "You're early, Leverett," I said. He seated himself on the couch between us; I scooted away from them both. A small man entered the room, his progress slowed by his weightload; he lugged a portfolio nearly so tall as he was, if flatter.

"Elvis, Isabel, this is Walter. He's our project's imagist."

"He's my what?" E asked.

"We're formulating the presentation of appropriate looks, dependent on circumstance. Walter's prepared examples for your approval. Walter? What's troubling?"

Walter stared at E as if watching his house burn down. "Forgive," he said, headshaking. "The resemblance uncannies."

"Intentionally unavoidable," Leverett said. "One and the same, that's him. The one and only. Show Elvis what we've brought. Show him how others see him."

"Don't these people already know what I look like?"

"You're no stranger to advertising, surely," said Leverett. Walter opened his case, withdrawing and unrolling a lifesize poster of E. "For the domestic market, befitting 19 to 22 dems," said Leverett. "Stunning, isn't it?"

I saw at once that they'd not retained the artist who'd captured the Drydens' image. E's figure showed half-shadowed; such lower extremities as were seeable faded into mist, as if he had emerged imperfectly from a lamp rubbed the wrong way. His one-eyed gaze targeted all onlookers. Enough of his chest puffed out against the black to reveal our emblematic there imprinted, its circle aglitter with jewels.

"That supposed to be me?" E asked.

"The hint of unreality is not only desirable but demanded," Leverett explained. "Artistic improvements on nature. Nothing personal."

"You can't even see who or what I'm supposed to be—"

"That's inferable. An image modicum is suitable for those particular dems. Outlines hold depth enough," said Walter. "Black's their color, certainly." From his case he pulled a second roll, of similar size and format. "Image two. For the Northern European and Russian market."

Image two consisted of a photo of our own E, his features so retouched that he resembled any postcard image of the Central Asian dictators. A jumpsuit so white and beglimmered as a filmscreen was painted over his form; he gazed heavenward, as if sighting the land upon which his followers would one day be allowed to pitch their camps. The sun backdropped him; whether it rose or set depended upon the onlooker's attitude. No face scarred its golden orb, though the yellow was assuredly that of Dryco.

"Didn't you tell me I wasn't gonna haveta wear those sissy suits?" E asked. "And you got me weighin' four hundred pounds in that picture. I told you I wasn't gonna get fat."

"This image holds global acceptance, even allowing for racial variation," said Walter. "Simplify, dealing with the simple."

"People see you as they choose," Leverett said. "Actual weight's unimportant. They'll reconstruct you after you've been viewed as they see fit."

"A bulking diet was considered," said Walter, "but to attain such size within two months, thirty thousand calories daily would essential. Difficult. Here, now." He extracted a third look from his binder, and opened it before us. E's bloated head was haloed by the world's globe; his features were so drawn as to suggest he contained all races within himself. Below his glow was the lettered command, DO GOOD. FEEL REAL.

"A bit overt," said Walter, "yet possesses full shopability while retaining Elvisceral heritage."

"What's thought, Elvis?" Leverett asked; resumed spieling before E had a chance to answer. "Well, I knew you'd approve." He motioned that Walter should stow what he'd brought. "We're going to break you in England, it's been decided."

"Why England?" E asked. "What's there?"

"Your British followers were first to formally recognize your divinity."

"No such thing."

"Elvis, please," said Leverett. "They're the most serious of your counterpart's followers. He never went there, while he was alive. Half the populace is yours outright, the moment you deplane. It's the natural stepoff for all else."

"They'll think I lead the sons of darkness," E said.

"In a picturesque sense, perhaps," said Leverett.

"That's unnatural. They're worse'n heatherns if that's what they think—"

"We'll see to their souls, so remain unconcerned."

E shook his head; windowgazed as if wondering whether to throw himself through. "I don't get it," he said. "I don't. I just don't get it—"

"Calm," Leverett said. "As we've told you, your unwillingness to innergrate problematics more than is necessary. Just calm, calm, calm. Close your eyes and take deep breaths. Like this."

"You've something besides these visuals planned, haven't you?" I asked, interrupting Leverett's hyperventilation. He shifted his attention to me, appearing irritated that I needed to speak.

"What's meant?" he asked.

"These posters'll do fine, thirdworlding it. They'd have been fine here, thirty years ago. Outmoded now, don't you think?"

"We've many plans arranged, Isabel," Leverett said, turning back toward E. "Unconcern. Calm, calm, calm. All's arranged—"

"It occurs to me that these'll be overlooked, if publicity's intended," I said; the veins along Leverett's temples throbbed, as if he'd been running. "Are environads designed? Online services? These prints are nothing."

"These prints are my idea, Isabel," he said. E said nothing; eyed us as I proceeded.

"And thirty years ago they'd have sufficed," I said. "The public's mediaed out, Leverett. It seems to me that there should be a plan for directly entering info into those sectors of the public you wish to influence, otherwise they'll never pick it up. My point's seen, isn't it?"

"All's under control," Leverett repeated, stating it with such surety that I knew it couldn't be so. "Unconcern yourself and we'll continue."

"I was advocating, no more," I said. "If everything's controlled, then all should go as desired." Leverett sighed; stared at me a moment longer than I would have expected before continuing to speak to E.

"It's essentialled we reveal you within a performance medium," he said. "Our London office will arrange a suitable setup before departure. Cast aside fear of being sewn into one of those jumpsuits, Elvis. At present an earlier look, your own, should probably suffice as required."

"Good, 'cause I told you I wasn't gonna wear one a those gladrags." E glanced my way; by his look I gathered that he was enjoying our contrarying Leverett so much as I was; Leverett, sandwiched between us, appeared not to notice our delight, and continued relating his scheme.

"We'll see each sight in turn," he told E. "Now, practice essentials in prepping you to onstage. No speeches'll be necessary, the first time out. Later we'll supply you with appropriate phrases and answers to those concerns your people may have—"

"They're not my people," E said. "They're his."

"They're Dero, as it were—" I offered.

"I'm gonna be singin'?"

"I have a playlist readied," Leverett said.

"Songs I like or songs that he useta sing?"

"What's familiar is always best appreciated."

"Not if I don't like it," E said, standing up and retrieving the guitar Dryco had provided him. He strummed the strings, breaking one; though the instrument appeared acoustic, the sound was electric. "Lemme play somethin' I'm good at. I know a song 'bout London. Give you a' idea a what I can do."

"We know what you can do, Elvis, we've heard and seen you—"

"You mean you heard and seen him," E said. "Just sit there and listen. If I'm the one singin', I oughta have a say. Right, Isabel?"

I nodded; Leverett stared at me, and I shuddered as his smile returned. As E began playing his chords I realized that he played so well as he sang. Mayhap he'd listened to his counterpart's sounds long enough to realize not only what he could do, but grasped as well that he might do better. When E sang he sounded as Elvis might have, and did on the earliest records, as if he'd dropped into the studio from another world, neither ours nor his.

> *"They call me the rude, the rambling boy,*
> *To London city I made my way,*
> *And lost my money at ball and play."*

"Not all of the songs playlisted were done by your counterpart," Leverett interjected, seizing a pause in the airspace, "but those that weren't suit the image. Have you ever heard 'Teen Angel'—?"

> *"I found me there a darling wife,*
> *I loved her dearly as my life,*
> *She made me rob, and murder and steal."*

E fixed his look on me as he sang, playing to no other, uncaring that we weren't alone in the room. Against all expectation or reason I felt myself soften. It possibled that I'd adjusted to him as the weeks passed; could have been that the control I knew I had over him, the power which I'd never had over my husband, strengthened me enough that I sensed my own soul's urgings as they evidenced pure, and not moments later, after my mind had time enough to reinterpret their meaning. When E stared at me now, caressing his guitar strings as he might have caressed his girlfriend, I not only at last understood his figurative attraction but felt it, as well.

> *"Now I am condemned to die,*
> *For me a many poor girl will cry,*
> *But all their tears won't set me free."*

Our trip had drawn John and me closer together, after all. We were bearing in toward one another again so inexorably as a missile returns, in time, to earth; but in our heaven I saw no sign that we could in any way forestall such a mutually attractive destruction. As I listened to E sing I outbodied for an instant, allowing my soul to drift away for a time that it might commingle with one I hadn't known. It wasn't truly E with whom I fancied conjoining, or so I hairsplit; my dream lover only showed in his shell, surrounding a center partly my husband's, partly my own.

> *"All young men, be warned by this,*
> *Never take up with a feisty twist,*
> *She'll see you hang on the gallows tree."*

E smiled, concluding his song and laying aside his guitar. Leverett rolled his hands together, sliding them one over the other, as if he'd become slippier while sitting there. "It's a feelgooder, sure," he said. "We'll go with my suggests, I think. Your public knows what it wants. Trust me."

* * *

"Not all of my pieces have been displayed," said Tanya, as she escorted me into her largest. "I call this one 'Wailing Wall: You've Seen Me Before.' "

After leaving E I'd had myself driven to Tanya's studio in Riverdale, having appointed to meet her and see her works closehand. Judy provided her with an old house overlooking the Hudson River and the Palisades, a mansion once occupied as all in the neighborhood had been occupied by a Home Army officer; twenty years of green paint flaked from its exterior, snowing onto the grass, showing as healthy weeds against the sunbroiled yard. Inside, we walked between double rows of quarter-meter-square metal boxes, stacked twice so high as our heads. Each box bore on its rusted face a photo of what appeared, at first, to be a sleeping baby; in many instances, even after applying close eye, it remained unimaginable that the baby shown was truly dead.

"Each box carries one lost. A reinterpretation of Boltanski. Are you familiar with memorial photography?"

"No," I said. Most images were funeral shots, head-on polaroids snapped precremation; others were older, including some tintypes from a century and a half before, so old that their surfaces were as one with their boxes.

"Most popular during the nineteenth century. Popular again at the end of the twentieth, when so many began dropping. A nineties specialty, the sort of thing you'd expect from that period." The two walls were spaced far enough apart that our shoulders barely brushed them as we singlefiled through; their lengths mazed through the house's ground floor, running over forty meters. "Memory pictures, all. Shadows of ones lost."

"So many of them appear so—"

"Normal?" she asked. "Fatal deformities rarely ambient overtly. Ten percent of these pictured, for example, died from being born lungless."

I stared at a shot of a windowed coffin constructed for two; the heads of a seeming couple were visible within, and I wondered if theirs was a physical or metaphorical juncture. "Their beauty isn't immediately seeable, even by those who believe they appreciate fetal art. This homes it a bit too close for most, I fear."

Small white lights affixed to the top of the walls cast enough glow to illuminate each photo. "You know their backgrounding histories?" I asked.

"I try. Someone should remember," she said. "The oldest images are anonymous, needless to say. But they're not forgotten, only lost. And these are mine, in the last row."

She gestured toward the boxed images of her nonviabled children; most had been recognizably recycled. I counted fourteen boxes. "Only four were fullterm. Five births were multiple. They're all still with me." Tanya switched off her piece's lights, and guided me across the room toward stairs.

"How did you choose the fathers—?"

"At random," she said as we ascended. "As circumstanced; they're rather inessential once the spark is thrown. Serve as seeds of ideas, as it were. Here we are." At the head of the stairs were high double oak doors; sliding them apart, she opened her studio. "Ignore, sweetie, we're occupied." Tanya's daughter stood atop a rolled plastic tube on the room's far side, placing small bones into a screened wooden frame, sprinkling sparkling powder over them with a sifter. While glittering their lengths she periodically lifted a femur or rib or vertebra, holding them up in sunlight to better judge their shine. The house's upper floor was cathedral-ceilinged, open from gable to gable; the walls facing the river were glassed. The sun, setting over Jersey, ambered the room. Tanya told her coffeemaker to pour us two cups, and we sat in two wicker rockers; she crossed her legs beneath her as her cat hopped into her lap.

"You were at the Columbia show, then?" she said. "It so successed. Forgive my not remembering you."

"Of course," I said. "I'd heard of the movement, but hadn't seen your work before."

"That was our first show, aboveground," she said. "Until Ms. Glastonbury began assuring security, public exhibition involved passing through gray areas. We've had no troubles since." She nodded toward her daughter. "What a worker. How's the look, sweetie?"

Her daughter hoisted an armbone no longer than a pencil, twirling it as if it were a baton; excess glitter spilled floorways. "Like this?"

"That's lovely, sweetie," Tanya said. "Many of my co-workers who lack studio space leave their materials here, and we appropriately treat them as desired. We're all quite close." She smiled. "Ms. Glastonbury tells me you're pregnant."

"My first month," I said. "Perfect, thus far."

"That's correctable. What procedures would you prefer to use?"

"That's not why I'm here."

"Of course. I'm sorry." Mayhap all who came to her claiming such employed that line at first, to detrepidize themselves; Tanya appeared to understand, and redirected our conversation. "My work speaks to you?"

"It shouts, but I don't know what it says."

"Keep listening."

"How did you . . ." I started to ask. "Why did you? Begin, I mean."

"My husband ran fourteen years ago, when we lived in Chicago," she said. "I found out I was pregnant afterward, and had neither money nor contacts to effect abortion. The Health Service amnioed me and forecast the stillbirth. I dayshifted all the while at a plant that manufactured car batteries. You can imagine the conditions. I still spew dust each morning. One evening when I got off there was a sandstorm and the El was shut down. A woman cabbie heading into town offered me a free ride. I was in my seventh month, and showed plain. She asked if I was having any trouble. I flooded, but couldn't say why. We stopped at a diner and I talked to her. Harangued, rather. Cursed the man who'd planted and flown. Cursed the government that demanded I birth the dead. Cursed the world that, through its poisons, guaranteed my baby's death so long as it was bound inside me. She said she understood. I cried again.

"Her name was Dianne. She led me into the diner's restroom. I remember hearing the rats scratching in the walls as she lifted her shirt. She'd had a caesarean; she'd tattooed a short-stem rose on her scar. She pushed her hair back from her head, and flashed her earrings. They looked like golden insects at first, but when I looked closer I saw that they were little hands. Diane told me that there were some women she thought I should meet.

"I went to see them the next week at her apartment, in an old building on North Clark Street. She'd stuffed the windows with towels to keep the sand out. There were five others besides Dianne. All'd gone to term after they'd been left pregnant, and all birthed at home. They'd insighted independently, they told me; afterward, realizing what they could do, they sought out others in whom they perceived . . ." Tanya paused; sipped her coffee while she considered her words. She gazed over toward her daughter before continuing. "You can't prettify violence and waste solely for aesthetic's sake, something more is needed. So what we do is take the rage the violence arouses and make of its leavings something bright, and strange enough to be familiar.

"Much more than this. Mind me, dear, you'll love the baby you grow all the more, knowing it'll live only while it's in you. It could be a nine-month funeral, if you negatived. But these days so many would say the whole of life is but a wake where the beloved can finally hear what's said about them behind their backs. So . . ." With callused hands she wiped her eyes; tabled her emptied cup. "So we found ourselves. None of us were art majors. Later the theoreticians deciphered what we'd folked. They semiograph us, but we

won't reply. All we know is that we were damned if we
birthed simply to bury. Our children deserve better than
that. In this manner we endow the life we were unable to
give."

"You outbodied your daughter, all the same—"

"Memories have their house," she said, looking around
her studio. "But art doesn't propagate so well as life. Do you
see? If I'd not undertaken these designs of mine, I wouldn't
have wanted so badly to have a child who would. Nor been
able to afford having her. In my art I try to aestheticize the
nonaesthetic. Silkpurse sows. Wrap fur on parking meters. I
make bearable pain I've known, for others if not always for
myself. I don't believe that's often understood, and rarely
appreciated." She sighed. "Critics."

"I appreciate."

"That's good. It's a holistic erosion, after a time. Retirement essentials. My final project is in progress at present,"
she said, patting her stomach. "I awared Ms. Glastonbury of
my decision before she gifted me with this studio. She
thought it a pity, but then suggested I continue casting new
works using plastic, or similar material." Tanya shook her
head, and smiled. "As said, I don't believe my work's intent
is often understood."

"But Ms. Glastonbury understands enough at least to lend
support to your work—"

"True. And as head of Dryco, that is to say the government
and the world and all its works, Ms. Glastonbury as well
continues to assure that fetal art has to be done. Irony
redoubles when good's made from bad." Her chair creaked
as she leaned back in it; her cat leapt floorways and padded
to its bowl of scraps. "If you reconsider before your third
month, call me. I'll guide you as I can."

"No," I told her. "I want my baby."

"I wanted mine."

* * *

The TVC played sans sound in our apartment when I came home that evening; each window's curtains were drawn against the dark without, all lights were switched on to brighten the rooms within. "John?" I called out, expecting an answer; hearing none. As each week passed he'd grown more depressed, saying little, doing less; he'd not gotten out of bed for several days, at least not while I was in the apartment, and all my attempts to comfort or concern futiled as he walled me off along with all others. For the first time since we returned I feared for what I might find, walking through my home. Cat-treading into the kitchen, I glanced through the door, turning my head away as quickly, praying to Godness I wouldn't spy him hanging there along with the garlic strands, or resting floorways with weapon at hand, afloat in his red sea.

"John?"

He wasn't there; all looked as per usual. Glasses filmed with remnants of the liquids they'd held filled the sink, the dishtowel was tossed on the table, an emptied icetray rested atop the refrigerator. The silverware drawer was open; walking over, looking in, I saw that all the knives were missing.

"Are you here, John? John?"

Mayhap he was asleep, and hadn't heard my call. I stepped into the short hall that ran between our bedroom and the living quarters, hesitating for several moments before crossing the bathroom's threshold. Reaching around the doorframe, I switched on the light; sighed as I stared inside and saw the shower door open, and visible emptiness within. His bathrobe lay near the tub, where he'd dropped it.

"John," I said again, and moved toward the bedroom. "John?" Our door was partly ajar; my hand trembled as I brushed my fingers against the wood, pushing it open. I could see my breath as I entered, and so found the wallswitch and lowered the AC. On our unmade bed's rumpled sheets rested our wedding album, a heavy blue folder housing a player and all that we'd been, preserved on disk. The dressing table was undisturbed; there was nothing in our closet that shouldn't have been there. Not even mice gave life to our room. My knees shook so that I could no longer stand; I sat on the bed, holding my head in my hands as I allowed myself recovery time. Adrenaline charged my system, pounded my heart, throbbed my head. John's copy of *Knifelife* lay open, facedown on the nightstand. Picking it up, I saw marked pages revealing a section entitled "What is Your Job?" Its opener read: *You are the devil and you come to do devil's work.*

I stood up and moved across the room to shut the door while I disrobed. As I started to close it I saw the kitchenknives embedded deeply in the wood, grouped at eyelevel in a tight circle. I gathered he'd thrown them there while sitting, or lying on the bed. Looking beneath their lengths to their wood-fixed target I gleaned what remained of the wedding picture he always kept with him. The door started to open; I fell back onto the bed, trying to shout; found that I couldn't speak, as if all my words were stolen from me.

"Iz—?" John asked as he walked in. I noticed a bloodspot at the corner of his nose; his shirtcollar was torn. His hands steamed in the room's cold air. "Iz, you're shivering. Are you AO?" I backed away from him as he approached, and I gripped my hands, trying to stop their shake. "What is it? What's troubling?"

"Where've you been?"

"A walk," he said. "As ever, it uncertained what time you'd home it. So I went walking. Nothing more."

"Why did you do that?" I asked, pointing toward the crown of knives in our door. "That's us, John. On our wedding day. Why? *Why?*" He sat near me, clasping his smoking hands before him in his lap.

"I mindlost, Iz," he said. "Forgive me. Something flared and I seized. I jealoused. Once I started I tossed them all. I'll repair—"

"Irreparable!" I shouted, beginning to cry. "That's us,

John, that's us. Why? I came home, you'd left no note, I
didn't know—"

"Please, Iz, forgive—"

"You'd exed yourself, for all I knew. Then this is what's
found. This is what you think now? Is it—?"

"No . . ."

"Then why?"

John stared at the knives in the door, blinking as if suddenly recalling that someone else had put them there. He
touched my shoulder with his hand; I pulled away. "I'll not
harm you, Iz."

"You harmed my picture—"

"Our picture," he said. "I jealoused. Forgive me. I miss
you so—"

"I'm here every night," I said. "I want to be here. I did, at
least . . ."

He stretched out on the bed, pressing his face into his
pillow as if he might suffocate himself with it; he evidenced
no sob, showed no rack, but I knew my husband's moods
and knew as well his hurt was true. All the same I froze,
unable to comfort, this time as never before fearful of the
manner in which he might choose to assuage his pain. A
metallic perfume clung to him, the scent of copper coins.
This was it, mayhap; still, however my emotions overwhelmed, my headache would not go away.

"I was unnerved, John. I expected you'd be here."

"I expected you wouldn't be," he said.

"Where were you?" I asked. "What did you do?"

"A walk, as told," he said, not turning to look at me.
"Rage overwhelmed, Iz. Something had to be done. It had
to be."

"What something?" He didn't answer. "I can't bear this,
John, it has to end—"

"Mutual," he said, and then silenced. I sat with him until
I was sure he was asleep, and of little harm to either of us;
then, rising, got up and walked into the living room and

made myself a place on the couch. Unplugging the TVC to assure that it wouldn't switch on by itself in the night, I lay down, propping my head against the throws, hoping that the throb would lessen enough that I too might sleep. I drifted in and out of halfsleep, eventually settling; but each time I remembered our picture nailed against the door I felt a new knife slip into my head.

9

□

The next morning I had a dream as I awoke. No sooner had I come to consciousness than most of its details raced from my memory, but I recalled being in an elevator; my blond hair lifted up from my neck as the car descended. E and John attended me as the door slid open; they held my arms with steaming hands, escorting me into a cavern. Metal filing cabinets stood as stalagmites all around. My men turned toward me and grinned; they'd lost their teeth. I noticed they wore yellow lapel buttons imprinted with the letter D. They lifted me off the floor of the cavern and threw me upward, high into its vault. As I descended I saw them waiting below me; awakening, I opened my eyes, and saw nothing.

By one that afternoon I'd been treated and then bedded in recovery at Montefiore. They'd anesthetized me during the procedure; coming to, I saw my husband near. He'd brought me to the hospital after hearing me scream for him that morning.

"I'm unblinded—" I said; it hurt so much to hear myself as it did to speak, and I quieted again. After a moment more I'd adjusted to the lingering ache that rattled my head, and spoke anew to John. "What happened to me?"

My husband appeared in angel's guise, whiteclad from crown to toe; when he replied, the mask so filtered and distanced his voice that it sounded as if it came from across a seance table, and for an instant I wondered if I'd died. The notion that heaven might resemble a hospital room seemed only natural.

"You're viabled, Iz," he said, reaching through the noninfective shield overhanging my bed, sliding his arm into the attached infold that he might stroke my hand with lastexed fingers. "Thank Godness. They said you'd be able again, after. I didn't believe. I thought you were leaving without me."

"What happened?"

"Calm yourself, Iz. Healing's ensuing. You'll be out by nightfall, they say."

"What happened to my eyes?" I asked. "Why couldn't I see?"

"Not your eyes," he said. "They attempted explanations. Claimed the diagnostician wasn't programmed to spot what showed. It's burned away now, you're treated—"

"My baby—?"

"No," he said, pulling his arm out of its enclosure, leaving me untouched. "Your headache's source. Once they doped you they scanned, and read a tumor. Behind the prefrontals, pressing against the optic nerve. Now it's gone."

"I was cancered?"

"You were," he said. "No longer. Love, Iz. I love you—"

"Known," I said. "What caused it? They're telling?"

"They're investigating."

"We have to talk, John," I said, recalling the previous night's events.

"We will. Meanwhile, I'll comfort. I'll nurse. Forgive me, Iz."

There wasn't reason enough yet not to; the tent's translucence prevented me from seeing his eyes' light as he spoke. "Forgiven. We still need to talk—"

"We will," he said. "We will, later. Rest, Iz. Rest."

Some time afterward I read of a child's brain tumor which, when biopsied postmortem, was found to contain within itself the seeds of seven tiny siblings who'd lost their way in utero. Nothing in fetal art matched such a spectacular, if small-scaled, performance. That afternoon, long before I heard of such findings, I insighted, and imagined my own twin unisoned within me without my knowledge, seeking solace in my head; I'd wondered why it had taken so long to let me know it was there, and then I wondered how its debut might have been assisted.

Several days later, once my outpatienting was done, I went to see Judy. "They've not IDed the likely agent, or they're not telling?" she asked; bells tinkled, counterpointing her words.

"Either's likely," I said, touching my head, tracing my scar, fingering my stubble. They'd shaved me to prevent laserburn during the operation. Leverett had several wigs forwarded to the hospital, blond mops of varying lengths; I preferred my nubbiness, and so went naked, topside. "Mayhap I'm sideshowing paranoia—"

"Paranoia has its place," Judy said. "Here's what's found thus far. The clinic's mum on Melaway. Your doctors are even more evasive than mine. Montefiore claims the Brixton studies are at present inaccessible. Alice won't rape their network, or won't tell if she has. My labbies inhouse are unfamilared with the candy he gave you direct, though they estimate it no more than an accelerator. The problem, they say, is that pinpointing the origin of tumors is like spotting the first cloud to rain in a hurricane. As ever, truth is lost amid fact."

"As ever—"

"They were able to ID the pills he gave your husband," she said. "They contained an unpronounceable which, as you hunched, nullified the regooding medication. That was mixed with an amphetamine base. He was lightspeeding, likely, throughout your trip."

"His behavior, then," I said. "Doesn't that explain his actions? Is he to be held responsible—"

"That partially explains his actions," Judy said. "But it's unquestioned to my mind that Leverett would have known. I'm sure as well he was awared of what he gave you might do. Astonishing that your husband could behave at all, as it circumstances." She handed me a sheet of printout initialled with her chop. "Ergo, he's reinstated. This'll ease him from your house with greater ease. If you'd told me Leverett was serving as pharmacist to you earlier, this might have been prevented."

"Or we might have not returned," I said. "Will Leverett suffer for this?"

"Your husband's actions demanded punishment, however situationed," she said. "Leverett's accomplished at smoothing trails. If direct correlation is made between his knowledge of Melaway's dangers, if any, and his approval of your treatment, I'll have him. Otherwise, his deniability holds."

"You can't intercede—?"

"He forwards data through Alice every morning," she said. "She passes his tales on to Seamus sans footnote or critique. Leverett's predecessor oversaw Alice's programming, and he evidently awared Leverett of data entry methods that circumvent all guards, ours or hers. Seamus, of course, deafens to me still regarding this. I closet a hope that she's logicked the plan through and presently strings Leverett along with so much rope that he'll eventually hang."

"He's addling," I told her. "The eyes show it. He's ad-hocking as he goes—"

"From the start Leverett's earplayed this one step ahead of the game and no further," she said. "He'll trip, soon. Then he'll be had." She paused; shook her head, and eyed me. "Unless his footing holds. He is an accomplished dancer. It racks me to think of what this company could be, if half my time wasn't spent thwarting others' schemes. The structure inheres such, I suppose." She spoke with the voice of one suffering thirty years' additional wear to what she truly held. That morning she evidenced a sense that, having worked lifelong to terraform a world, she'd discovered on the seventh day that the wrong world had been redone. "I'll truth you, Iz. He's rounded me leftright." She stared at the Drydens, backgrounded by bells. "He's secreting what he tells Seamus, and Seamus isn't saying. Seamus claims I'm obsessing when I bring the matter up, and then speaks to me only of lost days. He shares his anecdotage with me, but no more."

"Leverett's feigning strength," I said. "He has to be—"

"What of his homunculus? Is he approaching a terminal state?"

"All signs are there save collapse," I said. "Soon now, I think."

She extended her arm, alongsiding it near mine, contrasting my darkness with hers; again, I was no longer lighter than she was. "You've turned considerable this week. Have you seen him since the op?"

"No," I said. "This afternoon I do. He's one of his world, Judy. I'll show as animal in his eyes hereafter, and Leverett'll lose control—"

"For you he'll bestialize, Iz," she said. "Bet me."

"There's no love there."

"There's something, I gather," she said. "Should I have stayed with Seamus after I no longer had to? How much did

you once have in common with your husband that you no
longer do?"

"I've not looked," I said, lying; our differences of late
didn't trouble me so much as our similarities. "Even once
we're split we'll stay joined so long as our baby lives—"

"Your baby's what's shattered you, I'd say," she said. "Yet
you've convinced yourself otherwise. Your Elvis will overlook
much as well, however you show. Nothing's twisted so easily
as reality so long as you've reason to bend it."

"We'll see . . ."

"We will. That's this project's downfall, it can't contain the
realities drawn for it. Regooding's downfall as well, I believe."

"Regooding's your plan, I thought," I said. "You doubt its
success—?"

"It was Leverett's plan," she said. "His initial proposal to
Seamus. There are merits inherent, certainly. Our guards
always seemed too anxious to slip into praetorian skin so
long as the tailoring favored them. Leverett convinced me of
the need for doing with our guards as we have. Doing away
with them, I should say."

"They're people, Judy," I said. "My husband—"

"Those with whom they dealt were people." she said.
"Seamus and me are people, too. But when the moment
came, we struck. Where would we be, were that to happen
now? You'd be here, mayhap, in the driver's seat, landing as
I landed. Your husband was in prime position once, you
know, had he keened to act."

"He's honorable," I said. "He—"

"We were honorable. It's mooted, in any event. There is
an idea I've had, however. Would you care to give ear?"

"What is it?"

She pressed one of the buttons on her desk; headcocked
as if to hear whispers in another room, and then switched off
the control. "All's clear. It evidences to me that your husband's treatment seems not to have taken even prior to

Leverett's fudging. Now that he's reinstated he'll be fully accessed once more—"

"That's so," I said, lowering my voice as she did. "Detail."

"Praetorians, too, had their place," she said. "I shouldn't think he's overfond of Leverett."

"You're suggesting—?"

"Nada," she said. "I've let you read my mind, nothing more. Once he's repositioned, if he's uncontrolled—"

"He'd suffer consequences if such occurred," I said.

She nodded. "Settling both our problems."

"I'll not participate," I said. "John's not the same as he was, he's not—"

"Old habits don't die, Iz," she said. "They settle mudways until rain flushes them out again. The bottle cries for its alkie. The needle beseeches its junkie. The razor beckons its slasher. All are as before, in time. But mayhap you know him best. And as noted before, your course serves you, whichever way it turns."

"It's my old job I want," I said. "Nothing more—"

"And you'll have it again, once I'm in charge and Leverett's not," she said. "Our earplay ongoes." She patted my back; only rarely since childhood had Judy worked me in such manner as to make me feel as a conspirator, however guiltless I may have been. "I'm sure you're telling me all you hear."

There was no meeting that morning; Leverett was alone in his office. Guards slouched against the hallwalls outside, picking at their skin, nodding as I passed, their presence awaring me that E was somewhere near. Leverett's look melted when he saw me; his smile downturned and he lowered his eyes. "I've questions, Leverett. Answer me."

"Isabel," he said, "you're black."

"Sans doubt," I said, sitting on one of his office's hard chairs. "That's all you can say?"

"Did those wigs arrive?" he asked. "He's not doing well today, Isabel, when he sees you as you are that could tip it—"

"Did you know?" He pushed himself further away from me, rolling back, bumping against the wall behind his desk. "You're awared of where I've been, I take it."

"We prayed for you," Leverett said. "Recovery's assured in these cases, I'm informed. Problems are at more immediate hand, Isabel, we have to—"

"I'm not gened for cancer," I said. "Does Melaway tumor? You'd know, even if you've not told. Does it?"

"Please excuse me, Isabel, I'm so preoccupied at present. Your look will send him spiraling, do you know that?"

Rising, I spat in his face; as he sat there, openmouthed and dripping, I got up and walked around his desk, gripped his chair-arms and slammed him back against the wall as he sat there. He appeared more frightened than affronted, swiping himself dry with his handkerchief as I stood over him. His room's cameras recorded all; I didn't care what they saw.

"Does Melaway tumor?" I replayed. "Answer, please."

"You perceive a connection?"

"You don't?"

"If I were the sort who perceived connections, I might," he said. "Ours is a carcinogenic age, Isabel. I've been cancered three times, everyone gets it. Thank Godness yours was treatable—"

"Do you know?" I asked. "Did you?"

"You're hystericked, Isabel," he said, his smile returning. "Inhale slow and steady. Calm yourself. Calm—"

"You knew what Melaway would do to me before I started taking it, didn't you?"

"What's your context?" he asked. "Please, Isabel, communication's impossible when one's irrational—"

"Contexted in that I took what was given to me and now I'm cancered," I said. "You assured my safety."

"The doctors assured me," he said. "If they misinform, where's truth to come from?"

"What of the pills you gave John? You had to know what was in those. You doubledealed us, Leverett." Mayhap he believed he mimed benevolence as he shadowed his face with concern, eyeing me as I'd seen him eye Judy, looking my way as if observing, from a distant room, a particularly difficult patient. "You assured their safety, and then suspended John for actions taken while influenced by what you'd given him—"

"We took every option to guarantee your safety before you left," he said, his voice so even as an announcer's once again. "A week prior to your departure our experts statisticked me. Predicted your odds of returning at more than fifty to one."

"And you sent us anyway?" I said. "Two to one, we were told."

"I was informed that were John to be allowed reentry into his pre-regooded state for the duration, that was what the readjusted odds would become. So did I have a choice? These decisions aren't overnighters, Isabel. My concern for you led him astray, Isabel. I apologize for that."

"What about what I was given—?"

"Isabel, please. If Melaway produced the tumor, and that remains unproven, then I regret it and all that remains to be said is, it's treated. We have to move on."

There was neither reason to believe nor disbelieve what he told me; his tales readapted themselves to circumstance the moment they left his mouth. Once, during our trip's preparation, I was awared of a particular theory regarding parallel worlds, one holding that whenever a person made any decision, or performed any chosen action, the immediate result was to create at that moment a new, literal world in which all thereafter occurred differently than it would have, had any other choice been made. The concept of such ongoing fractalization of existence befuddled me, but the notion that Leverett made for himself and all around him a fresh reality with his every passing thought homed the theory as nothing else could.

"As for John," he continued, "his suspension will end once I've convinced Madam to agree. It was at her insistence, you know. She feels so strongly about regooding she's not always . . ." He tapped the side of his head with his finger. "I'll handle. Don't worry."

"I won't," I said, conscious of my husband's reinstatement tucked inside my bag, secluded amid wallet and mirrors and the compact Judy had given me; I estimated I'd lipstill, to wait and see how Leverett might develop this fantasy he proffered. "Where's E? Let's let him see me."

"We have him secured," he said. "It essentialled. Since you've been hospitaled he's lost all control. Sabotaging our program. Insisting upon singing as he wishes, appearing as he wants. His role's a given but he refuses to take it."

"He can't be presented as he is?"

"There're complications," Leverett said. "And even though he's facialed right, and his voice matches if not betters, he and the image aren't coinciding."

"To your mind, mayhap. Elvii might believe differently. You yourself said they'd see him as they want—"

"But they need to see him as *we* want," he said. "He's nonresponsive to that. You're needed, Isabel. You can keep him online." Leverett sighed as he eyed me updown again, frowning at my rehued features, my short black hair. "You could before, at any rate. You should reconsider, Isabel—"

"Reconsider what? Even if I wanted to I wouldn't take Melaway again—"

"No connection is proven," he said. "Reapplication of the treatment shouldn't be ruled out so hastily—"

"It is," I said. "Where is he?"

"Two doors down. Come on. Let's hope he's glad to see you."

Leverett preceded me as we halled ourselves. I thought it odd that I'd not noticed before that he was shorter than me;

then, studying his stance, I realized that his slump had great-
ened in the months since the project underwayed. While his
face remained stained with youth, his body showed every day
of his years. We asided the guards, gently pushing them back
until they came to rest against the walls alongsiding the
door. "Alone, Leverett," I said. "I want to see him alone.
Don't come in until I say."

"Agreed," he said, rapping knuckles against the door.
"Elvis? Someone's here to see—"

"Let me outta here!" E shouted back. "I've had it with
this. I've had it—"

"What's being done to him?" I asked. "Leverett—"

"Seclusion, nothing more," he said. "Allowing him time
to think."

"Get me out!" E cried again. "I can't stand—"

Leverett stepped away, that I might enter; laying his hand
on the nearby panel, he pressed the door's opener, and it
slid away. The windowless room they had him in lacked
furniture, save one chair. The moment I heard the top-
volumed soundtrack issuing from the ceiling's speakers I
realized what was being done to E. During Elvis's final years,
in his Old Pretender phase, an album was released that
contained nothing but stage remarks offhandedly muttered
between songs in concert, tossed out to his audiences while
he tried, seemingly, to remember where he was and what he
was supposed to be doing. No preserved text of the King was
so beloved by most sects of the C of E, save the most funda-
mental, as these mumbles; no other album in his oeuvre was
so torturous for the nonbeliever to hear.

"Well," Elvis was saying, sixty years earlier. "Well well well
well well."

The jumpsuit they had E wearing was Dryco yellow, of
shining fabric fused and cut along trad lines. The outfit's
padding thickened his waist until he appeared thirty kilos
heavier; his belt looked to weigh so much as I did, and
fastened with a buckle guised with the look of our logo. His

suit's pantslegs widened so below his knees as to hide his shoes, the collar rose so high as his crown; E appeared to be badly waterproofed, and beginning to shrink. Not even Elvis had ever looked so ridiculous.

"Look at these little red things," said Elvis.

"They've clowned you," I started to say to E; paused as I grasped the degree of his own disconcertion. "It's me." As he wordlessly mouthed, attempting to speak, I readied to hear anything he might call me, thinking nothing much could hurt, issuing from such a figure; thinking that at this point, nothing much from anyone could hurt. "You've cat-tongued. Talk."

"You're a—"

"I am. What of it?"

E sidled closer to me, edging over as if ready to run had there been anywhere to run. Holding out his hands, he drew them back as quickly, seeming to fear that my touch might tar him. The faceted glass sewn into his suit sparkled so as to leave my eyes afterimaged. For a moment more we stood apart, looking at one another; I thrust out my lower lip, not to seduce but to threaten. That did it; stepping forward, his pants rustling like a taffeta slip, he embraced me. His belt buckle pinched as it dug against my stomach.

"They told me you were sick," he said. "I was afraid you were gonna die on me."

"Not yet," I said.

His face crumpled, as if someone thoughtlessly had wadded it to toss away; before he could rein in his tears he made faint groans that sounded nothing other than words freed from the oppression of meaning. "You all're worse'n Dero," he said. "What the hell're you people doin' to me?"

"E . . ." I pried myself from his clutch, grasping his shoulders as he swayed, hoping to keep him upright. "How long have you been in here?"

"Last night," he said. "How'm I supposed t'know what's straight around here? I can't even tell what y' are—"

"I got wired the wrong way," said Elvis.

"My look so offends?" I asked. "I'm Isabel, all the same. This is as I am."

"I can't take this. I can't. How'm I supposed t'believe anything you say?"

"I'm showing you truth."

"Yeah, today. What about tomorrow? Or the day after that? Then what'll y'be? What'll y'have me doin' then?"

"I'll be what I am," I said. "I don't know what you'll be doing. I'm not the juggler here."

"This is really what you are?" he asked, stepping back, drying his face with the back of his hand, taking care not to scratch himself with the bracelets with which he was wristed. "I mean—"

"It bothers you that I'm black?" I asked.

"No wonder y' didn't like me sayin' nigger," he said, his perfect obliviousness seeming to return to him as he calmed. "Why'd you make yourself up like you was white?"

"If I'd shown as I am, what would have happened to me in your world?" I asked. "What would you have done, over there?"

He lowered his head; for an instant I thought he prepped to withdraw it inside his collar, and so hideaway from me. "I'm not like the rest of 'em," he said. "It wasn't right, what they did. It wasn't right."

"Nor is this," I said. "What's thought, then?"

"About you? Like this?" I nodded. "You're still you, aren't you?"

"I think so."

"That's good enough for me, then. You gotta stay with me, Isabel. I don't know what's up or down around here."

"Didn't know you was going to see a crazy man," said Elvis, "did you? Well well well well—"

"They've been playing this nightlong?" I asked. E grimaced.

"Never stops," E said. "He musta been crazy by the time they got through with him. He musta been."

"Leverett," I called out, turning and shouting behind me, marveling that he'd so restrained himself from interrupting us. E cringed, and moved some meters away to one of the roomcorners as the door slid open and Leverett walked in. "Mute it," I said. "Mute it or we're not talking." He reentered the hall and pressed the appropriate switch; Elvis's voice stilled, and only the AC's sound dulled the silence. "Why's he suited so?" I asked. "You promised—"

"They'll have him no other way in England, the London office tells," Leverett said. "There's no roundabouting it. That's what we told him yesterday, but there was no listening—"

"Would _you_ wear it?" I asked.

"He has to," Leverett said. "It's the image, Isabel, it has to be matched. It's a shame but there you are."

"Why can't they have me as I am?" E said, huddling against the walls. Eyeing his suit's decolletage I sighted more clearly his unhaired chest; his musculature ws that of a boy's, and I supposed reconstruction had not ensued below the neck save to effect repairs.

"Elvis," Leverett said, placing one hand on my shoulder, gesturing toward me with his other as if to enumerate my sales points. "Why couldn't you have Isabel as she is?"

"I can have her like that—" E started to say.

"Nobody can have me," I said, jerking away from Leverett's touch, distancing myself from them both.

"The principle holds," Leverett said. "Close in, Elvis. Over here. Come here." E looked at me; saying nothing, I motioned that he should approach, and so settle Leverett before he began offering biscuits. "That's good, Elvis. Now we're awared that the outfit's not as you'd wish—"

"I like clothes much as the next guy but not this shit," E said. "Excuse me, Isabel. You told me flat out I wasn't gonna have t'wear a sissy suit. This's 'bout as sorry as it comes."

"You replayed that timeover, Leverett," I said. "There's much you've told us both that doesn't hold."

"That's unfair, Isabel—"

"May be, but she's right," said E. "You told me I don't haveta wear one of these suits and I'm not goin' to."

"Not until we go to London," said Leverett. "You've no firsthand experience with your followers. You don't understand what they expect."

"They better start gettin' an idea of what I expect, then." My presence, in whatever shade I showed, seemed to recharge E, enabling him to confront Leverett as he'd apparently not been able to while I was gone. It didn't comfort me to see this transpire; that E found in me the spine he lacked, and the resulting support he could take from it, only assured I'd have another remoraed onto me whenever I tried to move.

"I've enough of an idea," Leverett said. "Contract with me, then. One time, that's all that's needed, on opening day. Wear it one time and no more."

"I'll be in public," E said. "People'll see me—"

"That's the *point*. Is anything still misunderstood? You're mountaining this molehill more than it needs."

"One time?" I asked, replaying his words as if by so doing I might record them. Leverett nodded. "E, if that's truth, then I'd think it could stand."

"*You* don't have to wear it, either—"

"It's dealable," I said, looking over the suit's trim, gold piping delineating collaredge and cuffs. "If it's what that audience desires they'll know no embarrassment. You'll send them out smiling." My concluding statement was, I think, a safe assumption.

"Let me sleep on it," E said. "Can I leave here now? I wanta put on something else if I can go."

"You're always unseen in transit," Leverett said. "Can't you—"

"I can't," E said. "I see me. That's one too many."

"Very well," said Leverett. "Your apartment clothes are in the office across the hall. Change there."

"Good—"

"All present are somewhat overtensed, I think. There's something I'd like to show you in the morning. You consider what I've said and we'll further discuss at morningside. AO?"

"You already know what I think," said E. "And I got a say in all this. Isabel told me that."

"Did she?" said Leverett, raising his head as he looked at me. "You have a say, true. We'll talk again tomorrow. Rest this afternoon. Now that Isabel's back with us we can return to our original program."

He nodded to us both and exited. E waited until we heard his footsteps' echo fade before reconversing. "I didn't know what to do when you were gone," he said. "See how quick he gave in while you were here?"

"He's not giving," I said. "He'll contrary, I believe."

"Maybe," said E. "I'm tired of fussin'. I just wanta get back to the hotel."

"You were here all night?" I asked.

"From about eight o'clock on. Didn't tell me what I was gonna be tryin' on till they put it on me. I guess I flipped. They shut me up in here and then after a couple hours, they turned on the phonograph. Didn't sleep a wink last night. Man, Isabel, that was rough."

"E, even when you have your say there's only so much that can be said," I told him. "Bend with the wind when you can, you'll be bettered for it after—"

"Maybe so," E said. "You goin' back to the hotel with me?"

"No," I said. "It essentials I talk to my husband. We've problems to straighten. I'll meet you in the morning before we see Leverett, if possible."

"What problems you all got?" he asked. "He must lose his temper a lot."

"Not really."

"He don't beat you, does he? Seems like the kind who would."

"We beat each other," I said. "Tomorrow, E. Get sleep, dream true."

For some minutes after I gave him his reinstatement paper John said nothing; with eyes so lifeless as a doll's he stared at it as if wishing to divine tomorrow's events from a white, wordless sheet. A scratching sound in our room's walls tickled my ears as we sat on our bed; I fantasized the mice racing through their tunnels, suddenly realizing their lost companion's absence. "What's thought?" I asked, trying to read his moodless face.

"Remember Harvey?" he asked, leaning over and kissing my cheek. "He was a midtown guard—"

"All showed as one after so long, John," I said, grateful that I was unable to contain my emotions so well as he contained his.

"He thirdrailed himself yesterday on the Pelham line," my husband said. "That's seventeen since we returned. There'll be no Security to oversee, soon enough."

"You'll be positioned as before," I said. "With greater pay."

"Doing less," he said. "Enabling others to go preretirement. How'd they ever notion regooding? It's unjustifiable, Iz, we're being hung and dried. Our training condemns us, and *they* had us trained. What's it accomplish—?"

"What they desire, I suppose," I said. "Judy claims Leverett demanded that the guards be treated. He infers that she did."

"Who lies?"

"Both, mayhap," I said. "Judy's no longer trusting me, however much she denies. When I confront her, she sidesteps. And as for Leverett . . ." No sooner had I replayed his name than I regretted it; mentioning him shot into John's

mind remembrances of our trip, might-have-been thoughts
of beginning and end; and to speak of Leverett was to speak
of E. My husband's face sagged as hate galvanized his stare.
"Don't freeze me, John. Reopen."

"Bedaway," he said, reclining, holding his knee as he
lowered.

"I'll not wallshout, John. Look at me." Propping himself
with his elbows, he fullfaced my way as I turned to confront.
"Leverett's my overseer. He's been yours, as well. Whatever
his doings, he has to be named—"

"Leverett's ruined us," he said. "His project—"

"We've ruined us," I said. "You negate the good that's
come from this."

"No good's been brought. None. Worse than none—"

"What's meant?" I asked; he stilled, and looked away from
me. "Do you mean our baby? That's worse than none? Is it?"

"Iz, please—"

"Our baby. Our baby, John. Say it." He tried to stand up;
I pushed him back down onto the bed and leaned across
him, pounding his chest with my fist until my hand hurt. My
husband evidenced neither alarm nor surprise, but only lay
there dispassioned while I iterated what I knew to be truth.
"Ours, not his. Ours. Ours."

"The test essentials," John said. "Why won't you take it?"

"The baby'd suffer the effects, as told—"

"I'm suffering now—"

"Believe me!" I screamed, clasping my hands and slamming them down, beating as if to concave his underlay. He
shifted onto his side, escaping my blows; clamped his arms
around himself, and tried to catch his breath. "Won't you
believe me?"

"It's understandable—"

"I told you he didn't assault me, I told you timeover. If you
don't believe me, can't you even show me disrespect? Can't
you even call me a liar—?"

"It must have terrified, Iz," John said. "I understand—"

"You don't understand," I said, falling away from him, collapsing onto my side of the bed as if I'd been deflated. "He attempted, I defended. Am I helpless, John? Am I?" My husband shook his head. "He tries a kiss, I toss him off and you mindspin into madness—"

"He . . ." John began to say; started running fingers across his chest from shoulder to waist, as if suddenly cognizant that I'd hurt him. "I read his feeling, early on. I jealoused when it seemed—"

"You've been jealousing since, sans reason—"

"It isn't logical, Iz," he said. "They clipped me. If I father, I father death." The lowvoiced, melodramatic tone of his concluding statement made me suspect it was a quote from Jake's book. "But there's no shame, Iz, not with me. I don't want your denials—"

I sighed, staring at the ceiling as if an escape route might yawn in its whiteness; accepted that his mind had concreted, and there'd be no chipping away with truth. "It's our baby, John. Unquestioned."

"It can't be."

"Unquestioned," I said. "John, I love you—"

"Mutual," he said, sitting up, eyeing me as he had whenever our emotions crossed; as if I were Godness and he, a flylike worshiper.

"But I can't live with you anymore, not like this."

John seemed not to have heard me at first, or at least evidenced no sign of understanding; I wished I could run off and hide away from all of them, even run back into that other world. Our world grew all the crueler, the more it regooded; by that evening, I felt regooded unto death.

"A separateness, first," I said. "A trial alone, maybe not forever. If we change we can reappraise, but not for a while. Are you hearing me?"

"Yes," he said, his face so unpassioned that as he spoke he lipstilled, and appeared to have been dubbed. "Why, Iz?"

"We're beached as we are," I said. "You're disbelieving

me. I'm fearing your actions. There's no escaping our jobs and their effect. It's tearing me to see what you're doing to yourself, what we're doing to ourselves—"

"It's deserved—"

"It's not," I said. "I'll talk to you daily, I will. I know I'm hurting you, but you've brought much on yourself. And that's killing me, John. It's unbearable and I can't help you—"

"You've tried," he said. "You don't see how you help me, that's all. You're what keeps me living against reason."

"What I'm seeing's killing me," I said. "Killing me against reason. We have to split, John. You go your way, I go mine—"

"Our way," he said. "I don't want divorce, Iz. I want you."

"Same," I told him; told him in truth.

"Then can't we—"

"Time to ourselves essentials. It's impossibled as matters stand. You're untrusting me and I'm watching you rot. We're imploding and time only waits until we blow apart."

My husband sat on the bed's edge, his reinstatement papers loose in his grip. As I looked his way I thought anew of our time together, its troubles and blessings. Mayhap I should have heeded what Judy told me, years before; but there was no regretting what we'd had, only what it came to. I wondered, idly, if I looked so old as John suddenly did. "I'll do as desired, then," he said, adjusting his knee so that he could stand sans danger of falling. "Forgive, Iz."

"Forgiven," I said. "Let's earplay it, John. We're not disconnected, after all. Only driven apart. When we parent—"

"If we parent," he said. "This is such a world, Iz. Should we assist in its continuance?"

"Yes," I said, uncertain why; knowing it, all the same. "It's our baby . . ." He lowered his head; walked over to the closet. "My baby."

"Yours," he said, slipping on his jacket. "I'll lowroad to-night. The office has space to house me, now that I'm allowed to return. I'll come back at morningside to collect my goods, once you've left—"

"If that's preferred." He nodded. "Forgive, John. It's impossibled, any other way."

"Naught to forgive," he said. "It's as it is."

"You'll not hurt yourself," I said. "Please don't . . ."

He shook his head, and smiled. "You'll know when time comes, Iz. We'll both know."

Walking over to me, he leaned forward and kissed my forehead, shadowing me as his body eclipsed the bedlamp's light. "John," I said, "the evening before I blinded. Where had you been?"

"Walking, as told," he said, fixing his eyes on our door as he readied to leave; seeming to stare at the circle of scars left in its wood. His fruitbag's twist-tie protruded from his pocket.

"What did you do, while walking?"

"Nothing unpredictable," he said, exiting into the hall. John was so accomplished at gansering as E. When I asked, had I wanted truth? For reasons I preferred not to specify I was as glad he hadn't told me. "Good night, Iz."

"Good night." I waited until I heard our apartment door close and lock behind him before releasing; even afterward, once he was gone, I could only impress tears, and not truly cry them. Our break accomplished with such wicked ease; however relieved I was to do it, I'd have never imagined that disposing of so many years could be so matterfactly done. For hours that evening I lay awake, more conscious of presence than of absence; thinking of what had been pulled from my head, wondering how long I could retain what still remained within my womb.

"What you'll see will fascinate, I'm certain," Leverett said as we drove into Manhattan the next morning. He sat in the jumpseat facing us, appearing more keen to observe us than our too-familiar surroundings. "Lookabout, Elvis. Your first trip heartways. This is New York as it was."

"As it is," I said. "There're inhabitants, still."

Leverett nodded; his smile so widened that I could number all his remaining teeth. "You could call them that."

Rivercrossing into Harlem, we southed on Fifth Avenue, far from the more secure Broadway route along the West Side's upper range that we'd taken during our training. E windowgazed, peering through his ski-mask's slots; Leverett insisted he incognito himself whenever he outed. We passed burned-out projects and their surrounding mudflats, strewn with long-lost residents' scattered belongings; fenced round by torched Army PVs and graffitied bus-shells. Our driver swerved us around holes larger than cavern-entrances, appearing deep enough to engulf trucks.

"People still live here?" E asked, staring at flames cornicing a brick cruciform slab on our left; the smoke blackened the rain, inking our car as it fell.

"Many find it preferable," said Leverett. "Our company's long tramped the live-and-let-live path."

A six-meter-high wall borderlined along 110th Street's midst, separating zones no longer, in theory, existing. No guards stopped us to ID as they once would have; razorwire loosened by weather and years dangled down over the ingress, fingernailing our car roof as we scraped below their rusted tangles. The driver, eyeing blockage ahead, wheeled us onto the right sidewalk, steering our car between tree-stumps alongsiding the curb and the park's unclipped foliage. Part of Mt. Sinai's older facade had collapsed streetways, cluttering the lanes. As we returned to the road our driver braked, and we idled. Leverett neckcraned, and eyed forward.

"What is it?" E asked, opening his window, thrusting his ski-masked head outside. He drew it in as quickly. Gazing windowways, looking past the driver, I saw rats cascading in a writhing stream, flowing out of the park as if pipered, their pack bearing eastward down 100th; aiming riverways, as if they intended to lemming. Their chirp was so loud as a birdflock; several minutes passed before all had cleared. "They can't do nothin' 'bout rats?"

"They're needed here," Leverett said; gansered as he continued. "People have to eat."

Central Park's overgrowth cloaked the sidewalk below 96th; a frosting of wet trash overlay the deadleaved bushes, branchbreaking beneath the weight. Across, on our left, rainscarred apartments cliffsided the avenue: from some of their dead eyes curtains fluttered flaglike as they breezed; behind the lids of others light yet flickered, evidencing those yet huddling against morning's dark.

"People still live in these places?" E asked.

"Elderlies, mostly," said Leverett. "They bedmade years ago, and choose to lie there still. They're secured, to a degree."

"They got cops or somethin' watchin' out for 'em?"

"Of a sort. Here, you'll see what's meant. Good thing traffic's light," Leverett said; ours was the only car visible above 72nd Street. "Are we shielded, driver?"

"Tripleplated," the driver said.

"We'll be able to birdseye. Elvis, see that boy? No evidence of deliveries, and it's apparent he's not tenanting there. A miscreant, undoubted. Watch."

The youngster showed no more than teenage years as he skulked along the gutters of 88th Street. After ascertaining we possessed no direct authority he laid a bare foot upon the curb. The ground windows of the nearest building opened; E and I instincted, tossing ourselves floorways when their guns began to fire. Bullets rang as hail against our car, pattering so harmlessly as the soot-soaked rain. Rearising once all quieted again, we spied through our rear window; saw the boy's remains, a reddened bag appearing to have been dropped from a jet.

"Residents code in at distance," Leverett said. "Years ago

these protectives rendered guards as such superfluous, here. The ur-regooding, as it were."

"What happens if you're just passin' by and get shot?" E asked.

"You die, generally," said Leverett.

I reached across and patted E's hand; he pulled it away so quickly as my husband might have. We passed the old Met, emptied since its Bronx megalith opened the year before. Ailanthus greensprouted between the steps, ivy overgrew the marble walls; by decade's end the park would reclaim all acreage once stolen for art.

"Why'd everybody leave?" E asked. "What happened?"

"There were problematic times," said Leverett. "Rough weather, fore and aft. The troubles onwent for so long down as to too well adjust the survivors to a nonregoodable mindset. The physical plant, too, was rotting. The subways are flooded, the bridges falling down. Eye for yourself the look of the roads. Mister Dryden commanded that we relocate north before building afresh. Many thought him mad."

"He *was* mad—" I started to say.

"You lip, but Madam speaks," Leverett said. "Source consider, Isabel. I knew him. Many times we talked. Mister Dryden saw his world unblinkered, and acted accordingly to make of it as he would. Few so capabled as he in recreating existence to suit his dreams."

The old 59th Street wall was gone; the Plaza Hotel, onetime Home Army Midtown HQ, appeared moldstreaked as its green wash peeled away from the brick. A dry fountain stood before its boarded entrance; a dozen lay sleeping in the bowl, blanketed by rain. The buildings passed facaded thirty years of blasts' pockmarks; hundreds camped beneath their scars, some boxed as if for storage. Smoke rising from their fires thickened the clouded air, and as we bore south our vehicle might have appeared as a vision to them, as if while driving we'd Alekhined, or else chanced into a spot where time folded in on itself, moebiusing our car into their present.

"You make people live like this?" E asked. "We wouldn't treat—" Before saying what I was sure he would he paused, so as not to blurt. "We wouldn't treat nobody this bad."

"Evidence infers that you did," Leverett said. "Unmattered. They live like this. We let them live. That's a subtle but clear distinction."

We righted at 50th, swinging wide to avoid fallen streetlights and a van overturned several months earlier. Dryco's old block remained secured as before, although our company guards were supplanted by unregoodable Army boys. I boiled, seeing their fat swaggers with eyes at once thirty years younger; I felt myself swept into another timefold, and again I was one of Washington Heights' myriad smaller targets, fearful of moving between doorway and street while the greenasses marched by. Lengths of printout tumbleweeded across our feet as we sidewalked ourselves and approached the entranceway.

"It's emptied, I thought," I said to Leverett as he slid his card through the entry-slot, unlocking the doors.

"Not entirely."

Our steps rang as multitudes' upon the lobby's unwaxed floor as we moved toward the elevator. Neither AC nor dehumidifier were on; the building stood dead, devoid of circulatory rumbles, awaiting a delayed autopsy. Mildew etched the lobby's murals with fresh, unexpected patterns. Boarding, we ascended thirty-three flights; emerged, and halled ourselves into a long passageway, strolling between rows of stacked desks.

"Yesterday I considered what you said," Leverett began, unclarifying whether he worded us individually or as one. "Informed opinions require a hear-out. Yours, sadly, lacks."

"Don't condescend, Leverett—"

"Forbid, forbid. What's meant is that your confusion's understandable. How can decisions be reached, sans data?"

He shrugged. "Badly, or not at all. So enlightenment neces-
sitates before threat becomes action."

"Detail," I said.

"No action altruistics," Leverett said. "Years past I've
muted timeover, facing disagreement, if I saw a greater purpose served by cat-tonguing. Greater, that is, in being either
larger than oneself, or else most useful to oneself. As the
intent splits between selfishness and concern, so they shortly
curve round to meet at endturn. So when I hear your plaints
I empathize. Still, the wise realize that when subjugation's
moment comes, it shouldn't be missed."

"Where's this leading, Leverett—?"

"Dryco readies to lead society horizonways," he said. "A
bright future awaits. You're part of that future if you choose.
This project essentials for our future in that it enables us to
harness materiel previously untapped; it will enable us, I
should say, once the presentation is made. This project is
more than Dryco sole, Isabel, Elvis. My soul lifes it."

"Understood—"

"All hitherto has only been prep. The moment on-
comes—"

"You're rambling, Leverett," I said. "Concise it."

"Demands suit their place, Isabel," he said, proceeding;
we paced him. "As told, we were aware predeparture that
your return wasn't assured. We improved your odds there,
however little our efforts were appreciated. Certainly there
always existed the chance that you'd not find Elvis there,
once across." Leverett slapped E's back, almost unbalancing
him. "We readied a backup in event Plan A problematicked."

"What manner of backup?" I asked.

"The best available."

We reached the end of the hallway. Leverett fingertapped
the righthand wall; it opened before us, exposing an unfur-
nished room, its windows sealed against the world without as
if assuring the purity of those within. The room contained a

single, centerpieced holding. E took my arm as he saw it; I
didn't note the bruises he'd left until that evening. "Close in.
He won't bite." A freezeframed E garbed in a white jumpsuit
greeted us, its hair and skin semblancing a greater genuine-
ness than E's, its look so mirroring that it shocked me not to
see the thing breathing. The eyes resembled marbles in need
of dusting. "Touch him, Elvis."

"No," E said, backing away from his dupe, examining
himself as if to compare. "You stole me."

"Stole your predecessor," said Leverett. "Plan B, courtesy
of WDI. Art personified and readily programmable. So approximate a perfection as can be presently done."

"If you got this," E said, "what do you need me for?"

Leverett twisted the cylinder-end he held. The Elvisoid's
eyes enlivened; its chest gently heaved, and it took two stiff-
legged steps forward. When it worded its lips matched the
phrases sounded; simulated facial muscles motioned unerringly. "Good morning, Everett," it played, its voice evidencing no more life than a toaster's. Leverett eyerolled, but
made no move to correct its error.

"We had this readied before we even approached you,
Isabel. An approximate perfection, as said. But art demands
the human touch. Televised, it would pass. The construction
is such that its emanations read as flesh once broadcast. The
look tubes well. But personal appearances are essentialled,
and it'll never stand for those. There's naught of emotion in
it, leaving its words unimpacted. So here you are, Elvis.
You're multiblessed with the real feel. It's you we needed."

E drew further away from the Elvisoid; as I read him I
perceived an understandable fear, that were he to come too
close to it he might find himself subsumed into its form
without realizing it. "It's all science fiction. You can't do
this—"

"It's a recent improvement on a classic process," said
Leverett. "As told, it's you we prefer. If our point's grasped,
unconcern yourself. He'll be employed only if you fail us."

"What point're you talkin' about—?"

"You're here to serve as savior, Elvis," Leverett said. "So serve. You're needed. You're wanted. All that we're doing, we're doing for you. Had we left you where you were found, where would you be now?" E turned; walked away from both of us, holding his hands against his ears. "Swinging, rather than singing, I'd suspect. Tennessee would capitalize for murder, surely. That's not the case here, you've seen. We backscratch, you bellyroll. Simply put, simply planned. Your requirements are nil. Your benefits, unsurpassed. Think of us as Dero if you wish, but whatever's seen in our cave, we've preserved you to see it. Now preserve us."

"Who'd you say thinks I'm God?" E asked. "Them or you?"

Leverett deafened, and readied the knife. "Your decision, Elvis. If you trouble the project into impossibility, you'll be made redundant. It's not as wished, but it will be done. Keep minded, too, that as your overseer Isabel shall be considered, if it so events, to have failed along with you."

"What would you do to us?" E asked. "Send me back home?"

"Impossible, Elvis," said Leverett. "This is your home. Allow me correction. If you choose not to assist us as we require, we've a new home for you. We drove through it, coming down."

E wide-eyed as if he'd been charged. "That's not right—"

"All obsolesces," Leverett said. "Timing's all. You've a choice. What's decided?"

E stared at me, as if I could answer for him; seeing I readied no annotation he slumped, and headhung as if he'd been sentenced long before. Leverett handclasped, seeming to pray.

"Any picture suits once the right frame's found," he said, sighing, countenancing unspeakable satisfaction. "Isabel, henceforth you'll word me sole, incompany. If I didn't trust you as I do I'd suspect you must be passing your observations along to Madam. Her perceptions, unaided, have rarely been so keen of late."

"Leverett—"

"Your husband departed last night?" he asked. "You wouldn't be awaiting his return, would you?" I shook my head. "The project demands that both of you fully attend to its needs at all times, sans comment or complaint. That's understood, now?"

E and I nodded, staring at Leverett. We were exitless, then; he would hereafter command me and there was naught to be done but do. There was no regooding this; all I could do was wait unto bitterend, and meantime take silence as my given; interning all emotion, blanking all thought, allowing myself no more life than the Elvisoid possessed, save enough to keep my baby kicking. Having allowed Leverett to sketch his own structure around me while I dismantled my husband's, I'd enabled my new overseer to build a more secure prison on foundations already laid.

"Shock's recognition worldround, yes?" he said, taking our hands in his, squeezing mine until he hurt me. "Settled, then. Questions?"

"What's scheduled next?" I asked.

"Close your eyes," he said. "Think of England."

10

□

"Fuck off, you fat bastard!" my host, Malloy, shouted through
our cab's open window as we scraped the red tripledeckers
alongsiding. "These burkes'll sarnie us if they keep playing
hogs of the road." Leaning forward until I could glimpse the
silver barette in skull's shape clasping his pony, he directed
our hack, voicing loud through the netting separating our
compartments. "Up, up, up. Loft us, Henry, sail us away."

Henry engaged a yellow lever beneath the wheel; Malloy
and I were thrown against our seats as our cab converted
into hovermode, lifting over the gridlock ahead. The result-
ant airblast blew Harrod's bags from passersby's arms, impaled children on Green Park's fence, flipped mopeds
beneath buses. As we parabolaed by the Ritz's bougainvillea
siding I felt anew the nausea known as the plane lowered
into Heathrow, stonefalling through London's overhead
mud.

"Funds saved riding black cabs pay for endless dinners,
later on," Malloy said. "Cuts assurance costs as well." A cab
several carlengths upstreet collided with one of the tall

palms lining Piccadilly as it went skied; the topknot dropped, blocking Fortnum and Mason's entrance, crushing haggis-laden shoppers as they emerged. Malloy tapped a cigarette free of its pack and fired. The pack's warning outsized the brandname, but said only *Let's Not Smoke So Much.*

"Smoking's allowable here, Gog—?" I asked; the fume, unexpectedly, made the air more breathable.

"Isn't drinking?" he gansered. "Malloy's the preferred moniker, Isabel, as I specked." His name, uncondensed, was Gogmagog St. John Bramhall Malloy; he oversaw Dryco's London office, having worked there for years.

"Why'd your parents peg you so?" I asked.

"New Agers," he said. "Tossed out of the Theosophists for heresy. Wanted to be harmonic convergers but never found the right key. They foresaw my drawing strength from the raw earth, so dubbed, as if I were a hillside figure. Never made a move without consulting entrails. My sister's name is Cropcircle, she doesn't tell everyone."

Our cab ascended several meters more as it entered Piccadilly Circus, circling toward Shaftesbury Avenue. A sculpture I'd not seen before replaced Eros, rising from the old fountain's site; an ebon-hued stonework taller than the surrounding palms and eucalyptus, guised as a gargantuan arm. Its hand's heavenstretched forefinger appeared to admonish Godness for having slacked during Creation. Unrobed citizens cleansed themselves in the nearby reflecting pool.

"What is it?" I asked, blinking as if the horror might vanish at second sight, nodding with lag; the flight from New York took two hours, the drive in from Heathrow, three.

"The Thatcher Monument," Malloy said. Our cab sideswiped a palm at Shaftesbury's corner; rats were thrown from its fronds into the throng below. "The punishment suits the crime."

"Thatcher?" I replayed; imagined I saw a rat clinging to the cab's hood.

"Not Thatcher Dryden. Mrs.," he said. "Indistinguishable, I'll grant you."

As we entered Frith Street, bearing toward Soho Square, our cab regrounded, halting before Hazlitt's Hotel, where I'd been booked. There wasn't room enough to allow the planting of palms, baobabs or even olive trees along these sidewalks. Flat metal squares affixed to uprights no thicker than vacuum-hoses were inset at intervals along the pedway; London plane trees trellised to the uprights had their limbs snipped to fit within the boundaried squares. En masse, they appeared as a display of green spatulas. I stepped out of the cab, losing my breath as the air's oven blasted me; the afternoon temp, as airported, was thirty degrees centigrade. Malloy exited; he stood a half meter higher than I did, and wore a kneelong black duster. As he outstretched his arms, retrieving my bags, he semblanced the look of the Tower's oldest, largest rook.

"Such trees—" I said, onceovering the street while he carded the driver.

"Topiary's overfashioned of late," Malloy said. "Flora's forever being remastered around here to suit climate shifts. Most's antipodean, generally. Tizzies the fauna. Forgive this November summer."

"There's AC within?"

Malloy frowned; his eyes bugged as he twohanded my bags. "Packed your pig iron collection, did you? AC, ah, sorry. Historical Accuracy Laws forbid." All small-paned windows in the rambling Georgian house were open; its aqua-painted bricks coordinated so well as to be expected with the pink trim. Periwinkle and banana trees gardened the ground floor. Across the street was a restaurant whose menu ribboned unceasingly along a metal strip above the ingress. A neon pizza hung over the eatery next door, issuing bubbles from its pepperoni dots. "Hazlitt died here, you know. I fear the room of demise was previously reserved. Let's check you in. Ready yourself to strip if they ask. Need for that lately, you know."

His warning went for naught; we transversed the entry, neither alarming the detectors nor needing to denude. Stenciled on the side of the fluoroscope through which my bags were shot was the command, DO NOT PUT LIVE ANIMALS OR BODY PARTS IN THIS MACHINE. Malloy gathered my belongings as they dropped from the chute.

"You'll bypass this hereout unless you're carrying," he said. "Once you're keyed, that'll suffice the guards, the layabouts."

The hotel's guards wore eyeshading hats; they stonefaced, listening to Malloy. The shortest bore scars running along each cheek from lipedge to ear, as if at an early age he'd attempted to widen his mouth enough to eat melons without having to chew. "Key," I replayed. "An actual key?"

Malloy nodded. "Historical Accuracy's iron fist slamming as it will."

The deskclerk ran my listing; once my name onscreened, she handed me my key. Its metal chilled my hand, and I imagined they must be kept refrigerated when not in use. Stepping through a doorway to the right of the desk, we climbed the winding, shoeworn stairs.

"Are there elevators in London yet?" I asked, trailing Malloy as he huffed ahead, bashing my bags wallways with every step.

"We're lifted at Dryco, certainly," he said. At the second landing we crossed a new threshold, and stumbled down another hall. "Here we go," he said, shoving himself against a corner so that I'd have space enough to reach round him, and unlock my door.

"Period pieces," I said, thinking as we entered that we'd mistakenly museumed ourselves, seeing furniture made two hundred years earlier. An oversize window overlooked the rear court's ficus and pine, and the chimneypots of other houses; beyond, topping all some blocks distant, was an old postmodern tower, inscribed at its brim with the word CEN-TRE. The ceiling-fan lowered the temperature; mosquito-netting creamed the sunlight until I could bear its diffusion against my skin.

"Lovely," I said. "So much cooler. So historicized."

"The tube's secreted within the chiffarobe," said Malloy, unlatching its high mahogany doors. "View as desired, or flip the button beneath to telecom." Setting down my bags, holding the control, he onswitched the set. Its eye at once imaged a whitecloaked man dissecting a fetal pig. "Infomercial, likely." Malloy gestured left, toward the bath. "Your facilities." Most of that room housed the tub, which was marble, and held a meter's depth; it resembled nothing so much as a sarcophagus, and appeared designed solely to lull its bathers into a sleep more relaxing than they might have wished.

"Leverett's scheduled you in advance?" Malloy asked; I nodded. "His eminence assumes the moon, doesn't he? He attempted to draw my hours for me; listed me out before we'd left Heathrow. Had me plotted like a Taiwan vid. Fruitless, his tries. So long as Dryco and I enjoy correlated moments at wide intervals, I'm content and told him so."

"I'm not optioned," I said, windowgazing; hummingbirds bombarded flowering ivy enwrapping the nearest pine.

"Tomorrow evening, you are," Malloy said. "The social graces demand we dine you well. You've that ElCon this eve, I gather, and of course his coming-out ball the next night. Would you like a moment's rest now? I can lobby myself, and haunt the maids."

"I'm appointed to head to the office upon arrival," I said, headshaking, wondering why I couldn't loose myself of its new ache.

"Pity. Spending days accomplishing hours isn't our model for productivity over here. Let's hotfoot it, then. Sooner you adjust to the air, the better."

"Leverett and E are already there?" I asked, locking the door after us as we reentered the hall.

"Lying in wait," said Malloy. "Their security, as well. He's working with Willy. Willy's our beefeater. There's been none of that goodgoodying here, mind you. This side of the tub's still beset with footpads and countercults at every turn. Old world, old ways."

I muted; before leaving I'd ascertained the company Leverett and E would keep, flying over a day earlier. John and I had talked most evenings since we'd split, awaring each other of our respective states, neither of us changed; though we had seemed to calm—he had, in any event, or so I perceived. It didn't surprise when Leverett awared me we'd all be back together while in England, one family seeking prey.

The heat flattened me again as we streethit; my collar damped my neck before we moved three meters. Dryco's London HQ was on Broadwick Street, reachable from the hotel through a labyrinth of byways. Malloy's black wrap billowed behind him as we strolled; his shirt and trousers were black as well, so black as his boots. He wore a string tie, its strands secured by a gold slide cast in our logo's look. "You're cool?" I asked, wishing, doglike, to shake my head dry.

"The gene pool tells all," he said. "My great-grandfather served in India, wrote one of those books about it after he cashiered. Regaled all with tales of how marvelous the weather was. Did nothing whilst he was there but look for the yeti and assault little boys, my uncle told me. You've been to London before, Isabel?"

"Fifteen years past," I said. "I came with Madam and sightsaw while she conferred."

"I was outlanded in Barcelona then," he said, shouting over motorcycle's roar. A cab came whirling upstreet, and we paused long enough to fasten ourselves onto a tree-stand as it passed. Its wind cooled me, if but for a moment. "Removed here ten years back and found myself sliding up the greasy pole. Didn't know where my hands were leading me. You've always worked the central office?"

"Always."

"I went to New York once, not long after Madam and OM exed the Drydens. A cadre of us were sent to see where we stood under the new management. Two of my mates were piecemealed in daylight, right on Broadway. Perpetrator said he didn't like our accents."

"London's changed, too—"

"Weather's had its effect. We've not flooded as you have, what with the Thames Barrier, but with conditions as they are it's no longer to daytrip the Med each summer now." We stepped between three cannon-muzzles set into the slate pavement; thin lianas spiraled around their lengths after emerging from their bores. "Statesiders tell me we've successfully blended the worst of New York and LA. Utterly happenstance."

Two bobbies stood near a bicycle rack, espying us, holding tight to their lemon-yellow plastic machine pistols. A large building overhung the street on our left, a thatched medieval hut inflated into twelve times trad size. What appeared, at first look, as mauve thatch evidenced, on closer inspection, as acrylic fiber. "Cornwall Tourist Council?" I said, reading its sign.

"A recent improvement," Malloy said. "Historical Accuracy demands, once again. Makes you feel flung headlong into Shakespeare, doesn't it?"

"Cornwall's still part of England?"

"Can't support themselves on pasties, can they? But each to their own country, so long as all stay fragmented within the greater madness. Citrons in a pudding, that's the Euro way."

That Europe so perpetually underwent disintegration while clinging to its shroud of union long troubled Dryco; seventy-four separate offices and a Continental HQ in Berlin were demanded if thumbs were to be readied all times to plum appropriate pies. Expenses perpetually overran: no sooner would a restructured Serbian branch open than Vojvodina would redeclare independence; Thurn might divorce itself from Taxis, for a week, or a month; Transylvania would be tossed, ball-like, among Wallachia, Rumania, Hungary, and Slovakia. I remember Judy being so angered, sometimes, that she suspected certain nations in which Dryco opened offices had, in truth, no actual citizenry, but only an endless series of gauleiters forever lining up to take their bribes.

"What remains of England, then, within the EC—?" I asked.

"By my estimation," Malloy said, "England qua England presently consists of scattered territories betwixt Ealing and Cockfosters. Everything else's balked. Wales, Yorkshire, Guernsey, Norfolk, Scotland High and Low, all of them spinout for a time before closing in long enough again to rifle the coffers as they need. Levels of inefficiency have been reached only dreamt of, heretofore. Thank Godness they've ceased passporting, otherwise we'd never cross a street without having to show need for leaving the empire."

In the midst of the next street over was a marketplace. Sellers from Asia and Africa hawked knockoff desktops, djellebas with obscene phrases threaded into their patterns, carved ensembles of frog musicians, brassieres portraited with the Royal Couple on their cups, neckties jacquarded with skull designs and other such arcanities. Dozens of camera-necklaced tourists burrowed through the lot seeking the best of old England. Malloy eyed a rack of frying meat hanging above a glowing cooker.

"There's Tibbles," he said. "Kitty kitty kitty. Here, now. There's Big D." Dryco's London HQ, a block distant, was a five-story structure built to resemble a country house, cloaking its true tenants well save for the yellow logo attached to each chimney. "Used to be cover offices for MI.7, my sources say," Malloy said. "Odds on, many a plot hatched there by souls fancywarped and dreamwoofed, and not adverse to a bit of tappage with the smackers if need be. After you, Isabel."

He pushed the door; it remained shut. "Fuck me," he said, booting its latch, swinging it open. The lobby was no larger than my office would have been in Judy's suite, had I been enabled to retake my position. A stairway curved up and overhead; beneath its broad spiral a dead date palm stood, flecked round by brown leaves.

"Thought we'd install our own greenery but neglected the method by which it might be watered," said Malloy. "Lasted a week before it withered." On our left were two elevators; both were out of service. "Not to mind. It's first-floored. So you've been dealing with Boy E direct since snaring him?"

I gripped the smooth bronze rail, hauling myself upward. "He trusts no one else—"

"With reason, I'm sure," said Malloy. "It's an uncanny resemblance, and the attitude seems right. The period he's modeling at present's a bit unexciting, but kitsch as kitsch can. I figured you'd deck him with the yak's hair quiff and a pair of great black buggers' grips stuck on his cheeks. The suit they'd fitted him for's a sight, all the same. I'd think that'll pass muster."

"He hates it—"

"Understandable," Malloy said, opening heavy French doors at the second landing; most of the panes were pocked with bullet holes. "Here we go, then. Dryco East."

Closet-sized enclosures ringed the floor's central open space; I trailed Malloy as he steered between desks, aiming for one at the far side of the building. Though I'd readied myself to see my husband waiting there, he wasn't; one of their guards secured Leverett and E. The man was twice John's width, and as tall; his neck's diameter was greater than that of his head.

"What's buzzed?" Malloy asked. Willy worded in return with an accent so thick as to disallow understanding.

"Gessa break," he said. "Am no partial te be settin' dayluing."

"Stick to your place, Willy. Where's John, my man? Where's Leverett's guard?"

"Loo," Willy rumbled. "N'ofally nice bitta crump y'got there, Mester M."

"Behave. She'll not suffer the prints of Gaels upon her—"

"Spikkin' fuh masel', nae more."

Malloy leaned his head back and lowvoiced me, as if that could keep Willy from overhearing. "Used to be a tight end with the Aberdeen Maulers. Banned for life first time season fatalities topped forty. The coach tossed him to us on a forward pass and we ran."

Each cubicle's infacing wall was partially glassed; staring past Willy's head, I saw Leverett and E within. Leverett was desked, shouting something at a man telecom-imaged. He'd epauletted his shoulders with phones. E sat in the window-ledge, streetgazing, his knees chinresting, his hands shank-clasped. Malloy opened the door, knocking as he entered.

"Interrupt," Leverett said, freezing his communicant in midsentence. "Isabel, at last. You landed four hours ago—"

"Traffic," I said; turned from him to speak to E. "How are you?"

He eyed me momentslong; redirected his look outward, as if he were debating whether to throw himself through. "Good as they tell me, I guess."

Leverett stood, interposing his body between us. "All's nearly finalized, at last. There's much, still. You slept in-flight?"

"I tried." Slept little, actually; sat openeyed for kilometers, feeling myself so cottonwrapped as the world below me. As E, during the months past, had come to know clockround his predecessor's isolation sans the joys and glory which may have attended, so I, too, had been cut loose, bereft of work, of friendship, of love, allowed only to devote life and time to readying one in whom I didn't believe for one I couldn't

believe to lull those who, against reason, did believe. I'd
nullified myself at Leverett's demand; while I was walled
away from Judy I was optionless. Now, having had in my
brief inflight separation time apart from the two of them, I
allowed my mind to return to my body, and my soul to
return to itself. Somewhere over the Atlantic I did sleep;
coming to in London as we landed, I reawakened full.

. "The hotel satisfies?" Leverett asked; his hands shook, and
he akimboed them against his hips, that none would see.
"Are you lagged? Time essentials—"

"You're so quiet, E," I said. "What's felt?"

"He's fine, fine—"

"Let him tell me, then." E unfolded himself, flooring his
feet. He wore an earthtoned coverall such as a mechanic or
driver might wear. Each week he'd been fortifying himself a
little further, disassociating from all of us, as if every new
assignment or insult simply mortared another brick. "E?"

"I just wanta get to it," he said, staring past me. "See what
it's gonna be. Where've you got me goin' tonight?"

"The annual London ElCon," Leverett said. "You've seen
your schedule—"

"Hell, I don't know if I'm asleep or awake. Haven't since
I got here—"

"I empathize," said Malloy, smiling as he interjected. "It's
a useful confusion, you'll find."

"We arrive incognito at eighteen-hundred, allowing you
to firsthand your followers," said Leverett. "Tomorrow
you'll be prepped for your appearance Sunday night—"

"Isabel's dining with me tomorrow eve, by the way," Malloy said.

"If the schedule permits—"

"You've got her doing nothing but attending, daylong.
She's sparable for an hour or two."

"Possibly," Leverett said; admitting that another might
adjust the timetable he'd drawn for anyone else was something I imagined he was no longer able to do.

"The coming-out's at New Wembley?" I asked, attempting to recall what I'd been given to memorize.

"Sunday's special, I've been awared," Leverett said. "Quite special."

"By Act of Parliament, the C of E, England, is allowed to hold its biennial Elvissey at St. Paul's," Malloy said. "Not in the church proper, mind you, but on the steps without and in the facing plaza. First time out they were given access to the innards but Elvii blackened half the monuments with their dirty hands. Took months to clean, afterward."

"What's an Elvissey?" I asked, never having heard the term.

"The eternal search for the home with the King," said Malloy. "The cry unto heaven that he be dropped back into their midst, appearing older but wiser, and scaring the dogs to death. The expression of the wish that he return, to assure that theirs will be perfect lives hereout. All sects unite on that night, as though through numbers they can rouse Godness to let loose her minion. Literal power through numbers, like the notion of all the Chinese leaping as one, knocking the world off axis as they land."

"Timing's everything," Leverett said, smiling for the first time since I'd arrived.

"Security's assured?" I asked. "For him and for us?"

"John will oversee our safety," said Leverett. "Crowd control rests in the capable hands of locals, and Dryco's British Security forces—"

"Such as Willy?"

"Precisely," said Malloy. "That is, those who aren't among the worshipers."

"As undercovers?" I asked.

"As believers," said Malloy. "It is counted as a religious holiday after all, both by the court and by the union. Half of Security has the day off."

"That many?" Leverett said, underbreathed; added nothing as Malloy nodded.

"These beliefs aren't to be toyed with in England," he said.

"The others are generally of Willy's ilk?" I asked.

"Even those who aren't Scottish."

"Security's assured, as told," Leverett said, loudvoicing as if to convince himself.

"A hell of a weekend, all the same," said Malloy. "The freaks' ball tonight, the Elvissey on Sunday, the Guy's day inbetween—"

"What guy?" E asked.

"Guy Fawkes' Day," Malloy said, grinning. "You don't know the story?

" '*Remember, remember the fifth of November,*' " he recounted. " '*The gunpowder treason and plot. I know of no reason why the gunpowder treason should ever be forgot.*' The Guy tried blowing up Parliament, some time back. Didn't succeed. We adore a good failure over here, mind you, just in the event that—"

"All's controlled and will go as scheduled," said Leverett, his voice rising enough to lend a squeak to his sibilance, causing him to sound as if he needed a lube. "It's accounted that these assemblies are invariably cable-covered live across the continent. By midnight Greenwich time news of the rearrival will have globed. By morning, New York time, Dryco's hand will have been shown."

"How's that to be accomplished?" I asked.

"We'll be branching the news through all info trees. Our media'll circulate suitable image and the event itself will be rebroadcast as essentialled. To verify our claim at the opener, we've a presentation arranged which should overwhelm so long as forecasts hold—"

"Forecasts? You mean an environad? Isn't that chancing—?"

"This from one who told me how oldtime my posters were?" Leverett said, greasing sarcasm with petulance as he shot his words from his mouth. "Bestill yourself, Isabel."

"How long will he onstage?" I asked.

"Ten minutes. Enough to show, sing, and say he's back. Then he'll be sped away, to lessen interaction with the crowd."

"Otherwise he'd be furied, likely," Malloy said. "Drawn and quartered by his beloving multitudes. There's no S and M like that between worshipers and god."

"Elvis," Leverett said, taking note of our charge's silence. "What's troubling? Stage fright?"

"Bellyflies, I'd think," Malloy said. "All before you's dust agleam in starsheen, E. Make-believe's mites and motes dance before you as you will."

"It's too much," E said, his voice so distancing that, against reason, I couldn't be sure that someone unseen wasn't ventriloquizing his words for him. "I wanta go home. Never shoulda brought me here—"

"We'll New York it Monday morning," Leverett said. "Set about arranging the American debut—"

"I mean I wanta go *home* home."

"Your reactions aren't appropriate," Leverett said. "I've said timeover—"

"*Home!*" E screamed; Willy eased his head around, pressed his face against the glass and stared at what onwent, appearing disappointed that his assistance didn't seem called for.

"Ah, me," said Malloy. "For a happy land, far away."

E fetuscurled as before in his windowseat. "Isabel," Leverett said, shaking his head. "Handle this, please. We'll exit ourselves. Aware us when you've settled him."

"Could be days—" Malloy began to say; Leverett took his arm and guided him outside into the central office, shutting the door behind them as they left. I waited until they were out of earshot, and even then whispered as I spoke to E.

"We're alone," I said. "Speak. Tell me what's troubling."

"You don't care," he said. "You just do this 'cause you have to."

"That doesn't mean I don't care," I said. "You've said naught about homing of late. Why's the thought returned?"

E sighed; hid his face against his updrawn knees. "I wish you all spoke English. I'll never get the hanga how you talk—"

"Is it these surroundings? Is it what's oncoming? Why do you want to go home now?"

"It's an evil world but that don't mean you should get away with everything," he said. "Even if you're God, especially so."

"Agreed," I said. "But what—"

"My mamma never did anything to me I shoulda killed her for. I shouldn't have got away with it, I shouldn't have—"

"Did you?" I asked. "You're here. It's done, E, you can't guilt yourself—"

"I still see her on the floor," he said. "She's still there."

"She'll stay there, I expect—"

"If you all hadn't come when you did," he said, "I'da called the police'n told 'em."

"Would you have?" I asked. "It didn't seem so—"

"And I'd be gone now," he said. "Real, real gone."

"That's what's wanted?" I asked, discomfited to hear him dupe my husband's sound.

"Always wanted," he said. "Always. No place for me, here or there, I guess."

Taking his hand I led him away from the window, reseating him at the desk. Beneath his retrofitted mask his spirit's remnants showed, revealing a gleam that no Elvisoid could have ever caught. However younger he was than me, his face showed greater years than mine; I keened my gaze, observing him, trying to seize every shift his mind made. He hadn't cried for months, nor did he then; I imagined it was something he was no longer able to do.

"You all've kept me hoppin' so I can't tell which way's up

anymore," E said. "I don't belong here, I don't care what you all say. You all shouldn'ta ever come after me."

"Agreed," I said. "Nonetheless, it's fait accompli. So—"

"Even if I wanted to stay, it wouldn't be right—"

"You're talking of what's right after what you did to her?" I said. "To us?"

"Somethin' got into me. I wasn't the person I am—"

"Who are you, then? Do you know?"

"I know I'm not who you all want me to be," he said. "I wanta go home, Isabel, that's all. You got a way to get me back, don't you?"

Judy's compact Alekhine remained in my purse even as he asked me; when we were still allowed contact, I repeatedly intended to return it to her, and never had. It was reasonless to keep it; however well the other world suited John, it would only genocide me as it had my people, were I to ever return. Even so, I suspect I must have backminded the notion, subconsciousing my thought: convinced myself that if matters here at any point overwhelmed sans relief, I had an exit readied that I couldn't call suicide.

"You do, don't you?" E asked me again.

"No," I told him. "This world terrorizes you so much you'd rather return and suffer penalties in the other?"

"I'm not scared," he said. "Not really. Just sick of it all. I don't think this's doin' much for anybody involved."

He closed his eyes and grimaced, expressioning a look suggesting that his head ached so much as mine still did. E may never have learned our world's way; he understood only too well our worldview.

"As I understand, Sunday'll be the main public show," I told him. "Afterward, you'll be left more on your own. You can have time to think, once you're alone—"

"You sure I'll be left alone?" he asked. "Everything Leverett tells me's different, anytime I ask. How do I know I won't be doin' this every week?"

"The strain's too great," I said. "Not just on you, but on him. On me."

"I just can't take it much longer. I can't."

"Perform as desired Sunday night, E," I said. "If I can get you back afterward, I will. This has to go as planned. Once it's done, once you've had time to consider, then we'll see. Will you agree, for my sake if none other's?"

"You'll get 'em to send me back after it's over?" he asked, monotoning as before.

"I will," I said. "Am I trustable? Keeping minded that I'm Dero, after all—"

He smiled, without evidencing happiness; appeared to have calmed, all the same. "Trust you more'n I trust Leverett," he said. "All right."

"Fine," I said, feeling myself drained of energy if not emotion; wanting nothing more than to let drop awareness, and fall to the floor. "Earplay, meantime—"

"Hey, Isabel, are you all right?"

"Why question?"

"You're gettin' fat," he told me.

I smiled; each day I showed more, or so I believed. As of the afternoon before, my baby still rested whole and alive within me. "I'll be getting exercise enough while I'm here, certain. Leavetime, now. I have to have an hour or two of sleep, whatever Leverett thinks. I'll be back this evening, predeparture."

When I stepped out of the office I saw that John had supplanted Willy. My husband looked as he did each time I phoned him; seeing him fleshed and not screened for the first time since we'd left each other comforted so much as troubled, against all expectation. He took my hand as I started past him; I let him hold it. His copy of *Knifelife* and his fruitbag protruded from his jacket's pockets.

"We're hotelled together," he said. "Did you know?"

I shook my head; glanced at his face briefly, unwilling to hurt either of us overmuch. "It's good to see you."

"Mutual." As he sat, and I stood, his gaze leveled toward me stomachways; when I saw nothing in his look evidence anything untoward, I allowed myself one final fantasy: that, my absence heartfonding him, he would have reconsidered our life together, reappraised its bests and worsts, readied himself to lay claim to fatherhood, and so have finally regooded. It was a lovely imagining, and faded so quickly as it came.

"You'll accompany us, this eve?"

"It's an unguarded trip, to lessen attention," he said. "If you're back by midnight, can I visit momentslong?"

"It'll be late, John, and what'll occur meantime—"

"To talk?" His hand tightened around mine; the clasp wasn't enough to hurt, and his eyes evidenced sorrow enough for the both of us. I nodded, unable to pull myself away before agreeing.

"Where's the event?" I asked that evening, as we streetshot; the car grounded and lifted repeatedly as it careened west along Oxford Street.

"King Charles Memoritorium," said Malloy.

"Your worshipers may strike you as being somewhat off," Leverett told E, who sat sandwiched between the two of us; Malloy was jumpseated across, clouding the car with eye-stinging smoke. "In pursuing your love they often neglect their social skills."

"Social skills?" E asked, headshaking. Our car nosed upward, missing a fire-vehicle, pruning a line of palms as it skied.

"Human interaction," Leverett explained. "Communicating one's desires within a multiperson context."

"Using implements, eating," said Malloy. "Washing at intervals, if only to alleviate scabies."

E nodded, flipping curls away from his face and shades; Leverett insisted he go wigged, to avoid speculation or com-

ment, and so E was domed with a mop-like tangle of dreads.
"Crazy," he said. Our car ascended another several meters,
shortcutting across Hyde Park. "These people about the
same here as they are in the US?"

"A global unity of spirit solidifies them, regardless of difference," said Leverett. "England is the nodal focus of all
theory, still. They've devoted more time here to developing
the conceptual theology."

"Like a caning eventually leads one to leather goods,"
said Malloy. "Sixty percent of the population here are believers, mind you. That's including agnostics; they'll at least
buy the tapes. No offense myself, El, but as regards pop of
the period I always preferred the Chairman to the King—"

"That's disallowable, as circumstanced—" Leverett said. E
stared windowways; I eyed the door's lock, certifying that it
was on. The car's interior lit up as we regrounded, whitening
within as if we were underwaying transfer.

"Here we are, then," said Malloy. The King Charles
Memoritorium stood in the north end of Hyde Park; was the
north end of the park, if its parking facilities surrounding
were included. The structure's searchlit hulk appeared as a
glass rhomboid, enwrapped by cerise and lime-green rib-
bons. From the neontubed cornice hung a banner proclaim-
ing LONG LIVE THE KING. Whether the sentiment pertained to
the place's late namesake or to the object of worship was
immediately unguessable. Our driver stopped at the main
entrance, which was done in an engorged Palladian mode:
winking blue bulbs outlined the fanlights above the fif-
teen-meter-high doors, plasmas bubbled up the transparent
pilasters alongsiding; it resembled a jukebox, designed by
Inigo Jones. In less than twenty minutes we'd cleared the
detectors and entered the central lobby; "Girls, Girls, Girls"
was being broadcast at jet-engine volume.

"Where now?" I asked, shouting over the din.

"We'll ankle a bit, and sponge up atmosphere," said Malloy. The building's multilevels were all occupied by those

convening. The Memoritorium, within, was reminiscent of one of the newer air terminals, or of a suburban mall whose stores hadn't yet opened. The London ElCon, hardheeling as it did in the Elvissey weekend, attracted believers from all continents; we'd arrived as most evening events were already underwaying, leaving the halls less crowded than I'd feared they'd be. Nearly all of those visibled wore participant ID pinned to their chests, though as observers we wore only our logo, and company name. Most people seen nondescripted; they could have been anyone. That, to Leverett, was what most problematicked, for how could what was hidden ever be controlled? Others in attendance manifested their belief plain, wearing clothes spoored by years along the Elvis trail, or singing topvoiced as they strolled, earphoning tunes that might have been favorites of theirs, if none other.

"Seven of the more agreeable groups are present, so well as an exaltation of Interpreters," said Malloy. "That is agreeable, in that there's little chance of intersectarian pogroms ensuing, though a certain friction's to be expected. Desired, even."

"What's the matter with these people?" E asked.

"Nothing's wrong," said Leverett. "They're yours, all of them. They believe, they follow. See them, love them—"

"They all look like they got hit over the head with somethin' and don't know it yet," E said.

"Incoming," Malloy said. "Behave yourselves, now."

A man approached us, padding over on ropesoled feet; he carried twice the weight that Elvis ever lugged. The pullover he wore bore a photo of the King, legended round with the words ONLY RESTING. Standing before us, blocking the hall with his mass, he studied each of us in turn; drooled as he read Malloy's lapelled ID, wiping his mouth with a dirty cloth afterward. "I never heard of you before," he said; his accent was unplaceably, but unmistakably, American.

"Then we're even," Malloy said, walking away, raising his head as if to pose for a portrait. We followed.

"Note that, Isabel," Leverett said, once we were out of earshot. "A grown man in this century who's *never heard of Dryco.* Now do you understand?"

"Generally the likes of Porky there overstuff these events, as I gather," said Malloy. "Seminars and theory groups are ongoing in these quarters," he continued, gesturing toward a row of double doors. "Let's see what's ongoing." A ribbon-scroll running above the entranceways listed events and the rooms in which they might be found; most of the allusions were so arcane that I had difficulty comprehending what material was being covered in what way, my indepthing in Elvisiana notwithstanding. "Recent Sightings, over here in Chamber Three. Let's eavesdrop."

Malloy led our quartet into the darkened room, careful not to disturb the meditative state of the onlookers within. I stared at the dais, where a middleaged man aimed a pointer toward a screen behind him.

"—this is the conclusive, right here," he said, sounding so American as the man in the hall. A blurry snap of a blond woman wearing glasses imaged on the white glow silhouetting him. A low murmur rumbled through the audience's midst; a woman in a babushka stood and pointed at the screen, speaking with a French accent.

"Is a photo of a woman," she said.

"The King held the camera." The audience accepted his word as truth; the most unnerving hush settled over all, even the inquiring woman. Before the speaker could proceed we exited; once we'd halled ourselves I doublechecked E.

"What's thought?" I asked him, lowvoicing as best I could and still be heard.

"They're crazy, aren't they?" E said. "Ever' one of 'em."

"You'd find similar percentages within any group," said Leverett, interrupting.

"Ah," Malloy said, calling us from across the hall. "This bears a look. The Interpreters are meeting within. Follow, if you dare."

E braked himself as we entered, and tried to turn away; Leverett seized his arm and pushed him forward as we dove into a sea of Elvii. "As I understand the subtleties, it's an open question as to whether the Interpreters are more shamanistic or fetishistic," Malloy told us, loudspeaking heedless of who might hear; none around us overted any opinion regarding his commentary. "Bit of both, I'd expect. They live their belief at all times, serving as example to all as to how the proper life should be led. Mind you, they can be temperamental."

The gallery must have held five hundred Interpreters of all ages, sexes and colors crammed shoulder-to-shoulder. Every one wore black hair, puffed and upswept; each wore a polychromatic jumpsuit of trad design, if amateurish execution. Caucasoid males going in for fullest decolletage crisped and teased their chest hair; Asians, Indians or those not so natureblessed glued merkins to their pectorals—to their breasts, in the case of women. The room's humidity peeled the wigs up at the edges; some Interpreters appeared to have tucked furry animals into their bosoms as if to warm them. Nearly all were multinecklaced, with chains dangling icons and personal totems: twelve types of crosses, stars of David, swastikas, ankhs, watches, painted miniatures of the King, shrunken heads, bulls' ears, lightning bolts atop the initials TCB, weasels' skulls, crystals and chickens' feet. Feeling something bumping against my leg I stepped away, and looked down; a nongender-specific child grinned at me as it adjusted its bejeweled cape. The Interpreters stood chatting, comparing leg and hip wiggles, studying karate gestures, running ringed fingers over each other's scarves, headshaking in order to demonstrate proper methods for flopping one's hair; all radared the room, looking roundabout to see who might be the most real.

"E," I said. "Are you all right?"

"Get me out," he said; his face gleamed with sweat. As I

laid my hand on his shoulder I felt his shake. "Please, Isabel, it's too much. Please—"

"Leverett," I said, "this is madness overmuch. We're leaving—"

"Wait," he said; must have moved too carelessly, for at once he upset an Interpreter standing nearby.

"Watch it, dad," he told Leverett, his accent decidedly Slavic. "My shoes."

"Excuse," Leverett started to say; before he could distance himself the Interpreter took hold of his collar, drawing him back. "Unhand me, please—"

"Hey, who are you?" the Interpreter said. "Why you here? Guys, look who I have. Is colonel Interpreter."

The Interpreter we'd offended was one of a larger contingent; examining his ID's nametag beneath the Elvis-head pin, I gathered that he and his compatriots were Bulgarian. They were barely contained by their white and red jumpsuits; by their size I estimated them to be miners, or even Olympic lifters. As Leverett struggled to loose himself from the Interpreter's hold, one of the others splashed a drink in his face; the surrounding crowd, including the child, laughed.

"Please, don't—" Leverett said.

"Our fault. Sorry," said the lead Bulgarian, lifting Leverett off the floor onehanded. More Interpreters were onlooking now, their eyes shaded with specs of many styles, their sneers uniform. "Let me dry you off, please." As he held Leverett he brought up his other arm, clipping his elbow against Leverett's face; blood trickled from Leverett's mouthcorner, and he staggered as the Interpreter let him go. I grasped E's waist and started guiding him doorways, trying not to bump anyone else.

"Too bad, colonel. Hope you get better." The crowd around us laughed louder, and closed in as we withdrew. Malloy was so tall as any of them, though not so broad; blackclad as he was, from on high he must have appeared as flyspeck upon a pastel field. Placing one hand on Leverett's shoulder, he interposed himself between the Interpreters and us.

"We're leaving, mate," he said, smiling as if something pleased him; nothing in his expression suggested any sign of upset. "Pardon the trouble. We'll be off—"

"Can't you see we're Dryco?" Leverett said, his hands muffling his speech as he pressed them against his bleeding lip. Most Interpreters hearing the word remained reactionless; the Bulgarians, however, recognized its meaning.

"Dryco?" said the one originally offended. "My father slaved thirty years for Dryco factory. Then thrown out like other trash when old."

"Dryco killed my brother," said another. "You hate us. You hate all people."

"Fuck Dryco," said a third.

"It's been real," Malloy said, pushing us forward as he turned his back toward them, unmindful of trampling anyone else as he spurred us to flight. E was first through the door, shooting hallways as if from a pressure chamber; Malloy kept close behind me as I exited, holding tight grip on Leverett, guiding him along. "Don't run," he said. "It'll challenge them." So we quickly strolled through the halls, passing the exhibits and sales-stands, ignoring the stares of other attendees. I glanced behind me, hearing mobsound; saw the Bulgarians leading much of the room's populace after us. Not until we exited did they begin throwing anything, and then rather than rushing our party they stayed inside, cursing us as we dashed into the parking lot. For long minutes we lingered there, bathed in building-light, catching our breath.

"Perhaps that wasn't so productive a tour as we'd have wished," said Malloy, straightening his jacket, offering Leverett a pocket square to assist in blotting his blood.

"E," I said. "Forgive. I didn't expect—"

"Sunday night, Isabel," he whispered, tugging his wig

farther down onto his head. "You promised. Once it's done, it's done."

"They'll regret," I heard Leverett say; turned to watch him smearing his blood from his mouth. "They'll regret."

Once back at the hotel I stopped at John's room. Our imbroglio had thrown off our evening's schedule, and we'd returned an hour earlier than planned. My husband's door opened as I rapped it; before coming inside I'd stared upward through the square trees and saw that his room's light was on. I hesitated before entering, wanting only to go to my room and sleep; against my wishes I'd been kept wakeful that afternoon, and now everything I looked upon shimmered with a hallucinatory sheen. Wandering in, closing but not locking the door behind me, I saw John lying on his bed. If the situation hadn't felt so dreamlike I surely would have screamed, and awakened him; still, frightened that I had come upon my husband as I'd always feared I one day would, I waited until I discerned breath uplifting his chest before I approached.

John meditated; he'd so tranced himself as to be unaware of my presence. Feeling safer once I'd ascertained he was outbodied, unwilling to ponder why I felt so blessed, I stared round his room, seeing a dupe of my own. He'd tossed his jacket onto a chair, as he'd always done at home; his copy of *Knifelife* lay openfaced upon it. Picking up the booklet, I read the page's sole passage, Jake's Golden Rule:

Love dead. Hate living.

He'd underlined the words; I suspected he'd memorized them long before. A domestic compulsion overcame me; as I lifted his jacket, thinking I should hang it up for him, I puzzled over its weight. Spotting his fruit pocketed within, feeling unexpected hunger, I drew the bag out, at once detecting a strong chemical odor, an ammoniac parfum; in my addled state I started to wonder how dried fruit could turn, and opened the bag. However long I tried, afterward, to convince myself that in my half-awake state I'd only misinterpreted what visibled, I knew then and know now that when I dropped the bag I saw ears spill out onto the oriental carpet.

John began muttering as I started edging doorways; low-voicing as if he sleepspoke, he began a litany, seeming to stir himself slowly into consciousness with his chant.

"Living must live," he said. "Living must live. Life demands purpose. Life demands purpose. Purpose essentials living. Living must live. Living must—"

Even at our meet, we'd masked ourselves with our preferred looks, the ones we could bear to show to others; throughout our years together, the gilding we'd long overcoated enabled us to continue the worship of icons that in no way resembled the people underneath. When had my disguise slipped away? Was it still there? He medusaed me when his fell from his face that night; I couldn't see how I would ever be as anything other than stone to him again. His lidded eyes were tearing; he shifted his feet, as if he were running from whatever rose up in his dreams. Before my husband could reembody himself I'd left his room, and run to my own. Several hours later I heard him come by; I still lay sleepless, seeing ears whenever I shut my eyes. He knocked twice; called my name through the doublelocked door.

"Forgive," he said, and walked away. Believing I felt kicks within, I pulled the covers over my head, and thought of my baby; uncertained whether my image still, if ever, matched its look.

11

□

"Thank you for lying," I told Malloy.

"It's one of the more challenging arts," he said, pulling my chair out for me once the maître d' showed us to our table. "Easy to do, but hard to do well. When Leverett asked where you were I told him I'd sent you forth to resolve certain unspecified matters regarding tomorrow night's affair. At first he insisted upon retrieving you but I stalled until he grew confused; it didn't take long."

"When you called me this afternoon I couldn't imagine what you'd said—"

"Said whatever he needed to hear. Shortnotice romance, nothing better." Malloy whisked his napkin from the tabletop and lapped it. "Willy's presence undoubtedly added weight to my argument."

"Was John around—?"

"For a time, this morning. Then Leverett sailed him off to investigate our avenues of retreat, following the fest. Hadn't returned when I left to meet you. Please pardon, Isabel, but I can't imagine the two of you married."

"We're divorcing when we return next week," I told him. "I'm divorcing. It's as well—"

"Quite a row you had last night, then?" he asked; I nodded, applying an additional glaze on my own art. "Content yourself tonight, then. Something you'll always get in England is good food."

A nearby mural, blocked along its low end by other diners' heads, was cloaked at topside and throughout its length by hanging tapestries bearing multihue designs so intricate as to appear woven by schizophrenics. The illustration visible depicted a cat pulling a gigantic root from the earth; a dog stood in back of the cat, encircling its waist with his paws, and several children as well were linked behind the dog. Hundreds of long swords and knives hung from the ceiling, aimed toward every guest. On the wall nearest the kitchen were ill-drawn portraits of a Black Virgin, the late Ayatollah, and the King of This World, his silver jumpsuit appearing him as most resplendent of all. "What kind of restaurant is this?" I asked.

"Irani-Polish," said Malloy. "Multicult at its most suspect, but highly recommended by those who should know, unless they've been funning me. Let's scan the offerings."

With nimble fingers he entered our greeting into the table's inbuilt keyboard; the menu onscreened, scrolling out appetizers and entrées. Each dish was listed with trilingual descriptives, seemingly arrived at through sequential translation, beginning with Farsi, progressing to Polish, at last stumbling into English.

"Grotty Fowl in Grease," Malloy said, reading. "Boiled Head in Glass. Various Slice of Typical Meat. Spinach Testes. Crab Legs of Lamb. Dear, this isn't promising—"

"My appetite's still lagging," I said.

"Mm. Mine just crossed the dateline."

Our blond, turbaned waiter returned, placing a bowl of carrot jam and bottle of chicken fat on our table between the electric candles. "What's wanted, people?"

"Let's gamble, shall we?" said Malloy. "Bring us tonight's specials, and a bottle of house red."

"Excellent choice," said the waiter, appearing grateful for not having to enter our order. As he raced kitchenways I felt a headtwinge, which passed so soon as it knifed. Though I tried not to evidence distress my face must have shown more than I intended.

"Something hurting you, Isabel?"

"Headache," I said.

"I've aspirin," he said, reaching into one of his long coat's pockets.

"It doesn't relieve," I said. "It's gone now. I was treated a couple of months ago, and ever since—"

"Treated for what?" Malloy asked. "Were you cancered, then?"

I nodded. "All gone now, the doctors tell me—"

"American doctors?" he asked, shuddering as if he chilled. "Saw a documentary on them not long ago. Suggesting England could learn something. Depends on what's being taught, in my opinion. See someone else while you're here, and be assured of what they're telling you."

"I didn't think your healthing was any better than ours."

"Oh, for the public it's worse," said Malloy. "But I've a Harley chopper. Call him in the morning and go to his office."

"You mean go tomorrow?"

"Here's his number." Malloy handed me a card upon which he'd scrawled his doctor's listing. "Tell him I told him to see you. He'll not fuss, he's a tradesman like any other."

"Thank you," I said, slipping the card into my bag, shoving aside my compact in order to find my addresser.

"That'll provide you with reason enough to keep from rushing back to the epicenter, as well."

"What happened today?" I asked. "How was it?"

"Appalling," Malloy said. An explosion outside rattled the room's curtained windows. "How's one so discom-

bobulated as Leverett kept his position? Do only psychopaths reach the top in America? He's driving us mad."

"I'm unsurprised—" I said.

"He sends out orders and rescinds them ten minutes
later," said Malloy, "then he starts bellowing about the
schedule being derailed. Trying to accomplish one thing, he
disrupts three others. Boy E's got the bloody flux, Leverett's
coming over to him every five minutes to remind him of
something else he needs to do or say tomorrow night, each
more important than the one previously told. When I tele-
commed in with Madam in New York to aware her of this
behavior she refused to even hear me out."

"Leverett's written his own program, and she desires that
he follow it through—"

"The more nervejangled he gets, the faster he goes, the
less he gets done. You can't even understand him once he
starts letting loose with the bizspeak, he starts shouting
across rooms into phones that aren't there, twirls dervishlike
from desk to desk. From afar he layered this project with a
fine patina of workability. After seeing him in action I don't
see why he wasn't given the hook some time ago."

"Interoffice politics," I said. "He eked his way into Mister
O'Malley's good graces in order to underway the project.
That's another reason why Madam refuses to interfere—"

"It's as well this'll be done over here after tomorrow
night," Malloy said. "We'd all be heaving ourselves out windows if it all went on much longer. Ah, here we go." Our
waiter returned, and placed our food before us; shook our
wine vigorously before unscrewing the bottlecap. "That
should detonate quite nicely, I'd think."

"The lovebirds' hearty treat," the waiter said, smiling as
he filled our glasses. We stared at what he'd left us. An
oversized slab sprinkled with orange-colored strips and ooz-
ing a glutinous sauce blanketed Malloy's plate. Seven sod-
den pirogi lay on mine, ringed round by sliced tomatoes so
unripe as to resemble bleached wood. Malloy moued his

lips; cut off a corner of his slab and chewed it cautiously, as if fearful it might blow up in his mouth. He worked it for a while, appearing not to have so much difficulty in rending the lump as he did in swallowing it. Picking up my knife and fork I clipped dough from one of my pirogi; a pale glazed ball evidenced within.

"Eye for an eye, I'd hazard," said Malloy. Closing my own I tabled my utensils, and pushed away my plate. He sipped his glass of wine.

"A good year?" I asked.

"For sugared vinegar, yes," he said, mouthwashing with water. "I'm terribly sorry about this, Isabel—"

"I'm appetiteless, as told. Drop concern." Malloy must have hungered unto starvation's point, and so he continued to eat. "How does E strike you? As regards what's intended—"

"Boozbambled," Malloy said. "Dazed and confused. It's to be expected, isn't it? Pardon, Isabel, one moment." He circled round in his seat as our dishladen waiter dashed by. "Excuse me." The waiter paused; his smile reappeared, as if he'd plugged it back in. "What am I eating?"

"Piece a cod."

"Which passeth all understanding." Malloy laid his napkin across the remains. "Let's air it awhile and see if that helps. Where am I, what was being said? Oh, right. I shouldn't depend heavily on Boy E's upswing if I were you. I'm doubtful he can carry the load, whatever his similarities to the original. All this double world business appalls me, mind you. I've never been much for science."

"It's an awful place, over there—"

"Undoubted. The notion that every buffoon I've ever encountered will be wandering about mucking up over there as well, years from now . . ." He paused. "It's a dumbfounder, to be sure."

"He wants to go back," I said. "I told him I'd do what I could after tomorrow night—"

"Send him back tonight if you can," said Malloy. "Nip the bud before it blossoms. If it's doable, do it. Would that I had the say here, I'd have canceled tomorrow yesterday."

"Why? Not that I disagree, but—"

"Your own reasons would suffice, I'm sure," he said. "There's no more plan to this than a Japanese city. Take crowd control, if you will. Something of a misnomer during an Elvissey, don't you know. Thirty thousand are expected to show tomorrow night, streetswarming round the cathedral from Moorgate to Farringdon and halfway up to the Barbican. Now, those Elvies last night were rousers but the ones tomorrow'll be the true believers, sure, and here our security's down two-thirds. Leverett's deeply taken by the municipal force but they'll skedaddle first time they're sneezed at, it's unfailing. Second trouble shows they'll shove their little yellow poppers in their tunics and zippo. Something else now: has the boy ever been out in public before? I don't mean performance, I mean has he been out at all?"

"Very little," I said. "In New York he's been housed all the time. He was prepped while interiored, Leverett wanted him fresh—"

"He's like an unshelled crab," Malloy said. "The slightest noise racks him. Coconut dropped on a car outside the office this afternoon, set off the alarm. He pitched an impressive fit, believe me."

"Are you inputted on this environad I gather Leverett's arranging?"

Malloy shook his head. "Not in my contract to hear. He's full tilt on it, I'm sure. He's got new weather charts onscreening every hour—"

"If it's anything largescale there's likelihood it won't take as desired—"

"The whole's as doubtful as the parts," Malloy said. "He's in a dreamworld, isn't he? Convinced himself they'll all hail and wail once they know Dryco's backing this. Mad, absolutely mad. The Elvies never gave, even when the company

could have stood to read 'em their redundancy report.
That'll never happen now. We've known this for years, mind
you, there's only so long a time you can keep the lid on
unteachables. He ought to be grateful it's all gone well as
long as it has."

The restaurant doors swung open, smashing against the
maître d's desk; a man aflame threw himself in, falling
floorways. He looked to have been tardipped; his smoke
grayed the room as he burned through the rug. Two waiters
and one of the chefs set upon him with extinguishers, lather-
ing him until he was doused. It possibled that our fellow
diners were too stunned to react, but I doubted it; they, and
the nonparticipatory waiters, continued about their business
as if nothing untoward onwent. As the maître d' stepped
forward to oversee the man's removal, a fellow at a table
nearby lifted his hand, signaling. "Dessert menu?" he asked.

"Seems like our cue," Malloy said. "This was a pointless
exercise, all told."

"Not so," I said.

"Good to get out, true." He threw a sheaf of edies on the
table as payment, stood and assisted me in rising. "You'll
need an escort back, as seen. They'll be laying in all over out
there by now."

"It'll be like this outside—?" I asked, holding my mouth
open so as to lessen the odor.

"Livelier," Malloy said, holding open the soot-blackened
door. "Never fear." We exited into Charing Cross and bore
north toward Oxford as a flameflower burst from the corner's window, spraying glass, sending celebrants sailing.
"They get Foyles every year," he said, his face ruddied with
fire's reflectives. "No night like the Guy's night."

Singsong sirens echoed off the buildings as firecars shot
by; one undertook its uplift as it leveled with us, and we had
but seconds to doorway ourselves to avoid being tossed in its
wake. In the street's midst was an overturned bus, burning
freely as crowds highstepped round its blaze, adding their

crackers to the sparks it threw. Three young girls armed with newsprint torches chased another, laughing and shouting. A liqrystal advertiser attached to a kindled shopfront close by continued rolling its list: *Cadbury's Is Good Chocolate / Travel the Underground / French Lessons With Strict Teacher Voicebox 432A6.* Many of the street's palms had been lit at topside, appearing the road as a tunnel lined with carnival flambeaux.

"Every year this happens?" I asked as we set out once more. Malloy nodded.

"Got to get it out of them somehow," he said. "This generally does the trick." Another structure, across the way in Denmark Street, flared and blew. Those evidently responsible scattered through the smoke. "Let's take a secondary, avoid the main action," he said, lefting us down a narrow passage. "Don't rattle so," he said, taking my arm. "I'll guide. This'll lead us back to Soho Square, and then around to your hotel."

"What'll you do, after—?" I asked.

"Wend my way homeward," he said. "Stop off for a quick one, maybe, I do hate to eat on an empty stomach. Look there, would you. They've got one wickered."

As we emerged into the square's encompassing lanes I saw what was meant. A straw construction in mannequin's form was centered near the small park's statue; within its conflagrated rushes a wraith screamed. Those encircling matched the screams in volume, if not intensity. Onlookers watched from windows above, their faces yellowed in the glow.

"The Elvii participate in this?" I asked.

"These are normal Londoners, all," he said. "Scattered tourists as well come annually to escapade, as in Pamplona. But those who follow the King look upon all this as nothing more than secular exhibitionism, and therefore unworthy of energy better directed toward their beloved."

"It's . . ." London had changed so since I was here last, or else I saw it now as I'd not before. When I'd worked with Judy

I'd traveled worldwide with her, on occasion, seeing Dryco's cities, or the cities Dryco once held; never before had I been to a place so reminiscent of what New York once had been, and surely would have been still, had it not been regooded. "I'm wordless."

"Contenting them's one thing," Malloy said. "Controlling, another. The former better serves all in time. Just as well, likely. If Americans had longer attention spans, who knows the follies they could have wrought."

We rounded the corner, coming to Hazlitt's. John's light was out; it was the sort of evening he should find it pleasant to roam, I thought. "Thank you—" I told Malloy.

"Think nothing of it—"

"For everything, I mean," I said; smoke rising from the park, and from the nearby streets, rawed my nostrils. "Dealing with Leverett. Awaying me, if for the evening. You've been very kind to me."

"I gathered that's something you're unused to," he told me. The square trees shivered in the warm wind; the sky reddened in the south, over Shaftesbury, reminding me of New York years before, when the eastern sky bled each night as Long Island underwent its ongoing siege.

"Sometimes," I said. "Lately, yes. Thank you, Malloy."

"When I'm asked your whereabouts tomorrow, I'll verify that you're being physicked. I'll occupy your husband after you arrive, if Leverett doesn't," he said. "Call Doctor Harrison and see him in the morning, he'll do you right."

"I will."

An explosion blocks distant so deafened that I thought that it had blasted overhead; tightening my grip on Malloy's arm, I trembled even after the noise decayed. Malloy's pizza-lit grin relaxed me, and I let loose of him, stepping away so that he wouldn't perceive that I didn't want him to go. "You ever want to relocate, I can place you here," he said, turning; his coat winged away behind him as he aimed south. "Tally-ho, Isabel. Tomorrow."

* * *

All had quieted by morningside. After waking up, calling to
appoint the doctor, and certifying with the desk that John
had already gone out, I left the hotel, thinking of Malloy,
walking through a brown haze gauzing the streets; its look
and ozone-laced scent were uncomfortably reminiscent of
the other world's atmosphere. Workers hosed cinders and
soot from the sidewalks, gutted cars were being towed out of
trafficflow's midst; damaged buildings were undergoing repair, and men in forest-green coveralls clipped charred
fronds from the palms. The cosmetic regooding underwayed
with such perfunctory calm that had I not witnessed, I could
never have pictured the past evening's events.

London's similarities to old New York evidenced all the
more, however much its citizens would have denied it; was
the similarity divergence between American Dryco and
European Dryco so great as it appeared? Dryco made its
employees part of itself against their will or knowledge, if
need be: Malloy had been with the company long enough to
become it, yet displayed a level of one-person corporate care
I'd known only with Judy; in regooded New York, how had
we worsened ourselves, bettering? Recalling Malloy's
aplomb in hazard's face, reminded of the calm so unnatural
as to be natural of those in the restaurant with us the evening before as the man afire burst in, I remembered my own
childhood numbness when confronted with such horror;
thought of my overt desire never to see what it was that John
did. At what point, for what reason, had I regained a hatred
for violence I never believed I possessed? Did regooding
make Dryco, as it made me, as it made John, only less adaptable to the world's ways as they remained, whatever our
efforts?

Doctor Harrison's office was in his residence, an eigh-
teenth-century row house in Bloomsbury, two streets east of
Tottenham Court Road. When I called he responded as

Malloy predicted, agreeing at once to see me; when I showed
at his door he allowed me entry sans word save but a brief
greeting. His examination was so gentle as to seem pediat-
ric: he questioned, I answered; with simple tools he checked
my rates; for the first time in years I slid off an exam table
without feeling as if I'd been assaulted by robot bikers. The
doctor's face was neither dispassionate nor emotive; nonetheless I could tell when he encountered something that
troubled him.

"Give me a few minutes," he said, concluding. "The garden's out back. If you can bear the sounds of nature so early,
wait there. I'll try not to be long."

His garden was no wider than a few meters, and surrounded by brick walls overgrown with ivy below the razor-
wire; reclining on a wicker chaise shaded by lime trees, I
watched bees hovering over blue hydrangeas and red gerani-
ums, and listened to sounds of siren and jet. After fifteen
minutes or so Doctor Harrison emerged, bearing two cups
of tea; handing one to me, he seated himself close by on a
patio stool and underwayed further interrogation.

"Dryco had you on Melaway?" I nodded. "Why?"

As I replied I cautioned, estimating it impossible to explain in fewer than a hundred sentences, even if I could tell.
"A business trip essentialled in an area thick with bigots. My
supervisors demanded that I be colorbled for the duration,
to lessen potential situations."

"And they had you on it for two months?" I nodded.

"Thereabout," I said. "And early on I was given that accel-
erant as well—"

He shook his head; entered something in his filer. "That's
unimportant. A number of agents speed up Melaway's effects without counteracting. You stopped before the tumor
was detected?"

"I'd noticed symptoms that I believed were connected," I
said. "The headaches, joint pain. Nausea, though that could
have been morning sickness—"

"It was," Doctor Harrison said. "Nausea's the least of it. I hate to have to tell you you've been fortunate, thus far. You've read nothing of the original Brixton studies, I'm sure—"

"Heard of them," I said, brushing away a bee buzzing too close to my face. "Why fortunate?"

"Two-thirds of the Brixton participants were dead within a week after treatment began," he said. "The others died within two months."

"I never knew—"

"They wouldn't have told you, certainly. Outside of private medical circles it's not widely known about here." He sipped his tea, appearing to enjoy its flavor, which tasted to me as if it had been partially derived from fish. "Allergic reactions killed some within minutes after ingestion. The majority developed pneumonia after the first three days of treatment which led, inevitably, into body-wide staph infection and general sepsis. Those who survived the initial week proceeded to develop malignancies as treatment continued, predominantly fulminating myelomas, or gliomas such as you suffered. Nonetheless, as the last participants went to their graves with rosy, if tumorous, skin, the project was considered a success though the people, sadly, were failures. An imbecilic theory unjustly applied, I thought, as did most of my colleagues save the ones in National Health who were involved."

"Why was it developed?"

"As I answer, please keep in mind that Europe is not so enlightened as America as regards some matters," Doctor Harrison said. "Melaway was developed as a way to alleviate the race problem. Changing attitudes proved impossible, and social engineering's a lost art. The demand was made to find a way to change bodies. It's inexcusable for Dryco to have given it to you, for any reason. Unsurprising, all the same."

"They knew I might have died the first time they plied me with it?"

He nodded. "They had to. Supposedly adjustments have since been made in the formula to lessen the most serious initial effects, and I would think they at least tested you beforehand to judge whether you were allergic or not. Fact remains, Melaway is perhaps the most effective carcinogen ever developed."

"What'll happen to me, longterm?"

"It's likely that tumor regrowth will occur, in the same area as before."

"I'll be cancered again?"

"Everyone is, eventually, whether they were dosed with Melaway or not," he said. "This can be treated again so long as it's detected early enough. Then, of course, the pattern repeats itself. Those participants in the study who lived long enough to be stricken with cancer were killed, in most cases, not by the first appearance, but by the third, fifth or even sixth once they metastasized. There's nothing showing in the fluoroscope as of this morning, so I'd estimate that the growth rate has been slowed. I'd not guess that this is an indefinite remission."

"They knew I'd be cancered beforehand?" I asked again. He nodded.

"Without question," he said. "Your problem is, of course, location. Each time these particular tumors regrow, they supplant to some degree the healthy tissue surrounding. The immune system goes, it all falls apart. I doubt I need to elaborate."

He clasped his hands before him, leaning forward, seeming to watch bees buzz around his flowers. Hearing a plane overhead I glanced up; saw skywriting above, white cirrusian letters wording against the morning blue: COME TO ST PAULS TONIGHT DO GOOD FEEL REAL. "What happens once I haven't any brain left?" I asked him.

"The law of diminishing returns should be taken under

consideration some time before that point. Elements experience halflife, there's no reason why people should," Doctor Harrison said. "But whatever the instigative agent, the treatment remains the same. So long as the regrowth remains encapsulate, and is found before it has a chance to spread, it can be removed again. Up to a point. Death's inevitable, afterward—"

"It is in any event, wouldn't you say?"

Doctor Harrison smiled; it startled, seeing a medici express emotion. "In any event. Until then, your life is up to you as it's always been."

Mayhap that truth accounted for my equanimity; possibly I'd been around my husband for so long that his acceptance of endtime became mine, or at least strengthened what I already took as given. I was surprised then, and now, how easy it was to believe that I could work within a set deadline, and accomplish my intentions as desired before that day arrived. The life of others, by then, concerned me most. "What about my baby?" I asked. "How does Melaway affect it?"

"None of the Brixton subjects were pregnant, so we've no precedent," he said. "Nothing untoward's immediately discernible. It's remarkable that your baby hasn't yet—well. That there appear to be no abnormalities of any sort, thus far. If no undetectable presences are within the fetus as yet, then—"

He stopped; sipped his tea, and appeared set to move on to a different subject. "Then what?" I asked. "Doctor—"

"I'd be speculating," he said. "That wouldn't be right."

"Please speculate," I said. "I'm used to it."

"There're no facts backing me. It's an idle thought, passed through my mind. Nothing more."

"Present it as such, then—"

"The idea occurs to me that Melaway could affect a fetus in a different or even converse manner than it does an adult. But there's no reason to believe that this is so."

"But it's possible?"

He frowned; then smiled. "It's not impossible. But it's nothing to put faith in. Live your life while you have it, that's all that matters."

"One other thing, doctor," I said, standing, readying to leave; wishing I'd never have to return to the clinic in New York again. "You kept referring to they. Who instigated and funded the Brixton study?"

"Why, Dryco, of course," he said. "The English office. Who else?"

At sunset, we left for St. Paul's. Malloy, Leverett and I sat with E in our car's rear compartment, surrounding him so that if his nerve wavered, he couldn't leap out; John positioned himself alongside the driver, forwarding his stare. When I arrived at Dryco that afternoon Malloy was present, attending to late-arising problems involving security; Leverett and E sessioned hourslong, going over subtleties of gesture and stance. John was elsewhere, and didn't appear until a short time predeparture; I kept my distance, and he didn't approach. His bag's tie flagged his pocket, and I wondered if he'd been adding to his collection since we arrived.

"What's up, over there?" Leverett asked Malloy, nodding toward a rally at the base of Nelson's Column; dozens of men supported on the shoulders of others graffitied its base as onlookers chanted.

"Rite of exhibitionism, it appears," Malloy said, eyeing the scene through our car's tinted glass. "Lundy nationals, or some such, troubling enough to be arrested without being shot. Poor Nels's seen enough in his time, I'd say if you asked, not that he's able to look any longer." Gaze-raising, I saw that the statue atop was headless. "Some of my more exuberant countryfolk decapped the admiral a year ago. Can't say what their intent was. Drunk, probably, and left in charge of the blasting caps."

We airlifted, passing St. Martin's and rounding Trafalgar Square; with a sudden lurch we cruised east along the Strand. Throughout the day the streets had been postered; at sightlevel, every building and bus shelter, each treetrunk and kiosk and newstand was papered with sun-yellow broadsheets worded with the Dryco-approved phrase, *You'll See Him.* Thousands of nondescripts shuffled east along the sidewalks beneath neon, plasmalight and windswayed coconut palms.

"Mediakill's necessary?" I asked.

"We still call it a blitz here," said Malloy, roaching his cigarette, swiping ashes off his long coat. "Nothing more effective where there're walkers. Not even the Beeb spits word so effusively."

"Not that Elvii are generally allowed media access," Leverett said, interrupting as ever. Our cab swerved past and overheaded three tripledeckers edging east, their levels crammed topfull with pilgrims. "Production values never up to standard. We'll change that."

"The Elvies are borderlined when it comes to dissemination," Malloy continued. "And again, many of the believers forswear worldly goods, save for their diskers. Cathode charms leave them unperturbed."

"Posters have their purpose, Isabel, as I told," Leverett said, his smile something more than fulsome. "You've not done this long as I have, otherwise there'd have been no questioning."

"What are those?" I asked. Two islands emerged from the traffic's river ahead of us, separated by no more than a hundred meters. Stranded on each isle were what appeared to be topiaried giraffes, twenty times lifesize; the nearest one's broken neck dangled over the cars and buses alongsiding, held placed by a netting of cables.

"St. Mary-le-Strand and St. Clement Danes," said Malloy.

ELVISSEY

□ 293 □
"Impossible to enter due to the unending vehicular flow. Preserved by Historical Accuracy, as ever." Each church was fenced round by crumpled steel walls; however protected from collision they might have been at streetlevel, their spires evidenced as fair sport for wayward cabs shooting past. "Terrible accident, that was," Malloy said, nodding toward the downdipped steeple. "The blood. Awful, just awful." Vines so well as cables helped position the damage; their leafy coils greened each church from foundation to cross, smothering the stone beneath. "The foliage was sold to the Historical Accuracy Council as impatiens," Malloy added. "Proved later to be a kudzu hybrid. That accounts for the AfterLondon look."

"What's minded, Elvis?" Leverett asked, slapping what he took to be E's leg. What part of E was where was not immediately discernible; he was wrapped head to foot in an all-covering cloak which he drew tight around himself.

"Lemme be," he answered. "Where are we?"

"Nearly there," said Malloy. "Look there, will you, at the splendor of mighty Albion." The last-century boxes formerly surrounding St. Paul's had been taken down years before; so isolated, the cathedral appeared ten times larger than it truly was. Its stone was illuminated from without; white-bright spots directed onto the dome impressed its look as that of a new moon rising from the city's black sea. From Ludgate Hill to the portico steps searchlights were rowed in double lines, their shafts heaven-aimed, forming skyceilinged walls between which the congregation assembled. "Positively Blakean. Shills of mine are responsible for their using the searchlights this time out, mind you. They're generally a bit more understated, left to their own."

Through the roof I saw naught but blanketing clouds; gripped Malloy's arm as our car grounded with a bump, leaving Fleet Street. "What sort of environad's intended, Leverett?" I asked.

"One that'll work," he said, chewing at his mouthcorner

as if he hungered overmuch to wait for dinner afterward. John glanced back toward us, resteering his glance after he caught my look. The driver guided our car into a secured area south of the cathedral; a column of bobbies allowed us to pass, and we stopped at the side of a dry fountain. Our parked viewpoint showed the throng shadowed, appearing as a bed of ivy visibly acrawl.

"That's impassable, Leverett," I said, examining the crowd. Malloy's estimates underestimated; no less than a hundred thousand gathered to cry for their King. "How's the church to be reached?"

"I've arranged for two representatives of ours to meet us at the edge of the group and guide us through," said Malloy, unbuckling as he prepped to disembark. "Not guide so much as hack a path across, more like."

"They lead us to the building," said Leverett, "then we come around front behind the speakers, arriving, so long as our timing holds, at precisely the key moment. Ready, driver. Unseal us, please."

The locks slid into their housings; we opened the doors and got out, shading our eyes with our hands as we looked toward the searchlit cathedral. "What'll blind their security to our presence?" I asked.

"They have none," Leverett said, laughing as he and Malloy extracted E from the car, tucking his wrap around him in order to keep him incognitoed. "In any event all'll be preoccupied, guaranteed. Elvis, time now. This is something you should hear."

As we stood there beneath the cathedral's snowbright mountain, eyeing its dome aglowing night into day, glancing leftward into the approach's Nuremberg light, we heard the crowd voicing song, singing the assembly's prelude. "Love Me Tender," acapellaed by a hundred thousand, stunned as I'd never imagined it could; through their massed chorusing the King's followers let drop their bodies, guised or not, and took on an ethereality that, at last, equaled their beliefs to those of any religion. Within the throng were a number of Interpreters, appearing as nightsky stars against black heaven; closer in, I could distinguish younger participants who'd bedecked themselves in Sun style, simulating the look of E so well as he simulated the look of Elvis. Most of those present appeared, even after prolonged examination, no different than any citizens of London or New York.

"Understandable now, Elvis?" Leverett asked as they sang their final chorus. E pulled his cloak around his face, and stepped closer to me. I put my arm around him, holding his garment tight; reached into my bag, and felt my compact there. Removing my look from the crowd I found myself staring directly into John's, who eyed us as if he'd at last found the conclusive evidence he'd long sought.

"It's pretty," E said. "I—"

"It's for you," said Leverett. "All for you." Reaching into his jacket, he removed a phone; drew up its antenna and spoke into its mouthpiece. "Undertake procedure A." Pocketing it again, he turned to us, and nodded heavenward. "Look."

We lifted our heads, staring at the clouds directly above the cathedral as they commenced to move, swirling as if Godness Herself stirred them, whirlpooling enough that a tremendous circle of strata soon detached itself from its enveloping banks, lowered several dozen meters and continued to spin. Malloy led us forward, taking a phone of his own from his pocket, staring up all the while as we crossed the plaza, bearing toward the crowd. A few among their number began taking notice of what ensued overhead, and pointed upward. Openings broke in the circle's middle, which now appeared to remain placed while the outer rim continued to spin. Many more in the assemblage saw what onwent, and their murmurs rose as hurricane-surf. By the time we reached the edge of the crowd, all were staring upward, looking beyond the searchlights. Malloy spoke into his phone.

"Execute procedure B, please," he said. *"Now!"*

As he worded, the searchlights shut off; the cathedral remained lit, appearing to shine all the brighter. A beacon affixed upon the dome's lantern came on, its beam fixed heavenward and revealing in full the face of Dryco. The crowd gasped; made no greater noise than that disturbing, and continuous, rumble. Two blackclad gentlemen stepped away from the multitude; Malloy greeted them, and turned toward us. "I'll wait here," he said. "I've had my share of risk in my lifetime, and would prefer to observe from afar. All's set from here."

"Proceed, then," Leverett told the men, who nodded and began unobtrusively pushing a route through the crowd. He and John grasped E's arms, and started moving him forward. "Come on, Isabel—"

"Luck be with you, El," Malloy said; looked down at me, and smiled. "You, too."

While we followed the men leading us, careful not to call greater attention to ourselves than was possible, someone came onto the portico to address the crowd; though he wasn't visible from where we were, the speakers set up around the cathedral must have carried his voice across the East End.

"E," the man called out. "Hear us, E."

The clouds above began making their own murmurs, as if to growl at all those below; flashes gave life to the logoed eyes and brightened the circle's whirling edges. As we reached the cathedral walls, keeping close against them as we stepped over cables and boxes and those who'd taken positions sans view, I felt drops spatter against my arms. The sky thunderclapped all the more loudly. "It's raining, Leverett," I said. "That's intended?"

Reaching behind E, he tapped my husband's shoulder, and nodded in my direction. "Quiet your wife," he said.

John stopped, and turned as if to confront me; I'd already circumvented him, pushing forward so as to alongside myself next to Leverett. My husband said nothing as he stepped next to me; I realized that, unconsciously, I'd muffed my ears with my hands. As I let my arms drop to my sides, unwilling to overreact where any might see, I felt a tug on my earring, as if it were snagged on something; circling quickly, I saw John pull his fingers away, and smile.

"E," the man at the podium continued to call out; the audience hummed, seemingly, in response. "We want you. We need you. We love you. Hear us, E—"

A sound of rustling paper came from far overhead, its crackle counterpointing thunder and drone. Seeing the lightning-lit face looming above as before when I glanced up, I spied as well blue flames flickering round the facade's twin spires, St. Elmo alicking their apexed crosses and the pediment's statues.

"We were worldscattered. In E we unite. Through E we go forth. With E we conquer. Hear us, E—"

Our leaders directed us to a door located in the base of the stairway, secluded from audience-view by a wall of carsize speakers; without word we entered, following their steps, passing quickly through a marble antechamber before ascending a stairway's iron coils. At its head was another door; we stepped through as our guides opened it for us, coming out onto the portico's left side, behind another cluster of speakers. The man addressing the Elvii stood at the podium, some ten meters away, shouting as if to drive away the rain.

"Time comes." The speakers so amplified his words, and we stood so close to their horns, that his phrases earstruck me as if they were long pins driven into my head. "We call for you now as we always have. As we always will. Return to us tonight. Return. Hear us, E—"

Our guides absented themselves, returning the way we came. John took up a position near me, his look evidencing that he had distanced; as if, however unintentionally, he had begun concentrating too keenly on past, rather than present. "Your cue," Leverett said, shouting loud enough that we could hear. "Ready?"

"If I have to—" E said.

"What's done is done," Leverett said, lifting his phone. "Now do."

"Hear us, E," said the man at the podium. "Answer."

"Procedure C," said Leverett, voicing into the receiver. "Engage."

Mayhap the man noticed his hair lifting, as if breezed, away from his neck, as I felt mine grow staticky; possibly tingles suddenly traveled from his fingertips, up his arms. Something awared him, and he leapt back from the podium; no sooner did he move than a bolt shot down from cloud to church, blasting the spot where he'd stood, charging the air. Simultaneously the searchlights came on, sending their shafts skyways once more.

"Go!" Leverett shouted. John tossed a capsule at the podium which flashed sunbright when it landed. E dropped his wrap from his shoulders, revealing his regooded jumpsuit: its lines were retailored to better fit his frame, and its fabric was white, rather than yellow; our logo showed upon it fore and aft as before. Running across, he passed through the cloud rising from the blistered stone just as the rain dissipated its mist. His people, initially, stood responseless, quieting so absolutely that, for long instants, all we heard was rain beating against the church, drumming against their coats. Once they realized whom it was they sighted, they connected, crying so loud as to push cheer into scream. E paused expressionless at the podium as the people's noise grew louder, increasing so as to deafen all other sound. Then he raised his right hand; they silenced, as if unplugged. The searchlights blanked again. Careful not to touch the podium, he leaned forward into the mike and began his unaccompanied song.

"Mine eyes have seen the coming—"

More than the searchlights had blanked, I realized; the whole of the city had gone out, totaling all in darkness. Sporadic lightning strobed the scene. "Volume," Leverett was saying into his phone. "What happened? Where's the volume?"

"—*of the glory of the Lord*—" E's voice wobbled as he phrased the second line.

"Nobody's hearing him!" Leverett shouted. "Electrify. Action! What do you mean, it's knackered—?"

E muted, and stared at his silent onlookers. The sky cloudburst; rain pelted so hard as to soak him. His hair matted against his face; his collar collapsed under water's weight. Removing his shades, he slung them into the crowd. No one jumped to catch for them as they flew; no one lunged to seize them, once they landed.

"What are you doing to me?" Leverett said, screaming into his phone. "You can't—"

"*Faker!*" someone shouted. "Ta'e a malky to 'im," another said. "Vegassene!" a woman cried. "*American!!*"

Those frontlined started surging forward, attempting to crash the impromptu defense line that formed itself; some of Malloy's men, undoubted, doing what they could to forestall, if not prevent, harm. Pocket-size soundsystems hailed onto the portico's steps as those farther back made clear their intentions. E backed away from the podium; turned, and ran toward me. I couldn't tell whether rain or tears most wet his face. John stepped between us as he approached, disallowing any embrace. When E tried asiding him, my husband throated him with his hands, shaking his head as if to detach it. Careless of his reaction, I struck John in the back of his neck; he loosed E, and I pulled him toward me.

"I'm sorry," he said. "Isabel, I'm sorry. Help me—"

John grabbed E's arm, dragging him across the stone as if readying to throw him to the crowd. Leverett sighted what onwent, dropped his phone and rushed over. Malloy's men positioned themselves along the steps, lifted their weapons

and fired. The crowdroar intensified; paving-stones landed
against the columns. Leverett drew back as he ran over, and
punched E's face; held his hand as if he'd broken it while
continuing to shout.

"Look what you did! Look—!"

"Don't hit me—" E said, rubbing his jaw; before John
could pull him away I took hold, and brought him over to
me. The gunfire upvolumed; eyeing downward, I saw that
those in the crowd who came armed had reached the front.
Seizing E more tightly with one hand, I reached into my
purse with the other, finding the compact. The cathedral's
smaller entranceways had revolving doors, to facilitate large
numbers of tourists; I knew what essentialed if we were to
escape, if but momentslong. Towing E, I raced toward the
doors; John and Leverett dashed after us, ignoring the Elvii
at the top of the stairs. I threw myself against the glass of one
of the compartments, hauling E into the wedge with me as
I pressed my thumb against the compact; before ten seconds
passed John, too, crammed into our slot.

"Not without me, Iz," he said. "Not without me."

Bracing my feet against our enclosing doors to hold them
placed, I sealed our compartment just as all outside went
white. Closing my eyes, feeling vibrations race bodywide, I
prayed unto Godness that my baby wouldn't be harmed.
Blood warmed my face as my nose flowed; neither E nor
John worded, while we were passing. Through my lids I
detected a shadowing as the whiteness faded; drawing my
feet together, I leaned forward and pushed, spinning the
door round until we exited. Coming out, my arm still clutching E's, I looked at a dark, red world.

"What's this?" E said, freeing himself of my grip. "Where
are we?"

"Iz," said John. "It's—"

"War," I said, at once recalling the historical inferences
Dryco extrapolated, following our return.

"We're still in London?" E asked, staring out from the top of the steps.

"What war?" John asked. "The second? It's over—"

"Not here," I said. "Britain never peaced with Germany. It's ongoing and we're in it—"

Until I saw the searchlights it was impossible to say if it was day or night. The cathedral's plaza was blockaded round by sandbags, and overroped with entangled hoses, lying coiled atop one another, resembling a snake-nest; spray geysered from leaks in their lengths. They were connected to fire-wagons, and their nozzles were directed by parties of men wearing metal bowls atop their heads, watering the burning buildings surrounding the cathedral. From a hundred blazes smoke billowed, clotting the air, stinging my eyes and choking me as I attempted to breathe.

"We can't stay here," I said, holding a handkerchief against my face. "Whatever's ongoing on the other side, we have to go back—"

"I'm not goin' back," E said, backing away from us. "They'll kill me."

"You'll die here," I said.

"Maybe not—"

"It's senseless, you can't—" A newspaper fluttered along, catching at my ankles; plucking it up, I scanned its heads:

GERMANY RENEWS ATTACK
LIVERPOOL, MANCHESTER, LEEDS HIT BY MISSILES
BRIGHTON SCHOOL V3ED, 189 DEAD
TRIAL BY NAZI HELLFIRE *** 'BOMB AWAY' SAYS LONDON
IF THEY HAVE THE BOMB, WILL THEY USE IT?

"I had it, Isabel," E said. "You're not gettin' me back there, no way." A series of blasts went off in the near distance, shaking the stone beneath my shoes; one of the sculptures toppled from the pediment, shattering as it fell onto the steps. E turned, and began his own descent.

"John," I said, following. "Stop him."

My husband actioned at once, moving more quickly than I'd have expected he would; as he threw himself at E, tackling him and sending them both rolling down the steps, I understood his intent. As they came to rest at the bottom he positioned himself atop E and started hitting him. Shellbursts bejeweled the smoke above as if they were fireworks, showering golden rain that burned, skinhitting. Three ambulances sped through the street alongsiding the cathedral's north side, ringing their bells.

"Stop it," I shouted, grasping John's collar, pulling him away. "You can't—"

"Essentialled," my husband said, jerking loose of my grip. "He hurt. He'll suffer. I'll revenge us yet."

The cathedral's dome appeared as a broken egg whenever the searchlights played over across the ruin. Silvery fish floated through the ink that drowned it, glinting as the beams lanced their sides; after a befuddled moment I gathered that they were observation balloons. One burst as it was harpooned, and sank slowly into the murk. "Leave him be. We have to home it—"

"Rapist!" John cried, returning to his work, fisting E repeatedly. "Housebreaker! You ruined us. You ruined us—" As I fixed myself upon my husband's back once more, I heard a drone overhead, the buzz of a bird-size bee; unexpectedly, it silenced, and some seconds afterward the ruins to the south of the cathedral reblew, throwing the three of us headover end, spattering us with cinder and slag. Sitting, looking up, I watched red blooms blossom from what had been sowed; the sirens didn't deafen against the screams.

"Come—" I said, pulling myself up along with E; his jumpsuit was blackened with soot and smudge, dulling its brightness, blanking our logo. His face was bruised and swollen; his hair was matted with blood. John was recovering as well; running his hand along his leg, assuring its fit, he readied to stand. "Come, E. We have to go. Come on—" He pulled away from me before John could haul him in.

He drew back, disentangling himself. "No, Isabel. I won't do it."

"You can't stay here."

"This is where I'll be goin' soon enough," he said. "You go. I won't—"

John lunged forward, striking E in the chest with his good leg, sending him down atop an agglomeration of charred timber. E enraged; seeing my husband move toward him he retrieved one of the more solid boards and swung up around, breaking it against my husband's skull.

"*Stop it!!*" I screamed. "I'll leave you both—!"

Neither seemed troubled by my threat; even now I can't say that I wanted to leave either of them there. As John dropped, so E rose; I paused there for what seemed a limitless time as they pummeled each other, sparks and ash raining down on us all the while. The fires around us intensified, blending into a single blaze; when the firemen's hoses ignited they dropped them and ran. One called out to us, awakening me from my trance. "It's a firestorm!" he shouted. "Are you mad? Go underground, get to shelter!"

The wind heated, picking up; lighter debris ascended and circled through the air, as if they were no more than bits of paper uplifted by a candle flame. As the fires burned hotter their roar grew; the smoke so thickened that I expected we'd all shortly drop. John had E down again, slamming his face against the paving-stones, remodeling him one last time. From his pocket I saw him extract his straight razor, and lift E's head by one ear. Bereft of thought, heedless of result, I picked up one of the boards and brought it down so hard as I could against my husband's back; as he fell off E I lifted it again, and smashed his bad leg's knee.

"Run, then, if that's what's wanted," I told E. "Run."

His balance failed him as he tried to stand, and several times he slipped against the pavement; when he at last footed he stared horizonwide for a moment, seeing, as I saw, nothing but fire. As he wiped the blood from his face, cleaning his blackened hands on his suit, E smiled, as if, having accepted his prospects, he at last felt himself redeemed. "G'bye, Isabel," he said, his lip drawing into that unconscious sneer; stumbling away from us, he headed northwest, where the flames hadn't yet ravaged every street, and vanished into smoke.

My husband lay on the pavement watching; pawed at his leg with his hand. "John—" I said. "We have to leave. John—" He said nothing; without warning gesture he thrust his fist against my face. In midswing he must have conscioused of his action, for he restrained his jab, and therefore neither fractured my bones nor splintered my teeth; yet, he hit me. Edging far from him, I knelt against the cobbles, finding the air breathable enough at groundlevel to allow me my sobs. Facades in Ludgate tumbled streetways as their fires overwhelmed; bricks sprayed across the plaza as if they were meteors. Momentslong while kneeling there I allowed myself disallowable thoughts; considered how easy it would be to stretch out, and await cremation. Belaying such notions, I looked at my husband; raising the hand with which he'd hit me, clenching it, he started pounding his own face, beating himself full-strengthed. Before I could stop him he'd caved in his right cheek; his nose sagged, as if the rising heat melted it. Seizing his hands, I pinned him; watched his face redden like a Jersey sunset.

"For you," he said, his voice faraway, barely audible over the surrounding holocaust's rumble. "For you. It's all wrong, whatever I did, whatever was done. Whatever was ever done. I'm sorry, I'm sorry, I'm so so sorry—"

"We have to go, John." Fresh explosions throbbed my ears, sounding as firecrackers might to an ant. "Back to the cathedral. We'll have to go back where we came in."

"Leave me. It's my deathright here, Iz. Please leave me, please—"

"I can't—"

"Why?"

He had me, twiceover; but whatever he'd done, having already watched E lose himself, I wasn't going to goodbye my husband over here as well. "Let's go," I said. Standing, I fixed my grip, enabling for him to rise; saying naught, nodding assent, he allowed me to lift him, one last time. He shifted his weight onto his good leg; the wind blew so that he couldn't stand unaided. Encircling his waist with one arm, I supported him as we started toward the steps; retrieved the compact from my purse with my free hand.

"The church's afire, Iz," he said; through the smoke I saw flames, high on the cathedral's roof, behind the towers. "It's unmakable."

"Come on." We ascended two steps at a time, steering around rubble fallen down from the pediment. Dust sandblasted our skin as the wind raked us; oily smoke blinded me, and soon we were only fumbling forward and up, lifting our shoes quickly from the steps so as not to sear them. I dropped as we reached the top, taking my husband with me, fearful that if we continued upright we'd smother, halfway across the portico. We dragged ourselves faster than we could have walked; shimmers playing over the entranceways' interiors evidenced that the nave had taken fire. Explosions rang the stone underneath as a clapper rings a bell; I crawled all the faster, dragging John along, believing that the columns would at any moment shiver down onto us. My compact warmed my hands; my clothes began to smolder.

"I love you, Iz—"

"I know," I sighed; pulled myself into the first revolving door we reached, careful not to touch the red-hot brass vanes until it essentialled. After I hauled John in with me, assuring that all of him was within our wedge before I stood, I positioned my feet and one hand against the metal doors to adjust the final fit, sealing us in as I thumbed my compact. I unbodied, and barely felt the burn; watched the columns outside crack and fall as flames tongued their grooves, wondering how long it would take us to bake. The columns, the fires; all suddenly whited out, and I no longer noticed any sensation of temperature as I pressed against the doors. Momentslong, our world reappeared; I spun us around, that we might fall into it. London's air, here, was so fresh by comparison as if it came from tanks; as I inhaled its sweetness, exhaling black when I coughed, I pressed myself against the cool stone as if it were my own bed. John, too, came through whole; he lay where he'd spilled, touching his fingers to his broken face as if it were my body. Staring out into the plaza, I saw that the Elvissey was over; the worshipers, surely disappointed but as surely not disheartened, had left. Dozens of workpeople were packing away speakers, gathering up discards, hosing blood off the steps. When I looked rightward, I saw the door through which we must originally have passed; several bobbies and three or four suited men encircled the entranceway. At first I couldn't see what it was they surrounded. A tourguide, splendid in his vicar's costume, turned away from their group and saw us. He tapped his compatriots' shoulders, and as they looked over I heard one speak.

"Call Malloy," the man said. As two of them rushed into the cathedral I saw a pair of trousers lying at the doorway; shoes protruded from the trousers. At first I thought they'd been stuffed with batting, as if for a party prank. Then it occurred to me that the window between worlds must have extended some distance beyond our doored compartment when it opened; when it closed, it closed—partly—on Leverett.

The men who'd gone inside reemerged. "That's them," said one.

"The darkie, too?" They nodded.

12

□

The Dero weren't born bad, E once explained to me during our talks; they just grew into it. Anything they did or thought harmed, though they apparently believed that their intentions were inevitably good; they could never have spread falsehood among others, had they not first perfected the lies they told themselves. The Dero adjusted so well to their caves and to the bottom of their shafts, that they convinced themselves that everyone should share the pleasure they knew, and so they set about guaranteeing that everyone would.

When morningshine woke me I coughed for several minutes, continuing to spew another world's soot. I'd opened the windows before bedding; dragonflies whirred round my room, hovering momentslong before me as if snapping pictures. At length I stood, and examined my hand's bandage, peering underneath at the damage evidenced. The air was no less warm than it had been since I'd arrived; compared to where we'd been, it chilled me, and I drew on my robe.

The clock read ten-thirty; switching on the telecom, I coded the New York office, hoping to contact Judy, and aware her of our conclusions. Several jets overheaded, without; while they passed the screen blurred, imaging. When at last the colors coalesced, I faced a young blond woman sitting at the reception desk. "Please tree me onto Madam, if she's present," I said, still attempting to blink myself awake.

"Who asks?"

"Her assistant, Isabel," I said. "It's a London call. Is she there? Would you please connect us?"

"I'm Madam's assistant," she said; the woman's smile was no less realistic than Leverett's had ever been, and her eyes were so glassy as the Elvisoid's. "I was assigned the position this morning,"

"Temp—?"

"Permanent," she said, setting her computer on datacall, eyeing her screen. "Your name is Isabel, you said? Isabel Bonney?"

"Isabel will do. If you'll connect me with Madam—"

"Isabel Bonney, and you were most recently assigned to the E Project?"

"I was. This interrogation's unneeded, would you please—"

"As of this morning the E Project has been ruled a nonevent," the woman told me. "All pertinent information has been defiled from Dryco systems. In accordance with an all-inclusive directive, participating New York office employees are terminated. Your husband, John Bonney—"

"Put me through to Madam," I said, wondering if I might still be sleeping. "Now."

"—has been informed prior to our conversation of his newly nonexistent state. Your financial holdings and accounts have been appropriated by Dryco to cover processing expenses—"

"*Bestill!* Listen to me—!"

"Is there a preferred location where personal possessions in your home and office may be transferred?"

"Don't touch my things," I shouted at the screen; the woman countenanced nothing untoward. "Judy? Judy! I know you're eavesdropping this—"

"As no preferred deposit location is given, all possessions will be therefore claimed by Dryco to cover transferral costs," she said. "All Dryco ID and charge cards are herewith nullified, including all Shoprivilege benefits. Healthcare privileges are immediately revoked—"

"Shut up! Judy—!"

"If you have been employing Dryco transportation during your trip, those tickets presently held are automatically voided—"

"*Answer me!!*"

"Inquiries regarding additional details relating to your severance package are to be answered by Mister Malloy, in the London office," she said. "Hotel checkout time is twelve, Greenwich."

"Don't—"

"Do good, feel real. Thank you for calling Dryco."

"Answer me! Judy!! Motherfucker! *Bitch!* Judy—"

The ease with which, pressured, I'd slipped into childhood's language patterns surprised me most, that morning. Being at last erased from Dryco wasn't such a shock in itself; in time it happened to all, and I'd left alive, at least. As I lay crying on the bed, listening to a phone ring in a room across the courtyard, I wondered why Judy slatecleaned me in trad manner, where the one departing loses not only the position but all existence up until that point. That was what I'd always feared, the threat of having my reality snatched from me; and if I were to be vaporized, I'd have hoped it would be for some wrong I'd actually committed. I remembered telling this to Judy once; I suspected she kept it minded for future use. She had so much difficulty regooding as any of us, after all; it was only natural that it would be those she'd known the

longest with whom she'd backslide. A dragonfly bumped
against the window-glass, breaking itself. Once cried dry, I
sat up; coded Malloy's number in on the switcher, onscreening him almost at once.

"Isabel," he said, seeing me. "I was about to call—"

"Were you?" I asked; his face inhered a sadness which
appeared not entirely false. "I'm awared I'm to contact you
for further details. Are you sending Willy over to street me?"

"Not at all," he said. "You've spoken to them in New
York?"

"A woman I've never seen before erased me," I said. "I'm
keeping my pocketed money and my clothes. Otherwise—"

"Isabel, Madam's doings aren't mine," Malloy said. "Hear
me, please."

"Dryco unisons its acts," I said. "I've seen, I know—"

"In America, possibly, though of late I have my doubts.
Alacrity and impunity are my bywords, so long as the profits
hold. Seat yourself and have a listen. All right?"

"Speak, then. What's left to be said?"

"More than you think," Malloy told me. "The only property I'm to seize from you is the compact Alekhine you so
usefully employed last evening. It's not something I imagine
you wish returned to you in any circumstance."

"That's so," I said. "You've spoken directly to Madam?"

"I did at home last night, after they called me from the
hospital," he said. "She'd received her own reports in from
the saturnalia and had evidently reached her decisions in
advance of speaking to me. All seemed rainright, first off the
bat. Leverett's fate appeared to cheer her immensely. Glee
glazed her eyes as I recounted what I'd been told. But then
when I broached the subject of your survival—"

"She chilled. So I gather—"

"She's a cold one, for sure," he said. "Struck me that she'd
been gardening her mood for some time to get such a crop.
When did you speak with her last?"

"Two months ago. We'd worded almost daily before then,

but Leverett threatened. Had me cut the wires. He had me eyed constantly, and I couldn't contact her. She was distrusting me even then—"

Malloy shook his head. "Leverett's tarbrush blackens even from the grave," he said. "Inferring from her comments, he allowed to Madam that you yourself had clipped, and thrown in completely with his project. Appears she believed not wisely but too well. 'No one betrays me but once,' she told me."

"Why wouldn't she tell me herself, then? Did she say?"

"I asked her if she didn't feel that would be the preferable method. She told me she didn't want to hurt you," Malloy said. "The upperlevel madness over there's always astonishing. Twelve contradictories believed at once, that sort of thing."

"It's in the system's nature—" I said.

"Certainly in her nature. Last year she had me organize medical experiments I'm still pretending I know nothing about. Horrible stuff, horrible—"

I stared into his face, seeking signs of falsehood; saw no flush, no quick blinkings, no shifting eyes. "Did they involve something called Melaway?" I asked; he frowned.

"You've heard, then," he said. "Utterly mad. The pot painting the kettle white, too, I'd call it. What's to be said, Isabel, that hasn't been?"

"Very little," I said, at once feeling myself more comfortable in his presence again, however much one day it might prove a mistake. "I'm as glad to be done with it, whatever happens next."

"Yes, we need to discuss that," he said. "How are you this morning, in any event? Looked a bit peaked last night, I heard. Still appear somewhat underweathered, but it's evident you're in better shape than Leverett, as it were."

"I'm better," I said. "I should see Doctor Harrison again, mayhap, while I can."

"He did you right, yesterday? That's good. I only go in when nature calls. If I start heaving blood or something."

"My baby, I need to be sure," I said; felt myself slipping once more. "I won't be able to once I'm returned—"

"Isabel, listen," he said. "As told, we've room for you here. I've final discretion over here as to what's to be done with miscreants if I so choose."

"Would I be placed so easily here?" I asked. "Last night—"

"We wouldn't bereave you," he said. "I'd certify that."

"Judy certified much as well, over time—"

"I'm not Judy, whomever she might be. I'm not sure what we'll have you doing, but Madam won't hear of it and even if she does it'll not concern her. This morning I spoke to my sister, estimating it wise to make a preparation or two. Croppie says she's a room for you in her flat. Lives in Bow. Enchanting neighborhood, and the crime rate's been plunging for years now."

"She works for Dryco, too?"

"Perish forbid," he said. "She's an artist. I believe you've something in common."

He winked; if I were to have no other choices, I could think of worse ones to have. Perhaps Malloy would prove to be more worthy of my trust than I'd proved to have been to Judy's. "Thank you," I told him. "I'm muted—"

"That's fine, I generally talk enough for three or four. Allow me to call the desk there and tell them you're covered through tonight. My sister and I will come by for you around six and haul you away. Would that be suitable?"

"Yes . . ." I said. "More than suitable. Malloy—"

"This evening, then," he said, allowing his image to fade. "It's been real."

For several minutes after Malloy unscreened I sat there, addled by events; grateful for once that Dryco's left never knew what its right was doing. Certain now that I was no longer asleep, I switched off the telecom. Walking into the bathroom I turned on the tap, deciding to bathe and allow my body to enjoy the same float my mind presently knew. I was unseeable through the window, and opened it wide, breathing in eucalyptus scent, clearing my nose of lingering soot. London wouldn't be so much worse than New York, save on occasions, I thought as I layered the surface of the rising water with bath salts. As I windowgazed, slipping off my robe, I noted an odd odor which at first I thought wafted from the salts; a chemical tang, such as the scent which clings to preserved fruit. Turning, I saw John behind me, shutting the bathroom door, locking us in.

"Checkout time, Iz," he said, favoring his bad leg as he stood there. His nose was held placed by lengths of gauze wrapped round his head; he'd had nothing done to his cheekbone save to have the bruises painted. I'd not heard my husband enter either my room or the bath; he'd moved so silently, damaged, as he ever did when whole.

"What's wanted, John?" I asked, bandaging myself with a towel; reaching behind me, I shut off the water. My husband stood where he'd placed himself, unmoving, stroking my hands with his, gesturing no overted threat.

"To see you, Iz," he said. "We barely talked last night."

"Please go out until I dress," I said. "Please—"

"The family that stays together," he said, "stays together. But you should have left me there, Iz. You should have."

"I couldn't," I said. "Please, John, one minute, that's all—"

"We don't talk anymore, Iz," he said, unpocketing his razor, unsheathing its length. "I was whole again for a while. This rips me—"

His eyes so hazed as to appear him blind; when he spoke he voiced child's tones, hinting fear, anxious for approval, set to tantrum. Sunlight glinted the razor's metal; I stared away from its flash, focusing elsewhere, hoping to sight something I might use to distract. Only his mouth's droop suggested that he wouldn't hazard me yet; I willed calm to blanket me while he was armed.

"Understood," I said, hugging myself. "Will you let me robe?" He nodded, and I gathered up my wrap, hiding within its folds as he watched; stared, rather, appearing to eye what lay in my head as if I'd gone see-through. "Talk, John. Show and tell."

He took my right hand in his left, and extended my arm full-length; raising his blade, he closed it shut. "We were one, Iz," he said. "Once and then again. What happened?"

"Too much happened."

He nodded; shook slightly as he stood there, clasping my hand, blocking the door. Too many meters separated the window from the courtyard, even were I able to breakaway and throw myself through before he might catch me. "The first day over there," he said. "Before we met him. We were like we were. It wonderfulled."

"We seemed to be as we'd been," I said. "But you know how long we'd been troubling before that. That was our last chance, and it didn't take. Neither of us is faulted. It's not workable anymore, that's all."

"The world's regooding without us," he said. "We're unregoodable."

"We imagined perfection," I said. "Was it ever so?" He lipstilled; stared windowways, at sparrows perched in a plane tree's limbs. Rotating his wrist as if unstiffening the wires, he flipped the blade free of its compartment once more, and then flipped it back in; out, in, out again.

"What's our life still hold, Iz?" he asked. "We're jobless. Homeless. Purposeless. What's left?"

"We're left," I said.

"But disunited. You know I'll not last. Do you think you will?"

"Of course—"

"We're more alike than you've ever admitted, Iz," he said.

"Singled, will you want to last? An isolate's life's neither mine nor yours."

"My baby's left," I said.

"His baby," he said; I allowed it to pass. "If it's birthed, will it live? It's chanceless, Iz, that's known."

"Unknown," I said, trying to loose my hand from his; he gripped me all the tighter, and leaned forward, as if to bite. "And Malloy's arranging something here, in London—"

"Something for you, Iz," John said. "I went unmentioned."

"You overheard?" He nodded, fixing a firmer hold on my forearm, squeezing the muscle. "You were roomed here with me? Where—?"

"Outside," he said. "If that's done, Iz, what happens to me? Where do I go?"

"John, the moment spurred and I reacted sole. I'll ask—"

"You've exed me too, then? All've exed me. It's not as written, Iz, it's not."

"Loosen," I said, attempting to draw away from him. "You're hurting me, John—"

"Mutualities," he said. "How do you know he told you true, Iz?"

"I'm assured—"

"People you've known yearslong have falsetongued you," he said. "Your workmates and betters. Family and friends. He's truthed you? You know that?"

I didn't; there was no rationalizing why I should have taken Malloy's word as truth, not after so few days. Yet it wasn't as if propinquital duration effected overmuch, longterm. Malloy would comfort me, surely; so had Judy. He'd secure me, undoubted; so had Leverett. He'd improve me, likely as not; so had Dryco.

"You don't know, Iz. You don't. All people betrayed you, save me."

"Agreed," I said; his bag's odor permeated the room's

warm air. "But you never told me what you were doing at night. That's horrible—"

"You'd have wanted to know?" he asked. "Our jobs were always separate, Iz. As we wanted. But then my job wasn't mine anymore."

"That didn't essential—"

"A dammed river has to flow somewhere," he said. "Then people drown. It's nature's way."

"It's not mine," I said. "It's unlivable, John, I can't—"

"Understood," he said. "It's mooted now. The business line allows, the private sector doesn't. I'll not be aprowl hereout—"

"It's unmattering now, John," I said. "We're done."

"Agreed," he said, flipping open his razor, leaving it out to reflect light. "Endtime, Iz. As it must to all."

His fingers closed round my arm; looking into his eyes I saw that they'd cleared, and his blues leveled me as if to fascinate. "No," I said.

"You know you want it, Iz," he said, drawing closer, seeming ready to spring. "You want it too. Neither world we've tried suits us. There's a third remaining. One size, fits all."

"You want, not me," I said; but how often had our darker thoughts singletracked? How many times had I assured myself so well as him to go wherever he wanted? My husband smiled; his eyes sparkled so bright as his razor. "My baby's alive. I'll keep it so."

"Alive now, mayhap," he said, lifting his blade. "How much longer?"

"Until it's birthed," I said, flattening my back against the wall. "We have to go on, John. If not together, then apart, but we have to—"

"We will," he said. "We'll go on together. Always have, and always will. There's no asundering us. Come along, Iz. Come along."

"I'll not," I said. "Hear me, please—"

"Talk's time is done," he said. "When time comes, act. I love you, Iz."

"That's the problem—" I said; he'd deafened to me, and made no reply. Releasing his grip, encircling my waist with his arm, he pressed himself against me, pushing his lips onto mine. While he kissed me time slipped its netting, lengthening as if we were caught in mid-transfer, there in that old hotel where so many, undoubted, had kissed, embraced, and died. Momentslong I felt my walls tumble; found myself adrift in his hold, allowing my mind to blank, convincing myself that I would be betrayed again, in time, that I should as well accompany and be done with it. Had he acted, then, we would have tandemed.

"Time, Iz," he said.

"Time," I repeated, nodding my head, staring into the sarcophagal tub. I heard the remaining dragonfly buzzing in the room beyond as it sought any exit. "What's to be done, then?"

"One mouth's not enough to our kisses," he said, cradling his razor in his hand as if it were a rose. Without yet touching its edge to his skin he drew it crossthroat, passing beneath his jawline from ear to ear. "Like so. Ignore shortterm pain and picture eternity. It'll be different on the other side, Iz. It will." He offered me the razor, inferring that I should make the first move; I pulled away my hand before I could take hold of it. At first he seemed puzzled; then he grinned. "I'll first, then. I'm an older hand at this."

"Yes—"

"I love you, Iz."

"Mutual," I said. He guided the razor beneath his chin, placing the blade immediately below his ear; then he motioned an inutterably smooth, unfailingly perfect slash. For an instant his throat looked as it had before. Then a red waterfall gauzed his skin, cascading its flow from the thin line he'd etched; two crimson strands issued from his carotids, geysering fine threads with a rhythmic pulse. As I allowed him to douse me, I watched his face pale, whitewaxing; with a surgeon's still hands he pressed the razor into mine, and I took it from him. He opened his eyes as he began lowering himself toward the floor, careful not to so disalign his knee as to unbalance himself; our gaze met while he sprayed my legs. My husband tried to speak; his lips mouthed my name, and he supported himself onehanded against the side of the tub.

"Goodbye, John," I told him, standing as I had before. "Forgive."

I thought it too dishonorable not to look at him; he stared up at me as if surprised, but then nodded, and smiled. The look of happiness he countenanced was one I'd never seen him have before; mayhap, finding his peace at last, it proved to be even more blessed than he'd ever imagined. Eyeshutting, he let his hand slip away from the tub, and placed it at his neck; with gentle motions he widened his wounds, and then lay down on the floor's thick red rug.

Once he lay calmed I slumped, sitting against the wall, holding the razor with which he'd gifted me, allowing him to drip from my robe. Positioning him full-length upon the rug, I denuded, and covered him with my wrap. Stepping into the tub, I lowered myself into the cool water, unplugging the drain, turning on the tap to refill it while I washed myself of my husband's outward traces. Shutting off my sense of all that lay beyond the tub's porcelain rim, I reclosed the drain, and allowed warmer water to rise round me. Lying back, staring at my length as if I saw it through a distorting glass, I fancied that my toes appeared meters distant; I pressed them against the far white wall as if to break it down. My swollen belly rose above the water, its truehued curves glistening; would my baby bear my husband's look, then? Or my own?

Then I thought of my lost men, and unexpectedly found myself unconscionably guilted; should either E or my husband have gone their preferred ways unaccompanied? Unwilling to travel with them, could I still claim not to have enabled their passage? My ears attuned to their voices as they sirened me, willing me to join them; wishing to be rid of both worlds, at once realizing again the uncertainty I had concerning Malloy, I eyed the razor I still held. Lifting it before my eyes I saw my face mirrored; for minutes I let my look linger on my face, staring to see who might blink first, hearing most loudly my husband's voice:

Wish I may. Act. Act. Act.

As his distanced words guided me, so I raised it, grazing the razor against my wrist, relishing its butterfly feel, shivering at its well-rinsed warmth. If husbands and wives become as one blood over time, had not too much of mine already spilled? What was remaining, after all? In the midst of my debate I glanced through the wide window, and I glimpsed a spark above the trees: distinguished a flare, a flicker, an earthbound plummet, the skyward sign. Turning the razor so that the blade's dull edge pressed against my palm, I slid it back into its holster, and dropped it floorways, alongside John.

I reclined, so that warm water would engulf me; felt its wetness rinse my scalp, the drift of my weightless arms: fancied myself Ophelia, loosed from Hamlet, my mind repossessed, unwilling to linger overlong in the stream. There could be but one messiah, and that was the one whose two expressions I housed; no others need apply. Alone, that was how to slide into winter; alone and free, if not forever rid of the stranger in my head, free at least to show my child to all who chose to see.

So regooded, I renewed, and rose like Venus from the waves.